Anniversary Edition
Volume :: Screams Beneath Pandora
Includes Realms and Galaxies :: Books #7 - #10
Felled Rage - Garren Waysixth - Care Ethaynen - Mermaid Mana

Thousands of years in the Future,
Human kind emerges from a second Dark Ages.
This time Magic survives.   Psychics are common.
Dragon, Elf, and Mer have not fallen into Myth.

"Your healing needs are on your back, eh?" The Blue Lady "tsked".

"Um, good point." Care turned over to his stomach. Garren mimicked him, giving Care the impression his mind was not really paying attention to their surroundings.

She walked around to the head of the bed carrying two sets of chain and bracelet bondage restraints. She wrapped the chain around the top slat in the headboard and asked for Care's wrists. He complied with a shiver of dread. "Um, tis this truly necessary?" He made a fist, but she waited until he relaxed his hands before the bracelets clicked and locked. She was no slouch to the tricks.

"Young one, you never Mage Healed before? Hmm, virgin? prrr," she grinned wicked amusement.

She snapped the same bracelet arrangement on Garren, then moved to the foot of the bed to attend ankles. She climbed on the bed, one knee between Care's legs and wedged her other knee between Garren's thighs. She threw herself forward and she landed with her body partially atop them both.

She pushed Care's hair aside and kissed his nape, then she bit him there. Care clenched his teeth to keep from crying out. He hoped the Healing would erase her teeth marks, he projected this thought very loudly in case she was telepathic in any sense. She licked at one of Garren's dried blood wounds.

She sighed and a forceful wind whipped the window curtains and filled the little room. Care buried his face in the bed covers. It felt like the winds high above the city. The wind became cold, wind from the mountains, perhaps? This new wind was laden with cool mist.

The wind grew heavier bearing cool moisture. Then, something gritty slapped at Care's skin. Sprinkles of it hit the bed covers by his face. Was it ... dirt? Common variety dirt like from the road outside in the cul-de-sac. Wind, Water, Earth, and Care squeezed his eyes shut; was fire coming next?

Lo, the dedication page:

03 November 2005

In Loving Memory of Indy Jones (1992 - 21 Nov 2005). My sweet, sweet Baby. I feel so bereft without you. You were my light and my love and my Jy

The characters and events in this book are fictitious.

Clipart in this presentation is from the Corel Draw Suite.
Artwork was created using Bryce 3d, Adobe Photoshop,
Creative Poser, (and one day Maya!)

ISBN 978-0-6151-3544-1

Library of Congress Control Number: 2007908480

Anniversary Edition: 2007

Published by Barista Witch Imprint,
Bon Coeur Publishing, Huntington NY USA

Distributed internationally in association with
Lightning Source Inc. (US), La Vergne TN USA
Lightning Source UK Ltd, Rooksley Milton Keynes UK

http://groups.yahoo.com/group/BonCoeurPublishing

::R EALMS & G ALAXIES::

VOLUME ANNIVERSARY EDITION

SCREAMS

BENEATH

PANDORA

BY

MISTY LARA PRENDVILLE
ELF PRINCESS

Contents

Allons	Human
	Sovereign Minister
Amé Asgothe	Human
	a Guard, perceptive towards Magic
Aneena	Immortal
	Mage Healer / Elemental Sorceress
Angélus, Ange	Human
	Minister of Royal Appointments
Ariel	Leonine Demon
	Greater Demon, an ancient felled angel
Atalaetia	Medusan
	Minister of Public Traffic
Barett	Human
	a bored Field Team Commander
Bel	Human
	Fleet Commander, ship 'The Equinox'
Brynnhilde	Were-Dragon
	Ambassadress from Castle Utfordring
Care Ethaynen	Mostly Human
	a Guard, Interesting hobbies
Caithlin	Mermaid
	enamored of the scent of virgin blood
Dana Atuin	Hybrid-Human
	a Guard, nice friend to have
Dawn	Hybrid-Human
	a Princess of Pan-Jupiter
Donné Ayfourth	Human
	fed up Field Trainer
Erin Tomick	Human
	a Guard Minor Telepath and Telekinetic
Fly13	Shuttle
	Lonely Entity in the Subterraneum
Freegelda	Were-Dragon
	Brynnhilde's little sister
Garren Waysixth	Human
	a Guard
Hannah	Human
	Minister of Housekeeping Affaires
Jace	Human
	a Guard stationed to Mare Ibrium
Jenny	Human
	a Guard stationed to Mare Ibrium
Jesse Nefeinn	Human
	Son of Nerrys and Nalira
Kanuenos	Humanoid
	Demon Summoner

Kerlin Lantanthen	Human
	Field Team Commander
	into the Nihera Circuit Rocket Races
Keyth	Human
	Fleet Commander assigned to 'The Halçyon'
	Astral Kinetic, telepath
Krizren ne Sara	Human
	Fleet Commander assigned to 'The Halçyon'
	Telepath bonded to Keyth, good cook
LeeAnne	Human
	Minister of Public Waterworks
Lisza	Human
	Commander, verily fun loving
Luna	Hybrid-Human
	a Princess of Pan-Jupiter
Methusem	Dragon / Mer
	Emperor of the Galactic Realm of Pan-Jupiter
Miassa	Mynx
	Jesse's bestest friend
Nalira Nefeinn	Human
	Married to Nerrys
Nerrys Nefeinn	Human
	Kinetic Construction Worker
Ole Nuben	Human
	Minister of Royal Crown Jewels
Pursy	Human
	guard assigned to Kraken's Team
Rhiannon	Mage-Elf
	a Guard with an erotomanic condition
Sable ne Redallion	Brown Elf
	Fleet Commander, ship 'The Nocturnex'
Starra	Elf
	a Guard assigned to 'The Equinox'. Likes Care's hobbies
Syra Nefeinn	Human
	Daughter of Nerrys and Nalira
Tamkin	Human
	a Guard 'Rogue Fielder'
Tane	Human
	Fleet Commander, ship 'The Solstice'
Tibetha	Mermaid, Water Demon
	pregnant Mermaid
Terriane	Human
	Guard paired with Lisza
Traci Lokden	Human
	a Guard, stingy with information
Vylara	Elf - Breath Magic
	Junior Minister, Assistant to Angélus
Wenrik	Were-Dragon
	Prince from Castle Utfordring

I. TERRA-DATE YEAR 215, DAY 142
Potens Cor
:: Celesterra Planet, Minister Angélus::

Minister Angélus was busy arranging his Emperor's appointment calends, when the planetary alarms sounded, the siren clamor scattered every thought in his head. "Eh?"

The young Elf woman sitting patiently in the visitor's chair of his office, gripped the arms of the chair.

Ange was pleased to notice she wasn't panicking. He tapped at his computer screen, the appointment schedule slid aside for an urgent news flash. The Planetary Shield Vale was about to be activated. All orbital travel was hereby suspended.

Orbital Antenna Station Mira Ibrium ::

Aboard the Orbital Antenna Station 'Mira Ibrium', a Barista Witch Spell brewed a mocha latté to order and set it on the side table next to a very good looking Human male. She made an effort to catch his eye to flirt with him, but he was too engrossed in his PDA.

Not one to give up on potential romance so easily, she tried to catch a flirtatious tease with his partner, Jenny; but the Guard was more interested in the candy dispenser.

'Ah well', the petite Witch returned to her Barista counter, hopped up on her stool, and waited patiently for a customer.

The two Humans on duty were dressed in the smart form fitting black uniform of the Royal Guard. Relaxing casual in a lounge of the station, Jace browsed the newsletters he subscribed to on his handheld PDA. His partner made her decision in front of the candy vending machine, perusing a cheap selection for her salary grade was too low to afford the finer chocolate snacks. She absently ripped open the wrapper, while gazing out an airlock window. The view of the planet below was spectacular with blue oceans, continental terrains, and wispy white cloud cover.

Mira Ibrium coasted along its second orbital pass of the day, shadowing above the equator plane of Planet Celesterra. The nineteen-story tower station structure supported a mounted parabolic antenna. The antenna preamp equipment, an amalgamate culmination of modern Magic and technology, was the main projector for Celesterra's planetary defense shields. Its debut was almost two terra centuries passed and over the time span the station was now more of a symbol of defense. No mortal in the present day ever expected to see the Planetary Shield Vale raised in their lifetime.

Jace tossed his PDA on to a cushioned seating sectional, sighing in boredom. He pulled his scrunchee hair tie off and stuck it in his teeth as he used both hands to finger comb out his shoulder length dark hair, avoiding the gaze of the flirtatious

Barista Witch. Jenny punched her pin code into the candy machine's dispenser for another snack. When suddenly! The last sound the Guards ever expected to hear screeched hard on their Human ears.

'WIRR_WIRR_WIRR,' The Planetary Alarms screamed!

The two Guards shared a shocked gaze lock before a call to action registered in their grey matter. They pelted as one to the corridor leading to the shield projector controls.

A very long corridor. Jenny panted, it had never seemed so long a distance before. Wishing ardently that she'd certified for gravity skates, cause then she would be at the controls by now. The wings of her vivid imagination propelled her ever swifter to the chamber at the end of the long corridor. She put all her energy into keeping up with her partner, arms pumping, as Jace put on an unexpected burst of speed. A fleeting thought flit across her mind that the disciplinary flogging they were going to be Writ for, for being errant at their posts would be the least of their worries.

At last!

They stormed the entrance at a dead run. The habit of drill taking over; Jace tapped the crystals in a sequence to activate the Machinery, crystals of many colors blinking in response. Jenny aligned the directional coordinates. They held their breaths, ready to gape at the awesome sight of the Shield Vale. Sweat plastered Jenny's fine blonde hair to her scalp and Jace's knees quivered.

Nothing happened.

The planetary shields FAILED!

Capital 'F'!

II. Terra-Date Year 215 Day 142
:: Celesterra Planet, Seaside Palace. Minister Angélus ::

"Who sounded the Planetary Alarms?!" A medley of voices cried.

Ministers and Junior Ministers scrambled from their offices, a few of the very elderly Ministers risking their health by being overzealous in their spirited determination to seek out the cause of disruption amidst the tranquil Palace Halls, their robe hems swept the marbled floorings.

"This must be an unsanctioned drill, eh?" A Medusan whined, her ophidian hairdo hissed and writhed, frightening a young Mynx woman into darting back into her office.

"He's gone, some 'un taken him!" A Minister in shabby mustard colored robes came crying down the hall, tears trembled on his paunchy cheeks; his overweight body reduced him to wheezing helplessly and he had to stop running. His watery blue eyes seeking for help, searched the crowd of faces. "Please, He's gone!"

"Isn't that ole Nuben, the Minister of the Royal Crown Jewels?" One Minister sniggered; the snigger turned to a gasp of concern as ole Nuben collapsed to one knee and cried in pain, unable to catch his fall. The formerly sniggering Minister rushed forward to help along with a few others. "Now there, there ole fellow. Explain all these hysterics?"

At that moment, speech became drowned out by the arrival of the Guard Force. Black uniformed Guards invaded the normally quiet halls, took up positions at the grand stairways, secured the invitingly open archways, and one Guard to every support column on the bottom level. Guards on gravity-skates skated for the upper levels and floated by the upper window casements, black uniform cloaks fluttering in the upper drafts, their negatron pulse weapons held point up and ready for a target.

Someone blessedly had the presence of mind to cut the siren clamor. The noise from the Guards diminished as they settled at their posts.

During all this hub-bulub, Minister Angélus, Ange to his friends, was elbowing a path through the crowd to his old friend Nuben. It was on occasions like these, Minister Ange missed his decades waned kinetic ability. Making a way through the crowd with a little kinetic elbow grease would have been so much easier, if not down right rude by modern standards. He felt a jostle at his elbow and found the young Elf woman Vylara at his side. "Oh yes!" She'd come today for an interview for he had a job opening for an assistant. At long last, he had been requesting an assistant for over a hundred terra years, now. It took too damned long for any request to get through the channels. 'Lucky for me I didn't die waiting for the approval,' he thought this with high humour. 'If you can't laugh at yourself, government life is the wrong career.'

He was still chuckling in a low voice as he reached ole Nuben. The gazes he drew caused him to realize that his chuckling coupled with his disarrayed shoulder length gray hair and hemmed too high robes (for the flood) must make him look unkempt and 'daresay' frumpy.

Minister Ange overheard a snide remark directed at Nuben and himself saying, "between the two of them, each with a foot in the funeral pyre". This criticism of his advanced elderliness made him wish for a trickle of his old kinetic ability; he would slap that huge tome the speaker was holding right into the speaker's face. 'Ah well, just as well I can't.' Minister Ange swallowed a fresh chuckle as he tried to soothe the distraught Minister Nuben.

"He's gone Ange, gone," Nuben stood leaning forward to rub his sore knee.   Seeing Minister Ange paying attention, he continued, "I laid out his sapphire diadem, the titanium one, you know, with the coral and diamonds set along the rim. Tis His favorite!"

"I know Nuben, it IS His favourite," Minister Ange heard a 'tch' in the crowd and he bestowed a scowling rebuke on the person. You could see signs of the forceful personality Angélus must have been in the vital days of his career.

"It matches the glowing blue aura of his power," Nuben sniffled.

"Yes, Nuben. Why are you saying He is gone?" Ange said kindly.

Nuben let go of his knee to grab Minister Ange by the arms. "Don't ya hear me lad? He missed His appointment for His fitting. He ne'er done that! And the conference today with Dragons, urgent it tis!"

"Ah yes, the Dragons. They are distraught about something. They will bespeak only with His Highness," Minister Ange already knew of the conference for his Ministerial position was that of Royal Appointments.

"Make way for the Sovereign Minister," an authoritative voice rang over the crowd. "Return to your offices."

The effect of this order went quite unnoticeable, it did however; clear a path for Sovereign Minister Allons. In honour of his Sovereign rank, his robes were less mustard coloured than the rest of the crowd, twas supposed to be gold, but in actuality, a bright yellow; his Sovereign title an honour bestowed for grand deeds done in the past. Only a very plain band of metal graced the Sovereign Minister's brow for anything fancier required ole Nuben's cooperation. Nuben was an affable person, however; once you've insulted him too greatly, he could bear a grudge forever. Nuben refused Allons the proper differentiation to which the Sovereign Minister felt he was automatically entitled. The rest was history.

"He speaks the truth, Our Emperor is missing, He's been taken," a breathless Human woman of questionable mortality rushed up to the small knot of conferring Ministers. She was Minister Hannah of Housekeeping Affaires and a most unusual guest accompanied her.

Minister Ange gaped just like the rawest of the Guards were doing from their security positions. He recognized the Grand Dame Brynnhilde, not to give the impression the Great Lady was in any way grandmotherly. He'd met her only once before, a time before the conquest.

He swept a low old fashioned courtly bow. "Greetings Your Greatness, Dame Brynnhilde and on behalf of our Emperor, Regards to Castle Utfordring. Regards to your Dragon King."

He politely tried to keep his gaze on her face. Brynnehilde's fair statuesque body stood unselfconsciously nude, but for some jewelry set with precious stones on her ankles and wrists, a belt of silver strands encircled her waist in loose abandon. Her full breasts accentuated the curve to her hips and balanced her long legs. Bright gold tresses draped down her arms and passed her hips, a shade to invoke envy from a solar hydrogen star, her tresses crowned by a diadem of sparkling diamonds and rubies. Her irises were the brilliant cobalt blue of the Dragons with a pupil of purest silver. Her two sets of wings folded tightly to her back, Minister Ange could not see their gossamer like membranes to describe their colour. He knew they would be iridescent with whirling glyph designs that were as unique to every Dragon as fingerprints were to Humans. To sum it all up, Grand Dame Brynnhilde was a 'show stopper' to the beholding eyes of Humans, Elves, and a good many other sexually compatible species.

She inclined her head slightly. "Angélus?" Her drawling husky voice lilted on a questioning note.

"You remember me by name, Great Lady?" Minister Ange said incredulously. "But I was young and dare I say, mayhap, handsome back then?" He smiled to show he could be as self-deprecating as the next Human.

She returned a strange smile. "I have come to bespeak to your Dragon King, we must have words for a grievous harm has been done upon us."

"Ahem," Sovereign Minister Allons interjected by clearing his throat, drawing up his slim figure to his most commanding dramatic impression with one shoulder pushed forward, deliberately theatrical. "The Dragon King you speak of is our Emperor, is He not?"

She nodded, the weight of her golden tresses shifted, covering her breasts.

"It has come to light a mystery has shrouded our Emperor. It is unconscionable that he would miss a conference with the great Dragons."

"He is taken, I tell you," Hannah's dark eyes flashed with stormy anger. "I went into the Eternity Chamber to announce Grand Dame Brynnhilde's arrival," she said this with a quick curtsey to the great Dragon Dame. "I saw something strange. I saw Emperor Methusem like a shadow disappearing into the center of the chamber, vanishing into a mist."

Dame Brynnhilde closed her eyes at this announcement; a frown line appeared on her forehead.

"Great Lady, does your great knowledge extend to understand the meaning of this mist?" Minister Ange asked urgently.

"I know what it means," Sovereign Minister Allons spoke with little patience at being ignored in favor of the Dragon. "He's crossed into the Crossroad Corridors. What makes you think he was taken by force?" He put the question directly to Minister Hannah.

Hannah grabbed a handful of her full skirt in a move to hide her irritation before she answered in a calm voice. "Because, He is not here, He is always diligent in his responsibilities."

"That is no token of surety. He could have left to follow after an emergency. Nevertheless! We must find him. We will start a planet wide search. On the chance this whole affair is a diversion of some enemy, we will allow only Senior Guard rank and above in the search. The rest of the Guards are to stake their usual posts." He took charge in a manner most heartening to the growingly fearful.

Grand Dame Brynnhilde opened her eyes and said, "there has been unusual traffic in the Crossroad Corridors of late. If twas One of the truly powerful treading those pathways, its dread passing would have defied even our Dragon senses."

"Are you able to tell us in which general direction this traffic was heading?" Sovereign Minister Allons asked with false humility.

"The subterranean passages, a portion of it sprawls below Celesterra City, I recommend you start your search there. I will join with my Dragon kin and search Dragon Lands. I Aft-Gleam an impression of celestite crystal and strontium rock, there are many mountains of such rock in our lands." The Great Lady took her leave without further ado, exiting via the southwest archway. She passed under a pillar of sunlight streaming from an upper level skylight; the sunlight revealed silver skin tones like brushed silver glitter sparkles.

Sovereign Minister Allons turned to one of his assistant Ministers, "call a meeting of Field Team Commanders. Let us organize this quickly. And send a preliminary team to the cave bluffs."

"Minister," Minister Ange called as Allons moved away, "I mean, Your Highness!"

The Sovereign Minister spared a moment, "I don't have time to spare for you right now Angélus."

"What would you have me do to help?" Ange used his most persuasive voice.

Sovereign Minister Allons rocked back on his heels, studying the elderly Minister. To be fair, Allons tried in his way to be kindly as he said, "You are the Minister of Royal Appointments, you should rearrange those appointments, or surely chaos will ensue, more chaos than there is already." And with a condescending smile, he returned to matters at hand.

Minister Ange stood rooted to the spot as everyone else went about their business. The Guards on duty stayed at their positions and after a few moments he had only Hannah and Vylara for company. "Well," he said wistfully, "Ole Nuben will need us to steady his nerves." He turned, turned again, 'til he had Hannah doing it too when he turned a third time.

She quickly surmised, "Nuben, where is he?" Hannah clasped her hands tightly together.

"You live at this Palace Dear Hannah," Minister Ange said in a wavering voice. All this worry was exhausting, it dawning clearly for the first time that something awful may have happened to his beloved Emperor. "Are there secret passages to the Subterraneum from within this Palace? Surely Nuben must be headed for such a passage?"

One of the Guards spoke up, "ho, Minister Ange!" A Guard waved.

"Oh, Dana, is it not?" He addressed a tall blonde Guard of Hybrid-Human parentage floating near the skylights on gravity-skates. The Guard did a little meaningless dance with his feet and his elevation came down several levels.

"Yep, ole Nuben went towards the Antiquities Wing. Do you think he's putting himself in danger? We can assign a couple skaters to look after him," Guard Dana offered.

Minister Ange shared a worried look with Hannah, reading similar thoughts to his own in her eyes. He understood ole Nuben's sentiment for he loved Emperor Methusem just as dearly, like a son. It felt awfully close to snitching, but Ange knew ole Nuben would die in the Subterraneum trying to find Methusem. Methusem was immortal and had a chance of coming out of this ordeal unscathed, Nuben wasn't and wouldn't.

"Yes Dana, thank you," Ange absently scratched his ear.

Guard Dana waved to two Human women skating tight to

the upper windows, motioning them to join the search party. The Minister had a fanciful idea of what Nuben would make of Lisza and Terriane, a verily fun loving pair.

"If there is an entrance to the Subterraneum down in the Antiquities Wing, it couldn't hurt to search a little ways." A little gleam sparkled in his eye.

"I'm coming, too," Hannah brooked no argument.

"And me," Vylara spoke up for the first time.

"What? No Vylara, tis much too dangerous for a civilian."

"Minister," the young Elf woman spoke with steadfast conviction in her sweet dulcet voice. "You saved my ancestress at great personal risk to yourself."

"I'm afraid my memory has waned with the rest of me, but I don't see what that has to do with 'the price of chocolate on the outer fringe'," he frowned slightly.

"I'm going with you; nothing short of force will stop me. I must remind you that I am graced with Breath Magic, so you'll have to pit a Magic User against me."

"Dear me! Really now!" Out of the corner of his eye, he could see his dear friend Hannah had taken quite readily to the determined Elf maid. "Let us go then." He could not deny such ferocious conviction. Surely no harm could come of allowing her to follow.

After the little party walked beyond hearing, one of the Guards remarked to those nearest him! "Thereon bound upon a rescue mission to save our Emperor from something too powerful for the Dragons' perception; Minister Caretaker of the Royal Crown Jewels, the Minister of Royal Appointments, and the Minister of Housekeeping Affaires."

"You have to admire their brave hearts!" A Guard named Traci replied with great affection for the three Ministers under discussion.

III. TERRA-DATE YEAR 215, DAY 143
:: In the Subterraneum. Minister Angélus::

The small entourage of would be Emperor rescuers tread their way through the Palace corridors in search of the Antiquities Wing, with Minister Hannah leading the way. She paused at a junction in the corridors, unsure of which way to turn.

One of the Guards commented that the Palace didn't seem this labyrinthine from the outside.

Distracted by the chatter, Hannah huffed in irritation, her bosom rose with her deep inhalation of breath, tightening, momentarily, the fit of her gown's bodice. The hem of her old fashioned embroidered skirts, layered in shades of lavender, swept near to the floor. A scarf length strip of lace held back Hannah's cloud of brunette hair, floating to her waist. "You only see the top six floors of the Palace from outside. We're built into a bluff, remember? You have no idea how deep the Palace goes."

"Sorry Minister," Lisza mumbled, flashing a quick grin at her partner Terriane, disabusing any notion of sincerity in her apology.

Minister Ange imagined Lisza must run rings around her grandparents.

The two uniformed women were both strikingly pretty with dark loosely braided hair. They wore red lip colour and eye make-up, black eyeliner drew emphasis to their mischievous expressions. They did not look like sisters, yet, were so alike in attitude they could have been. Their form fitted black uniforms accentuated their curvy hips, their uniform cloaks hit them at mid-thigh and hid any curves they may have had in the rear department. The Guards looked to be in their late twenties.

Vylara seemed to be a decade younger in age, yet carried herself in a way as to give an impression of dependable maturity. She was dressed in a conservative job interview outfit, long green tinted tunic layered over a calf length light green skirt.

Hannah was saying something in a soft voice to Vylara, smiling kindly at the Elf maid and Vylara shyly returned the smile.

Minister Ange took note of this exchange, heartily pleased. He decided Vylara would be perfect for the job as his assistant. He would offer her the position as soon as palace affaires were sorted.

While their small group was deciding on which direction to take to the Antiquities Wing, one of their fellow Ministers came rushing up. The approaching woman was elderly with close cropped gray hair. From under the hem of her robes, Ange caught a glimpse of jogging shoes.

"Ministers!" She skidded to a halt in front of Ange and Hannah.

"Minister LeeAnne, how good of you to join us," Ange greeted. He overheard Lisza mumbling, 'good traction'.

"I've come to tell you," Minister LeeAnne took a deep breath, "Princess Dawn has gone into the Subterraneum with ole Nuben."

"The Princess?!" Ange exclaimed. This was startling news. But of course; the Princesses must be worried sick for the Emperor. Lisza was drawing out her PDA to relay this bit of news to the Guard's communications broadband.

"Are you going into the Subterraneum?" LeeAnne didn't wait for them to answer. She beckoned the group to follow her, "before the Princesses left to follow their purpose, they used their Magic to activate the Portways in the Palace."

"Portways within the Palace?" Ange had never heard of such a thing.

"Shortcuts!" LeeAnne became a little impatient, when the group didn't follow her fast enough for her sense of hurry. She beckoned once more, made a sharp turn and walked into a wall. And promptly vanished.

Ange dipped his eyebrows into a deep V. The wall was plain, or rather, as ornate as any other run of the mill wall in the Palace.

Vylara approached the spot cautiously. She leaned her face close and huffed on the wall. Her Breath Magic in action. The wall rippled, a mirror appeared, reflecting a surprised looking group of people. "This portal is made from Crystal Magic," Vylara commented in a hush voice.

"Eh?" Ange cleared his throat. "Isn't the Emperor constantly scolding his daughters to not rely on Crystal Magic?"

Lisza shouldered her way to the front of the line. "I'll go first."

She walked without any show of hesitation, right into the mirror.

A PDA blerpied. Everyone checked their pockets. The noise was coming from Terriane's hip pocket. She tapped on her little PDA screen. They heard Lisza's voice saying, "tis okay. Come on through."

One by one, they passed into the portal. Ange closed his eyes, not completely trusting the Magic. All worked out well, they stood in a corridor much dimmer than the one they'd left behind. Were they deep underground? Ange had never been privy to this part of the Palace.

LeeAnne called at them to hurry forward. Shortly after, the

group stood before a solid metal door etched with runes.

"A Mage tongue?" Ange asked.

"An ancient one," Hannah commented. She used one hand to gather her skirt in a nervous gesture. At her touch the door swung open. It tore from her hand and opened with a loud ringing bang. A stinging wind ripped through, it hit them like a slap in the face.

The women weren't showing any fear, Ange's nerves were emboldened by their courage. He braced against the wind, the wind lessened once he'd stepped through the door.

Beyond the door, a tube like tunnel stretched in two directions. A transit station platform led up to a shuttle waiting patiently with it's ramp extended as an invitation to passengers.

Ange speculated, he'd never seen anything on their Planet resembling this technological design. "Who built this LeeAnne?"

LeeAnne shushed him.

Ange was taken aback. He couldn't remember the last time anyone had shushed at him. "Really now. I say."

"Please, Minister Angélus," LeeAnne said in an overly formal tone. "Fly9 is friend to Our Emperor. Please, be polite."

What did she mean? Ange scratched at the day's worth of bristles on his chin. Be polite? What difference could it possibly make? As if ... could this machine be sentient? A merry twinkle glittered in his eyes as he looked his supposition at LeeAnne. When she nodded, Ange's eyes twinkled all the merrier. This made two Palace secrets he'd learned today. Being privy to Palace secrets was always a pleasure.

"Our neighborly Dragon Dame mentioned gleaming an impression of strontium rock and celestite crystal. Is there an area concentrated with it, where we could start our search?" Ange suggested to the group.

"An area such as you described, I believe," Hannah hesitated before blurting, "is in the Pandora's Peaks mountains. Under the relic ship."

"Pandora's relic ship?" Ange pierced Hannah with a shrewd gaze. Ange had an inkling he was learning one of dear Hannah's secrets, even more precious than a Palace secret. His fingers itched for his diary. He feared he would forget these new secrets by the time he could tap it into his PDA.

"Aren't we here to follow after ole Nuben? And the Princess Dawn?" Lisza interrupted.

Ange turned to Lisza, "ole Nuben was present to hear the same clue we did. Don't let his usual impression of befuddlement fool you. Nuben has survived tumultuous times you young people can't even imagine." These younger folks had no idea of what life was like before Emperor Methusem conquered the Planets.

Lisza batted her eyelashes at the Minister.

Most likely the same look she used on her own grandfather in the middle of a reminisce about the old days. And for her patience, her grandfather would follow the tale with a few illumes to send her shopping at the galleria. Ah yes, the mental picture was clear as a sunny day in Ange's mind..

Minister Ange overheard Terriane whispering to Lisza, "do you have a bad feeling about this?"

Lisza boarded the shuttle first.

Since, this expedition was his idea, Ange insisted he board immediately after her.

Vylara politely deferred to Minister Hannah.

Terriane boarded last.

Ange was delighted to find the inside of the shuttle rather cozy. Two sets of benches faced an opposite pair. In all, the seating could accommodate eight moderately sized Humans. Soft lighting illuminated the décor of browns, yellows, and orange.

The Guards stood near the nose of the craft, Vylara sat next to a window, the rest arranged themselves comfortably. Once they were settled, the shuttle seemed to sense they were ready, it pulled in the ramp and the door whooshed closed with a metallic thud.

Ange was amused to see Terriane twitch a hand over her hip holstered negatron hand cannon. Lisza was a steady presence, giving Ange an impression the young lady might be commander material.

The shuttle began its subsurface journey, accelerating. The force of the acceleration was not enough to push Ange's head against the head rest. He leaned his head back anyway and tried to formulate a plan of rescue.

Nothing could be seen from the window, Vylara leaned her face toward the window, Ange felt quite confidant she couldn't view any more clearly the passing of the tunnel. Every so often, the tunnel outside seemed to open up to give glimpses of cavernous spaces, they sped by quickly and it could have been his imagination.

The uneasy quiet was interrupted by conversation between the two Guards. From the gist of it, Ange ascertained a Rogue Fielder by the name of Care Ethaynen had engineered a new hand cannon proto-type they were 'psyched' to try out.

Ange chuckled. He was familiar with Care Ethaynen, incorrigible, but; very capable, his loyalty to the Emperor above reproach.

There came the sound of a peculiar thump outside the shuttle. Everyone silenced their conversations to listen intently. Just as Ange started to relax, a sound of a scratch on the metallic hull raised the tension level.

What would happen if the shuttle decided to stop in the bowels of the planet? Ange decided this pure conjectural happenstance didn't bear contemplating.

Vylara tightened her curling fingers on the edge of the seat cushion, otherwise, she displayed no anxiety.

Ange rose to his feet to move to the nose of the shuttle. If there were windows, he could find no means to uncover them. His telekinetic powers had waned over the decades, he could still sometimes "feel" objects with his mind, even if he couldn't move them. He put a hand on the inner hull and pushed his telesense through the hull. "Oh dear!"

The two Guards reacted to the "oh dear".

"Oh dear, what?" Lisza harried Ange for an answer.

Ange didn't wish to frighten the ladies. He 'tch'd at himself, recognizing symptoms of chauvinism. These ladies were fully trained Guards, much more capable of handling physical threats than he himself could manage.

♋

Vylara pretended not to be worried, conscious she needed to impress Minister Ange as her prospective employer. She noticed Minister Hannah was tracing her finger tips over the embroidery in her old fashioned skirts, embroidery depicting squiggly lines suggestive of a mage's script.

Hannah winked at Vylara.

Vylara rubbed her upper arms, feeling the pinpricks of building magical energy. "Ma'am, may I inquire..."

"Please, my dear," Hannah said kindly, "address me by my name. Hannah. Ma'am makes me feel old. I'm not yet five hundred."

Vylara swallowed her astonishment, not wishing to be rude. To her own eyes, Minister Hannah appeared no more than 40 terra years at the most. "Hannah, may I ask, which school of Magic are you conjuring?"

Hannah winked again, she leaned her rosy lips near to Vylara's ear and whispered. "I'm a Page Whisperer."

Vylara blinked and turned to the little shuttle window to smile privately, feeling gratified by Hannah's confidence.

Then ... something ... with teeth ... bit at the window from outside. Vylara shrieked, she became all embarrassed by her lapse of composure as Minister Ange came running in response.

♋

"Oh dear," Ange repeated his earlier exclamation, pressing his face to the window to see what was out there.

The thumping and scratching intensified. The shuttle tilted, the occupants held on to the seats.

"Minister, maybe you shouldn't do that," Vylara was very uncomfortable with the Minister pressing his face to the window. "What are they? Are they drakes?

Hannah answered, "no. Drakes are sweet creatures in comparison. Those are demonoid minions."

"Demonoid minions?"

Hannah finished tracing a series of squiggly lines on her skirt. A wall of flame erupted outside the window.

With Ange's telesense, he sensed the flames surround the shuttle. "A fire shield," he exclaimed. "How did that happen?"

Those words revealed to Vylara her prospective employer had no inherent sensitivity to Magic.

The shuttle righted itself. A respite from the thumping ensued. They felt the shuttle veer sharply, changing course.

"Does this mean we aren't headed toward Pandora's Peaks any longer?" Ange asked the shuttle.

For answer, the shuttle decelerated with a faint whining sound.

The group waited. A light grew outside the window, next they knew, the shuttle pulled up to a platform similar to the one from which they'd originally disembarked.

The shuttle let down the ramp and slid open the hatch.

"Wait here!" Lisza commanded, the Ministers brooked no argument.

The Guards activated their gravity skates with deft stepping motions and glided down the ramp.

Ange, Hannah, and Vylara sat calmly.

"Who is fooling who?" Ange remarked, he forced his keyed up muscles to relax.

A quarter mark later, the Guards returned with bad news.

"There is a rune door like the one in the Palace," Lisza said matter of fact. "There was a cave-in. It's solid rubble, no way out."

Ange addressed the shuttle as polite as could be, "excuse me,

Fly9? Beg pardon. We need to depart at a platform with an egress to our Planet surface."

The lighting flickered.

"I guess Fly9 heard us," Lisza drawled, an accent colored her diction.

A hair raising wail came from the distance.

Lisza whipped out her PDA. She tapped at her PDA's little screen to call a friend. "Hey Dana, did your training classes cover demonoid minions? Are they vulnerable to negatron hand-cannons?" She spoke into her PDA as if she never had a doubt in her communication equipment. "Dana?"

No answer.

The Guards examined both their PDAs and discovered they couldn't hail anything, not even the central dispatch computer.

"This can't be," Terriane tapped rapidly on her screen.

"Is it possible they're both broken?" Vylara shyly offered the suggestion.

"No," Lisza hesitated.

"Say it. We can handle bad news," Ange coaxed.

"We're being jammed. Something is deliberately sabotaging our comm-link."

"Jammed? As in jamming *technology*?" Ange became seriously subdued.

Any harboring doubts as to the validity of their rescue efforts, were now undoubted. Communications jamming could only be a deliberate act of an enemy. Was an invasion pending? The second howling wail, sounding not so distant this time, was all the more imperative for this new realization.

"Please Fly9," Ange said more urgently. "Please, help us escape our pursuers. It was said you are friend to our Emperor. We serve Emperor Methusem, we put our trust in you for our mission to protect Emperor Methusem from harm and deliver him safely from our enemies."

At first it seemed the plea would go ignored. The lighting flickered, the hatch closed, and the shuttle renewed their journey, gently accelerating. They all breathed a sigh of relief.

The Guards sat this time, Ange had a feeling they were mentally preparing for a fight.

"Hannah?" Ange said in his most persuasive voice. A voice that in his heyday was claimed to have swayed whole council meetings. "Does your Lore knowledge extend to know the meaning of these demonoid minions? Is it possible our whole planet is infested with them?"

Hannah's expressive dark eyes softened, gazing into Minister Ange's age lined and handsome face. She was not immune to his winsome ways; she knew, he knew.

Ange knew Hannah's will power was great enough to withstand his most persuasive arguments, she only acknowledged him out of the fondness of centuries of having been friendly to each other; he knew, she knew.

♋

Vylara looked down at her feet, a little despondent on seeing Minister Ange's heart leaning. She had half hoped, well, she pushed the hope aside.

♋

"I don't believe we have to fear an infestation. Minions have to be summoned. A Summoner would not call forth more then it could control," Hannah held her hands together tightly in her lap.

"A Summoner?" Ange traded looks with the Guards. They shook their heads, as baffled as he.

"Surely, Angélus, you remember. I'm sure you've been around, since the day?"

Ange scowled fiercely under the strain of trying to recall. "I'm sorry." He shrugged apologetically.

"There was a to-do a few centuries back. The Aristocratic Archon had issued forth a bounty on a troublesome Demon Summoner of the time. I wasn't in a position to learn all the particulars," Hannah continued in an even voice. "After all the trouble, there was a story out of Castle Utfordring. The Demons are ancient adversaries of the Dragons. A demonoid minion sworn to the Summoner attacked a Dragon cub, killing the cub.

I can't confirm any of this, mind you.

Twas said, the Dragon King of those lands, Lord Fafner, held the Summoner Kanuenos accountable. There was a battle.

I can't recall a hearsay nor trouble reported of the Demon Summoner afterward."

Hannah's enraptured listeners leaned back to digest this story. The few centuries back bit had Lisza and Terriane impressed.

Ange scratched at his chin bristles, clearly, he couldn't recall the events Hannah described.

A whine from the shuttle rose in pitch. They were accelerating all the more rapidly.

"Is Fly9 literally escaping our pursuers?" Vylara held on to the seat.

"How fast can those minions fly?" Terriane said aloud.

"An ambush may be ahead," Lisza speculated. "If I were piloting, I would go as fast as I could to crash through them."

"This doesn't make sense," Ange's mind spun scenario after scenario. "Supposedly, this Summoner is alive after all. And supposing our Emperor is being held captive. Why would it waste its minions on us?"

"Maybe, it means we're hot on their trail?" Lisza guessed.

Ange shook his head, then his gaze fell on Hannah. His heart leapt into his throat. A tiny worry wrinkle marked her otherwise serene face. Dearest Hannah, she was the grandest Lady he'd met in near three centuries of life. Too much of a Lady to include the juicy tidbits in her tale telling. He'd known her long enough to know she kept her secrets close. Did this Demon Summoner have a history with Hannah? It all didn't make any more sense, even with Hannah in the middle of some great secret. Never the less, he had to get her up into the daylight where the Guard forces could protect her.

Had she been aware of the minions before she'd volunteered

to come on this scatterbrained rescue party? It didn't seem likely, she'd been as surprised as the rest of us. Or had she fooled him completely?

All thoughts scattered when the shuttle pitched to the side, a stomach gut feeling of suspension heaved at his innards, then Fly9 landed on its side, tossing its passengers to the bottom. The hull scratching screech hurt their ear drums as the shuttle skidded on its side. The small group bated their breath, waiting for the shuttle to stop. The shuttle finished its momentum and with thundering hearts the group recomposed their senses. Light shone through the window, which was now the ceiling to their orientation.

The shuttle hatch opened.

"We'll check out the situation. Wait here," Lisza nodded to Terriane. The Guards skated up and out.

Terriane returned first. "There 's another shuttle out here. It's right side up. I'm going to carry you one at a time, Lisza has her hand-cannon to give us cover. Come on!"

"Take Hannah first," Ange helped Hannah to her feet amid her "but, but", "shh, no more buts."

Terriane didn't argue. "Step on my feet. There you go, left foot, right foot." Terriane pulled Hannah against her front, spooning Hannah. Once Hannah had dutifully placed her petite feet atop Terri's insteps, Terriane lifted Hannah up and out of the shuttle.

From the window, flashes of amber light were the only clue to Ange and Vylara that Lisza was firing her weapon. Ange exchanged looks with Vylara, appreciating her bravery in this situation.

"I feel bad about leaving Fly9 like this," Vylara confessed. "It put itself in jeopardy to save us."

"Yes. When all this is over, we'll inform Emperor Methusem. He'll know what we can do to help Fly9."

The lights flickered. The shuttle seemed able to appreciate their sentiment.

Terriane returned. Vylara knew better than to argue, she copied Hannah's position and the two women left Ange alone in Fly9.

Lisza dropped into the hole, "it's clear. Come on." Lisza pulled Ange on to her feet and spooned him. He was taller than she, Ange tilted his head down to let her be able to see forward. He wasn't too elderly to be able to appreciate his position. What a delightful woman! He chuckled.

Outside the shuttle, they glided on Lisza's g-skates towards a shuttle on the opposite side of a platform. Ange had only a brief glimpse of a dead thing with wings, it was a steaming pile of burnt critter. Lisza steered directly for the open ramp of the new shuttle.

Ange hopped off Lisza's feet and thanked her politely.

The new shuttle went through the motions of departure and started a steady acceleration. This shuttle had no whines. The ride was so smooth, they had no sensation of moving.

"Welcome friends," came a mechanical sounding voice. "My name is Fly13."

"Thank you for your timely arrival Fly13," Ange bowed deeply in the direction of the shuttle nose.

"All in good time," the shuttle answered.

"I am curious," Vylara said timidly. "Fly9 didn't talk to us?"

"I know. Tis truly sad. Fly9's vocal modules were extracted long ago."

"Oh, how horrible!" Vylara said.

"Fly9 will appreciate your kind sympathy, young Lady."

"Fly13," Lisza did her best to match Ange's polite formality. "Please, I am curious to know where our journey is leading us?"

"Your wish was to free our friend Methusem. We travel to Pandora's Peaks, under the relic ship."

"Thank you very much, kind Fly13."

Ange saw Vylara and Hannah whispering together at the back of the shuttle, he took the opportunity to whisper to the Guards. "We have to bring Hannah beyond the reach of those minion creatures," he put all the imperative he could muster into the plea.

"Hannah?" Lisza whispered into his ear. "Do you think they were after her?"

"I'm not entirely sure," Ange confessed. "No offense, but I can't think of any other person here who could possibly be of any significance to these creatures."

"You think there may be more to the story she was telling us earlier?" Lisza nodded.

"Understand, we may never know the whyfors. As immediately as opportunity presents, you can speedily carry Hannah to safety on your skates."

The Guards started to protest, Ange interrupted, "if my theory is correct, danger will follow you. You will be in greater danger than Vylara and myself."

"What plot are you three hatching?"

Ange startled guiltily as Hannah interrupted them.

"Minister Hannah," Lisza tried to defuse the tension with a show of her usual bravado, one hand on her hip and looked coy. "Could you think of any reason why the minions would be targeting you?"

Hannah's dark eyes flashed with spectacular temper, which she turned on Ange.

Ange's throat went dry, too dry to swallow.

"And you told them," Hannah nodded at the Guards, "to save me and leave you behind. Didn't you? And what about Vylara?

"You are avoiding Lisza's original question."

Hannah answered with a straight face, looked Angélus straight in the eye and confessed, "I cannot think of any reason why demonoid minions would be targeting me."

Ange's face fell. He'd been so certain she would confess.

"Angélus, stop looking at me like I ate your last cookie. I am telling you the truth. How do you know you aren't their target?"

"There is no rational reason why they would be after a

Minister of Royal Appointments."

"More than a housekeeper? Mayhap they're hungry and we smell a tasty treat?"

"Yes, I concede the point," Ange backed down in front of her temper. He knew, she knew, he was conceding no such thing. Would he ever learn the secrets to her mysteries?

♋

Hannah's expression passed a look of shutting down. She withdrew to sit on the last cushy seat bench in the rear of the shuttle.

Vylara followed Hannah, sitting beside her and almost afraid to disturb Hannah, she said quietly, "are you very angry with Minister Angélus?"

Hannah shrugged one eloquent shoulder. "No, not really. If he didn't act the infernal busybody, I'd have to wonder who the imposter is and what did he do with our Minister."

Out of sheer curiosity, Vylara asked, "has such a plot ever taken place?"

"Supposing it had, then I suppose they succeeded," Hannah chuckled at the audacity. Hannah looked up to see her chuckle had raised Ange's hopes. He offered her a little apologetic smile. Hannah appreciated his wisdom to not push the matter.

"You throw an impressive fire shield."

Hannah startled, she'd almost forgotten the Elf's presence.

"Why thank you, dear," Hannah twisted to sit sideways on the bench. "And are you preparing any of your Magic to ready a defense against what chases us?"

Vylara blushed and bit her lower lip, she tucked her long dark hair behind her pointed Elf ears. "I fear by the time I am close enough to use my Breath Magic, the fight will be all over for me."

"Nonsense. Anyway, not to worry, our Guards have proved very proficient with their weapons."

"Yes," Vylara's voice rose in pitch with enthusiasm. "Lisza was amazing, not one shot wasted."

"Yes," Hannah agreed. After a few moments of quiet, she said, "this morning, you mentioned something about Minister Ange saving your Ancestress at personal sacrifice. Would I be prying if I asked you for the tale?"

"Of course not," but before Vylara could reply further, Fly13 announced their imminent arrival.

"Please, save your story for when we are safe at home," Hannah requested.

The passengers had no sensation of slowing down. One moment the hatch was closed, next it was opening.

The Guards exited first.

Terriane poked her head in to inform them the coast was clear.

Vylara shuffled her feet down the ramp, giving Ange and Hannah an opportunity for private conversation.

Minister Angélus swept a low old fashioned courtly bow to Hannah. He offered her his elbow. "May I have the privilege of escorting you, my dear Lady?"

The Lady in question huffed at him at first. But, then Hannah dipped into an old fashioned courtly curtsy, one hand on her skirts. The spirit of the gesture lifted her heart. She crooked her fingers on Ange's elbow. Together they stepped into the deep space like quiet of the Subterraneum with all the aplomb of entering a Palace Ball in full dance.

Hannah scolded Ange before he could even think of it, "don't you dare start dancing."

"In deed," Ange chuckled. "Please save that dance for me when next we revel at the Palace Ball."

Lisza and Terriane were giggling helplessly, agreeing they never knew government Ministers were able to act silly.

"I sure hope those minions aren't flitting nearby," Lisza slapped her knee, trying to regain some seriousness, afraid she wouldn't have steady aim, if she was laughing.

Ange graciously thanked Fly13. He offered his free elbow to Vylara. The trio followed the Guards.

Lisza tried her PDA with a hope it would work this time. Communications were still down, but the scanner was functioning. "Oh yeah," she cheered. "We know where we are!"

"Tis a pleasant relief, eh?" Ange remarked.

Lisza and Terriane slowed their pace a few times, trying not to be too noticeable about it. Minister Ange was showing signs of fatigue, they guessed he would collapse before he complained.

"Ah," Lisza exclaimed. "Our scanners are picking up two blips."

"Our erstwhile Minister Nuben and Princess Dawn?" Ange was dismayed to hear a wheeze in his voice.

"Princess Dawn's vital signs are totally unique," Terriane said.

"Yeah. As unique as her twin sister's," Lisza drawled.

"Are you making fun of me?" Terriane slapped at the area of Lisza's rump.

From there, the two women were slapping at each other as they led the way. They also sounded like they were arguing over who was the more obtuse.

Ange surmised this by overhearing phrases beginning with, "oh yeah, well, remember the time you ..."

"It would seem," Ange commented to Hannah and Vylara as Lisza and Terriane were both doubled over with giggles. "We've expended their attention span for decorous behavior." He chuckled. The two Guards were lively. If you had to be in a dark and scary Subterraneum, they were pleasant company to have along.

They hadn't gone far when Hannah took her hand away from Ange's arm to put both hands on her skirt. She absently picked up the her pace and was soon caught up to Lisza and Terriane.

Ange strained his ears to hear if Hannah was having a conversation with the Guards.

Several steps behind, her hand still on Minister Ange's elbow, Vylara thought maybe Minister Hannah was preparing a helpful Spell by tracing the embroidery on her gown.

Before any Spell could be conjured by the Page Whisperer, a thick black shadow figure jumped in front of Vylara and Minister Angélus. It instantly solidified into solid rock, blocking the passage. Vylara and Ange became separated from the Guards and Hannah.

The thing not only blocked the passage, it blocked the only light, the glow cast by the Guards' gravity skates.

Vylara used her Breath Magic to cast a simple Glow Ball, but a Magic more powerful slapped down her Magic, snuffing it out.

IV. TERRA-DATE YEAR 215, DAY 143
:: North of Celesterra City, Cave Bluffs. Garren ::

A range of bluffs holding back the Adrianna Sea girded the northern coast of the continent near Celesterra City. Markedly above sea level, a preliminary base of operations was setup in a wide cave entrance to the Subterraneum Passages. This area was restricted to a minimum rank of Senior Guard.

"Haven't we detected Our Emperor's vital signs yet? He is the only half Dragon half Mer on the planet," a haggard Field Commander demanded from a Guard working at a computer console panel. The Guard mumbled a reply.

Across the cave, Garren Waysixth, a junior ranked guard of age 29 reckoned in terra-years, shyly crowded a Senior-Tech by a keyboard. He contributed his own finger typing to the Tech's in an effort to ascertain the best starting place for a search and rescue effort. The Elfin Tech gave the Human an encouraging smile, perfectly willing to share his station.

"YOU THERE!" The haggard Field Commander snapped at Garren.

Garren shook his hair-braid back in irritation, but otherwise ignored the snap.

The Field Commander came up beside Garren, reaching a rough hand to turn Garren; alas, he missed.

Garren anticipated the move and nimbly reared beyond reach.

"Who is your Commander?" The Field Commander demanded, sensing a potential troublemaker in his midst.

"I am unassigned," Garren faked an air of authority to which he had no claim.

"This mission is designated for Senior rank and above, only. We don't have time for overconfident under-graduates." The Field Commander puffed out his chest and pointed to the cave exit. "Vacate My Field of Operations, NOW!"

Garren's stormy-gray eyes flashed with a quiet rebellion. "I will search for Our Emperor without your by leave! My loyalty is directly to Him."

The Field Commander was not cowed, he had the epaulette pin and this firebrand with the combat trained physique did not. "The only reason I'm not having you escorted to the stasis cells is because I can't spare the personnel power. Mark me! You haven't heard the last of this. You'll be brought up on charges of Contumacy!" The Field Commander shouted to Garren's back.

For the Junior Guard had already penetrated into the tunnel system, alone in the dark for loyalty to his Emperor.

V. Terra-Date Year 215,Day 143
:: Celesterra Subterraneum. Emperor Methusem ::

"Swear Fealty to me!" The Emperor of the Galactic Realm demanded.

"They will not obey you, You Tyrant," a scathing Humanoid did not look up at his prisoner as he said this. He was intensely studying a computer panel.

A silvery shaggy furred Demon swung its ponderous leonine head toward its Summoner, its forked tail flicked at the ground stirring a sound like a whip crack.

A Spell-induced grogginess slowly relinquished its dark power over Emperor Methusem's returning consciousness, quite surprised to find he had succumbed to a Spell, since he was normally resistant to that sort of occurrence. He peered about the unfamiliar surroundings. It was an odd rock formed chamber this odd assortment of life forms were occupying; littered with rubble, smashed furnishings, and an eclectic mix of Magic arcania and advanced technology. Closing his eyes, Methusem could not telesense anything beyond a warding Spell entrapping him. He felt fairly certain these renegade Demons had not managed to smuggle him off planet or to escape his Guard Forces; ergo, this creepy ponderously quiet dungeon must be deep below the planet's surface.

'Dragonpoo', Methusem cussed. No one could say, what race had originally carved the network. There were remnants of things, unlike the friendly entity Fly13, things best left buried. And Methusem had an awful idea that he might be joining those buried remnants.

"Are these Demons enthralled to you?" Methusem tried asking politely, a little charm couldn't hurt matters.

"Bah, enough questions! Be it known, our ilk shall never accept your rule!"

"I gave your ilk plenty of time to evacuate this planet. Don't blame me."

The humanoid kept his tongue quiet a moment, then despite his resolution to not parlay away any information, spat; "It is YOU who needs to evacuate this GALAXY!"

"Who are you, Human?"

"Hah!"

Methusem lapsed silent to focus his concentration on his bondage predicament for chains and shackles suspended him by his wrists, pulling his arms taut. His lithe figure felt little strain from weight, but time and gravity would add agony to the position. Two more chains and a spreader bar forced his legs apart by the ankles, effectively suspending his nude body in a spread-legged position; highly undignified for his Royal Personage. His long midnight dark hair caused a tickle down by his thigh, a need to scratch the itch spot excruciatingly intense. Methusem's two hearts beat a hiccup out of unison.

If only these Demons would enter into the warding field, the critters would then be rendered vulnerable to Methusem's power. And he would use his power to crisp them into little Demon fritters! Oh yes, he would, eh! What kind of condiment to flavor Demon fritters? Would they be tasty or have a singed fur aftertaste? His gaze accidentally locked with one of the greater Demons, the eyes of the leonine Demon flamed like two glowing coals. There was something naggingly familiar about those eyes.

♌

Meanwhile; the Summoner reading his console instruments, perceived a flaw in the restraint system. If the Tyrant perceived the flaw! Fighting back a surge of panic, he had no doubt the Tyrant would feed him to the Dragons if freed. He mentally considered options. It would be best to kill the self-proclaimed Emperor immediately, alas, how to kill this damnable creature beyond resurrection?

A deep growling voice said slowly, so low it would hurt a Human's ears, "Kanuenos".

"Quiet you fool!"

"Is that so? You are Kanuenos! Never heard of you!" The Emperor twitched an ephemeral smile.

The Greater Demon whip cracked its forked tails, striking Methusem's bare legs and missing the itchy spot. A rattle of chains was the only sound in response.

"Bah, wasting your time. He can outlast more pain than you can gift him with, Ariel," Kanuenos returned the favor of naming names.

A small gasp came from the Emperor, not induced by physical pain. Was there history here between these two? Kanuenos studied the Greater Demon Ariel; this ancient Felled Angel was not so powerful as to resist a summoning charm; unless Ariel had answered at his own will and reason, no matter, laying this conjecture aside for futurity.

'Would feeding Demon blood to the Emperor unbalance the Tyrant's powers with its draught of demonic power? Twas impossible to drain the Tyrant's powers, but could he be fed power to the point of overbalance?' Kanuenos stared with eyes wide and bloodshot at his prisoner. Two centuries culminating to this moment and here it was arrived. Two centuries of study, summoning Demons and digging deep into ancient lore.

Grandmared of a Dragoness and born of a Mermaid mother, poised the Tyrant in a balance between two adversarial realms, both a Dragon King and a Demon Lord combining the ancient rivals into a grudging truce. The audacity for such a creature to claim dominion over Pan Jupiter Major! It was Kanuenos's pet theory that the mere presence of too much demonic essence in the Realm plane would upset Methusem's balance and overwhelm the tyrant's 'so called' sanity, out of balance and weak the Emperor would be and vulnerable to eternal death. And now Kanuenos hesitated in fear, too afraid to test his cherished theory.

Kanuenos paced, coming to stand in the chamber's center and facing towards Methusem's in bondage body. "What would happen if I cut out your heart?"

Methusem smiled a slow smile and spoke softly with dire promise. "It depends which you take."

"What if I cut out both?" Kanuenos startled, a bit disturbed upon realizing he had muttered his rhetorical mutterings aloud.

"Why don't you find out?" Methusem said sweetly.

Even the Demons winced nervously. One of the ovine Demons made a noise suspiciously like a 'baaaa'.

Kanuenos muttered, "so sweet voiced and so pretty," yet, the subtle threat chilled him to the marrow. His lore knowledge ran deep. Lore said, 'the Were-Dragons cannot hear a lie.' If they cannot hear a lie, than logically, they would not know what it was to utter a lie, yet; the Mer folk were the epitome of duplicity.

All he had to do was prevent Methusem's delicate girly wrists from slipping the shackles, and then order his demonoid slaves to collapse the passages. The Royal Guards would never find their Emperor. He rummaged in the debris piles, until he found an interesting item; a plank made of dead tree material and as he lighted on two long nail spikes, more ancient lore chunked into his mind. The humanoid's eyes were all for the Emperor's face, while he handed the spikes to the Greater Demon Ariel.

Ariel lifted his upper body, a bright flash of light flared and dimmed to reveal Ariel in humanoid form, a man beast with a head much like his Demon form.

Methusem's Dragon-Heart knew no fear, but his Mer-Heart feared the ancient Felled Angel Ariel. A scream spilled from his throat, his Dragonish cry sending echoes into the passages. "Someone HELP me! Someone PLEASE!"

"Ah-ha-ha," Kanuenos waved merrily, "take your time Ariel. Meet me at the gate's mouth when you're done destroying this vile creature. You vile creature," Kanuenos nearly choked on his next words, "you who buried your own sworn friend alive."

"NO!" Methusem cried, but knew the words had to be true for his Dragon heart was incapable of hearing a lie. It was a weakness he'd never regretted.

"Yes! You made yourself forget with a Spell. Revoke your forget Spells and drink the horrors of your life."

Methusem didn't want to believe, he touched the power within his flesh and felt nothing of Forget Spells. He sighed in relief. 'Perhaps, the Demon Summoner is trying to demoralize me into becoming self destructive.' Perhaps his Mer heart was allowing the lies to reach his Dragon heart. The sobs spilling from his throat were from his Mer heart as the Felled Ariel began its task.

The Demon Summoner tarried long enough to watch with infinite glee, the spikes driven home and then he departed.

♌

Emperor Methusem was sobbing even while Ariel finished its work and floated to the ground. He was unable to strike back, which meant IT was the caster of the warding Spell. None of the lesser entities came close. One by one they fled away, until it was only Ariel and the sound of Methusem's strident breath.

"Why? We have no duel between us," Methusem felt weary and very heavy.

"Swear Fealty to me," Ariel's eyes flamed like strange glowing coals, his voice not so deep sounding in humanoid form. He stood proud, covered mostly in silver fur, a very Human looking oversized penis thick as his wrist lifted erect.

"What?" Methusem felt cold running like broken glass into his limbs. He screamed again, begging for help from somebody.

"I will release you, if only you will vow your undying loyalty to me." Ariel rose into the air and leaned his face close to Methusem's ravaged with suffering face.

"Never!" Methusem sobbed out a brief litany of expletives.

"You would rather suffer this then worship me? Am I that anathema to your Dragon essence? You, who are an abomination of Demon and Dragon vile union!" Ariel rose higher into the air, fire flamed around his body.

"Help me." Methusem panted and felt one of his hearts falter.

"Promise your love to me. Together, our combined powers will pierce the Realm vale. We will fell all what hast not fallen from atop the highest of choirs."

"NO ...I will ... lay ... with you, not for ... power, but for truce, if only ... you will release me from this torture," Methusem whispered, his head resting like a dead weight on his shoulder.

"You think your empty lust could possibly tempt me?" Ariel blazed in fury. "Agony consume you." Upon those last words the Greater Demon fled away on the sound of Methusem's last weakening scream.

"Fall to Erebus, damn you Ariel. I curse you," Methusem screamed, knowing full well the Curse could not escape the warding Spell.

VI. TERRA-DATE YEAR 215, DAY 143
:: Seaside Palace Council Chambers. Kerlin Lantanthen. ::

Senior Guard, Kerlin Lantanthen, shook back his chest length red hair with a snap of his neck, wincing, too fast a snap, his neck muscles protested. He suppressed an 'oww'. He stood leaning against the back wall of the Council Chamber, arms folded.

Close to two hundred people packed the ornate room of the Seaside Palace, crammed together in a standing room only crowd. Most of the attendees were clad in the black uniforms of the Royal Guard, with some splashes of gold robes worn by the government ministers.

At the front of the room, a formal table occupied a raised dais. Sovereign Minister Allons presided over the meeting, his chair pushed back and he was standing mid-table. To either side of him, sat Senior Ministers facing towards the assembly with their elbows on the table. Two of the Royal Fleet's top Star Commanders were seated amongst the Ministers; Commander Bel and Commander Tane for their ships were newly returned from their deep space assignments.

From where he leaned, Kerlin could not hear what was being said at the 'Head' table. Minister Allons was treating the Emperor's unexplained absence as a war act. Kerlin was not ready to believe anything could overcome Emperor Methusem's powers. Kerlin shook his head, clasping his hand firmly to his aching neck.

A voice from the crowd shouted something about wasting time in Councils, when they should be out searching for their Emperor without delay. Kerlin recognized a Field Team Commander as the shouter; the FTC forced his way to the front of the crowd with his Field Team close behind.

Kerlin's brown eyes crossed paths with a senior guard named Pursy. Pursy was a Human on Kraken's Team, and he was the instigator behind the team's most obnoxious pranks. Kerlin looked away in disgust after Pursy made a sexual tongue flicking gesture.

A minor commotion at a side entrance to the Council Chamber drew Kerlin's attention. Another 'below Senior Guard rank' attempting to crash the Council Meeting, after Minister Allons had decreed only Guards 'senior rank and above' were allowed to join the search and rescue. There'd been a string of them the last time marker, but this Guard sounded overly persistent. Kerlin glimpsed a snow blonde head, the rest of him hidden by the two door Guards. More people were becoming distracted by the commotion.

Kerlin felt totally sympathetic to the younger Guards, bereft of the comforting security of their Emperor's presence upon the seat of Empire. There had been no war in their lifetimes, no war for two terra-centuries; the conquest by their Emperor had been the last. A Realm at peace! Many of the Royal Guard – Guardians of the Realm – lived under a mantle of complacency and did not have the mindset for war. To-Terra-Day could be the beginning of a rude awakening.

Being currently unassigned to a Commander allowed Kerlin a certain degree of autonomy, no one would miss him. Someone needed to assume a big shoulder to cry on role for the younger ones. Kerlin raised a foot to kick off the wall in a toe-shoe position; the winking lights of his gravity-skates stringing along the soles of his uniform boots ran a random-dazzle color display. Rather than push through the crowd, he skated up perpendicular to the wall and glided to the side entrance. Kerlin calmly ex-scuzied himself passed the door Guards, his shiny black uniform cloak fluttered gracefully in a breeze from the hall.

In the Hallway, he confronted a Human male with long streaming snow-white hair hanging loose in a breach of uniform protocol. Technically, Senior Guard Kerlin had the authority to Writ the blonde, but hey; Kerlin wore his hair loose, too. Under the veil of blonde hair, gold irises shimmered on a pale alabaster complected face. The young man was very slim for a Human.

Beside this vision a female of the same age and coloring hovered nervously; she wore the blue uniform of the Junior Guards. She spun around and hurried off down the marbled Hall.

Kerlin privately thought the whole Palace décor overly marbled to a fetishist's extreme.

"Pré!" The male Guard called after the fleeing girl to no avail.

He can't be more than 18 or 19 terra-years, Kerlin decided, yet the blonde wore the black uniform of a fully vested Guard. The uniform's epaulette pin did not have a Commander's insignia on the setting, ahah, unassigned. The gold eyes and complexion gave away the blonde's origin planet. Humans inhabiting the planet StrataTerra had been isolated for so long; they had evolved their own racial traits.

"Hi, I'm Kerlin," Kerlin smiled kindly. Meeting the worried gaze of the Strata-Terran, Kerlin felt twice his age, though Kerlin was no more than a decade older. Kerlin held his hand out for a wrist-to-wrist greet, but the blonde rudely ignored the gesture.

"I'm Amé Asgothe, and I'm ..."

Kerlin forestalled the rest of the statement, beckoning Amé to leave earshot of the door Guards. They walked, until they turned a Hall intersection and were beyond view.

"It's no use, there is nothing you can do to stop me!" Amé blurted out defiantly.

"Stop you from what?" Kerlin put a companionable hand on Amé's shoulder.

"Searching for Emperor Methusem!" Amé's eyes narrowed, indicating a fierce stubbornness.

"Sounds like a great plan to me," Kerlin stepped back and

folded his arms; his brown eyes warm with sympathetic kindness.

"We're going into the Subterraneum passages then, we should requisition weapons!" Amé nodded, to his mind Kerlin's receptiveness made practical sense.

Kerlin smiled and shrugged agreement. "And since we're going underground," he put a hand to his smooth chin, - face rather heart shaped -, thinking aloud, "we should bring along a Negatron Tunnel Blaster."

"Ah, I can tell right away you're Commander material," an elderly woman with close cropped gray hair and wearing a mustard yellow minister's robe practically pounced on them from seemingly out of nowhere. 'How did she sneak up on us?' Kerlin did not recognize her, nor apparently, did Amé.

"You'll need my authority to access the weapons; you don't have a Commander to give it for you."

"We can't argue with that," Kerlin acknowledged, "Minister …?"

"Call me LeeAnne," she started them walking towards an offshoot wing of the Palace.

Another elderly Lady Minister rushed up. "O fantastic Lee, you found some."

"Some? You mean us?" Kerlin smiled, amused by this.

"Yeah, well," LeeAnne answered his quizzical look. "You're quick, intelligent, and unassigned. We can't trust Allons to get the job done."

Amé spoke up. "Did you mean Kerlin or both of us?"

"Oh Amé, we're well aware of your special relationship with Methusem," the two women smiled reassuringly.

LeeAnne's friend hesitated, "I dunno Lee. Mebbe this be too dangerous."

"We can handle it," Amé was very quick to say.

"What exactly can we handle then?" Kerlin already knew he would do whatever task the Ministers set him to, but a little caution would be wise.

Taking a deep shrugging breath, LeeAnne checked for eavesdroppers, then began, "three of our Ministers, the Princess Dawn, and a small escort of Guards, went into the underground passages. We're not saying they disappeared," Minister LeeAnne quickly added, "we're just out of communication with them."

"We think this means they are hot on the trail of where-ever Methusem is being held."

Kerlin remained silent a moment, try as he might, he could not follow their logic to that assumption.

"You said three Ministers?" Amé spoke with no small concern.

"Yes. Minister Angélus, Minister Nuben, and Minister Hannah," after reciting the list LeeAnne's friend betrayed her fearsome worry.

Kerlin found this news quite remarkable. He knew Minister Ange, kind of a busy body, but Kerlin was quite fond of the old good hearted Minister. And the Caretaker of the Royal Jewels and the Housekeeper were also out of communication?! Ah, that's right, these three Ministers would be intimate with the Emperor on a daily basis. And Princess Dawn? Kerlin remembered hearing gossip, Princess Dawn was magically adept. The most vulnerable of the missing were the Ministers.

"Come on, let's hurry!" LeeAnne prompted, they all sped to the Weapons Clerk's Office with as much alacrity as the Human ladies could muster.

Kerlin and Amé waited outside the weapons claim lobby, while the Ministers went in to sign for the equipment. Would the docket clerk ask questions or just hand the stuff over? Kerlin was very curious to know, but let it go.

There were Guards standing on a line outside the lobby doorway all waiting to claim weapons, the tail end of the line reaching to the inter-floor lifts. Kerlin felt fortunate to have the Lady Ministers using their authority on his behalf. Amé stood quietly near his elbow, withdrawn into his own private thoughts, a pinched expression discouraged idle conversation.

Kerlin studied the waiting line of Guards, he observed many wearing the epaulette pin etched with Commander Bel's insignia. He was about to go up and say 'Hi' to a female Elf, Kerlin liked to introduce himself to fellow red-heads, he sometimes entertained an idea to start a Red Headed League; for fun.

Before Kerlin opened his mouth to say anything, he caught the gist of a conversation the Elf lady was having with a Human male next to her. From the gist, Kerlin THOUGHT he heard the Human propositioning her and he THOUGHT she told the guy he would have to have sex with her brother first, then, IF her brother gave his recommendation, she would consider the guy's proposition.

A male Elf bearing a twin's resemblance to the girl, stood by an open window at the Hall's end. The upper floor Palace corridor caught a refreshing cross breeze; the Elf leaned into it closing his eyes, looking very peaceful.

Kerlin forwent pondering the gist of the girl's conversation for the Lady Ministers reappeared. Kerlin and Amé quickly shouldered the equipment the ladies dragged out and they hithered off to Palace halls they'd never before been privileged to hither.

They crossed into an area known as the Antiquities Wing. Not another person in sight, their steps echoed. The way was confusing and Kerlin briefly considered that if the Palace Halls were confusing, how was he ever going to navigate the Subterraneum? But, their gear included scanning equipment and Kerlin was pleased to note everything they carried had been covered in training classes.

"This is it," Minister LeeAnne suddenly announced, standing in front of a heavy closed door. Runes etched the metal, probably a mage tongue.

In the unoccupied area of the Palace, their breathing sounded amplified. Amé's eyes were opened very wide, Kerlin noticed. Amé did not complain, he readjusted the Negatron Pulse Rifle hanging from a strap on his shoulder and took a deep breath.

Kerlin nodded his readiness to the Lady Ministers and through the final threshold they crossed, and immediately there upon a stinging wind slapped them in the face, ugh.

An artificial subway tunnel presented itself, facing in two directions from the little platform they stood upon. It seemed to reach into infinity. It was perfectly round and smooth. It looked a perfectly wretched place to have to walk. Kerlin wore gravity-skates, Amé did not.

LeeAnne did something Kerlin found quite spectacular, she put two fingers to her lips and sounded a long piercing whistle. She repeated this odd gesture thrice. The acoustics of the tunnel amplified the whistling echoes.

LeeAnne's friend huddled into herself, looking frightened. "You aren't obligated to do this, you know, we can turn back."

Kerlin, to be frank, was sorely tempted to go back, not sure anything could make him step into the dark windy night of the subway tube. What in Astra's name lived down here? Celesterra was not a planet free of dangerous insects and rodent critters.

A strange machine like sound approached from the left tunnel. And a single bright light appeared, very tiny at first, it grew as it came closer. A frightened 'yip' came from Amé.

Very soon, the source of the noise arrived. It was a tube shuttle, a very strange looking shuttle of no recognizable origin; to Kerlin's imagination the plates on the nose of the thing resembled a face. It stopped at the platform and a hatch slid open and a ramp slid out like a monster opening its maw and lashing its tongue.

"Fly13," LeeAnne called, "tis good to cya!"

"LeeAnne," a mechanical voice answered. "Ah yes, it be disturbing times if the rumours be true!"

"Fly13," LeeAnne said in a very formal tone. "Please carry

these two brave Guards safely to our brave friends whom you carried yesterday."

"Will do, LeeAnne," the strangely mechanical voice replied. "I volunteered to stay active for these such times."

"I?" Kerlin couldn't contain his wonder. "This machine said I?"

"Please, Kerlin," LeeAnne said, very politely, still in formal tones. "This machine is sentient. It is friend to us and our Emperor."

A sentient machine! Kerlin slapped himself to make sure he wasn't dreaming. He enthusiastically bounded up the narrow ramp, Amé trailed with more reluctance. The inside of the shuttle was lit to a satisfying degree; soft yellowish lamps cast their shadows on the walls. Two rows of cushioned seats were available; Amé chose a seat directly next to Kerlin. They shrugged their equipment and Negatron rifles to the floor. Kerlin reclined into the seat, stretching his legs out comfortably. The shuttle closed up its hull and made a strange hissing noise.

The shuttle accelerated steadily. They shot down the tunnel and with no external frame of reference, they had the illusion of no movement at all. Kerlin nattered gaily with Fly13, while Amé remained in silence. The young Guard fidgeted with a silver bracelet chain he wore on one wrist, another breach of uniform protocol. StrataTerra, Amé's home planet, was the haute couture fashion center of the Realm.

Kerlin quite enjoyed Fly13's conversation; the shuttle was well conversant in all the current literature and had some interesting opinions. He would like to cultivate Fly13 as a friend, if it was manageable.

A map would be great, Kerlin looked around the shuttle, seeing only yellow walls, orange panels, and the brown seats. He checked the time on his wrist worn time-marker, they'd been traveling like this for well over 2 marks. They could be anywhere on the planet by now.

"Excuse me Fly13," Kerlin interrupted a dissertation on the

origins of the piccolo. "Do you have a map or something to show us where we are?"

"Oh, my dear man," Fly 13's mechanical voice stressed. "I should have anticipated your need."

"No bother friend," Kerlin sat up.

One of the orange panels slid open to reveal a holographic projector. A complex assimilation of lines appeared, drawing and again drawing upon itself, until the map expanded to fit the small area in front of them. Kerlin gaped. It appeared the network of subway tunnels encompassed the globe. Once the lines finished drawing, a surface terrain map began superimposing the subway map, with a big orange 'You are Here' dot.

Kerlin's heart rate quickened and he surrendered to Amé's hand slipping into his, not so blasé now about the trip.

They were heading straight under the shadow of Pandora's Relic Ship in the mountain range known as Pandora's Peaks.

VII. TERRA-DATE YEAR 215, DAY 143
:: Under Pandora's Peaks. Kerlin Lantanthen. ::

Kerlin and Amé disembarked at a station platform very similar to the one they'd used at the Palace.

"Thank you for our safe passage, Fly13," Kerlin bowed.

"I shall wait for you here, until I am called for, elsewhere."

"Thank you Fly13, I feel better knowing you're here," Amé said in a respectful tone.

Fly13 closed up, pulling in it's ramp. The lights shining from the shuttle winked dark.

"Supposedly, this is where our Ministers were left off," Amé headed for the only exit from the platform. The rune door stood open.

Kerlin followed, holding his PDA at eye level, he tapped the instrument into scan mode.

Beyond the threshold, carved stone steps led upwards. Just as Kerlin started to wonder how the elderly Ministers had fared on these steps, they reached the end and the underground trail leveled. The ground underfoot was covered in powdery fine dirt. Kerlin shined a hand held light beacon on the ground and they could make out faint traces of Human sized footprints.

"Fly13 did not lead us amiss," Amé picked up the pace as they followed the footprints.

Kerlin checked his PDA, there were no signs of life registering. Not so much as a rodent. Was there a predator eating up all the rodents? Had it run out of food?

They came to a turning point in the passage, the passage veered right, but the footprints did not.

"Huh." The footprints led directly into solid rock. The scanner picked up a hollow passage yonder the solid rock; no life signals.

Amé leaned his chin on Kerlin's shoulder, standing on tippy-toe behind Kerlin to share a view of the PDA screen. "Should we look for a detour around or blast through the rock?"

"Did Magic do this? It doesn't look like a cave-in. What say you?"

"I'm perceptive towards Magic and I'm not sensing any," Amé revealed. "I agree this doesn't look like a cave-in."

Kerlin rubbed his chin. "Illusion?"

Amé took a cautious step backwards. "Have you ever heard of Demonoids who can transform their flesh into rock?"

"No," Kerlin retuned his PDA to scan for any and all known forms of energy. "How do you think a Demonoid would react to a Negatron Tunnel Blaster used on it?"

"By becoming angry and eating us."

"We're in uniform, I doubt it could take a chomp out of our hides," Kerlin tried for this bit of bolstering courage.

"Or it could swallow us whole," Amé gulped. "You outrank me, call it."

Kerlin couldn't imagine Amé ever uttering those words. He ran the PDA close to the rock, there were positively no vital signatures coming from the rock.

He used the PDA to scan up a map of the area. It's field of influence didn't reach far enough to show where the passage would end. Just then, an energy signature blipped.

"What was that?" Amé pointed to the mini screen.

"A negatron sig," Kerlin answered.

"From a Guard issue weapon?" Amé didn't sound happy.

"Amé, Minister LeeAnne said a guard escort was with our missing Ministers. This could be them."

"Or it could be a guard search and rescue party with the authority to escort me off the field. I'm below rank for this mission."

"Amé, I'm sure they are too busy to escort you off," Kerlin sympathized.

"Well, I know Emperor Methusem personally, He'll reverse the below rank decree once we rescue Him. I just have to avoid anyone who would throw me into a stasis cell."

"By the Vale, would they really put one of our own in stasis" Kerlin swore at the ridiculousness of it. He smoothed his hair back. He started them walking again, moving towards the negatron energy blip.

"Aye," Amé was learning to appreciate Kerlin. "Our Emperor should make you Supreme Sovereign Command-Second, then you'd have rank over Minister Allons."

"There is no such rank."

"There aught to be! And, I'm going to suggest it," Amé shrugged his rifle strap more securely over his shoulder.

"You're whimsical," Kerlin grinned. His grin died as the PDA mysteriously went dark. "What's this?"

Amé checked his own PDA. No power. Their light beacons went dark next. They stood within the amber glow of their negatron weapons.

"Whatever it is, it can't suck the energy out of negatron weapons," Amé swung his rifle forward to double check it.

"It would seem not," Kerlin held his PDA to his ear, listening intently for any telltale energy hum. All he heard was a strange far off scuffling sound.

Amé huddled against Kerlin's side. "That wouldn't be what a shape changing rock Demonoid would sound like, if it was walking?"

"We're not completely in the dark. Let's quicken our pace a bit, eh," Kerlin moved forward.

They jogged. The passageway curved up. They paused after they realized they weren't hearing the strange scuffling sound anymore.

"What if?" Amé said. "What if our Ministers were eaten by something?"

"Amé," Kerlin began, "we read a negatron sig, I'm pretty sure it means they're okay."

"Not really. It just might mean the weapons weren't digestible."

Kerlin stood quiet. Was he less brave than Amé by refusing to contemplate the possibility? In the quiet of only their breathing, the scuffling sound started approaching again.

"We should capture it for interrogation," Kerlin said.

"Capture ... it?" Amé tightened his grip on his rifle.

"Yes. Anything in this area is suspect. It might know something we need to know."

"If you say so," Amé locked his knees, ashamed to show knee quivering fear in front of Kerlin.

"I'd feel better if we had some cover," Kerlin brought his negatron rifle around and held it close to his chest, pointed down the passageway. Now that they were waiting for it, the scuffling sounded a long way off.

"Too bad our PDAs don't run on negatron particles," Amé broke their waiting silence.

"Mine does," Kerlin shrugged.

"Senior rank guards are equipped better than the rest of us," Amé pouted.

Kerlin grinned in the near dark. It was an extraordinary pout from what he could see.

"This means our PDAs probably aren't drained. Something is interfering with the power flow to the cpu."

"A strong jamming signal could do it," Kerlin mused. He shifted his weight. The scuffling thing was taking awhile, yet, he wasn't quite ready to run to meet it.

"Are you a scientist?" Amé asked.

"Me? No. I'm certified in a few technical skills tracts, enough to read our instruments. I can't fix them."

"I'm not a scientist, either; I can't wrap my head around base 42 math. I'm certified in cartography."

"After a deep space assignment, eh?" Kerlin leaned against

the rock face.

"Maybe. What's the focus of your training, then?

"I'm into physical training, gymnastics and acrobatics."

"Really? So, you can climb walls and cliffs? Sounds interesting," Amé complemented. "You're certified in gravity skates, eh? You probably don't have to do much climbing."

"I guess it doesn't make much sense," Kerlin shrugged. "It's basically a family tradition."

They interrupted their conversation when the scuffling noise stopped. They strained to listen. In a few moments, the noise started up again.

"Taking after your father, then?" Amé resumed their conversation.

"My mother, actually," a tender smile touched Kerlin's lips.

"Is that ...," Amé leaned close to Kerlin's ear. "Is that a tattoo under your hair?"

"Why yes. How can you see my tattoo in this dimness?"

"I can see your aura, it paints a light around your silhouette. You look brighter to me in the dark."

"You see auras? A remarkable talent," Kerlin was impressed. He scratched at his hair grown over his tattoo, above his left ear. His mother would be upset if she knew he hadn't kept to tradition. Most of his young life, his hair had been buzzed close to his scalp.

Amé held out his wrist. "I apologize for my rudeness, earlier. I'm very pleased to make your acquaintance Kerlin."

Kerlin smiled and grasped the offered wrist, letting the pulse in his wrist rest over Amé's, even though he couldn't feel the pulse through their uniforms.

The scuffling sounded much, much closer now.

Amé took back his hand, so they could both grip their rifles. "Capture, right? Meaning, we can't hurt it."

"Correct, we need it to answer our questions."

In the tense silence, a new sound intruded.

"Huh?" Kerlin pushed off the wall and gave a listen. "Do

you hear singing? It sounds very pretty," Kerlin leaned toward the sound. The opposite direction from the scuffling.

"Mermaids. Ignore it mate! They're Demons, you know." Amé gave Kerlin a push to try and break the Spell.

Kerlin staggered a bit, then started moving towards the singing.

♋

"Kerlin, stop!" Amé suffered a pang of angst. He swung his long blond hair behind his shoulder and followed Kerlin.

For some reason, Kerlin wasn't bumping into rocks. He squeezed through a tight rock formation and kept going. The Mermaid's Siren Song was leading Kerlin unerringly through the labyrinth of underground passageways. A bit of sunlight was soaking through the dimness.

Amé realized they were nearing an exit. Their beacon lights winked on and Amé pulled out his PDA to see the instrument was functioning normally. Most bizarre. Not as bizarre as watching Kerlin succumb to the lure of the Mermaids. He seemed too practical, not the type who would be spelled.

Amé followed Kerlin out into a cave entrance area, over the lip of the cave entrance, he could see blue ocean. An artificially made pond took up the center of the entrance area, barely roomy enough for two Mermaids.

Two Mermaids lounged on chair sized rocks, wearing the loveliest scarf dresses Amé had ever seen. Amé felt a twinge of envy.

The Mermaids both wore their hair very long, thick tresses spilled to touch the fins on the end of their dolphin like tales. Necklaces of precious stones laid over their full breasts, no attempt at modesty was made to cover their nipples under their dresses. Bangle bracelets of mythril metal made pleasant bell like sounds as they raised their arms in a welcoming gesture at Kerlin.

Their sensational singing toned down to a hum, the power in their song raised ghostbumples on Amé's skin, but he did not succumb. He'd had sex often enough with Emperor Methusem, that his intimate nearness to Methusem's powerful effulgence had bathed him and imparted to Amé some resistance to Magical attack. The Mermaids seemed to sense this and concentrated on Kerlin.

One of them started to shimmer a glowing mist of light around her tail, as the light spent itself, two legs were now spawned from the Mermaid's hips. She stood, the scarf dress flowed down her length, showing a provocative long line of skin.

Words were now being sung within her hum. "Come to me lover."

Kerlin took one step forward, then stopped in a lurching motion.

Amé saw Kerlin's eyes roll up like he was about to faint. Kerlin stood his ground and snapped out of it. Expression animated his face once more.

The standing Mermaid lowered her arms. She pointed at Amé. Her voice was less pleasant as she said, "you I understand. ... How is he resisting me?" Her bangles chimed as she swung her pointing finger at Kerlin.

"I'd say," Amé answered for Kerlin, "he isn't interested in sex with you."

"Sex!" Kerlin looked genuinely surprised.

"I'd say," Amé said to the Mermaids, "sex hadn't even occurred to him."

Kerlin looked a bit bashful. "Is their a problem?"

The Mermaid's expression was priceless. She sniffed the air. Amé laughed at her.

"I would gander," Amé paused, but Kerlin nodded at him to continue. "It's probably related to your regime of rigorous athletic training. Runner's high, so to speak. Your endorphins are exhausted from exercise, not leaving you wanting in the sex department."

"A challenge," the Mermaid who hadn't transformed her tale

into legs said. "If I wasn't pregnant I would try all my persuasions on you."

"Congratulations! My sincerest regards." Kerlin refused comment on the challenge thing.

Both Mermaids were scenting the air, making them appear more carnal.

"What is it? Do you smell rock Demonoid?"

"A rock demon?" The Mermaid crinkled her nose. "There is no such thing."

Kerlin and Amé looked at each other. No such thing? Then what had been the cause of the scuffling noise following them?

"I smell something exquisite."

"Rapturous."

"Sublime."

"Amazing."

The two Mermaids ran out of words, seeming to swoon.

"What is it?" Amé was almost afraid to ask.

"The scent of virgin blood."

The lovely Mermaids smiled, their eyeteeth elongated. Their seaweed green eyes had no whites to them.

Kerlin stared at their teeth, learning something new about Mermaids. Amé swung his negatron rifle to point it at them.

"Relax, we will not harm him," they spoke in unison. They sank into the water.

"May I ask, why not?" Amé moved a little in front of Kerlin.

Kerlin reacted to Amé's move. "I appreciate the sentiment, but I believe I'm safe."

"Indeed, we would be in so much trouble with our betters if we despoiled a virgin," the Mermaids' spoke with no little disappointment. "You are not for the likes of us."

"Should we tell Chantal about him?" The pregnant one asked her companion.

"No, I don't want a hand in harming him," the one with legs let her face sink under the water surface.

"What harm?" Amé demanded.

"I'm Tibetha," the pregnant Mermaid said.

"Don't give them your name," Amé warned Kerlin, being careful not to say his name.

Just then! A large shadow passed over the cave entrance. A shadow the size of a flying shuttle. A figure in full guard uniform started to enter the cave, but then turned back to speak to somebody.

"It's Commander Barett. I can tell by his aura, he is *not* happy," Amé said quietly, he put up his rifle, not sensing a threat from the Mermaids.

"You overestimate me," Commander Barett was saying to someone they couldn't see around the turned edge of the parapet.

"Your Permit of Residence for Celesterra is temporary. You'll have to return home to Quinterra Planet one day. You left a lot of unhappy people behind," said the voice of the person they couldn't see.

"Quinterra will nevermore abide the pleasure of my company, I feel most assured on this point."

"Your Goddess gives you long life, doesn't she? You should feel assured on nothing."

Commander Barett turned his back on the person. When he faced Kerlin and Amé, he wore his usual amused sneer. Hiding whatever his true emotions were, perfectly.

"You're intentions toward are helpful Mermaids are honorable, I hope?" Barett came around the edge of the little pond.

"This one is more infatuated with our dresses," the Mermaids giggled like Elf maids.

Cdr Barett took one look at Amé's epaulette pin to learn Amé's rank. "Ahh, below senior rank. Shall I Writ you a caning?"

"Actually, we're not on the 'search for Emperor Methusem mission'," Kerlin stepped forward.

"Am I supposed to believe you?" Commander Barett said

with some amusement.

Kerlin shrugged his Negatron Rifle into his hands, very casual like.

"Who issued you weapons?" Barett said, eyeing the weapons and other gear they carried.

"Minister LeeAnne. Has Minister Angélus, Ole Nuben, or Minister Hannah emerged from the Subterraneum?"

"Don't tell me they're missing?" Barett seemed genuinely dismayed. "What has gotten into people? Don't they trust us to find Our Emperor?" Barett stopped mid-rant.

Kerlin merely looked at him.

"This is because of Minister Allons. He doesn't inspire confidence in his competence," Barett added. Held his hand close to his chest over his heart.

"Why are there Mermaids involved in our field operations?" Kerlin said.

Barett made a show of tolerating the question. "They are using their Siren powers to help rescue our Guards from the Subterraneum. As you've probably discovered, our instruments aren't working underground. Their song leads our people out. And unlike your companion here, some of our 'below senior rank' have gotten themselves in over their heads."

A flicker in Barett's eye betrayed a worry. Or maybe two worries, Kerlin thought, it was hard to be sure.

"And when your Mermaids lead them out, you'll be the first one here on the scene to cane them?"

Barett's expression didn't change.

"The incoming shuttle is bringing Fleet Commander Tane to this field site, he'll outrank the rest of us," Barett shrugged. "If you intend to continue with your search for our Ministers, you should both leave now before he circumvents you."

"Would you happen to have a spare PDA that works under the mountain?" Amé said.

"I shall accompany you," the Mermaid with legs said. "We wouldn't want anything to happen to you and my powers may be helpful." She sniffed the air and fluttered her eyelashes.

Barett raised an eyebrow. "Do we not need the power of both of you to sing our friends to the surface?"

Tibetha argued, "Chantal is very near. She would help me sing. Your virgin friend here will need one of us to run interference with our Siren song, or he will be swayed from his purpose, anew."

"A virgin?" This was said from the cave entrance. A Guard they didn't recognize stood there, by his voice Amé and Kerlin knew he was the one who had been making vague threats at Barett.

They heard more voices. Kerlin and Amé quickly ducked back into the passageway, the Mermaid followed them.

"What's your name?" Kerlin asked politely.

"An odd question, when you won't tell me your own," her sweet voice was smooth sounding.

"We could call you, hey you, then?" Kerlin teased.

"Heyu? No, I want a prettier name."

"Kerlin."

"No, I want something more feminine."

"No, that's my name. Kerlin."

Amé rolled his eyes, but kept his peace.

"Thanks for putting your pointy teeth away," Kerlin teased.

She sniffed. "Yes. It's an effort on my part." She seemed comfortable with his teasing.

"Why is it Mermaids aren't attacking our young for virgin blood?" Kerlin felt a need to know.

"There is no potency in blood of the young. There would be no bonding."

She sniffed in Amé's direction.

"I'm not a virgin," Amé declared.

"No. You have the scent of Dragon King all over you. It has a special enchantment all its own. I've never been close enough to sniff your Dragon King. Once upon a time, I was at the court of the Dragon King, Lord Sigurd." She shuttered.

"I take it, it isn't one of your favorite memories," Amé said. It was not hard to notice her reaction.

"If you are ever graced with an invitation to Lord Sigurd's court, don't go, trust me," she said.

Amé slipped his fingers into her hand. She was pleasant company.

She seemed uncertain how to react to the gesture. After a moment, she let her hand settle comfortably with Amé's hand in her gentle grip, being careful not to crush his bones.

"Are you going to tell us your name?" Kerlin ducked for a low hanging rock, he was able to straighten again after several steps.

"Caithlin," the Mermaid said with a trace of shyness.

"What a beautiful name."

She dropped her gaze, looking demure.

They came to the point in the passageway they recognized from earlier, and sure enough, their lights and instruments went dark. Caithlin's pale skin gave off a soft glow. They could see for several steps ahead and behind them.

"Your skin is shining through the dress," Amé remarked. "I didn't know Mermaids wore clothes. It's very lovely."

"Thank you," she smiled. "I won it at a Festival."

"What did you win at?"

"I lured an Elf male with my singing."

"Uh, what happened to the Elf?" Not sure he wanted to know, he glanced at Kerlin for comfort.

"He won a prize, too, then he went home safe and sound." She smiled at the release of tension in Amé's body language. "That's a lovely bracelet you're wearing."

"Oh, this old thing?" Amé sounded very pleased at her comment. "It's only silver, nothing as fantastic as your mythril bangles."

"I'll trade you one?" She offered.

"Really? Are you sure?"

Kerlin watched with quiet patience as they stopped, waiting for the two of them to exchange bracelet for bangle.

"Here, you can have one, too," Caithlin offered a bangle to Kerlin.

"I have nothing to trade," Kerlin declined.

She looked disappointed, then said, "it's just as well. If Chantal ever saw my bracelet on you, she'd discover I hadn't told her about you."

"I can't understand how my state of virginity would interest anyone," Kerlin complained.

"You can't?" She laughed.

"Here it is," Kerlin said with relief for the change of topic.

They had come to the point where the footprints they'd found earlier had disappeared into the solid rock face. Only, now, the rock face was no longer there.

"By the Vale," Kerlin exclaimed. For the first time on their mission, he felt nervous.

"The scuffling we heard, it was the rock trailing us. I'm certain of it," Amé turned to Caithlin. "Are you sure Demons or Demonoids can't shape change into rock?"

"I've never heard of any," her delicate sharp looking teeth sucked on her bottom lip. "I am a Water Demon," she gestured at herself. "I've met Fire Demons. I guess, it's within the realm of possibility, there could be Terra Demons. There is Lore of a Tempest Demon, once upon a time, no one knows what happened to it."

"Alas, we can follow the footprints," Kerlin mentioned the bright side.

They followed the prints, until the prints disappeared into another rock barrier.

Kerlin and Amé eyed it suspiciously.

"Do you still want to interrogate it?" Amé whispered.

"Do I hear sarcasm?" Kerlin teased. One look at Amé's face and he stopped the teasing, seeing Amé battling with his fear.

Caithlin sniffed. "I'm not smelling Demon."

"And I'm not sensing Magic," Amé added.

A rumble sounded. A tremor deep in the heart of the mountain rock.

"It's not a cave-in, is it?" Amé's heart pounded. They were a long, long way down. "What happened to our Ministers? Please, please, don't' be dead."

"No, it's not a cave in," Caithlin was breathing fast.

"Let's not panic," Kerlin spoke calmly.

"What is it then?" Amé didn't believe her.

"It's a roar."

"A roar?"

"Yes. A very powerful entity. I'd guess it is quite ancient," her lip quivered with fear. She slipped her fingers into Amé's hand, he squeezed her fingers, drawing courage from her and projecting courage at her.

Kerlin felt a little left out.

"What do we do?" Amé turned to Kerlin.

Before Kerlin could answer, they heard a scream. A terrible anguished scream.

"Did that scream come from our side of the rock face, or the footprints side?"

"This side," Caithlin said.

Amé panted with emotion. "I've never heard Methusem scream, but, ..."

"Truly?" Kerlin felt his own emotions rising and ready to spill over. Panic wouldn't help. They had to stay focused.

"I smell Humans. Humans with the same smelly clothes you two wear," Caithlin's eyes were drowning pools of seaweed green. A puddle of water started seeping out by her feet.

"They must be our Guards. Caithlin," Kerlin looked her straight in the eyes, trying to gauge her sincerity. "Could you, I mean, would you, lead our Human friends here? Lead them to the screaming?"

She slowly nodded. The puddle expanded under her feet, then; she seemed to finally notice it, and it stopped growing.

"Aye," Kerlin nodded to acknowledge her help. "I would be grateful enough to let you have a nice tasty snack of my blood."

She started to shake her head and nod at the same time. She calmed and smiled at him. "Blood the red of brilliant rubies, like your hair. I make no bargain with you, I will help you for the sake of your Dragon King. Indirectly, he has done much for me in the past, in my time of darkest needs." She nodded once more. She sped off, her scarf dress flowing behind her, and she was gone.

♋

Deep in the Subterraneum below the mountains of Pandora's Peaks, Kerlin and Amé faced each other as the dying echoes of a Dragonish scream pierced the darkness. The two Guards clutched their Negatron Pulsar Rifles tight and ran toward the general direction of the sound.

The next scream came so anguished, Amé had to brush a sleeve to his cheeks for his gold eyes shimmered with tears.

The screaming echoes waned.

They stood sweating in the dark underground passage, huddled in the glow of their weapons, straining to listen. The next scream made them agree to separate, each desperately following an echo.

Kerlin's PDA scanner blerpied. 'What was this?' His PDA was now functioning. Did this mean the source of the jamming had gone?

Kerlin followed a passage leading closer to some very peculiar vital signs. The sounds of screaming became muffled sounding and feeling lost he almost turned back.

Scanning behind a barrier of sheer rock face, alien signals blipped on the mini-scanner. This was beyond coincidence.

Kerlin shrugged the gear pack off his back. Quickly, methodically, and with no room for emotion, he setup a knee-high tripod, mounted the Negatron Tunnel Blaster, and keyed up the operating controls. Remembering just in time to energize his safety helmet by activating a crystal embedded in the collar of his uniform, Kerlin started blasting a new tunnel through the rock. The Pulsar energy lit up the tunnel with eerie amber light. Finally, his tunnel broke through the barrier, it was still smoking wisps of steam as he stepped into it, crouching low.

As fast as he dared, Kerlin stepped free and straightened. Kerlin saw Amé running in from the cave tunnel entrance.

Kerlin fired his weapon at a fleeing beast like humanoid figure disappearing into a mist. Too late! He missed his target.

They stood in a hollowed out chamber of mountain rock, it could have been natural, or artificially made, it was hard to tell. Kerlin looked up for the first time, after hearing a strangled sounding cry from Amé and following his gaze. The sight of their unconscious Emperor's crucified and mutilated body, hanging from chains near the ceiling, shocked them beyond bearing. Kerlin numbly moved forward.

"Wait," Amé cried out. "I'm sensing a Spell Warding."

Kerlin squinted; he could see no trace of tell tale signs of Magic, he was not sensitive to Magic use. "We have no choice; we'll shoot the chains and hope the fall doesn't ..."

Feeling helpless, Amé nodded.

Their Emperor's legs were held spread apart by a spreader bar attached between ankle manacles. Together, the two loyal Guards fired their Negatron Pulsars at the ankle manacles. Kerlin felt the blood drain from his face upon seeing their most powerful rifle class weapons had no effect through the Magic ward.

A clatter of bootsteps preceded three more Guards on the scene, correction two Fleet Commanders and one Guard. Kerlin recognized the Brown Elf Commander Sable and the all too Human Commander Tane. And one more Guard Kerlin failed to recognize, perhaps an Elf by the look of his alluring features, the Elf's wavy blonde hair being thick enough to hide his ears tips. No sign of Caithlin the Mermaid.

Kerlin's heart filled with a sudden surge of morale as the Elf chanted in a low mumble rhyme and emptied fists of colored light at Emperor Methusem. Having cast it, the Elf collapsed in a heap. Kerlin surmised the Spell must be beyond the Elf's casting level.

The Spell must have performed something visible to Amé for he raised his weapon to fire once again at the chains. Kerlin followed suit. The spreader bar fell and Methusem's legs swung free.

Amé let his rifle clatter to the rocky ground. He ran to Methusem, flinging arms around Methusem's nude thighs and bearing the Emperor's weight on to his shoulder; Amé's slim figure barely a mite fuller than their Emperor.

Commander Sable moved to stand under Methusem, behind Amé, ready to break Methusem's fall.

Kerlin and Commander Tane fired negatron pulses to break the last remaining chains at Methusem's wrists. Commander Sable neatly caught Methusem's upper body against his chest, his cheek pressed against the wood plank across Methusem's back.

They gingerly lowered Methusem's limp body to the ground.

Before Emperor Methusem was completely prone, a glow of pure cobalt blue light brought Methusem's aura into the visible spectrum, lightening the Emperor's flawless coppery coloured skin to a sheeny gold. Light sparks traveled long strands of Methusem's knee length midnight dark hair, his hair started to float as if they were under water.

The light of their Emperor's Dragon Magic became so intense, the rescuers had to wince away, tear ducts working ceaselessly to protect their retinas.

The Healing glow finally dimmed to a comparative candle glow, when the rescue team could see from their watering eyes again, they beheld their Emperor sitting up freed from his torture and appearing healed and well, and not particularly happy looking.

Between one breath and the next, Methusem fled away with

the speed of a wind gust, and without a word of thanks.

An Aura Flash of Dragon Magic

VIII. Terra-Date Year 215.Day 143

Methusem's telepathic hearing screamed.

Minister Angélus ... pain ... death - chill.

Methusem navigated the complex system of passages, a glowing body of light, flying on currents of channeled power; hurrying, his old friend's life fading fast. Throwing open his telemental powers Methusem could feel his Guards and questing way, way above their planet's atmosphere; he sensed the utter failure of the Planetary Shield Vale. Inconceivable!

Shivering, Methusem's questing touched on the astral shadow of the Relic Ship. He now knew, this was not the Subterraneum network under Celesterra City, this place was within Pandora's mountains; so nicknamed for a Relic ship parked upon the mountain. The ship was partially embedded in rock outcroppings, nestled in a crevasse in between two mountain peaks.

The relic ship was closed up tight and an impenetrable gargantuan fortress, not even the Dragons knew how to unlock this lockbox. No activity had ever manifested, Pandora's Relic Ship was presumed empty; which was just a presumption. The immortal Pandora could be in their filing her finger nails and whiling away all eternity as much as anyone knew; for sanity's sake, some Relics were best left un-delved.

To tell the truth, privately; a chill of fear disturbed his Mer-heart in regards to that ancient Relic. The Great Knowing would occasionally whisper Pandora's name to him. He had at one time, decades ago, cast a Spell to search out Pandora. The Spell was out there in the Realm somewhere, alive and kicking and still searching.

Alas, almost to his Minister's position, Methusem's hope flared anew in his hearts. An Elf was tending to the Minister, yet; Ange's life continued to slip away.

Methusem vowed to better reward those who served him well. And also to belatedly grant Minister Ange all the long list of petition requests the Minister had submitted over the last century. Methusem gathered his circumbiant energy to become solid flesh again as he reached the end of a passage and passed into a cavernous area. Rock crystals glittered from the natural formed walls.

Minister Angélus lay propped in the arms of an openly weeping Elf maid, his breathing labored and eyes filming over within the final moments of his life, yet his eyes flickered in recognition when a shining thing knelt at his side, recognizing the pure cobalt glow of his Emperor with power upon him.

Between ragged sobs, the Elf-maid explained, "we became separated from the others. Then an awful voice came from the darkness, it said Our Emperor is destroyed." She raised her tear soaked lashes, addressing Emperor Methusem with eyes full of hurt. "It said we would never see you again. There was some kind of power in the voice, it hurt terribly. The Minister clutched his chest and collapsed."

Methusem dropped to one knee as he listened to her words, his sheen of long midnight hair cloaking his nude figure. His peridot eyes changed to the vibrant green-blue of the Dragons, pupils transmuting to silver, winds of power wafting from his warm and again warmer skin. The chamber was large enough for Methusem to let loose his two pairs of wings, which he doth did so; sheath glows sprang from his back and solidified into his Were-Dragon wings. The top border of his wings matched the color of his skin, the wing membranes gossamer thin like wind sailing material coloured by iridescent blues and golds with silver glyph patterns that were unique to every Dragon like fingerprints on Humans. The partial transformation to his

Were-Dragon form brought forth a great host of Methusem's Dragon power to the physically tangible realm.

Methusem cosseted his Minister's trembling hands with his own elegant hands and pressed them to the heated skin of his torso, near his Dragon's heart.

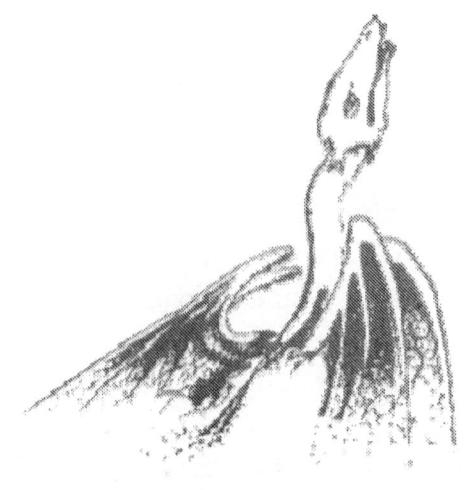

"Feel my heartbeat,
my friend
Listen to the drum,
The beat song
Strength and heat,
Ember of fire and life,
Mote flesh daren't depart,
Human heart to Dragon heart."

IX. TERRA-DATE 215.143 LATE AFTERNOON
:: By the Vale, Kerlin ::

"The reason Methusem went off so rudely like he did, he was racing to save Minister Angélus, who was dying. Methusem made it in time and saved the Minister with dragon healing magic."

Kerlin handed his negatron weapon over to the weapon's clerk in charge of the temporary Field site. Commander Kraken tried to cut the line in front of Kerlin, but Kerlin stepped around him without glancing at him. "Amé, I wasn't faulting our Emperor for rushing off." He pushed up his uniform sleeves and unfastened his uniform at the collar, the mountain air was invigorating.

Amé fidgeted with his new mythril bangle. They hadn't seen a sign of Caithlin, and by unspoken agreement, they hadn't asked anybody after her. Commander Barett was also inconspicuously absent.

"Anyway," Amé continued, "He sent a ride for you, to take you home to Celesterra City, or Nihera City, if you prefer."

Kerlin, "well ..." Their Emperor had personally sent a ride for him?

He stopped as another blonde, long haired youngish man strode up, hand outstretched for a wrist to wrist greet.

"Pleased to meet you, Commander Kerlin."

"You're Tommy! The 2nd in place racing pilot!" Kerlin said in surprise, grasping wrists with the pilot.

"Yep, that's me. Maybe, next terra-year, I'll finish in first place," Tommy held Kerlin's wrist firmly, feeling Kerlin's wrist pulse beat against his own.

Kerlin was sure Tommy could feel his pulse beating, rate speeding up from the excitement of meeting a professional racing pilot. Wait ... Commander? He turned to Amé who seemed to have all the answers to-terra-afternoon. "He called me Commander. Amé?" Kerlin stopped, not yet letting go of Tommy's wrist.

"Yep, we both be promoted to Command rank," Amé acknowledged.

"How can this be? I don't have Command training."

"You have some training classes in your credits. They're preparing a special training class to bring us up to speed on the fine points."

"Oh."

"Field Team, Commander Kerlin," Amé teased, "has a nice ring to it."

"You should drop the 'l'. Kerin sounds a touch manlier," this was said by Commander Kraken moving to stand next to the racing pilot.

"I prefer my name the way my parents gave it to me," Kerlin turned his back, not letting Kraken near the pilot.

Amé smirked.

Kerlin said, "Amé, don't you need a ride, too?"

"Not yet. Some of our Jr Guards went in to the Subterraneum by their lonesomes to join the search. Not everyone has come out, yet."

"You're going back under the mountain to search? I should help."

"Nah, we have it handled. Later."

Amé waved as Tommy urged Kerlin to follow him to the field site parking area, around a projecting ridge of the mountain side. The mountain was scarce with flat areas to land a vehicle.

"Well, I'm not truly famous. How did you recognize me? Do you hobby race, then?" Tommy asked politely, gaining his hand back.

"No, someday I will. All my down time is spent in acrobat training."

"You mean like tumbling?"

"My top feat is a triple-sault with a half twist." Kerlin laughed "Can't quite reach that 2nd half twist to make it a full revolution, unless I'm in low-g. Actually, with the excitement in my heart right now, I might manage a full twist."

Kerlin whistled as they rounded the outcropping and he saw the racing rocket. They were going to ride that beauty?

Tommy said, "you're in the navigator-seat for this ride."

"Me?"

"Yes, you. We'll do a scenic detour and cruise by the Vale."

"Literally?" 'By the Vale' was one of Kerlin's favorite expressions of frustration. The Vale was a gas cloud beyond orbit, towards their sun, within the gas cloud was an asteroid field. The Nihera City rocket race course navigated the asteroid field.

Kerlin took a moment to admire the little rocket, while Tommy scuzied himself to utilize the field site's porta-potty. He walked a circle around the rocket to study it from all angles.

The rocket was laid on it's belly, its length equal to three moderately sized Humans laying toe to head. Height wise, the rocket reached to Kerlin's shoulder. The nose rested on two gear flaps. Fins attached to the tail end, one on top, one starboard, and one aft. A corkscrew spine spiraled the rocket's body shell from fore to stern, winding to disappear under the rocket.

Under the coating of air friction resistant gloss, the rocket was painted in bands of black and white to its mid-section, followed by a black and yellow checkered pattern. The fins were decaled with a busty Humanoid female form in silhouette.

Remembering the friendly Fly13, Kerlin wondered, if the rocket might be hiding sentience, but the silence wasn't broken by the rocket.

Tommy returned, "ready?"

Kerlin nodded, his heart thudding.

Tommy tapped a touch pad by the rocket's hatch, a third of the way down it's length. The hatch opened with a barely detectable click. Tommy reached in and grabbed shaded goggles. He rummaged in a compartment and brought out a second stretchy band with goggles. He handed it to Kerlin. "You climb in first."

Kerlin mimicked Tommy by donning the goggles. He settled it on the bridge of his nose. Once he had it settled, all kinds of stats displayed in his peripheral vision field. It displayed arc degrees and depth of field measurements, depending on where he focused his eyes.

Feeling a heady rush of anticipation, Kerlin put a hand on the rocket's inner frame. An inside layer was like an inner shell, disembodied from the outer hull, supported on magnetic bearings. The inner shell checked before it dipped below the bottom of the open hatch, about knee high from the ground. Kerlin saw a lead with a carabiner hook, preventing the inner shell from sinking. Kerlin realized the outer shell of the rocket could twist and revolve without taking the inside occupant along for the spin. He backed in to the rocket on his hands and knees, it wasn't possible to stand up in the rocket. Following Tommy's instructions, Kerlin passed his legs into a five point harness. Fastened securely, he felt like he was wearing a girdle.

"Umm, is there somewhere to stow my uniform cloak?" Kerlin asked hopefully.

"Sure."

Slipping his uniform cloak from its fastening grommets, it took some wiggling to pass it to Tommy.

Kerlin surveyed the instrumentation within reach. He'd taken basic piloting classes in guard training, he was reassured to find he recognized the gizmos and knew he could operate them. But, he found he was actually useless at the controls.

Tommy climbed in, in front of him and activated the power.

There was little indication they were lifting off the ground. Kerlin's stomach dropped, a sensation he was accustomed to from flying on his gravity skates.

The plates protecting the nose of the rocket parted to reveal a window. It looked like the hull window was at least 3 layers thick. Taking into account the inner and outer shells, he couldn't' figure out where the third layer was coming from. Tommy settled in his own harness, so that he was situated with his head lower, giving Kerlin a mostly unobstructed view.

The planet fell rapidly, first there were clouds, a few blinks later, they were approaching orbit. Kerlin had been to orbit before, he was expecting to see all the traffic. They passed one of the orbital farms, a quick glimpse showed the harvesters at work. Their planet's smallest moon went by on the left.

"Care to listen to some music?" Tommy's finger hesitated over a touch pad.

"Sure."

Kerlin's eyelids drooped dreamily as the sweet sound of string symphonies filled the little racing rocket.

⚮

Kerlin wondered if it would be rude to grab Tommy into an all embracing hug. He'd just experienced the most fantastic trip of his life. Tommy had navigated the entire Vale asteroid field, as if it had been a real race. Kerlin was shaking in reaction from drowning in adrenalin. It was more intense than his experience in the Subterraneum, even more than when he had thought he was going to be crushed to death in a cave in.

"No matter how many times I fly it, it's as intense as the first time," Tommy put an arm around Kerlin to steady him. Tommy reached into a pocket and brought out an engraved chip. "And here is a season token to the Nihera Races."

Kerlin felt touched beyond words by the gesture. "I don't know how to thank you."

"Just enjoy."

"When are you racing?" Kerlin didn't want to let go of the

pilot. He had a million questions.

"Actually, I'm off to test out the new racing course at Tylwyth. It's an opportunity I can't miss."

"Oh," Kerlin couldn't hide his keen disappointment.

"Well, you're a Field Team Commander. Maybe a mission will come along near Tylwyth?"

"Tylwyth is half a solar system away."

"Half a solar system isn't too far what with today's interstellar ship speeds." Tommy drew Kerlin into a brotherly hug, patting his back for an exponential hug increase factor. "Anyway, this means my Hotel suite will be unoccupied. I've already told the Hotel to expect you. My room is at the Hotel Looloo. Enjoy, ok?"

With a last hug, Tommy released Kerlin and started walking back to the parking lot.

Kerlin didn't move, until Tommy was beyond sight. He sighed. His legs were feeling spongy, he found a bench by a lovely fountain. Stray mist from the fountain cooled his face on this hot summer day in Nihera City. Here he was in Nihera City, without any luggage. He would have to buy all the necessities. And, he would have to buy all the paraphernalia needed to enjoy the races. Life was good.

He pulled out his PDA to check his money balance. Clueless as to what a starting Commander's salary grade offered. He tapped his PDA to deactivate scan mode. His inbox of email flashed at him. He'd never seen so much email in his inbox in his entire career. What was going on? His eyes skimmed a quick scroll. He noticed an email from a Rogue Fielder, overcome with curiosity, Kerlin read this message first. It was from a Rogue Fielder named Care Ethaynen. Kerlin thought he couldn't be any more surprised. It was an application to his Field Team.

"Huh." Kerlin attempted to access the Commander's Registry, but his login was denied. He scrolled further into his email and found one from the Emperor. Kerlin felt his heart rate quicken anew. Technically, he was nominated for a Field Team Command. His promotion was not yet confirmed. A nomination from the Emperor was a sure thing. It would take a few terra-days for the process trail to wind it's way to the proper desk. A quick by-note under the Emperor's signature informed Kerlin his new salary grade had been retro-activated.

Kerlin first sent a 'Thank you' note to Emperor Methusem, playing down the awestruck emotion. The next thing he looked at was his money balance. Kerlin whistled with pleasure at the figure amount scrolling on the mini-screen. He calculated how long it would take him to save up for a hobbyist's racing rocket, taking into account his not so thrifty spending habits.

He felt tired. All the excitement and exertion catching up to him. Even too tired to look for the Hotel Looloo. Too tired to lift his head, it was an enormous effort to look around for a hopeful sight of a hotel sign. He spotted one, one of the taller buildings in the historical city of Nihera. It would have been a long walk, but he was wearing his gravity skates. If anyone of rank caught him skating in his exhausted condition, he could incur a hefty painful Writ. He twitched his feet to activate his skates, they lit up.

Halfway to the Hotel, and he hadn't see a sign of anybody else on skates. His luck must be holding, it seemed the Guards local to Nihera City weren't certified in gravity-skates. In his home city of Celesterra, he would have been busted by now. He was too tired to pull off any fancy skate moves. Almost too tired to ask for a room, when he reached the Hotel.

The Hotel employee seemed to understand. She called for an employee to escort Kerlin to a room. He was too tired to undress himself. A Guard he had never met before came into the room.

The Hotel employee was saying, "thank you."

Apparently, they had found someone to help manage Kerlin through his exhaustion. His uniform was already unlocked, all it needed was someone with the know how to pull it down his body. It took his last waking moment to unlock his boots. Kerlin fell into a well deserved sleep.

The Guard and the Hotel employee finished undressing Kerlin, pulled the bed sheets to tuck him in, turned down the lights, turned on the air cooler, and quietly left Kerlin to his privacy.

ഷ

Kerlin slept peacefully, stirring occasionally to shift his body to a new position. His favorite sleeping position was to lay on his left side, knees tucked up level with his waist. One hand lay cupped on the pillow next to his face.

Shadows shifted in the room, the closed transparent sliding doors to the balcony kept the noises of the seaside city at bay. The quiet whisper of the air cooling vents masked the murmurs of the hotel guests comings and goings out in the hallway.

In sleep, a little smile softened Kerlin's lips, a hint of pleasant dreams.

A barely audible click of the room's door handle did not disturb the sleeping Commander Kerlin. A silent shadow entered the room.

A figure passed under a splay of sunlight coming from the balcony door. The light touched on the ankle length seaweed green tresses of the Mer woman. The eyes of the woman remained shadowed. Fair skin showed between the draped lines of her scarf dress, spun of blue and green sea-silks by non-human hands.

Her upper eyeteeth elongated into fangs. She brought her wrist to her teeth, vital blue veins faint under her pale skin. A gentle prick of a tooth and blood welled on her wrist.

Careful not to spill the precious fluid as she moved her wrist, she brought it close to Kerlin's lips. She turned her wrist to let her blood drip between Kerlin's softly parted lips. Kerlin licked at his lips and crinkled his nose in reaction, but did not wake. He unconsciously turned his head to face towards Caithlin and settled.

Caithlin fed more of her blood to Kerlin's mouth. She whispered, "it is said, he who drinks of given Mermaid blood, will forever hear the eternal lapping of the ocean's voice in his dreams. And his sleep will always be restful."

She continued feeding Kerlin, waiting to see him swallow no less than three times. "I can not protect you from Chantal, our Queen's favored. But, I can give you this small measure of strength to resist her Mer powers."

Kerlin licked at his lips. Almost woke. His dreams were pleasant. He resisted the urge to wake and floated back to sleep.

Caithlin watched him sleep for a few moments longer, then, took her leave as silently as she had intruded.

X. TERRA-DATE 215.149 EARLY MORNING
:: Seaside Palace, Celesterra City, Minister Ange ::

Minister Ange smiled cheerfully at his computer monitor, lots of colourful fancy paper strewn about his antique desk. Promotion Certificates of Commission, lots of 'em. 'New commission appointments are always a pleasant contemplation for a sunny day.' He beamed an excited smile at an artisan chiseled sapphire sculpture of marine mammals at play, a get-well gift some of the Guards had chipped in their salaries to buy for him.

It did not escape his keen notice that these newly commissioned Commanders had been involved in the Subterraneum rescue. One promoted 3 grades in one sensational swoop; this'll set all the Junior Guards dreaming. Hmmm, details withheld, of course, exciting his curiosity all the merrier. And one demit! Hmph, not so much a surprise there.

He idly rubbed his fingers over the polished wood sheen coating his new desk, tracing the delicate scroll detailing under the beveled ledge brushed with amber highlights. The drawer handles, all seven for there were seven drawers in all – three to a side and a shallow center drawer, winked a milky mythril. The piece gleamed exquisitely in the noonday light filtering from the wide windows of the Seaside Palace chamber.

The Palace was ideally situated atop Celesterra City's highest bluff, the view sported recreational craft lazily skipping the sea waves, sea-eagles hovered the sun-warmed breezes appearing motionless in mid-air between downdrafts. A solitary Dragon flew circular laps; Minister Ange imagined some nervous craft skippers making for the docks as a result.

He sighed.

It was rather a boon to be nigh on two terra centuries of seniority, plus the good fortune to have good friends still active at the Palace from his vital days; he had been among the first of the new Ministers appointed to the new government. He bore witness to the day Methusem, an adolescent then, had strolled in the vaulted entrance of the old Aristocratic Archon and declared himself Emperor, immediately sitting proprietarily upon the Throne of Prophecy and divested the Aristocrats of all authority.

His old friend Nuben, appointed Minister Caretaker of the Crown Jewels, had way too much time to putter around the closeted artifacts. Minister Ange considered the appointment to be an unacknowledged kindness done on Methusem's part. Emperor Methusem's conquest had been very timely for old Nuben; indeed, Nuben was nearing the end of his usefulness at the time and had been on the docket for the next shipment of slaves to be shipped to the slaughterhouse.

Minister Ange shuddered. He did not wish to spoil this wonderful day by remembering the days of Aristocrat rule. Indeed, his own appointment, Minister of Royal Appointments, he chuckled aloud, was just as pointless - he chuckled aloud again at his own pun - or would be just as useless, except that he spent most of his time sticking his nose in Royal business everywhere, much more gratifying then puttering in closets. To each his own, he'd gotten caught at it a good many times, alas.

He chuckled long and heartily. He noticed his new assistant did not even look at him funny, she'd quickly become use to his quixotic ways.

Hmm, and Hannah, no reminisce was complete without Hannah. Hannah had actually been hanging in the slaughter chains when the Emperor's take over had shut down all the machines. Minister Ange had always been quite intrigued by how Methusem had managed that massive machine shut down, something deep and he had never been able to delve deep enough. Methusem had declared droids illegal labor and deactivated them shortly after routine had settled, effectively ending the servitude of these artificial life forms. Ange suspected some kind of alliance with the machines had made the conquest of the seven Pan Jupiter Major planets plausible, even for an immortal, conquering seven planets was still a major undertaking.

"Well," he said aloud, ending on a satisfied sigh.

Hannah was now the Minister of Palace Housekeeping Affaires. She was in charge of all the Palace household functions. By appointing Hannah Minister, and not just a housekeeper, assured Hannah she was no one's servant, serving none but the Emperor, her devotion to Methusem completely unvitiated.

This desk in this room must be a gift from between old Nuben and Hannah. They alone knew how much he'd wanted this second story corner office, a wrap around balcony opened to Sea Vistas and he could view the coastline, positively brilliant lit up by the city at night and scrumptious with colours upon sunset and sunrise. An adjacent chamber was furnished for his sleeping comfort, it had a balcony too and a small hearth for chill nights, when a small controlled fire made for a cozy elemental evening. He'd have to request a pyro-kinetic to come light it for him tonight. Not that it was chilly, but it would be quite a luxury to see fire again.

As his chuckle finally faded to a quiet hum Hannah bustled in, she never needed an invitation to enter and it was her prerogative to enter anywhere she willed. She was dressed in the style of the old-fashioned court ladies, a pale pink on pale lavender gown with ivory lacing and embroidered squiggly lines. Those squiggly lines may mean something in some archaic mage tongue; the Minister could not name it. He watched her with quiet adoration as she bustled to the balcony doors and threw open both sets of doors. A mere strip of ivory lace tied at the base of her neck swept her hair behind her neatly, where it floated down her back in a dark brunette cloud. Some bustling of material made her skirt gown trail a little bit behind her, accentuated by rustling noises as she walked. Very lady like slippers shod her feet, these also were embroidered with squiggly lines, he could just see her dainty toes peeking beyond the hem of her long skirts. Many of the Lady Wives of the Ministers from his era dressed in this fashion and the modern husband and husband couples were adopting the gown as fashionable.

Ange sometimes regretted never marrying.

Hannah's even features did not set her apart, yet her vitality sparked off the very air of her aura around her, you sensed a force of personality held in check; it was there when she smiled at you. He knew her to be at least 5 terra centuries in age, which suggested more than just Human genetics at work for she appeared to be on the younger side of Human middle age. And he felt infinite gratitude to Hannah for her kindness to his young new assistant.

It was still a mystery to him why Hannah had been sent to the slave slaughterhouse, that heinous fate had been used for the unwanted, the lame, and exhausted to uselessness labourers. It was not a mystery he could solve by simply asking her. In the chaotic first days of the conquest, she'd been discovered lying on the tiered steps of the Archon Basilica, badly battered and succumbing to death. Methusem had adopted the healing of her and had straight away established her in charge of the Palace domesticities. Ange hummed innocently as she gave him a piercing look with those remarkable dark eyes of hers before she strolled out without a word, she was a woman who only spoke when she had something to say. Hmmm, Ange bet she carried the answers to more than a few of his dearest mysteries.

Ange sighed aloud, this time with a self deprecating air, he would marry her without hesitation for he had lost his heart to her many a terra decade ago, alas, he knew her heart belonged to the Emperor with all the power of platonic purity. Over the last two terra centuries, no rumour whispered of a lover for Hannah.

Sunlight streamed in from the freshly opened balcony doors, the scents and sounds of the nearby sea borne into the lofty room on wonderful heartfelt peaceful breezes. The breeze renewed his satisfaction in finally being given this perfect chamber, his petition for this long unoccupied chamber at the Celesterra City Seaside Palace granted only yester-terra-day. The most beautiful Palace in all the Realm.

There were plans being drawn up for a Winter Palace near the planet's Southern Pole, he hadn't managed to muddle in that project yet. ON speculation alone, expansive winter sports resorts were already under construction, raising a demand for telekinetic construction workers and bringing in an influx of families from the outlying planetary and lunar settlements.

"Yes. Tis a wonderful contemplation."

"Minister," a dulcet female voice intervened upon his attentions. He swiveled in his brown cushy high-backed chair, - brand new and measured to suit - to bestow a beaming encouraging smile at his newly appointed assistant.

"Yes Vylara," he said in a most gentle voice to the Elf sitting at her desk.

"One of our brand new Commander commission-ees is headed toward a Disciplinary Hearing. He's facing a Writ for corporal punishment."

"Eh? My dear girl, did you say Writ? Before his Hearing? We must put a stop to this insanity! This must be addressed immediately, send a Belay Order," Minister Ange hopped to his feet, feeling spry for his elderly age, owing his fresh health to his Emperor's Dragon Healing Magic. "Actually, send the Belay Order and let us reinforce it with a personal visit. There is some petty vindictiveness at work here; a Belay Order may conveniently be overlooked 'til too late."

He out raced his assistant to the curtained egress of their Palace office chamber. Hmm. "Vylara please, grab the epaulette pins, there's a dear. And away we go. Let us hasten along."

Minister Ange smiled so hard he almost tripped as he heard his demure young assistant mumble, "aye you're just showing off" as he outpaced her best efforts to match paces.

Their slippers made nary a sound on the marble floors of the Palace, which was the reason for the slippers; the need for haste prevented a change to outdoor footwear. The milky white marble of the Palace floors were accented with lightening shaped patterns of pale blues, mauves, and pinks. Vaulted ceilings of the finest art, hand drawn and intricate inspired by Dragon wings, defied description by merely a few brief comments. Much of the stone artwork and architecture were remnants of the past.

The newest editions to the Palace halls were the skylights. Emperor Methusem wanted light of the sun, moons, and stars to grace the halls. Infrequent bridge spans connected the east and west offices. There be no such thing as walking across the hall on the upper levels. Minister LeeAnne, Minister of Public Water Works, had submitted a petition to install swing ropes from the top ceiling to swing across on like jungle vines; the submitted petition was politely sitting in some clerk's slush pile. Minister Ange chuckled even as he ran the length of the hall; Minister LeeAnne was certainly a lively lady, her talents wasted on fribbles.

We would see what muddling could be engineered in LeeAnne's area, a governorship vacancy would soon be opening up on Mariterra planet, and perhaps she would be an ideal candidate. He must send in a nomination.

Chuckling slowed him up a pace and Vylara was catching up. Feeling revitalized Ange picked up the pace another notch, thinking how fun it felt to run again. They came to a grand curving staircase, taking the shallow steps at a run and rounded a left at the bottom.

He paused at a fairly busy corridor intersection, lackadaisical fellow Ministers benignly witnessing this untoward burst of energy. He slowed with barely a wheeze at the entrance to the Hearing Chambers, dismayed to find it empty. "This does not bode well. Why would they not host the Hearing here?"

Vylara caught up and perceived the situation with the quick reaction she had earned her job by; she hurried to a kiosk mounted in a wall recess. "They made a last moment transfer to the Collier Building."

His dismay deepened, the Collier building was halfway across Celesterra City. Being appointed within the artistically breathtaking Seaside Palace was certainly luxurious, but it did set one apart from the heart of affaires.

"Quickly, no time to lose let us to the fastrafts," referring to the Ministry's zippiest mode of technology powered transportation around the city. Hmm. "Except for the Guards on g-skates," he said aloud with a twinkle in his eye as Guard Traci dove air skimming through a broad window from atop a grand stairway; a practice highly frowned upon by our esteemed colleagues. Traci draped his uniform cloak behind his shoulders and landed. He twitched his feet in a little meaningless tap dance, until you noticed the wink of g-skate lights lining flush to his boot souls.

&

Traci caught quick movement on his peripheral vision, seeing the Minister hurrying towards him with assistant in wake from the entrance to the Hearing Chambers, he immediately leaped to the conclusion Minister Ange was all ready aware of the situation. Right or wrong, a harsh punishment was about to be mete out under vindictive judgment. He'd already made the personal decision that if the officiates in charge were not held responsible for their abuse of power, he would resign his hard earned commission in the Guard.

Garren Waysixth

Born Terra-Year 186

Race Human

Mission Specialties: Night Vision
Combat Training

Permit of Residence Planet Celesterra

Planet of Birth Quinterra

XI. TERRA-DATE YEAR 215, DAY 149
:: Collier Courtyard. Garren's Disciplinary Writ ::

Garren Waysixth swallowed convulsively.

Dana Atuin finished reading the Writ of Sentencing aloud, glaring at his handheld PDA, the bearer of bad news. The closest person to someone Garren could call a friend, Dana's long blonde hair was sopping wet as if he'd dashed straight away from a shower and he was not in uniform; which would keep Dana barred from attending the hearing. Somewhat relieved, Garren expected the hearing to be humiliating enough without his friend witnessing the punishment.

Garren nodded to indicate acknowledgement of the news. His mind and spirit balked and his face felt warm with shame. He fought a strong inclination to psychologically disassociate from the whole proceeding.

"This is NONSENSE Garren," Dana was still talking and leaning close, being a full head taller than Garren, dripping the odd drop of herbal scented water on his Human friend.

Garren knew Dana to be a hybrid-Human; other things preoccupying his mind stopped the stream of thoughts on Dana's genetic traits.

"They can't issue a Writ of Sentencing BEFORE they hold the hearing, this is illegal. My friend Traci is skating gravity to the Palace as we speak to bring your plight before the Ministry in person." Dana stopped, highly indignant on Garren's behalf, his light brown eyes welling with concern. He knew Garren well enough now to know the Human's posture to be a front to cover the insecurity behind an unperturbed facade. Garren was a Human from the planet Quinterra and near to 29 terra years of age, but still only a Junior Guard. Dana peered again at his PDA. The Writ for Garren's punishment read: stripped to the knees: 50 welts.

"Is that excessive for crashing the rank's party-line?" Garren intoned flatly. "I imagine the Ministry is too busy governing our planets to bother with a Junior Guard's hearing."

"This isn't fair Garren," Dana repeated as his gaze followed Garren's to a black uniformed figure.

The black uniform in question was being worn by a Human named Care Ethaynen, a certified disciplinarian. Care turned and noticing Dana's attention, waved and sauntered up, craning his neck in all directions, scanning faces as he approached, holding a bag on his shoulder with one hand on it to steady the weight.

"You're going to give your neck whiplash." Dana smiled at Care's easy mannered charisma.

"Tee hee, I'm hoping to catch up with Krizren," Care's yellow eyes smiled wickedly. "He was asking me to top him and I thought maybe he staged something to get in trouble. You know? He likes my toys," shrugging his shoulder bag meaningfully. Celesterra sunlight gleamed in Care's glossy brown hair, streaked with amber highlights, complementing his mocha brown complexion, the sun also brought out Care's light freckles generously dusted across his cute nose and cheekbones. "Or Starra, she's been disciplined twice since I came off Assignment."

"You've been planet-side since the Kin Holidays, eh? Is it true you're giving up the Rogue Fielder life?" Dana found Care's lifestyle a fascinating study.

"Well, I might apply for a Field Team assignment. Maybe I'm not all that anti-social."

"Ahh," Dana discretely tipped his PDA towards Care and showed him the Writ.

Care peeked quick, looked up, shook his head and looked

again, then stared at Garren. "Ach, no, I refuse to do you."

"Why?" Garren had never been rejected by a disciplinarian before. He crossed his arms and regarded Dana's friend, head tilted sideways and his hair floating in a breeze.

"I only discipline Guards who like it. And never a Junior," the 22 year old stated.

Despite himself Garren responded, his eyes flashing with keen intelligence. "Isn't that the anti-thesis of a disciplinarian?"

"Maybe it's a bit unprecedented, eh? But I didn't get Discipline Certified just to qualify for Rogue Field Assignment; I did it for my friends who appreciate my efforts."

"So you're saying," Dana stared at Care as if he was something good to eat. "Being disciplined by you is better than sex?"

"Hmm, well false modesty doesn't become me, does it?" Care chuckled lightheartedly.

Garren could not quite smile; he was not into pain - not even the erotic kind - and even less into being stripped in front of the very people he detested, knowing they would gloat. Dana's smile faded. Garren wondered if Dana was telesensitive in any way. "You seem to know exactly when my thoughts are sour."

"It's not hard to read your body language Garren," Dana was all sympathy.

"I should work on that. In case I get interrogated by enemies of the Realm."

Dana shook himself in dismay, flinging more drips of water from his hair on to his friends.

"This is highly irregular, this classifies as down right abuse," Care remarked, reading deeper into the Writ. "Do you have a plan?" He didn't know Garren, but he knew Dana well enough to sense something a foot.

"Not a grand plan. Traci is skating to the Palace to find a sympathetic authority figure to void the Writ and re-authorize this hearing under an appeal for an unbiased judgment," Dana answered for Garren.

"So you need a play for time? I can stall."

Garren was cautious to feel gratitude to this Senior Guard with the bag of disciplinary implements tottering from his shoulder. "How?"

"I'll go through the motions, at the last instant, balk. Then they will have to bring a second disciplinarian in. It will all take time."

"Can you stall so Garren doesn't get stripped?" Dana knew Garren was too conservative to be comfortable naked. "Oops, can you believe this? Someone wants Garren whipped pretty badly." Dana pointed to another well-known disciplinarian Guard.

Garren recognized Senior Guard Erin from a few field exams Erin had hosted.

"I respect his work a lot," Care mused.

"From spectator view or participant," Dana teased.

"Muwahahah," Care laughed. "You know what?" Care turned serious, more serious than usual for someone of his disposition. "This whole situation is too illegal. I'm going to countermand this order."

Dana raised his eyebrows. "Can you do that?"

"Yes."

"No," Garren interrupted his friend's enthusiasm. "A Senior Guard needs a qualifying cause to counter-order my pre-existing orders and there isn't one."

"How do you know that?" Dana's light brown eyes ogled with the conclusion he'd jumped to. "You've been studying the Commander's registry!"

"You hacked the Commander's Registry?" Care's eyes sparked with hero-worship.

Garren swallowed.

"Woah, the o Sacred database," Care intoned. "Garren, I want to save you from this. Anyone who can hack a computer like you can does not deserve this punishment." And he seemed to mean every word.

"Listen, as humiliating as this whole scene is, I don't want to be known for being afraid of a whip," Garren's cheeks burned a flush of pink. "Anyway, I didn't hack the live database."

Dana and Care waited.

Garren sighed. "It was just an overlooked hardcopy." He stopped talking.

"What's a hardcopy?"

Garren remained silent, he unexpectedly started experiencing one of those crystal clarity of moments. The banter between his concerned companions became a pleasant buzz. He lifted his face to the Celesterra sun, luxuriating in the kiss of her light, the clear weather sky deep in a dream of blue, an orbital station pale and visible passing in its lackadaisical orbit; to gazers below just another moon.

The trio stood in the cobble stoned courtyard of the Guard Administrative Center. The five-storied Dumier building, where certification exams were held, faced north. To the south of the quad, stood the three-storied Collier building looking oh so innocent in its brick facade, smallish and squat, its rear exit a dual door aperture tall enough for the taller races to not have to duck. Or almost, Garren twitched a grin as one of the hearing officiates clunked her forehead on the arch bend, her Medusan snakelets hissed in aggravation.

Shouts and excited screaming were a soft background sound from a May Ball game outside the walls of the quad.

Flower baskets decorated window ledges, varieties of which he couldn't name; his home planet Quinterra did not cultivate these. The heady flora perfumes tangled with a strong breeze laden with salty ocean scents, a faint waif of herbs from Dana's freshly washed hair, and a faint waif of cooking smells from a mess hall.

A gust chased the breeze, lifting Garren's hair. Leaving his hair unbraided and free was the only token of Garren's defiance at the whole maltreated affaire. A Writ of sentencing, before the disciplinary hearing even commenced, quietly he started to seethe with the injustice of it. He would go thru with the whipping and then use it as grounds to charge the petty Field Commander with Misuse of Authority.

"I can guess what you're thinking Garren," Dana interrupted the fine temper Garren was working up. "That Field Commander knows he's on dodgy ground for a hundred petty instances. He wants you humiliated, because of his misguided pride, no matter the penalty to his failing career. The best you could do to defy him would be to not be at this hearing at all."

"I agree with you," Care swept his hair behind his ears, a fresh gusting breeze made the gesture futile. "But, Garren still has to weigh the risk to his reputation."

"Why?" Dana protested.

Care skipped the rebuttal. "Dana, if I talk Erin into declining, who is next on the Disciplinary delegation list?"

"Care, I'm not privy to that info," Dana handed his PDA to Care.

"Ugh, Commander Kraken is next. I recommend you stay with Erin on this, Garren," Care's voice was full of sympathy. He handed the PDA back to Dana.

Garren darted a glance to follow a new figure walking into the Collier building and felt a tingly sensation prickle his nape hairs. The figure belonged to a trainer from the Guard Center, one he'd run afoul of on several occasions. Garren's seething temper was replaced by a drowning feeling of hopeless despondency, these Officiates on the hearing panel were here just to gloat over his humiliation. "Maybe I don't belong in the Guard," he swallowed to mask his depression, shaking his head in answer to Dana's exclamation of protest. "I'm only a Jr, if I can provoke this much hostility, how will I fare as a fully commissioned Guard?"

But, Garren continued silently, 'then my Permit of Residence for Celesterra Planet will be voided.' After living on this lovely temperate Planet, returning to Quinterra Planet would be miserable. Not to mention the horror of facing his relatives again. He had conveniently forgotten to mention to anyone back home he'd planned to ditch Quinterra Planet.

"Garren, you know you are welcome to make my home your home, no matter what you decide," Dana clapped a long fingered hand on Garren's shoulder.

Truly appreciating Dana's friendship, Garren tried to invoke a smile and failed miserably. He had only ever wanted to be a Guard. Could he live with himself under a banner of total failure? "Let's go through with this farce, I'll resign my Commission docket before they start stripping me for the bench."

"OK for plan B, what about plan A?" Care proposed this, "Well, I can give you a countermand, because you shouldn't know that I don't have a qualifier."

"Yeah, but," Garren countered, "then you'll be disciplined for breach of protocol. The punishment would just be transferred to you with an addendum making it more severe."

"I'm OK with that," Care winked mischievously.

"No way!"

"Yes way."

Care grabbed the PDA back from Dana's inattentive grasp. He tippytapped on the mini keys, at the last keystroke, Garren's own PDA blerpied.

Garren pulled his own Junior issue PDA from a hip pocket and tapped the mini screen display. In BOLD caps read a priority order to report to an exclusive training exercise on the far outskirts of ZangShe City. Issuer: Rogue Fielder SrG Care Ethaynen.

Dana grinned as Garren tempestuously keyed in a Decline citing prior Orders.

Care wordlessly tippytapped more keystrokes, on the last, Garren's PDA blerped.

Garren read silently, Dana reading over his shoulder, "DISCIPLINARY HEARING DOES NOT OVERRIDE COVERT

TRAINING EXCERCISE. REPORT TO TRAINING LEADER DONNÉ". Garren pointed to another member of the hearing officiates entering the Collier building, then typed: DECLINE. HEARING CONVENE IN PROGRESS.

Care frowned, still in the spirit of trying to rescue Garren, typed; Rare TRAINING OPPORTUNITY. FIELD EXCERISE IN ARCHAIC ARMS.

As Garren read this it gave him pause. He'd just recently Certified in Archaic Swordsmanship and an opportunity to put his training to field exercise was a powerful lure. With an expression full of regret he DECLINED once more, this time because he wanted to spare Care a disciplinary action, he could not seriously believe anyone would be OK with 50 welts. Or more since Care was deliberately endeavoring a breach of protocol. After Garren hit the SEND key, Dana's and Care's PDAs blerped almost in unison.

Care handed Dana's PDA back to him and whipped out his own PDA. He "tch'd" then started a rapid tippytap, then his PDA blerped again. He paused, made a noise of pleased surprise then tippytapped some more. CLICK

Garren's PDA blerped again, he smiled gamely, if nothing else this was an interesting distraction. Garren got a jolt of surprise as the next message read from Field Team Commander Kerlin, ordering him to report to this Field Exercise with SrG Donné. A full FTC had all the qualifying authority necessary to countermand pre-existing orders for a disciplinary hearing.

Care held up his PDA for both Garren and Dana to read: I AM HAPPILY PLEASED TO CONSIDER YOUR REQUEST TO TRANSFER TO MY FIELD TEAM. I AM AT THE ROCKET RACES IN NIHERA CITY. PLEASE JOIN ME IF YOUR TIME IS AVAILABLE. SIGNED Cdr Kerlin Lantanthen.

"Congratulations Care, woah, Field Team!" Dana saluted. Dana leaned closer to read Care's PDA, letting his now dry hair to swing forward to block the mid-morning sun, which was now bright enough to create a strong glare on the mini screen.

Garren started keying in an ACCEPTANCE to Kerlin's orders, he really wanted to do this Field Exercise. Before he hit the SEND key, a voice commanded, "Jr Guard Garren! Belay what you are doing!" An officiate of the hearing had come to call him for the Hearing Commence.

Garren tapped off his PDA and deposited it into his pocket.

Care stepped in with a mite's worth of prevarication, Dana beside him, "Senior, Garren has been recalled by my Commander, Cdr Kerlin's orders take priority over this hearing."

The Senior Officiate scowled most maliciously, ripping into his own PDA screen, tapped forcefully into the delicate instrument.

Care and Garren's PDAs blerpied. Garren didn't bother to re-activate his own as Care read aloud, JR GUARD GARREN, HERE-BY SUSPENDED FROM DUTY 'TIL DISCIPLINARY WRIT SATISFIED.

"Of all the blasted, conniving, falaetin'..." Care blew a fit. Dana's hand on Care's shoulder held him back from saying more. By the look on the Senior's face, Care had just made a serious enemy. The Senior Officiate beckoned Garren to follow him into the Collier Building. With a bearing as commanding as any Fleet Commander, Garren followed as if this was any normal errand.

As Garren followed the Senior, all he could see of the officiator's uniform was his gray cloak and braided topknot. The gusts whipped about the blue wispy sky neutral in its majestic wonder, the colorful aviary life fluttered as always between the flowery hosts and just ahead of them; the Disciplinary Guard, whose work Care admired, proceeded them into the dark maw of the Collier building.

&

Garren was directed to wait in a secretary's reception room before the doors to the Hearing chamber.

At the moment, he had only Erin for company. The tall disciplinarian Guard stood leaning against a wall with his bulging shoulder bag, which he let drop to his feet. Erin was thin, brown eyed, with a long brunette hair braid reaching to his waist.

"So." Erin spoke.

Garren let the syllable hang in the air. He had no desire to converse with the man who was about to whip fifty welts into his flesh.

"So," Erin repeated. "Are you gonna quit the Guard?"

Garren shifted his weight to one leg, thinking, Erin must be a telepath.

"It's okay," Erin continued the small talk. "Every Guard thinks the same thing standing in this waiting room. Deciding if they're going to throw away their career rather than face the consequences of defying our protocol statutes."

Still silence from Garren.

"You must have done something pretty outrageous to be sentenced to fifty welts."

Despite his mood, Garren answered. "You mean, you don't know the charges against me?"

"No," Erin raised one expressive eyebrow. "They don't tell us. They don't want us judging. We might balk at performing the sentence."

In his thoughts, Garren said silently, 'or knowing which official we pissed off.'

"So, it's a conspiracy against you, is that it?"

"Stay out of my mind," Garren felt the edge of a fine anger flushing his face.

"I can only communicate in pictures," Erin declared.

Garren didn't believe him.

Erin turned his head towards the sound of voices approaching. He whispered, "you're a friend of Care's? Do you want me to single tail whip you like I'd do it for Care?"

Garren conceived a notion there was a whole sub-culture going on within the Guard, one he'd been completely oblivious of up 'til now. "Do it like you'd do it for Commander Kraken, as if you'd ever get the chance to perform a sentence on him."

Erin whistled, a mocking sound.

Two Guards of the Court Executor branch showed up, garbed in full uniform tailored to show off their muscle. They flanked Garren to escort him into the Hearing chamber.

"What are you two here for?" Garren's voice came out hostile.

Erin tried not to smirk as he said, "they are here to help you strip to the knees, in case; you have trouble undressing yourself."

Garren remained stoic, praying to show no emotion at all. The door to the Hearing chamber swung open on hinges and in they went.

Someone was speaking, but Garren tuned it all out. He counted several faces sitting at a curved table, giving the officiates a close up and personal view of the object in the center of the room. His mind barely registered the Medusan Minister, the Field Commander who'd charged him with Contumacy, and Fleet Commander Tane. Garren saddened for he'd heard Tane was a decent personality.

In the center of the gray room a block was set, the block once knew life as a ship's negatron cannon casing. It was a little taller than waist high. Garren could see the restraining cuffs grommet attached to the case.

The tiresome legal speeches finished and Garren saw one of the Court guards reaching for him. Garren quickly put his fingers to the collar of his blue juniors uniform and started the task of undressing. He pulled the sleeves down in rough jerky motions, then pushed the uniform down his legs. He yanked his uniform boots off, tossing each to the corner in turn. When the boots were gone, he finished yanking off his uniform and tossed it to the corner, too. He stood completely nude in front of the court and pretended not to care.

♌

No one said anything. Commander Tane was looking down

at his PDA and didn't watch as Garren was bent over the block and cuffed into position.

☙

Garren was fastened tightly, he found he couldn't even twitch. It was a battle with his own body to not show any reaction to the chill in the air, he concentrated on not letting his ass twinge at the thought of what was coming.

The vulnerable position he was in made his mind flash back to a painful memory of two terra-years ago. A memory of his father and cousins tying him down into a subjugation position in front of the Altar of Ares.

Something deep in his mind stirred, as if the god Ares himself was only waiting for Garren to call upon him. A voice without sound said, 'oh yes. Let us wreak some vengeance here.'

Garren squeezed his eyes shut and braced himself as the first fierce sting of the whip hit his bare ass cheeks. He hissed, Garren hoped it was too low for anyone to notice.

The voice in his head said, 'swear fealty to me. Become mine. Channel my power to punish thine enemies.'

"They aren't mine enemies," Garren held his breath when he heard the whistle of the whip about to strike again. He withstood it without a hiss escaping from his lips. The pain wasn't anything too terrible, he dearly wished he could rub the sting away.

Garren felt the roll of something inside his skin. Ares rising.

'No!' Garren cried silently. 'You agreed to leave me be. I want no part of your priesthood.' Garren felt a smile come to his lips, deriving a bit of comfort from Ares good humour as Ares mildly swore in mild exasperation. It was good, when defying a god, said god is amused by said defiance instead of angry.

Then, something else stirred in his mind.

The third strike of the whip flicked it's third burning welt.

Garren became conscious of the air outside the building. But this was a sense of thunder and rain storm, and Garren knew it to be a bright and sunny day out.

Ares stirred again, 'Pazu, is that you?' The impression Garren felt was cynical amusement. 'Garren, my sweet male concubine, you certainly know how to pick up strays.'

'Concubine? I absolutely doth protest! Don't even start a rumour! This is what insanity is like,' Garren scoffed. This imaginary conversation in his mind was his psyche's attempt to hide from the external pain and humiliation of submitting to the whip.

'My thane,' came Garren's imaginary conversational voice, again. Even knowing it was imaginary, Garren vehemently replied, 'NO!'

Garren heard Commander Tane's voice rising, thankfully, from the outside of Garren's head. "I can't find the Hearing record of this sentencing. What is the file name?"

After the fifth crack of the whip, Garren struggled against the cuffs holding him down. His depression metamorphosed into a quietly contained rage.

A commotion of sound started up, intruding on Garren's internal dialogs.

"Stop!" Garren recognized the voice of Commander Tane.

New sounds of commotion came louder.

THE SKY RAINS MY TEARS AND THUNDERS MY ANGER

:: Dana Atuin and Care Ethaynen::

Dana sighed heavily, upon rapidly fading hopes of saving Garren from this injustice. "You said you respect Erin's work?"

"Yeah, he is a minor tele-kinetic, so for a fact, welts won't go any deeper than they need to be to show," Care shaded his eyes with one hand.

Care lowered his hand, a passing cloud shadowing them

from the sun. He wracked his brain for what to do, some Rogue Fielder he was, he was supposed to be quick thinking and pro-active to sheer emergency. When did the integrity of the Guard deteriorate this wrongly? These were the people training up the Guards of tomorrow. What would the next class turn out? Garren as a Jr Guard was a prime candidate, but he was mature, the younger Jrs would be more impressionable to petty jealousies and vindictiveness. Care shivered, becoming aware of a rapidly developing chill in the air. He looked up to see what a moment ago was pure beauteous blue sky now gray and cloud filled. A minor roll of thunder precipitated a flash of lightening in the distant horizon.

Dana muttered beside him.

"What did you say?" Care prompted. Not expecting a reply, figuring it as rhetorical.

"The sky rains my tears and thunders my anger." Dana repeated.

"Why does that sound familiar?"

"It was Our Emperor's speech when he claimed Dominion over our planets."

"Ah, history, you think this weather is one of Our Emperor's famous temper-tantrums?" Care gaped in awe. "The last one on record was way before we were born. What could it be about?"

Dana shivered, then jumped in happy relief. "Finally!"

A Ministerial fastraft was at present landing in the center of the courtyard with Traci at the pilot controls. The fastraft was a very basic boat like design, two benches with safety grip bars and windscreens aft and fore, the steering controls comprised of a single handle centered from the floor. A thumb-convenient wheel on the steering handle provided pitch control.

Minister Ange hopped off the raft unaided; a nice feat for an elderly Human, his gray locks a contrast with his spry manner. He tripped on his vanilla linen robe, catching it in his slipper heel, but his Assistant's hand steadied him. He was distracted by a play of distant lightening with a grave air of concern that accentuated the age lines in his face. He was finely aged enough to remember their Emperor in younger less mature days. He turned to his young female Elf assistant. "Can you take a conjecture at what this flash storm means?" Minister Ange nodded to indicate the sudden dismal shift in weather. The young Elf woman shook her head after a moment of delayed reaction.

Dana repeated the axiom as he and Care joined the little group. "The sky rains my tears and thunders my anger."

:: Minister Angélus::

"O Yes, quite," Minister Ange beamed in praise for Dana's apt timing.

A PDA blerped, everyone checked his or her pockets, the call was for the Minister. His assistant answered it for him; she exclaimed with delight and then quickly curbed her reaction as befitting her Minister's new authority

"Well, what is the message Vylara? Are we being called away from this matter for something more urgent?"

"Um no, your Highness."

Minister Ange peeked his eyebrows into a deep V. "What??"

"You are hither-to offered the appointment 'Sovereign Minister of the Royal Fleet'." She smiled, she couldn't help it. "Your decisions are fully supported by Our Emperor."

"O my! My stars! Astra grant me guidance!" He threw his shoulders back, fixing his posture, but then forgetting to hold his posture only a moment later. "This makes everything all the more interesting. Yes, yes, tap the Acceptance key on my behalf. Would you Vylara? There, my dear girl." He startled at the scrutiny he was being treated to by Traci, Dana, and Care.

"Hee hee," Care broke the silence first. "Well, you are our favourite Minister."

"Ach, incorrigible as always Care," Sovereign-Minister Ange grinned back. Adding sternly, "this is not a popularity contest." He was unable to suppress an ear-to-ear grin, ruining the stern impression. "Ah hem, well, shall we? Let us put this honour to some good this afternoon. After you?"

A greatly smiling Care and Dana led the small entourage to the Collier building entrance; the courtyard filling with astonished spectators, the freak lightening storm not withstanding amazement. Everyone with the minimalist gleaming skills began brewing premonitions.

The lobby of the Collier building was no more than a square with room for a receptionist table and a few stiff backed chairs. The small group squeezed into the lobby, to Minister Ange's keen mind resembling a boisterous rabble.

A pretty Human male receptionist smiled disarmingly at Dana. Minister Ange looked to observe Dana's reaction, even while scolding himself for being a busy body; not much of a reaction, Dana returned the smile only politely. Minister Ange bided an amused smile; the tall blonde Guard must be used to this sort of attention. Dana was pretty, even featured, and slim in an elfish sort of way. Traci stood over Dana's shoulder, hair tight in a long thick auburn braid and body type more muscular in a not bulky way. Traci's most alluring feature was a pouty turn of lips, in older days, considered quite an attractive feature. The young people today did not seem to pay all that much attention to pouty lips, nor the neat turn of calf; which was a shame.

Ange was curious to know if his assistant found anything attractive in this pair, but she did not display any surreptitious interest. He rejoiced to be working with such an able minded assistant and a little saddened that she was letting her career outshine the youthful perks of life. He did not have the authority to promote her to a Minister position, only the Emperor could grace such an appointment, he would do his best to advocate an appointment for her. A Sovereign Minister would be expected to engage only Senior Ministers as Assistants-In-Chambers. He did not envisage any need to be so strict to conventions, a Junior Minister would do.

Sov Minister Ange came out of his reverie, realizing the assembly of Guards were waiting on his lead. "Admit us into Jr Guard Garren's hearing, please." Adding the please to be polite, he was ready to drop the pleasant-tudes if necessary to carry his authority, dearly hoping to not have to resort to rudeness.

"It is an unpleasant hearing, Minister," the receptionist squirmed in his swivel chair. "I can bring out whomever you wish to confer in the reception office across the hall."

"Quite. I intend to confer the whole hearing. Guide us to the appropriate hall."

The receptionist stood hesitantly. "In my experience here, the Ministry has never been involved in Guard discipline," the civilian had half a notion they were thrill seekers.

Dana 'tchd' aloud, reminding the Minister of the secret and no-so-secret telemental talents available. Hmm. He stored the thought away for future reference.

"I have not stepped within these halls, since the first days of the conquest. We shall see what the near future holds. Well, twice I have asked you to lead us to the hearing."

The receptionist gulped. He would be sorely depressed if he lost this receptionist position. The Guards were very picky in their promiscuity and this position was perfectly suited to his tastes. Without further ado, the slutty receptionist led the small group to a chamber in the west wing of the building.

As soon as the Sovereign Minister recognized the chamber they were headed to, he threw dignity to the shadowy corners and ran the corridor length, reaching the door to the Hearing Chamber first; tickly pleased to find he was as fast, if not faster, than all these young trained physically fit Guards.

Ange felt an unexpected urge to attempt his old tele-kinetic ability, which he'd despaired of ever using again upon decades of waning strength; but this new vitality gave him inspiration to try. He squinted and projected a focused kinetic pulse at the sealed chamber door. The door thumped loudly and shuddered; however, it failed to open. Encouraged by this evidence of results, he poured more of his minds electric synapses into a ferocious effort of will. The frame around the doors splintered. Minister Ange sighed upon realizing the failure; the wood must undoubtedly be reinforced with poly-metal. He turned to ask the Guards to do the honours, when he noticed they were standing agape at his powers. He restudied the doorframe and decided; perhaps, it was an impressive feat after all. Encouraged, he kinetically heaved at the door – frame and all - and shoved the assembly aside.

There was another little unattended receptionist area before the Hearing Chamber. Sov Minister Ange jogged at his memories, at a loss to recall the original purpose of this building. Perhaps it was time to tear it down. There was no necessity to hold disciplinary hearings behind sealed doors and shadowed halls, when there was a perfectly lovely Palace with chambers set aside for such things.

Care stepped to the fore, "I know the key code." He approached a wall set terminal and tapped at it. The inner chamber doors swung open.

An argument was taking place, so heated none of the inside occupants immediately noticed the intrusion.

Ange first searched the chamber for Garren, realized he didn't know what Garren looked like, but then spotted him anyway, unless there was another discipline-e, this had to be him. He was bound bent over and naked to a waist high crate that once knew life as a ship mounted Negatron Cannon casing. In the old vernacular, this used to be called 'kissing the cannon' and he was outrageously shocked to find this still in use. Two brackets fastened Garren by the knees to the near side of the crate; Garren's shoulders were drawn forward, so he assumed Garren's wrists were fastened similarly to the far side of the crate.

The disciplinarian, SrG Erin stood with a single tailed whip trailing in his hand. He did not look comfortable, nor was he wearing his usual smile.

The pronounced oddity in the room however; Commander Tane assigned as one of the hearing officiates was standing bodily shielding Garren from the whip in Erin's hand, both Tane's arms out to garner more space between the whip and its victim.

Commander Tane noticed the new group first.

The Minister fancied he saw an expression of vast relief in Commander Tane's eyes. Erin noticed them next, echoing the same palpable sense of relief; he started curling up the whip to stow it away.

Minister Ange winced, he counted five angry red welts striping Garren's bare bottom, apologetic, not as terrible as 50.

ß

Care Ethaynen was speaking close to Garren's ear. "We're getting you out of this Garren," Care's voice whispered. "Sit tight, while we spring the cuffs. Urr, sit tighter, I meant." A teasing note filled Care's voice and Garren felt a friendly feeling toward Care.

Care lost not another moment to free Garren. It became obvious Care was intimate with the room for he seemed to know the key codes to interrupt the magnetic seal on the fastenings pinning Garren's wrists to the crate.

"Halt, no one ordered this sentencing Writ satisfied," Minister Atalaetia stood up. Her hair, no not hair, tentacles waved about her head in agitation.

Care blithely ignored her and freed Garren's wrists. Garren did not move to stand up, nor move at all.

&

Commander Tane motioned Erin to assist Care in assisting Garren.

Quick witted that, Ange felt he should have made the gesture and was glad to credit Commander Tane. The Sovereign

Minister's thoughts flashed on the spanking brand new ships currently being fitted in South Fleet Bays. Sovereign Minister of the Royal Fleet made it his responsibility to commission qualified Fleet Commanders for those ships, 'Oo, which was going to be a lovely exercise.' A flitting thought made him wonder what happened to the erenow Minister of the Royal Fleet? Did he get fired? Usually a Minister died un-retired in his or her Ministerial position.

"Minister Angélus, what a surprise to find you here," Minister Atalaetia spoke for the assembled hearing. Out ranking everyone else present made her the forward choice spokesperson, or judging by the sullen looks of these officiates, they did not appreciate Ministers spoiling their little party.

Ange shuddered. It brought back awful memories of the old Aristocrat parties, when Aristocrats ruled the planets, 'o the bad old days'.

"Not as surprised as I am to find you here," Minister Ange pierced her with his shrewd gaze.

She smiled, easier to notice as her many tentacles stopped agitating, the tentacles looked like invertebrate complete with little fanged jaws on the ends.

"It is rather breaking protocol to find a Minister of Royal Appointments at a Jr Guard's disciplinary hearing," her logic almost debugged his own logic.

"Wouldn't the same protocol apply to you, Minister Atalaetia, Minister of Public Traffic?" He stressed the 's' in Minister.

"I am invited to officiate here," she deemed this not all at odds.

"Invited by whom, may I inquire?"

No one spoke.

Hmmm. Ange checked on Garren's progress and saw his knees still fastened to the crate. Minister Ange readied a kinetic pulse, thinking this was show-offee, but there was a time and a place for everything. He kinetically ripped the fastening grommets from the crate.

Garren involuntarily jerked as the pressure on his kneebacks disappeared. He'd been fastened very firmly.

Ange was well pleased at the gasps he provoked from these derelictions of duty. He sincerely hoped Garren would not be bitter over this incident. Well, Garren's triple promotion and Commission Docket were issued directly from the Emperor; it should cheer Garren considerably.

The Guards went to help Garren stand, Garren shook his head politely and straightened up by himself, he staggered a little, Dana reached out to catch him and found the offer unnecessary as Garren pulled his will together and controlled his shaking legs despite his undoubtedly flooding endorphins levels.

Care murmured, "I thought the Writ said stripped to the knees. How come he's totally naked?"

Erin shook his head, admiration evident. "He stripped before anyone needed a reason to touch him. Very spirited it was."

Dana and Care shared grins, and over hearing their exchange of words, Minister Ange felt heartened. There was obviously something extra to this Jr Guard's psyche; oops, Commander now. Dana handed Garren his uniform, the blues of the Jrs. Garren thanked Dana, draping the apparel over his arm and making no move to dress.

Minister Ange reasoned Garren felt it would look furtive to dress in front of these officiates. He became amused to see his young assistant, who had been oblivious to the Guard's charms until now, drinking in Garren's figure. Looking at Garren as unbiased as he could manage, he had to admit the Human to be exquisitely proportioned. The Jr, Ooops again, Commander, trained with archaic weapons, chiefly the broadsword as he recalled, certainly doing no harm in the muscular look department. The tapering of his shoulders to trim hips, the ideal of modern beauty, and the angry red of the fresh welts drew attention to the accentuation of perfectly contoured buttocks. And other proportioned details of physique embellishments the younger people would find interesting of note.

These observations brought Minister Ange to a realization he never would have considered before. The panel of officiates, the tables set up in a semicircle around the crate, were treating Garren as a piece of meat for their entertainments of whim. Minister Ange almost staggered, raising his fingers to his forehead, gripping his temple as if it hurt. These Guards were dedicating their lives to their Emperor, to their Realm, and to life and liberties charted in the Bill of Personal Rights.

A babble of voices started up from the members of the panel, excepting Commander Tane. Tane stood in the middle of it all with an expression of profound boredom and distaste very evident, this Commander who protected this Jr Guard from the very people who should be his haven, not his pain. These were the people the Guard could not afford to loose. The Guards who would not just accept, but speak out, if the Guards did not protest injustice and maltreatment, then who would? The Guards who, if no one listened or cared would abandon their commissions in disgust or turn mercenary and leave it to the self-interested, like the Aristocrats of old who molded society with decrees to their own selfish benefit and only back breaking labour fit for the rest. Minister Ange tuned out the babble; maybe it was due to his new feeling of robustness. There was a time for political games and savvy and this was not such a time.

He walked to the rear wall; feeling healthy and vital, he prepared a new pulse of kinetic energy, this time confident in his recovered ability. Using the fine tactile detail he had been capable of decades ago, kinetically tapped a tiny shadow covered terminal, using his Minister's override code, programming the shutters to open, shutters unopened since the building was made. The shutters creaked, groaned, and protested; yet doth did open. To the Minister's mood, the shutters flung open seemingly joyous.

The sun kissed day he had woken to was now a dismal rain, a pattern empty of rhythm and with a frightening unnaturalness. They way it used to rain before the weather control stations were dismantled.

He turned his back to the wide-open window, his light colored robes and gray shoulder length hair moving with the gusts parrying the room, the rain and gray skies behind him.

"Will you deign to inform us why you are here and accompanied by these Guards, Minister?" Minister Atalaetia resumed her spokesperson role.

Unfortunately, he had no authority to reprimand her in any form, except to monitor her actions in the proceeding terra days to come.

"I was originally coming hear to inform Jr Guard Garren of his promotion," he reserved the rest of that statement for a more private moment. "And to inform the Field Commander here of his demit," Minister Ange disdained any familiarity with the harried Human by saying a name. "In light of what has transpired here, or rather came to light today, for this smacks of long practiced caligula-ism, I find it would be a boon to the whole of Celesterra if you were not privileged to our governmental bodies at all."

A collective gasp resounded. The Guards did their best to hide smiles behind coughs.

Minister Ange pointed a finger at each of the panel in turn, excepting Commander Tane and the besnaked Minister Atalaetia. "BY the authority invested in me, I here-by revoke your Commissions. And subsequently, if you are on this planet with a temporary Permit of Residence, these Permits are here-by rescinded. This will be done immediately." Minister Ange hollered out the open window at a knot of Guards standing under a south side awning, who were watching the building trenchantly for activity. "Guards! To me! Escort these disgraces off the grounds." He turned to the stunned collection of people. "There, that should do it." He shared a beaming smile with his assistant. She was so new to the position, yet had a complete grasp of all the fine intricacies of the affaires of the moment. She discretely nodded at Garren and motioned discretely to her robe's pocket hiding Garren's new epaulette pin.

The Elf maid spied a quick look at Garren, the mistreated Human looked like a vessel of barely contained rage. Her heart skipped a beat.

"You can't just fire us!" A Field Trainer burst out.

"O YES I CAN. My Writ of Authority from the Emperor says I may ... and it is done."

"We do not fear the Emperor," a voice rang out.

"Indeed; because he has guaranteed you personal rights and liberties, and because he does not wish you to live in fear of him. How can you in your former positions of authority, not understand that these rights were not granted you so that you may abuse the rights of others and mete out injustice?"

"We are essential personnel, the training regime will collapse."

"You think you are indispensable," Sov Minister Ange's eyes twinkled, it was absurd, he felt no sympathy for them in the slightest. "Is bad training better than no training? I donan think so," he slipped into the dialect of his long ago youth. He dismissed the ex Officiates from his immediate attentions.

"Garren, may I have a private word with you?"

XII. TERRA-DATE 215::149 Mid Afternoon
Castra Urbs Certamen
:: Public Transit Plaza. Care Ethaynen::

Care Ethaynen stood at a kiosk reading the public transit schedules, searching for the fastest transport to Nihera City; a city on the far side of the planet.

A circumbiant gloom cast its melancholy on people. The normally thriving public station was doing a dead of night type of business with a sparse crowd of mainly Humans and Elves, families and rambunctious teenagers. The dress ranged from form fitting silks to shapeless cloaks, modern and the arcane intermingled. It was not wise to judge a person's age by their appearance. Indiscriminate Magic was not legal in public thoroughfares; therefore, the local activity was exclusively mundane. Or aught to be! Care was sure the Mages, Witches, and Clerics; stretched the legalities as long as they didn't get caught.

Care shook his head at the kiosk display. The express launches were all finished for the day. The next launch made local stops around the planet. 'Dragonpoo,' he mumbled with ire, no luck. 'O Well. What to do with the rest of the day?' He'd left his bag of discipline toys at a locker in the Guard Administrative Center or he might have called Krizren and offered to make him happy.

It could be fun to crash Garren's promotion party. Care now wished he'd stuck around to find out Garren's new rank. Poor man! Having to go through the mockery of a Hearing today. Care wiggled his butt, feeling an empathetic twinge on his bum cheeks. Nice! Wearing his most comfortable waist cropped organic fibred t-shirt and tight fitting canvas pants, must have made the wiggle stand out for he heard a voice behind him.

"Woah, cute dance, do it again!" A voice prompted Care's ridiculousness.

He turned to find another Guard behind him. The prettiest Elf male he'd ever seen. They were both of a similar height. The Elf's long thick blonde hair braided into two sections hid his ears; aqua-green eyes with a slight mermaid-ish tilt drew all your attention. His epaulette pinned him as an unassigned Guard and a tiny engraved squiggle line indicated Magic user.

Care just kept smiling at this vision, insatiably curious to find out what he was into. 'Wait, did this Elf just call me cute?'

"Umm, I'm looking for a transit to Nihera City, have you seen anything on the schedule?" The Elf blinked long eyelashes at Care.

"O no, I'm out of luck too, the last express left and the locals will take terra days to circle the planet," Care cocked his best jaunty smile, a smile that usually scored for him. "I was just deciding what to do to make this evening fun and unforgettable."

The Elf, refreshingly in Care's opinion, didn't even pretend to miss the meaning. "Don't you even want to ask my name first?"

"No, why?" Care shrugged. "You didn't grow up on Celesterra!" He made it a statement; cultures varied drastically, especially in the Guard, etiquette Writ couldn't cover everything.

"Actually, no. I'm Rhiannon by the way," Rhiannon held out a hand hesitantly for a wrist to wrist greet, a lot of people wouldn't grasp the hand of a Mage. But obviously, Care was unlike a lot of people, for he grasped the Elf's hand with no hesitation. Rhiannon grinned widely. He took a liking to this

Human.

"Care," Care beamed. "Pleased to meet you, Rhiannon."

"Umm, you can call me Rhi iffn you like, just think of all the consonants it will save you." Rhiannon shrugged back a shoulder bag he was carrying, standard gear for a Guard to tote his uniform around the galaxy.

"It never occurred to me to count my consonants," Care brushed his brown hair behind his ears. The gusty winds had died down for a while now and the hair stayed for a few moments.

"Were you going to the Rocket Races?" Rhi grew a little shy at the avid attention Care was giving him.

"To an interview actually."

"With Commander Kerlin by any coincidence?" Rhi said with excitement.

"Hey, wouldn't it be something if we were on the same Field Team?" Care felt his luck changing. Luck was a fickle thing, not something to waste time chasing.

"Yeah, we have to get to the interview before someone else gets the appointment, everyone's hot to be on Kerlin's Team." Rhi craned his neck at the sky, gazing longingly at the transit ferries.

"Right," Care fleetingly considered rejoining Minister Ange with Rhi along. Yet. He feared Commander Kerlin might be swayed either way if he knew Care kept lofty company. 'All right, just pretend I'm on a Rogue Field assignment. What would I do to get somewhere in a hurry?' Care chatted internally. The fastest mode travel was via Space Vessel. How would it go over if he borrowed a Scout ship? He slapped his forehead. Of course, he could just ask. Who to ask? Lessee, Traci was a pilot.

"You have an idea?" Rhi said hopefully as Care whipped out his PDA.

"Mebbe," he tapped some, then spoke closely into the PDA's nano-mike. "Traci, you online friend?"

Bweemeep!

"Oh! You again! Hullo friend, aww, are you missing me since this morning?" Traci's good humoured voice squawked crystal clear in all its nuances from Care's PDA.

"Da thump, da thump," Care thumped on his chest with his free palm. "Be still my racing heart."

"Lemme guess, ya need a ride to Nihera City?" Traci impersonated a Gleamer in trance.

"O Traci," Care disguised his voice as a lovesick teenager. "Actually, a ride for two?" Care winked at Rhi listening silently by.

"Hah, you work fast," Traci sounded normal again. "Can you and your friend make it to the South Fleet Bay?"

"Um," Care spied a public fastraft, the zippiest means of travel in Celesterra City. "Affirmative, we can ride a raft to an outskirt shuttle to a port canoe." Care's heart did a for real thump thump. "What's at the Fleet Bay? Huh? Huh? Stop holding out on me." He started jogging to the available raft pedestal, waving at Rhi to follow.

Traci took forever to answer, drawling, "well, our friends from Mariterra Planet, Krizren & Keyth offered me a float in their new commission."

"Woah, they're going Deep Space?" Care figured there had to be more to it for Traci to be dragging it out this long. Care's emotions were very mixed, excited yet sad; it could be terra years before he saw Kriz again.

"They are assigned to..." Traci cleared his throat.

"Enough, is Dana still with you? Put him on."

"No, he went home for a change of clothes. He's taking Garren to Nerrys & Nalira's for a quiet evening."

"Huh? Who would want a quiet evening?! Aw, is Garren still hurting? Did he go to a healer? Or, doesn't Nerrys have an eligible daughter?"

"It was more the shock of his promotion I think."

"Really?"

Care and Rhiannon were climbing the two steps into the raft. The whole craft was basically a poly metal construction; two mounted benches with gripbars, seatbelts, and windscreens behind and in front, and topped with a canvas canopy in red and white stripes.

&

Rhiannon was new to the city; travel brochures mentioned the red and white stripes meant this raft was for public use. Trivia funneled across his thoughts as he eavesdropped on Care's PDA conversation.

ß

"Shock?" Care switched the raft's autonav to manual, flicking crystals on the dashboard.

"Yes."

"Traci!" Care swore, these monosyllables were a strain on his swooping emotions. "Are you always this fun at a party?" He rolled his eyes playfully at Rhi to let him know this banter was normal.

"I know what kind of fun I'm gonna have at Krizren's party. He likes that I'm broad, tall, and strong." Traci waxed loquacious a sudden.

"Yeah? Why is that you figure?" Care adjusted the steering stick, driving daringly fast for not being in uniform. He watched Rhi to see how he was taking the ride. The Elf was calm as could be, no white knuckle grabbing at the handlebars. Care's interest quickened. Why would an extremely pretty, Magic-using, iron nerved Elf be unassigned? And apprehensive over an interview? Something wasn't copasetic here.

"Do you want to drive Rhi?" Care offered.

"Okay," Rhi put a relaxed left-handed grip on the steering shaft.

Care leaned back to relax and gave his attention to Traci's exasperating word play.

Rhi steered the raft up to a third story elevation and careened the next turn - midair- at a hard tilt. Care reflexively grabbed for the handlebars as his backside slid across the bench, until the seatbelt checked his slide. The raft straightened and Care eased his death grip and noticing knuckles pale against his naturally medium brown skin, burst out laughing.

Rhi kept his attention on the mid-lane, he smiled at Care's laugh, not getting the joke.

"Is there something you wanna share?" Traci talked over Care's fading laugh.

"Never mind," Care grinned ruefully. "You were saying about Garren's promotion?" He wanted to save the Krizren's likes chat for later. Care pondered Garren's promotion. Shock? "Did he get promoted straight to Senior Guard??"

"Nope."

"No, Nah. Jr Commander?" Care shared a meaningless eye meet with Rhi.

"Nope."

"No, nah, no. Commander?" This had to be a prank.

"Senior Commander! ... Senior Fleet Commander!"

No wonder Traci wanted to milk this bomb for all it was worth.

"And," Traci had another bomb to lay, "assigned to The Halçyon!" Traci obviously couldn't stand the suspense anymore.

"The Halçyon? Woah!!" Halçyon was thee premiere Scout-Class Command ship, the most coveted assignment among the space fleet wannabes of the Guard. It was a well-known secret the Emperor hid himself aboard Halçyon, when he was hiding from pestering petitioners. It was a nugget of knowledge the Palace Guards kept quiet about. The rest of the Guard pretended not to know.

Care whistled in sympathy. He'd once used a docked ship himself, though for his cause he was hiding from a very aggressive ex-girlfriend. He hadn't reported her, because he couldn't blame her. At the time he had been practicing one of his Rogue Fielder undercover disguises. The disguise had worked all too well.

"Hey" Care said aloud. "We're going float on the famous Halçyon? Do you think Kriz will take us to Nihera City? It's a pretty important trip for us."

"Sure. Orbit, then to the farside. Nothing to it." Traci chuckled. It was going to be a fantastic(!) night or day, depending on which side of planetary orbit they'd be coasting.

Care looked to the sky for it became dark all of a sudden. Clouds rolled across the sky, fast, thick thunderheads, sort of frightening and ominous.

Our Emperor again? What was going on at the Palace to upset Methusem so? And, if it wasn't the Emperor, did they have an uncontrolled tempest kinetic on their hands messing with the weather?

Traci logged off, "cya soon."

And right away Care's and Rhi's PDA blerpied. Rhi landed the fast raft before he drew his PDA. It was the same message on both.

An Emergency Drill to test the Planetary Shields scheduled for 3 days hence. Care winced, "tis going to be utter chaos." Though, he understood the necessity for it.

They climbed out of the raft, walking towards the outskirt shuttle about 300 steps away, just as rain started up again.

"Perfect. Lessee my assignment in a planetary emergency is to ... oops I forget ... um ... o yes ..," Care said rather facetiously. "Secure the drinking water. I suppose it's pretty important, I'd rather be in combat." He looked at his now rain drenched Elf companion. Neither of them hurried. It was scientifically proven by some bored students, running in the rain does not mean you get any less wet.

"At the moment I have no assignment," Rhi answered in a strange voice. "That could change tomorrow, if Commander Kerlin accepts my application. Go ahead ask!" Rhi listed his head to the side a little, thinking Care looked very cute all wet. Care's glossy shoulder length hair normally hid a lot of his face, his yellow eyes looked supernatural in the rainy weather.

"Ask what?" Care teased then thought better of it, this seemed to bother his companion a lot. "OK, why aren't you assigned?"

"Because no one wants me, I'm a liability on a Field Assignment." Rhiannon shrugged his carry all more firmly on his shoulder, his boots sloshing rainwater.

"No one? Come on." Care couldn't imagine what could be a liability for a Guard. "You're a Senior, aren't you? Obviously someone didn't find you a liability." Care used both hands to slick his drenched hair back, squirming as rain dripped into his cropped t-shirt and down his neck, now regretting not wearing a uniform. Uniforms never get drip down the collar.

"It is a new promotion. I was in the Subterraneum, when we rescued Emperor Methusem."

"Weren't we all?" Care became uncharacteristically solemn a moment.

"I threw the dispell, negating the warding holding Methusem prisoner." Rhi stared at his feet.

From his manner, Care could tell Rhi wasn't revealing this as a boast. Whatever he'd witnessed in the cavern seemed to disturb his outlook.

"The Palace hasn't released details, it must have been horrific," Care petted Rhiannon's arm. "Your promotion to Senior Guard came directly from Emperor Methusem? Awesome honour!" Care waited, almost to the shuttle now. "And the liability is?" Finally giving in to impolite curiosity.

"I'm a ..." Rhi raised his face to the rain then blurted, "an erotamanic."

"Huh?" Care didn't bother to conjecture.

"Erotomania, I like sex way more than normal for my species."

Care didn't respond at first. What would it be like to be on a Field Team, in the field with an over-sexed Elf? Hee hee. He danced a little dance in the rain, shouting. "Yes!" He leapt about, raising his arms to the raining sky.

This time Rhi did stare at Care.

"I'm Okay with it. Believe me," Care laughed. "Anytime you need it!"

Rhi didn't react the way Care anticipated.

"You say it now. It won't last," Rhi was too young to talk so sad.

Care shook his head, his spirit buoyant, only time and experience would prove his sincerity. Rhi climbed into the dry outskirt shuttle, a craft little grander than the fastraft, well dry until Rhi sat in it in his rain drenched apparel. No one else was in view, people sanely staying home in this insane weather.

Pausing before boarding, Care turned to gaze at the City. His City! Viewing it from the outskirts here, layers of building obscured the heart. The Emperor had dismantled the lost in the clouds sky-high buildings long before Care had been born. Only a small section of the old city remained. The Mynx population sequestered themselves in the old derelict buildings. They wouldn't be coaxed out.

Streets that 200 terra years ago were dust trails, today were now neatly paved with sparkly Evening Stones.

Care's throat chakra tightened with love for his City. Born 22 terra years ago, raised here, lived all his life here among the Humans, Elves, and other races calling this place home. The tamed and untamed creatures, the aviary life, flowers, trees, and sea breezes; the shops, malls, and theaters; sunsets and sunrises; Care loved every pebble. He would give his life for the folk and creatures living here, no hesitations or qualms about it.

Care smoothed his hair behind his ears and then climbed into the waiting shuttle.

XIII. T̶ERRA-DAT̶E 215.149 MI∂ AFT̶ERNOON
Audi Alteram Partem
:: Celesterra City, South Fleet Bay. Garren ::

Garren waited at the gated entrance to South Fleet Bay, and waited some more. He fidgeted with ill fitting disposable clothes he'd bought from a vending machine. Gazing out at the ships berthed in the bay, his heart pounded heavily in his strong chest. Assigned to the Halçyon? Too preposterous to imagine!

The great South Fleet Bay sat off the coastline of the southern peninsula of Celesterra City. Reserved for Royal Fleet ships, Halçyon had a permanent Docking Permit.

Garren looked keenly round him at the infinity of activities, which were making the pre-launch ships ready for a long indeterminate period of service in distant – and likely uncharted – deep space.

The closest vessel to view 'The Solstice" berthed and submerged to her 'waist line' in the waters of the bay, she was currently in the process of re-supplying for deep space. Port ferries hovered over the water, gliding in both directions; no ship would go deep space without an adequate supply of, among other things, commercial chocolate and fresh water. In Celesterra City, the water sourced directly from mountain runoff. Garren shared the common distaste of recycled water. From his vantage point, he could not see anyone supervising the embarkation of stores, not wise for you could end up running out of chocolate somewhere beyond the heliopause. 'Then where are you?'

Under the competent command of Fleet Commander Tane, 'The Solstice' was a Ship of the Line one model release behind the latest vessel design. Recent rumour hot off the gossip broadbands said, Commander Tane had turned down an offer of a newer ship. Garren felt no criticism towards Commander Tane for refusing the upgrade, – a Fleet Commander of impeccable integrity; Garren was ready to defend the commander against any criticizer.

It was still an astonishment to Garren that he was now of equal rank with Fleet Commanders Tane, Bel, and Sable; as a Junior Garren hadn't met any of the other Fleet Commanders and felt wary of them. Fleet Commanders on long deep space assignments were granted an autonomy that must be hard to relinquish once returned home, even with communications technology available today. He had to admit; he was unpopular with many in the Fleet due to his stubbornness and lack of social schmoozing skills.

Why had Emperor Methusem chosen him for The Halçyon?

Garren had been only 7 of age in terra years, when the Emperor had come to his home planet of Quinterra for a groundbreaking ceremony opening a Guard Administrative Center. Built on the nearly perpetually cloudy Quinterra, the Guard Administrative Center was a center of light and modern thinking. The Emperor's new buildings had gleamed and with the Guards dressed in form fitting black uniforms with capes rippling in Quinterra Planet's blustery winds, had created an indelible impression. His ambition to join the Guard had been touch and go in those days for you needed an actively commissioned Guard to sponsor your candidacy; and his family had been quite dead set against supporting Emperor Methusem. The Emperor had taken all power away from the Aristocrats at the time of the conquering. Many of those Aristocrats were still alive, being able to afford the life prolonging potions, or rather used to be able to afford. Heh-heh!

Garren shifted his weight on to one leg and folded his arms. Reminiscing on his home planet could ruin his mood on any day, no matter how transforming the day. The only thing he could thank his home planet for was his night vision, which was better than an Elf. He could not see in a complete absence of light, but if there was a little, he could see in dim light quite clearly. It would be an advantage on a pre-technical world, but with modern gear, night vision did not add significantly to his stats.

He reconsidered his earlier question, why had Emperor Methusem chosen him? It couldn't be for his personality, no matter how much he regretted it, Garren refused to change for people who didn't like him. Among the generally extroverted personalities among the Guard, Garren was, umm, to be self kind, what word ...

"Misfits," spoke a voice behind him.

Garren managed to hide his startlement and casually turned around. A Guard he had never met before stood outside the lobby to the gate entrance area. This outspoken Guard was decked out in full uniform, standing amid a pile of luggage and many cartons. He appeared Human, near Garren's own age, fine dark hair cut in a trendy wispy style shorter on top and shoulder length for the rest. Light brown eyes lit with sensitive humour regarded Garren with a keenness to which he was most unaccustomed. Garren shifted his gaze to the Guard's epaulette pin affixed to the uniform neckline at his collarbone. He was expecting to read the symbol for a minor telepath, and not at all surprised to read the Senior Fleet Commander rank, but the last symbol was a surprise for he'd never seen it outside of a training manual. Garren blinked, making an ardent effort not to be rude. There was a good chance this rude eavesdropping telepathic person would be his shipmate.

"Yes, I'm Keyth," Keyth held out a hand.

Garren clasped wrists with Keyth trying very hard to keep thoughts clear of his mind.

"I'm only a minor telepath. I wouldn't ordinarily read you, but it seems when you're distressing you broadcast," Keyth smiled.

Not at all reassured by this last comment, Garren did his best to deal with it. "You're really an astral-kinetic?" Garren felt impressed despite himself.

"Yes."

"What's your range?" Garren asked, imagining what it must be like to be an astral-kinetic on a deep space assignment with an uncharted galaxy to explore.

"I can leave my body here and send my consciousness as far as the orbital station," Keyth smiled. "Any further than that and I could lose touch with my body and become lost."

"So, it's bloody dangerous," Garren re-measured his first impression of Keyth to a higher level of impression. The courage it must take to make such a journey. "Did you say 'Yes'? Meaning we're going to be shipmates?"

"Yes." Keyth chuckled.

"Are you a misfit too, then?" He seemed very likeable; Garren hoped he continued to be fortunate in this regard.

"Absolutely! By the way, I read your complete profile in the Commander's Registry," Keyth remarked by way of casual conversation. He sat on a carton and gestured Garren to pull up a carton and seat himself similarly. "Unless, you haven't been to a healer yet?" Keyth's eyes crinkled at the corners and dimples appeared.

"Great, a joker," Garren sat; hiding the sore twinges coming from his sore bottom, despite the fact Keyth would likely be telesensitive to pain.

"Oh, I'm not empathic to your pain," Keyth drew a bar of chocolate from a satchel at his feet; he broke it in half and offered a piece to Garren.

Garren accepted with polite thanks. He took one bite and it tasted deliciously smooth and rich. This must be an expensive variety. He made an assumption that Keyth enjoyed his Senior Commander's salary grade.

"Are you fond of jokers? You must have a preconceived opinion of our fourth new shipmate then, eh?"

"Hm?"

"Does that non-committal noise mean you haven't read the Commander's registry? It was the first thing I did when I made command rank. I guess you had other business on your mind today, or not on your mind, butt your other end," Keyth laughed.

Garren took another bite of the chocolate. The worst part of being disciplined was not the punishment itself; it was all the wisecracks you had to endure afterwards.

"Okay," Keyth took pity, "anyway, Amé is coming deep space with us. My tether-mate is not happy about it, I can tell you."

"Your tether-mate?" Garren swallowed his chocolate down.

"Krizren is my telepathic tether-mate. He's coming deep space with us, too."

"Krizren?" Garren remembered hearing the name this morning, but could not remember in what context.

"Who else?"

"That's the lot of us," Keyth finished his chocolate and pulled another bar from his satchel. He shared this one, too.

"Thank you. What do you mean? Halçyon is designed for a crew of twenty-seven, they can't send just four Guards into deep space," Garren's suspicions floundered. It made no sense.

"Actually, four Fleet Commanders and someone begs to differ. Have you made the acquaintance of Minister Ange? His promotion is wonderful news, isn't it?"

"I wish he'd get here already, I'm anxious to tour Halçyon." Garren tried adjusting his seat to ease the soreness on his bottom, it didn't help. "So, we're senior fleet commanders with no crew to command." Ready for a change of subject, "I see you have all your things ready." He nodded to indicate all the cartons.

"Oh no, this is all for the party tonight?" Keyth smiled warmly.

"Party?"

"Yes, you can't receive a commission like this and not celebrate. Invite all your friends to come aboard," Keyth became very animated.

Avoiding mention of friends, Garren replied, "you really think I want a whole night of enduring whipping wisecracks? I guess my profile didn't reveal much about me." A hand brushed his shoulder in sympathy.

Keyth patted Garren's stiff shoulder a couple of times then pulled out a third bar of chocolate. "Here."

"You know, it isn't that the Hearing was unjustified," Garren uncharacteristically ranted a bit to his new shipmate. "I did crash a mission meant for above my rank, I did deserve something, it's just that ..." Garren stopped himself, appalled that he was ranting to a relative stranger.

"Go on, I'm listening," Keyth prompted with kindness and not a trace of pity.

Garren's emotions felt a little wrought, but he managed to continue. "They sentenced me without hearing me say a word in defense. The Writ was so harsh and the officiates who showed up had no business there; it was like, everyone who dislikes me just showed up to gloat at my expense. And ..." He stopped mid-rant. It was so unfair, 'so life is unfair'.

"I'm so sorry Garren, here, let this cheer you up," Keyth held forth a beverage container.

Garren thumbed open the spout, expecting something in the way of alcohol. It wasn't alcohol, "this is genuine chocolate ... milk? This stuff is frikkin expensive, I couldn't possibly!"

"Yes you can, enjoy!" Keyth smiled.

He accepted the offer and drank the chocolate milk; it tasted great, refreshing and smooth textured. "What produced the milk?"

"Zabarleek, it's a hydroponically grown fruit of the gourd genus."

"I haven't seen any farms on this planet," Garren never noticed before.

"All the farms are hydroponic, mainly in lunar orbital stations and some bordering the Dragon lands. I'd hate to think what would happen if the crops failed and we couldn't feed the Dragons," Keyth lost his appetite for more chocolate as he contemplated Dragon dinner, even though no one had been Dragon dinner since the last of the slavers went down the gullet.

They sat in comfortable silence. Sea birds cawed overhead, nothing in the bay 'cept smooth hull to perch their little talons upon. The winds gusted, the clouds remaining from the earlier freak storm overcastting the afternoon; or temper tantrum as people speculated.

Garren breathed deep of the air, he'd been deep space only once before, a very cheap transport vessel from Quinterra and he'd stayed in hiding for most of that voyage. Would the ship's environment smell anything as good as this sea air? He glimpsed down at his wrist worn mark-meter, it read five marks into the afternoon. 'Minister Ange was taking a long time.'

"What's the matter?" Keyth saw Garren bouncing his heel, an impatient gesture.

"I'm supposed to meet Dana in a little while and Minister Ange isn't here yet." Garren took a deep breath and relaxed. Dana would understand. "You say your tether-mate has some discord with Amé?"

"I didn't say discord, I said unhappy about it," Keyth said. "Amé has a reputation as a practical joker, you know."

"We'll have a lively voyage then," Garren savoured another long drink of the chocolate milk. He wiped his upper lip, making sure he didn't sit in public with zabarleek milk on his face.

"Do you see the bright side in all things?" Keyth leaned back to tilt his face up for a sky bask.

"Who me?" Garren sat incredulous. "Must be your influence. So, how do two people become telepathically tether-bonded?"

"Well, it's a long and interesting story. I should pen a book about it," Keyth smiled with his eyes closed. "Ahh."

"There won't be any sea breezes aboard ship," Garren watched Keyth enjoy the few streaks of sunlight breaking amid the cumulus cloud layers.

"No, but there'll be the Pearl Chamber's Storm Sanctum, if you feel a need for weather."

"Right," the Pearl Chamber was something Garren looked forward to experiencing, the living energy source powering the Fleet's ships.

"The Commander's Registry didn't list you for a special Ability," Keyth opened one eye to regard his new shipmate.

"I don't have one, just blood and guts combat training," Garren half smiled. He added, "and night vision."

Keyth opened both eyes to witness this. If a half smile could transform Garren's face so, what would a full smile do? "You must be a latent at least, I'm sensing something there."

"There is nothing special about me ... anything ... trust me on it."

"You know, I remember Emperor Methusem's temper tantrums and to-terra-day didn't feel like one. Extreme stress can bring out a latent and you were extremely stressed this morning, around about the time of your suspension?" Keyth quirked one of his rather straight lined eyebrows.

Garren could only gawp. "Now you're being outrageous, how could you even hint that I had anything to with the weather?" He laughed, not realizing it had been a long time since he'd laughed last.

"Why? Maybe it is part of the mystery? Why are four senior commanders newly assigned to float the premiere virgin ship of the Royal Fleet? And on no particular mission? Halçyon has been sitting in her berth since her debut half a century ago."

"My part of the mystery has nothing to with any special ability from me, especially, weather! So, extreme stress can bring out an Ability? Is that how you and Krizren became mates?"

"It can happen from any extreme emotion, or fantastic sex between latents!" Keyth rummaged in another of his satchels, ready for another chocolate snack.

"You mean you and Krizren are? Oh," Garren blushed in embarrassment.

"What's the matter?" Keyth looked at his companion in some perplexity. "Does it make you uncomfortable? I thought you young moderners intermingled."

"Not on my home planet," Garren shrugged. "And why are you calling me 'a young moderners'? What does it mean?"

"It's slang from my home planet, Mariterra."

"Mariterra? I've never been there. Mariterra was the planet that took the longest to stamp out slavery, eh?"

"Is it? I shall bow to your knowledge, its modern history hasn't been a focus of my learning," Keyth's PDA blerped and he became absorbed in his mail.

Garren noticed the sun was a well arced 4/5ths of the way down from its zenith. They would be sitting here in full dark before long. And there goes the Orbital Station on its last pass of the day, to a sky gazer below looking like a small moon.

"There! I just invited Traci to our party tonight," Keyth's PDA tapping sounded merry.

"Traci helped save me this morning, he brought Minister Ange," Garren wondered, if after today, he could count Traci as a friend. And Care, he was a likeable fellow, despite having strange tastes. Ah, that's who he had heard Krizren's name from.

"Of course you can," Keyth said in a gentle voice.

"What? Oh. Am I distressing again?" Living with telepaths!

"And Krizren is an After-Gleamer, he can see your past. Do you have expectations of privacy? Don't worry," Keyth said quickly, seeing Garren become genuinely upset. "I'm only teasing; he would never pry into your privacy."

"Are you and Krizren both from Mariterra Planet? Did you grow up together?"

"Yes, we're both from Mariterra, but we grew up in very different lives. Krizren was raised by a very sheltering Momma in a secluded mountain environment with plenty of streams and meadows. You should see his dreams about it sometime, twas absolutely beautiful." Keyth's eyes misted a bit.

"What about you?" Garren asked gently.

Keyth appeared about to answer and then didn't say anything, he was a bit surprised that someone of Garren's commanding manner could sound so gentle.

There came a noisy commotion from the far side of the gate. Garren strolled to peer between the gray bars of the gate. A dockworker was swearing at a lumpy lift machine. The dock worker started yelling, "can you believe this machine chose today to defunct? The thing is nearly four centuries old. Do you know how long it's going to take to get a permit for a new machine? They are so blasted stingy widd'em."

Someone beyond sight mumbled in response.

The dockworker continued, "what are you planning to do? Spell every supply parcel to the ship berths?"

Garren sat down again, speaking to Keyth, "that could slow our launch." He smiled.

The transformation to Garren's face was everything Keyth expected. Garren was stunningly handsome.

"Don't worry," Keyth wasn't talking about the machine. "Krizren and I have a healthy relationship, if you catch my meaning. We won't call Deep Space Etiquette on you. I can't speak for Amé, true, if he calls etiquette on you just point him mine and Kriz's way."

Garren sat stone still, recalling all the complicated social writs for long deep space assignments. Especially with a crew of only four, Humans and Elves have a record of going wonky mental alone in space void with only each other for company. The most infamous case of Deep Space Stir Crazy, the logs of the Old Renown crew were classic training reading.

"That goes for you too," Keyth continued with a teasing grin.

"You can go wonky with only yourself for relief, if you catch my meaning again."

A loud rumbling hum saved Garren from thinking up a witty reply to that. He looked beyond the gate to see a machine rolling on casters, clinging to its last expectations of life. The huge thing had to be even more ancient than the defunct machine.

The port's public lanterns winked on, this was premature since dusk wasn't quite descending yet upon the bay. Activity at the Bay began winding down for the day. The Celesterra workday was rather short, Garren mused, not criticizing it. Citizens were guaranteed food, water, shelter, and a tunic and shoes. But if you wanted chocolate in your diet or silky evening clothes, you had to work for the money to buy luxuries beyond the bare necessities. And some people were fine with the bare necessities, though most people worked at jobs. People earning money now did many jobs that used to be the purview of droid servitude. Garren smiled to himself, when he had first come to Celesterra to join the Guard, he had heartily expected to fail and end up serving snack trays for a street side snack vendor.

Garren ran his splayed fingers through his hair, pulling it back, his hair a medium sandy colour with blue highlights glinting in the descending sun's valiant light beams piercing the vale of clouds. He concentrated on not distressing. 'Do I have any expectation of privacy? Do I care? Not that I have any secrets to keep.'

This was something he needed to decide before signing on for assignment with telepaths, it hadn't occurred to him 'til now to doubt if he should accept the offer. He grazed a peep in Keyth's direction and felt his heart thump as he saw the friendly Human now looking cool and distant. Had his thoughts offended?

He sat down heavily, ignoring the searing discomfort from his whipping. 'Do I really care if my shipmates share my most intimate thoughts? Can I accept a casual touch from a friend and not feel threatened by a presumption of sexual overture? Would it really be so impossible to be close to someone?'

Feeling despondent, exhausted, and burdened with emotion; Garren dropped his face into his open palms, trying to hide his turmoil from a telepath. As IF!

Garren felt an arm wrap around his back and an arm wrap around his chest, arms that tightened in a way meant to give comfort. He felt soft hair touch his forehead and tickle his hands. He tensed, so tense he expected to feel muscle knots in his calves, the kind of muscle knots that hurt a LOT.

"Garren friend," Keyth mumbled low into Garren's ear, softly, "you know you have the symptoms of someone who has been abused as a child." Garren made to move, but Keyth held him tighter. "I want you to know, I can't promise that I won't be offended sometimes. I can and will promise you, I will never stay offended long and will not stop being a friend. If you weren't so terribly fortified against hearing my telepathic sending, you'd be aware of Krizren's presence sharing my mind and making the same promise to you."

Garren stopped moving and after a few moments Keyth loosened his hold, keeping one arm around Garren's shoulders.

"There," Keyth made light of the moment. "Are you totally embarrassed?"

A crackle of thunder made them both startle and peer upwards; the sky looked ready to rain again, or was it another of the Emperor's tantrums?

"It's not me," Garren said jokingly. "That was a joke." He waited for Keyth to agree, and waited. Sigh. "I'm not ready to be a Senior Commander, maybe I'll never qualify."

"You do qualify, you are strong and decisive, and I bet you'll be fair, and I will trust you to Guard my back," Keyth's stomach rumbled. "If they don't get here soon ..."

"You know what I'm wondering," Garren started to say.

"No, I can't hear your thoughts at all right now," Keyth stood up to pace the waiting area. "Let's go in the lobby, the rain is going to start."

They went in and found the receptionist desk unattended. Nobody was about and there were no food dispensers, not so much as a morsel of candy.

"We can break into the containers of party food as a last resort," Keyth grinned, not kidding. "What were you wondering about?"

"Oh," Garren sat in a soft chair. "I wonder why some few have these special Abilities like the telemental powers or can wield power in the mage tongues. The majority of us, Humans like me," Garren emphasized. "Can only bleed, sweat, and toil."

"I can't explain why all of us can't do these, but I can explain why some of us can," Keyth slumped in a seat.

"Huh?"

"Imagine a world where no one could use Magic or possess the psycho-kinetic Abilities," Keyth folded an ankle over one knee.

"A very dull world," Garren felt more comfortable not moving at all.

"But explicable. Imagine a world like ours where some of us are Magic and some aren't," Keyth readied for a brief lecture. "What do you know of ancestral Earth?"

"Only that it existed," Garren trained his intelligent gaze on Keyth, settling as comfortably as possible for a long afternoon natter.

"Well, know that ancestral Earth was once similar to us in its diversity of Magic and Humans with mental powers. Earth was a crossroads between several dimensions and there were some interesting intermingling of unlikely bedfellows. However, the Humans with none of these special Abilities became fearful of those who did, fearful, hateful, and vengeful and the killings began."

"Killings?" Garren said sharply.

"Killings and burnings. They were so vengeful, they burned these people, burned them alive, even the helpful ones and the

Healers."

"Do you have nightmares knowing this?"

"A few," Keyth admitted. "The Kinetics and Mages used their powers for defense of course, but during this time, disease was also rampant upon the denizens of Earth and between the fires and the disease; they perished. Much was lost, the way of herbs and the green witches perished, or became so fearful of the fires they gave up their art and the art all but died. There were then no cures for the disease and two thirds of the Earth denizens died."

"Do you feel silly relating a factual account with all this flowery tale telling? It sounds like a fable," Garren wished he hadn't said that. To his own ears it sounded offensive.

"There is nothing wrong with silly. I enjoy silly and it makes the relating of the facts enjoyable," Keyth suddenly felt twice Garren's age.

"I'm sorry," Garren felt like a kid. "If they all perished and we are descended from Earth, why do we still have Magic? Was it dormant and became reborn after the burnings and disease stopped?"

"Honestly, it could be true, but there is a more direct explanation," Keyth paused to tease, "see, you're doing the flowery talk too."

"Tis catching pray continue."

"Tis true Humans are all descended from ancestral Earth," Keyth sat up for the next part. "We did not all descend the same path, we came by different routes."

"Huh?" Garren leaned forward, intent on the next words.

"There are two paths that I know of that were told to me, there may be more."

"Who told you?" Garren made an educated guess.

"Methusem," Keyth answered.

"That was my guess. So what were the two paths?"

"The survivors replaced Magic with machines, eventually overpopulated the Earth and headed into the space void for breeding room."

"Ugh, I hope I'm descended from the other path. What was it?"

"During the time period ancient Earth historians label the Dark Ages, even though the sky did not darken, Humans were harvested as slaves and food staple by planet hunters. Not just Humans, I mentioned Earth was a crossroads, some of our other species like the Mermaids were also taken, to the point when all became afraid to venture to Earth and they began sealing the windows to the Crossroad Corridors.

Not only was the Magic lost, the peoples giving Earth its magnificent diversity also vanished, the Mermaids, Nymphs, and Dragons became myth and legends to the Human survivors.

The only reason Humans were not harvested to depletion was because the disease discouraged off the slavers. At some point the way to Earth became lost, and with the crossroads cut off, Earth became a myth from the opposite side, too."

"So, you're saying the disease that claimed two thirds of the Earth's population was ultimately, its salvation?" Garren's physical discomforts became forgotten during the listening.

"And to compound their woes, the misguided Humans blamed the feles, - they called these helpful fellow creatures cats -, and killed the feles in masses. The natural prey of the feles, the real purveyors of the disease, ran rampant and unbalanced. That's why we have no descendents of the feles on Celesterra."

"And the ancestors who left for breeding space didn't bring them?" Garren had trouble being sympathetic to the burning instigators.

Keyth yawned, "I don't know, I never thought to ask Methusem. We should be thankful we have equus among us today."

"Keyth," Garren bowed low from his sitting position. "Thank you. And I enjoyed your way of telling it. Emperor Methusem passed all this knowledge to you? You must have spent a lot of time together."

"Yes, we..." Keyth paused.

Garren leaned forward again, willing the words to spring forth.

"We were slaves together, on ... Mariterra, when we were kids."

"Keyth, but," Garren gave his new shipmate the benefit of the doubt, "that would have been before the conquest, you would have to be over two terra centuries old. Are you?

"No, I'm only 27, so is Krizren. Can you figure it out?" Keyth smiled encouragingly.

Garren's mind raced. He wanted to believe. How? If Keyth was truly 27, then the only way he could only be 27 and be born before the conquest, meant; temporal travel? How? Garren knew the Crossroad Corridors really existed for he'd seen one of the immortal Guards step in and out of one. Walking the Crossroad Corridors could bring you to the far hemisphere in a matter of steps, in some cases, between planets. Could these corridors cross time too? As far as he knew, the only thing you needed to travel the Crossroad Corridors was a window to them.

"You came forward in time?" Garren answered.

"Woah, you figured it out without boggling your mind," Keyth's stomach rumbled again.

Garren shifted in his seat, inflaming his discomfort now that he wasn't distracted from it anymore. He sank into private reverie, his chin sank to his chest, and he nodded off into a fitful nap. He jerked awake from a tap on his shoulder. Keyth stood over him.

"The rain has not yet begun. I'm not waiting for them any longer, let's go ahead to the ship," Keyth beckoned.

"Can we do that?" Garren rubbed a knuckle over his eyelids.

Keyth thought the gesture boyishly cute. "Yes, we have Access overrides."

"We do!?"

"You really should read your own stats in the Commander's Registry."

"Aye, I should do," Garren grinned. At last, they were going to board their new float.

They first asked a dockworker to open the gate.

"No can do," was the reply.

Keyth trotted over to the gate's keypad and started tapping into its controls. Garren assumed Keyth had the access code, but soon realized Keyth was attempting to hack the security system ... successfully. The mechanical gates parted and the two Senior Fleet Commanders breached the South Fleet Bay. "Can you deliver my stuff here to 'The Halçyon'?" Keyth hollered at the heretofore unhelpful dockworker.

Seeing two intruders on the restricted side of the fence did not raise the dockworker's suspicions. He motioned to a fellow worker to bring up the ancient lifting machine.

Garren and Keyth climbed into the nearest canoe. They looked for the steering controls, but could find no visible way to power up or navigate the silly thing. An elderly Elf came huffing up. "It's be-spelled," he explained. "You're lucky I stayed for overtime." The Elf climbed into the canoe, his wide girth making the canoe unsteady, he expertly settled in the middle of the craft and it soon steadied. "Where to?"

"Halçyon," Keyth answered.

"Woah," the elderly Elf smiled wide, well versed in the Guard slang. "The premiere float of them all. Settle in, it's a quarter-mark's ride." He closed his eyes and concentrated his will, this being the way to push and steer the canoe.

The canoe was wide enough to sit two abreast, but Keyth and Garren chose to sit opposite each other. Garren's back turned to the fore; he couldn't watch their approach to Halçyon. His heart pounded with anticipation. "Have you been aboard her yet?" Garren posed the question to Keyth.

"Uh yep!" Keyth nodded, a secretive grin twitched his lips. "I helped Methusem with some of the modifications."

"Modifications?" Garren let a thrill of excitement jolt his nerves.

"You are aware Halçyon is behind by five release models? Anyway, Methusem fitted her with some secret surprises. Shields, advanced weaponry, accelerator mods; he likes hiding things like that. He figures, what our enemies don't know, can hurt them. Even the newer ships are more powerful than their Commanders know." Keyth sat back, it was fun to watch Garren's jaw gawping amazement. "Come to think of it," Keyth pulled out his PDA from his uniform's hip pocket, "I wonder who the new ships are launching under." He did some fingertip dancing on the little PDA screen. "Hmm."

"Well?" Garren didn't enjoy suspense.

"The lovely Commander Bel accepted The Equinox. She's a beaut!"

Garren figured out Keyth meant the ship was a beaut. "What was her last ship?"

"The Isabeau. Tis a shame beyond bearing, but The Isabeau is being decommissioned. She's going to the pasture." Pasture was the Guard's euphemism for the junkyard. "Makes me want to cry."

And he seemed serious; Garren watched Keyth's eyelids tighten. "Who else?" Garren asked to divert Keyth's attention away from the sad fated Isabeau.

"The Nocturnex, hmm, is now commissioned under, hmmm, Commander Sable," Keyth read aloud. "What do you think of Commander Sable?"

"I don't know him," Garren said, throwing a look over his shoulder to check their progress along the bay, Halçyon was not yet in sight. "He's a brown Elf, isn't he? I've never met a brown Elf. I'm not even sure why they soever distinguish themselves."

"Yeah, me neither. No one calls Rhiannon a fair Elf and he is certainly fair," Keyth smiled the secretive smile again.

"What is your opinion of Commander Sable, then?" Garren's hair whipped about in a brisk sea breeze, he struggled in vain to hold it down, but his hair was too thick and full-bodied for the struggle.

Keyth gave into the lure of gossip. If you can't gossip with your shipmates, then with whom can you gossip? "Well," and his voice took on the charisma of a bard.

Quietly, Garren figured, maybe that's what he did as a slave-child, told tales to amuse his Owner. Garren cringed just thinking of it, it was beyond his wildest reckoning to imagine living as a slave.

"Are you OK?" Keyth asked in concern. "Do you need a cloak?" He detached his uniform cloak and over Garren's wild protests threw the cloak over Garren's shoulders.

"Thanks," Garren muttered, feeling utterly ridiculous and embarrassed, at least Keyth hadn't telepathically heard that last thought. On the plus side, Garren drew the cloak high to cover over his hair to keep his hair from blowing in his face, thinking he must look like a wild harridan; not that a harridan had been seen in decades.

"Well," Keyth repeated and continued. "Commander Sable is like me and Krizren, he's from the past. He did not come forward in time; he was discovered in a stash of slaves stored in stasis."

Garren's jaw dropped in absolute horror. "Slaves stored in stasis?"

"That's how they were stored, you didn't have to worry about feeding them or them escaping and it kept the meat fresh on the foot."

Another wave of horror made a tremor under Garren's sculpted musculature. He appreciated the knowledge Keyth was imparting, but all this new knowledge would definitely ruin sleep.

"Am I disturbing you too much with this, should I stop?" Keyth let a look of guilt creep into his expression.

"No, please continue, it's just," Garren groped for words. "They don't go into this stuff in Junior Guard training."

"That's right, you don't have Commander training," Keyth mused. "Then why do you seem so knowledgeable concerning

Commander's etiquette?"

"The story?" Garren prompted.

"YOU, you hacked the Commander's registry, didn't you!? No wonder you're so blasé about reading it now, you've been reading it for what? Terra years?" Keyth looked suitably impressed.

"I never looked up Commander Sable or how slaves were transported," Garren decided denial would be futile at this juncture.

"Well, I gave you the gist of it. Sable is from the past and no matter the training, he still has the subconscious mindset of people from the past. They have a different regard for the sanctity of life and don't respect it."

"Go back to what you were saying about meat fresh on the foot," Garren disguised a fresh tremor by drawing the cloak tighter.

"Some Humans were used as farm bred food, very salty I heard too. And brown Elves, well, their hair is very luxurious, meaning their hair makes finer pelts then most mammal."

"No, now stop," regretting asking for that clarification, a sharp queasiness hit Garren's stomach hard. He dropped the cloak and leaned over the side of the canoe and heaved his meager snack into the bay waters.

At the sound of the retching, their mage pilot rose from his concentrated magical trance. "Oh, young man that will not do, no way to be greeting your new Mistress. There she be!" The elderly Elf threw an arm gesture to the wind.

Garren stood too fast and neatly fell over the side of the canoe. With very quick reflexes Garren found a chance to admire very quickly, Keyth grabbed at Garren's arm before the canoe went beyond reach and pulled the wet and bedraggled Commander from the waters. The flimsy disposable clothes Garren had bought earlier in the day, for he had not wanted to endue his inappropriate junior's uniform, shred apart from the water.

Keyth quickly draped the cloak around Garren's wonderful body, sheltering him from exposure to the sea breezes and present company.

'Now I'm naked under a man's borrowed cloak,' Garren wondered if the day could bring any more humiliating embarrassment, then he winced. "Oww." The salty bay water did nothing to ease the welts decorating his bottom. From Keyth's expression, Garren could see his shipmate immediately jumped to the correct conclusion prompting the 'oww'.

"Let's get you aboard and see to your problem, I hold a minor medical certification. Not the same as a Magic User healing, but scientific medical technology works just as well on something like this," Keyth drew the folds of the cloak around Garren as the new Commander chattered from nauseous reaction.

"No, that's not necessary, I just need dry clothes," Garren stubbornly resisted, thinking the heat from his embarrassment at being treated like a child should dispel the cold, only it didn't work that way.

"I can tell right away our ship life is going to be interesting," Keyth remarked.

XIV. Terra-Date 215.149 Mid Afternoon
:: Welcome aboard Halçyon, Garren ::

The canoe departed with its pilot, leaving Garren and Keyth standing on a water-floating platform marking Halçyon's berth. The Halçyon was submerged up to her 'waist line', towering over the two Humans by the height equal to a six story building, an equal mass refracted under the waves with the clear water and cloud strewn sunlight magnifying her under belly. A gilded ledge girded her middle, about five steps deep; a plaque attached to the hull near a small hatch in the gleaming silvery reflective ship read simply 'The Halçyon'. Not in fancy lettering, yet it made a deep emotional impact on her newest charges.

The ship recognized them without any need for tapping override codes into keypads; Halçyon's computer opened a hatch to an airlock and seemed to Garren's fancy to willingly embrace her new men.

"O yeah, I will always remember my first step aboard Halçyon," Garren remarked sarcastically as he stepped in, dripping the water of the South Fleet Bay into Halçyon's airlock. His eyelids drooped in relieved pleasure. Lockers in the room beyond the airlock held some loose fitting clothes in several sizes. Nothing fancy, draw string jogging pants and short sleeved crewneck shirt; Garren climbed into the dry clothes in some haste, feeling a little shy dressing in front of Keyth. He sighed. The fabric was soft as a kiss and immediately warming to his shivering skin. With a great big 'thank you' Garren handed Keyth's uniform cloak to its owner.

"This is it," Garren said, stamping his feet briskly to warm up faster.

"Yep."

"We're here," Garren rubbed his upper arms briskly.

"Yep."

"This is Halçyon, our ship." Garren thought that if Keyth wasn't there, he would throw himself to the floor and weep.

Keyth's expression softened.

"Am I broadcasting again?" Garren winced in embarrassment.

"Yep. Garren," Keyth began and was at odds how to word his thought, "you don't have to be embarrassed in front of me. We have a long time together ahead of us. Even though we've met only a few marks ago today, we need to come to some understanding between us."

"Aye," Garren said slowly. "I remember this afternoon and … I … that hug was sorely needed." He rushed the rest.

Keyth spread his arms wide, inviting a new hug.

Garren hesitated in dismay, but really did not want to offend and at least he had clothes on now. He walked forward into a friend's comforting embrace. The urge to weep came and went and came back again. It had been a long trying last several terra days, more trying than usual for he'd been suffering harassment for most of his training days; and then during the rescue search he'd gotten lost in the Subterraneum wracked between doubts. Then there was the whipping this morning and almost abandoning his career in the Guard; then the promotion; and then falling into the bay and having a rant and emotional breakdown in front of a total stranger. Keyth's arms tightened. 'OK' not total stranger, his shipmate. He took a deep breath and exhaled slowly, exhaling the tension. Keyth's hand started rubbing Garren's back as you would soothe a child.

"This really makes me doubt my quality as a Senior Commander," Garren murmured, revisiting these doubts.

"Why? You have to be big and tough? As a minor telepath, I can tell you, even the toughest most hardened on the outside Commanders are internally wracked with self doubt, fear of inadequacy; fear of failure, and fear of being exposed as cowards."

"You're making it up."

"No, I am not."

"It's a Bard's tale."

"Garren, I say it like it is," Keyth gave an extra tight squeeze then released his shipmate, keeping a hand on Garren's arm to steady him. He recognized medical symptoms of battle fatigue in his new shipmate; it was worrisome to find Junior Guard training could put someone into this state. "Feel like visiting the galley first? I'm starving. Are you sure you don't want treatment for your wounds?"

"Wounds? You say it like I've been on the battlefield. It's just a chastisement. I can't imagine how many Guards are walking around with the same discipline reminders on their bodies right now."

"It is rough, what do you do though? You fire a guard and you've wasted all the years of training, you suspend them or confine them and you're down a resource. Unless it is criminal, then of course they should be arrested and expelled from the Guard. For infractions like having a drink on duty, propositioning a whore while in uniform, skating out of uniform; you'd think a suitable chastisement would be a deterrent. "

"Have you met Care?" Garren said with amusement.

"Yes. He's 'played' with Krizren, my tether-mate. Tis because of Guards like Care, the new discipline implement is going into use."

"Oh no, what implement is this?"

"It's a tawse with very high prolonged sting value, exCESSively painful, yet does minor physical damage."

"What about mental damage?" Garren didn't like this news one bit.

"The concept is to make you think before you do something to disgrace your uniform. For Commanders, the chastisement levels are much higher; we're more likely to get the new tawse used on us. On the upside," Keyth grinned, "there are a lot less people who can Writ us for an infraction. You especially will be safer aboard Halçyon judging by your discipline record." They both paused on the last remark.

"Wait," Garren stopped, stunned. "You don't think Emperor Methusem promoted me just to protect me? I can not accept this."

"Garren," Keyth said carefully, realizing how seriously Garren's pride augured his future. "We're misfits, remember? That is why we are here. And if you don't mind me saying, the four of us are extremely loyal to our Emperor, and I suspect, our sense of justice and fairness seems superlative to the people administering our current protocol statutes.

There is rumour flying proposing putting a cap on how many new candidates one Guard can sponsor."

"What? Why?" Garren remembered his own difficulties in finding a sponsor.

"Suppose, one person with an agenda sponsors a gaggle of kids into the Guard, learning our weapons and using our own training against us."

"I can see where this line of conjecture is leading," Garren said numbly. It was entirely plausible. What better way to attack your enemy than from within? His mind began dwelling on a more personal level; denouncing ordainment into his family's religion had begun his real troubles. He could not imagine any effort on his relatives' part to infiltrate the Guard just to get back at him, though; Garren realized he was probably the only person in Quinterra history to reject the Order and survive.

"Anyway, let's go break in the Galley," Keyth interrupted his companion's brooding, the look of terrible sadness on Garren's face heart wrenching to witness, Garren's face transforming smile a ghost of a whisper. "And as a medical technician, I recommend you finish the nap you started back in the gate lobby."

"Aye-Aye, Commander!" Garren dragged his feet, sadly, paying little attention to his new ship in his present state of weariness. He swung into depression, the weight of it dragging his feet to something painful. 'Is it possible to have a future? Will every new friend I touch be in danger?'

&

His second nap of the afternoon became too brief too. He was not deliberately wakened, the loud and happy voice of Sov Minister Ange preceded the procession of new arrivals. Garren barely stirred, when he heard them come nearer the recreation chamber. He and Keyth had chosen the closest room to the galley, flopped down on the padded lounge chairs and snoozed. Keyth took longer to come alert.

And sure enough, Sovereign Minister Angélus led a small entourage into the rec chamber.

"How did you know we were in here?" Keyth pretended annoyance at being woken.

"Our Emperor said you'd be in here," Ange chuckled; he so enjoyed surprising these young people. "Here is Dana," he motioned to the tall blonde Human following immediately behind him. "And Traci you already know. And may I have the pleasure of introducing my new assistant, or should I say, our newly appointed Junior Minister Vylara." He bowed as he said this and the young Elf woman smiled shyly at the august attention.

"Hi," Krizren entered next, going straight to Keyth to plant a swift kiss on his forehead. He looked around. "No Amé yet?

It'll take him terra days to pack his wardrobe. This must be Garren?" Krizren asked Keyth, while walking over to Garren.

Garren raised his eyes to a Human male close to his own age. A clear and candid gaze regarded Garren from eyes the pure azure of the sea at its most bedazzling majestic blue. Garren met an honesty in those eyes he could never have imagined in a fellow Human. Krizren was fair with the healthy glow of an outdoor earned tan and from under his sunlight gold hair the hilt of a shoulder-holstered baldric and broadsword parted the long blonde locks. From sitting down, Garren judged Krizren to be a tad taller than himself and a tad broader in the shoulder width department, similar in body weight and physique and well toned, the kind of physique you developed from long terra-years of broadsword practice. Krizren's soft pale blue tunic with cloak and dark gray fitted leggings set off his coloring to full advantage.

Before any another word could be said, Garren blurted, "is that a broadsword?" He sat up straight, ignoring pain twinges, "I mean, hullo pleased to meet you and share this voyage with you."

"Voyage to where I wonder? Yes, this is my broadsword. Are you certified too?"

"Yep. What level are you?"

"Master."

Krizren held out a hand to clasp wrists, clearly not assuming the slightest offence by Garren's brusque greeting.

Garren offered his own hand for a wrist-to-wrist clasp greeting. Krizren's grip was very firm and Garren wanted to match it. He let go, sooner than was polite, he was afraid Krizren would assume there was an attraction on his part. When Krizren turned his head to share a look with Keyth, Garren then recalled that Krizren was a minor telepath, and then the further realization dawned, that not only was Krizren a minor telepath, he was also bonded to Keyth, which meant Krizren had shared his whole afternoon with Keyth; from his moment of weakness, the hug, the dunk in the bay, the borrowed cloak, being naked under the borrowed cloak, and the second hug.

Garren flopped down on to his back and lay flat out on the padded lounge chair, closing his eyes in embarrassed weariness. Keyth was right, he did have to stop with the embarrassment or it would be a long and unduly stressful voyage. He cracked open his eyelids and Garren saw Krizren looking down at him with those eyes that must surely turn the Women witless, the smile filling Krizren's eyes and pursing his lips was a smile of pure sympathetic understanding.

"Ah, well all the introductions are sorted, except for one," Minister Ange said pleasantly. He turned to his assistant and added, voice filling with high amusement. "Is he arrived?"

Garren rolled on his side, tucking his bent elbow under his head, wondering if the last of his shipmates had arrived. Instead, someone totally unexpected entered the chamber, not a sound of footsteps to mark his entrance. Garren beheld his illustrious Emperor; Methusem's presence filled the chamber. Too stunned to move, Garren barely took in Methusem's sylph like figure clothed in a knee length blue tunic and naught else, medium height, and fine midnight dark hair streaming loose to his mid-thigh. Methusem's light copper color skin looked flawless, and Garren knew his Emperor's peridot eyes could change depending upon his Spell casting.

There was no hesitant awkwardness in Krizren's greeting, he simply walked up to Methusem and threw a welcoming embrace around him. They stood relaxed against each other; Methusem's hands reached around Krizren's back and returned the embrace, leaning into him like a long lost friend. They didn't say a word and Garren figured they were likely bespeaking telepathically. Well, Krizren was a good choice for Halçyon; Senior Fleet Commander, Certified Master Swordsman, minor telepath, and what else; oh yeah, after gleamer able to see the past. Garren had no idea what kind of limitations an after gleamer could have on their Ability to delve the past.

Keyth made an exaggerated show of heaving himself from his seat and took his turn embracing Methusem, eerily silent.

"Ahem," Minister Ange interrupted, "now, now, it is not polite telepath's etiquette to bespeak when there are non-telepaths in company." He said this in a mock scolding manner.

The elegant Dana dropped his tote-carry to the floor and shyly approached Methusem for a close conversation and a hugging squeeze.

Garren closed his eyes, feeling way too weary for this ensemble moment. Unexpectedly, a very warm hand touched his forehead.

"Hello Garren," Methusem's lightly accented voice spoke softly. He kneeled beside the chaise to meet at eye level. The next was spoken directly into Garren's mind and startled him into opening his eyes wide. 'I am so very sorry. I'm afraid I didn't find out about the Hearing until too late to stop it.'

Not trusting to telepathic speak, Garren spoke aloud, "it's OK, I deserved it."

"No you didn't. I reversed the minimum rank decree as soon as I returned to the Palace. I am sorry to say, you were the only one not spared the discipline charge. We made quite a shake up in the ranks over it. There was some arguing over the reversal for it undermined Minister Allon's authority."

"I lost my way in the Subterraneum," Garren admitted aloud.

"I know. I am so sorry."

"Did you have anything to do with the rescuers finding me?" Garren wondered for he had gone in quite alone and would rather have died before calling for help.

"Yes. Now, let me call healing Magic, no reason why you should suffer this ignoble pain a moment longer."

Garren watched a dazzling light show as Methusem's peridot irises transmuted to the cobalt blue of the Dragons and pupils transmuted to silver. Never in his life had Garren thought he would ever witness this up close and personal.

Everyone in the room waited respectfully.

"Well Garren," Methusem bespoke. "When I am not in my Dragon body, I cannot avail the full host of my powers, therefore, I need to touch you to heal you."

"What do you mean?" Garren said aloud in some alarm.

"I need to touch your bottom, so if you would kindly drop your trousers and turn over."

"Oh no, I can't let you befoul your sight on my awful body," Garren protested in horror.

"There is nothing awful about your body," Methusem refuted calmly, the cobalt blue of his power seeping from within growing brighter, flashing his aura into the visible spectrum.

Garren quailed. He couldn't do it.

"Garren, another time we will have to discuss what made this shame of your body, believe, as the young people say, you are scrumptious," Methusem couldn't fathom the unwillingness on the young Commander's part.

Still stricken with horror, Garren pulled his knees up and clenched tight.

Methusem turned to Minister Ange. "Is he defying me? This is quite remarkable." If it were not so heartbreaking to find Garren so upset over this, he would have been pleased. He knew Garren was spirited; it was one of his most endearing qualities.

"Garren," Methusem said firmly and gently, "turn over, this is an order." During this delay, the power accumulated and a wind started emanating from Methusem's skin. It felt so very physically pleasant to call forth the power, too much power though, and his form would transmute into one of his Were-forms, Dragon or Mer. As a Merpage breathing air was quite impossible and the ship's water pools were currently empty; he would suffocate; a painful experience he did not wish to suffer ever again. And there was not room enough in the chamber for his Dragon form, he would be crushed by the metal walls and his bulk would crush everyone in the room with him. "No more delay Commander Garren."

In a desperate plea, Garren asked, "may I turn over and then drop my pants?"

"Would it help if we were alone?" Methusem shrugged apologetically; he slipped an arm under Garren's knees and an arm behind his back and lifted the protesting Human up into his cradling arms and carried him into an attached ante-chamber to the rec room. There was a gaming table for a clutter free surface, Methusem gently laid Garren's rigid form on top of it.

Garren felt ashamed of himself, this was no way to act in front of his Emperor who was only trying to heal a whipping. "I'm sorry, I know I shouldn't be like this." He put trembling fingers on his pants drawstring and couldn't continue.

"I know. Tis ultimately remarkable." Methusem put his own fingers to the task of undoing the drawstring, the glow of his power painting a blue light on everything, including Garren's skin. Garren was naked under the pants and he shivered as Methusem pulled them down. He quickly turned over, laying flat and closed his eyes, his hands clutching hard to the side edges of the table.

"This will not hurt a bit," Methusem climbed on the table and straddled his unclad thighs against Garren's exposed calves. Methusem let his head fall back as the power poured over his skin and pooling the warmth of it into his palms before he leaned forward to place his open palms directly on Garren's bare bottom and gently over the first of the welts. Methusem's very long midnight hair fanned around them like a curtain.

Garren felt the healing warmth near to his skin, then touching him, the heat poured into his flesh. He writhed and bucked, gripping the table hard to control his body movement and managing to stop writhing. The moans and pleasure noises struggled from his clenched lips. It felt so good. The brushing warmth went deep, deep, filling him from the inside out. The pain disappeared like it had never been. He expected the pleasure to stop at that point, but Methusem pushed his hands up Garren's back to his neck and shoulders and then down again over the entire length of his body to his knees.

Anticipating the protest, Methusem answered, "I need to put this power somewhere and you've managed to pull a few muscles with your fighting me."

An orgiastic scream he could not prevent broke from his mouth, Garren's face went scarlet with embarrassment even as he writhed anew. The healing power flooded his skin; touching and warming and Garren's body was helpless to resist its natural reaction. And he was all too aware of the telepaths in the next room, sure they were aware of everything.

Methusem laid his length along Garren's side, drawing the Human's face near to snuggle against his neck, running long tapered fingers through Garren's hair and smoothing and rubbing his nape to bring soothing calm. "It's alright, it is okay."

Garren rested against the mighty strength of his Emperor, letting weariness drain away under the soothing petting and healing warmth, the urge to weep vanished with all his anxieties. Laying in the encircling protection of a Dragon King, knowing nothing would hurt him as he lay here.

"Shh, you can sleep," Methusem brushed a gentle kiss on Garren's hair, snuggling for a nap.

After a little while, Krizren crept in quietly, not quietly enough. Garren rolled over to pull away from Methusem who was almost asleep; he hopped off the table, pulled his pants up and tied the drawstring.

"Yes Krizren," Methusem spoke aloud softly with eyes closed.

"I have a stomach ache, I was wondering if you might heal me?" Krizren sounded like a little boy asking for cookies before dinner.

"Your tummy?" Methusem laughed. "Alas, come to me." And the Emperor held open his arms for Krizren to lay encircled within them.

Methusem was ready with power by the time Krizren settled himself in position. Krizren was by no means quiet when the healing touched him, he seemed to exalt in grabbing at the sides of the table and wailing at the top of his lungs, really letting go.

Garren envied Krizren a little for it. He sauntered back into the rec room. Minister Ange and Jr Minister Vylara were sitting at a table talking quietly together, Dana and Traci were lounging in the chaise chairs, and just then Care and another were entering the room. They were dripping wet.

"Did you fall in the bay too?" Garren grinned.

"No, it's pouring rain out there," Care answered in high humor. "This is Rhiannon, if none of you have met."

Garren glanced over Care's Elf companion, seeking Rhiannon's informative epaulette pin. 'Mage!'

"Yayy Garren, I heard you weren't coming to the party, glad to cya here," Care wrung his shoulder length hair out, squeezing out water by twisting it tight.

"I'm not staying, sorry Care, but Dana and I have other plans." Garren held out his hand to clasp wrists with Care and then a hesitant Rhiannon. Dana and Traci broke their private conversation to do the same.

The four made their way to the galley next door, where Keyth was spreading out some party snacks; chips of many different colors, dips for the chips, and warm fresh baked chocolate cake. "Krizren actually baked this, we're lucky there was any batter left to bake," Keyth scooped a bite of cake with a small spoon before the cake hit the table. Care, Dana, and Traci dove for the chips straight away; Garren and Rhiannon sat at the table by the cake. Keyth served them up slices before they finished pouring out caramelonade drinks.

"Mm," Rhiannon mumbled with mouth full of cake.

"Elf, you be a mage? Do you know any Witch's Spells to brew this caramelonade into macchiato?" Traci asked shyly.

"I keep meaning to learn, but not at the moment. Sorry." Rhiannon shrugged apologetically.

Garren made too busy with eating cake to say anything. It was delicious, light, and fluffy. This adds another talent to Krizren's long list; it was not a bad thing to go Deep Space with someone who can bake excellent chocolate cake. Keyth flashed Garren a wide smile. Garren rolled his eyes, living with telepaths!

"I didn't catch your name?" Traci said to Rhiannon from where he stood behind Keyth's seat.

"Call me Rhi, short for Rhiannon," Rhi helped himself to another slice.

"Rhi," Traci leaned forward, putting a hand on Keyth's shoulder. "You were the one who freed Methusem from the enchanted prison?"

Rhi nodded, his suddenly tearful aqua-green eyes a dominant feature upon his fair face. The tears ran unheeded down his cheeks, clearly not yet at terms with what he had witnessed in the passages.

A small snack dish of assorted chips and creamy dips tossed down on the table, followed by Care seating himself. He clumped his elbows on the table a chip held in his lips, he looked ready to say something looking at Rhi, but whatever it was, he swallowed it with the chip.

Dana and Traci sat down next, looking very splendid in their Guard uniforms, full of high spirits and chips. "Woah, did you make this dip homemade?" Dana asked Keyth as he chewed with a crunching noise.

"Huh?" Keyth came out of his pre-occupation, "nay, my tether-mate did. He has cooking talent."

"Is this cooking or alchemy?" Traci winked to add weight to the compliment.

"So, what are your plans Dana?" Care's smile faded a bit, he darted a concerned glance at the now tear dry Rhiannon. "We're going to miss you tonight." He couldn't manage to say this without twinkles of mischievous gleam in his eyes.

"I promised Nerrys a ride home from his construction job

and he invited us to dinner," Dana added a mischievous twinkle of his own. "Erin lives in the same building."

Garren surprised himself by not wincing at the name. Erin was the Disciplinarian who had administered the whipping that morning.

"Are you going to take the Certification test for the new tawse?" Garren asked politely.

"Nay," Care shivered.

Meanwhile, Keyth had been thinking through how Dana was to carry both Garren and this Nerrys. "Are you certified for skates Garren?"

"No, I don't have the knack for them," Garren admitted.

"I'm going along to lend a hand, or rather, two arms and my feet," Traci interjected.

"O, but you're here for the party tonight, aren't you?" Keyth raised an eyebrow.

"Wouldn't miss it! I want to get a change of clothes, I can't wear my uniform all night or I'll be Writ for disgraceful activities on duty," he laughed heartily.

"Ah, there you all are!" Sov Minister Ange came in. "O, no, no more Writs today, please. O, please do not get up, no, no, tis not necessary. See, I'm sitting down too." He beamed a great smile at everyone in turn, his merry wink settled on Traci.

"What?" Traci swallowed down a chip, choking.

"What happened to your Guard like nerves of steel?" Care teased.

"You'll know in a mark," Minister Ange said mysteriously.

Dana slapped the table with both hands, "TRACI! Remember we agreed if either of us made commander we'd make the other command-second. Remember?"

His mouth gaping, Traci stared at Dana without comprehension. "Surely, you don't think I -"

Before the sentence finished, Emperor Methusem crossed the threshold of the galley with a disheveled looking Krizren trailing behind. Keyth smiled, "complements to the chocolate chef."

Krizren responded with a lazy wave and lopsided smile, leaning his bum against the wall. All the seats were taken.

Traci looked at Garren sitting at his left, "do you want to sit on my knee?"

"What? No, sorry, I mean thanks, but ..." Garren quickly raised a glass of caramelonade to his lips.

"I'll park a knee Traci," Care piped up. He waved his seat to Methusem.

Garren accidentally let drink down the wrong pipe, stinging his nostrils, wondering if he could ever become blasé with the Emperor of their galaxy casually sharing a galley table.

"Want some cake?" Keyth offered.

"I thought you'd never ask," Methusem eagerly grabbed the offered plate with his kinetic powers, floating the dish to rest on the table in front of his face. He dipped long elegant fingers into the chocolate and ate from his fingers.

The group waited for the announcement, sharing Traci's astonished excitement.

Minister Ange folded his hands, posing as for a portrait in patience.

Methusem stuck a thumb in his mouth to lick chocolate frosting, when he lost a child like silly giggle; the breathlessly waiting group realized they were mistaken in their Emperor's supposed ingenuousness.

"Well, I must start the speech by saying, some decisions are very difficult to make," Methusem laughed happily, "these weren't." He closed his open palm and opened it again and held up a Commander's epaulette pin followed very slowly by his alternate hand holding forth a second epaulette pin. He kinetically floated one pin to Traci and the second to Dana.

Dana gawped, "really? You can't mean me? O, I couldn't possibly qualify!" He bowed his head in humility, his long blond hair spilling into his lap.

Methusem winked and smiled.

Dana's only sad thought was that he and Traci would have to be on separate teams now.

"You can work as a recognized joint team, but you'll need to decide which one of you will give the no gainsay orders during an emergency. And I have a very important first mission for you, so if you could form up your teams as soon as humanly possible, it would be greatly appreciated."

"A mission, can you tell us a bit now?" Traci leaned forward in his seat.

"Quite," Minister Ange leaned forward too, even more keen than Traci. "Anything to do with what upset you this morning? The Dragons, per chance?"

Methusem considered a long moment, the only sound during the pause made by Care loudly crunching chips.

"Incorrigible Care, you're doing it on purpose!" Minister Ange laughed, breaking the tension as they waited for Methusem to make a decision.

Traci jostled Care, who was sitting on his leg, by tapping his foot. Another source of crunching sounds made them look at Vylara helping herself to a plate full of chips with a dollop of dip on a corner of the square plate.

"Care? Are you rested from your last Rogue assignment?" Methusem broached. "Are you ready for a new mission?"

With much personal angst, Care admitted that he was interviewing with Commander Kerlin on the morrow and didn't see how he could accept a new mission just now.

"Commander Kerlin?" Methusem smiled warmly. He closed his eyes as if lost in a gleamer's trance. "A most excellent match, I sincerely hope Kerlin accepts your application. And you too Rhi?" Methusem turned to the fair Elf.

Rhiannon nodded shyly.

"Which reminds me, I have a gift to give you!"

"Please, don't make me a Commander," Rhi held his hands up to feign warding a blow.

Methusem stopped in the motion of standing up. "What? O,

I've just been teased, haven't I?" He could not hide his pleasure.

Witnessing Methusem's pleasure at being part of the banter, Garren recognized the fellow feeling. The Emperor of the major galaxy really just wanted to be treated like everyone else. It was an eye opener and made Garren feel more comfortable, not only in the Emperor's presence, but also on a personal level. Tension flowed away and his eyelids drooped, he felt so exhausted. He should have been more accepting of the healing for then this exhaustion wouldn't be so persistent.

Methusem stood and made as if to reach for a pocket, except the plain blue tunic he wore had no pockets. A small bag flashed into the visible spectrum, and from this enchanted pouch he withdrew a small hard covered book a hand span wide and two hands in length. The worse for wear book clearly an antique, he handed the book to misty-eyed Rhiannon. "You'll need this too," and Methusem gave the Mage Elf the enchanted pouch. "The book is a grimoir of minor healing spells." As Methusem said this he darted a teasing look at Care who groaned, of course Methusem was aware of Care's predilections. "You know, I would never interfere in a Commander's team picks."

Rhiannon nodded, understanding without being told that Magical healing would add a major asset to his stats for team picks.

"What dark fantasy is this?" Methusem asked Care directly.

Care hid his face in Traci's neck, flaming hot in embarrassment, grateful for his naturally brown skin. "Nothing," they all heard a muffled mumble.

"You want me to spank you over my knee? I am your ultimate authority figure?" Methusem said this with gentle amusement, careful not to sound derisive.

Care pulled Traci's uniform cloak to completely cover his head.

Garren clucked his tongue in sympathy. 'Living with telepaths is tough.'

"Actually with the harshness of our new Discipline implement, you will need me for your Certification Exam."

Vylara paused in a chip crunch and squeaked a "Huh?"

Minister Ange patiently explained, "some of the exams, like Discipline or Hairdressing, you need a volunteer to be a subject for your efforts."

"But," Care showed his face, "we can't let the Emperor be used for an exam like that."

"Why not?" Methusem argued, his lightly accented voice lilting. "I can heal straightaway. You are going to certify, aren't you? The new sentencing standards go into effect tomorrow and no one is certified yet. Only Commander Kraken is signed up for the exam and I am the only volunteer available. I was hoping you and Erin would be up for certification, also."

Care was stuck on the news concerning Commander Kraken, "NOT him. Please, you can't let him touch you!"

"Why? You do not like him?" Methusem turned perturbed eyes on Minister Ange. "Kraken isn't corrupt, is he? This is too great a blow upon everything else."

"No, I don't believe he is corrupt, he is just stern," Minister smiled benignly. "Not too stern for all tastes, he does have a team together. There is no evidence of abuse among his team, either."

"O, what a relief!" Methusem exhaled sharply. "Will you do it Care? I would consider it as a personal favor."

"I haven't even seen the monstrous thing yet," Care argued lamely.

"It's nothing complicated. You administer it with a strapping motion. There are two certification levels, one to satisfy a Writ for five and one to satisfy a Writ for fifteen."

"Fifteen?!" Minister Ange surprised everyone by this outburst. "I've witnessed how painful this thing is, it could conceivably drive a fragile mind mad."

"This thing is the last level of chastisement for our Guards. This punishment will be for civilians, also, the last and final sentencing before banishment from our Realm of Planets." Methusem almost lost his desire for chocolate cake. But since Krizren was the cook, he wanted to enjoy it. A piece of fluffy cake levitated from the serving dish to his little plate.

"Did you decide if you mean to give us a hint concerning the mission?" Traci cupped his new epaulette pin in his hand.

"May I?" Care offered.

Traci happily gave Care the epaulette pin.

Garren offered to pin Dana's new epaulette pin for him, too. Their uniform necklines had a grommet prepared specifically for the epaulette pin for their uniforms were proofed against piercing weapons.

Amid all this activity, Methusem hesitated. "Let us suffice to say, I cannot afford to have the Dragons upset with me. I am in too much danger now with what 's after me, well, more dangerous than usual."

Minister Ange grabbed Methusem's elbow in surprised reaction. "What danger? From whom? The kidnappers? We failed to catch the culprits."

Speaking very slowly, Methusem explained. "A Felled Angel of Punishment, now lives the existence of a Greater Demon, Ariel has appeared in our Realm; a most ancient and powerful entity."

"But, what is a Demon?" Rhiannon whispered.

"This one is a dimension traveler of the worst sort. Right now, I have no sensing of IT crossing the corridors with impunity. I need the Dragons to keep watch; they can perceive the comings and goings in a manner most mortals cannot."

"How do we protect you from it?" Garren clenched his fists.

"You cannot protect me from this," Methusem whispered.

"We are assigning Guards within the Palace itself," Minister Ange informed them.

"They can do nothing, they will only get killed." Methusem said this with an air of a standing argument.

"We'll have warning if something untoward reveals itself.

Better than waiting for ole Nuben to realize you'd missed your new crownlet fitting," Minister Ange bit back a harsh criticism. This situation was delicate indeed.

"I vow to give my life to protect you all," Methusem raised his voice over their protests. "I will give it again and again, but I need time to resurrect and in the interval it will be the Dragons to engage the Greater Demon in battle. They are ancient rivals."

"Why are the Dragons upset? What can we do?" Minister Ange willed the Emperor to spill all.

"No, not today," Methusem smiled. "I'm not even sure Ariel is a lurking threat, but I can't leave our planet for the Elf Ambassador's coming summitry 'til I am sure. In the meantime, if we can hunt the Summoner Kanuenos, he is not too mighty a foe for our Guards. The Summoner has roots on our Planet, or he would have evacuated during the time of the conquest with the others."

"We'll locate this Kanuenos," Dana said with conviction.

The small party sat in pensive silence. Blerpie! The sound came from somewhere indeterminate. Keyth checked with Halçyon's security computer. "The girls are here!" Keyth announced with pleasure, reviving the party spirit.

"The girls?" Traci was quick to reply.

"Starra and Kylie were in the mood for chips," Keyth teased.

"Starra!" Care perked up. In his opinion, she was the prettiest Elf in the whole Fleet. And she often played!

"Starra!" Methusem sounded just as pleased. "Let us make sure there are plenty of chips for this party."

Garren regarded his new shipmates, curious what they had to say about the girls. He found Krizren flirting heavily with Vylara and Keyth smiling at the pair.

Dana brushed a reverent fingertip on his new epaulette pin. "We have to go pick up Nerrys," Dana said with little regret. He would have loved to stay and party, but he loved spending time with Nerrys and his wife and kids.

"Please convey to them my fond wishes," Methusem stared

into space then broke into a wide grin, his peridot eyes sparkling with affection. "They do not know it yet," he chuckled. "Nalira carries a new child. A girl. You can break the news to them if you wish."

"Yes," Dana exclaimed. "Fantastic." He stood up and found his long fine blonde hair had landed in some chip dip. "Aw. Sticky mess!"

Dana was not a sticky mess fetishist.

COUTEAU DE CHASSE

XV. TERRA-DATE 215.149 EVENING
:: Night in The sky above Celesterra City. Garren ::

Traci, Dana, and Garren took their leave of the Halçyon party, Traci promising to return as soon as possible.

It was Traci who carried Garren aloft with Garren's heels poised on Traci's boot toes and with Traci's arm around Garren's waist to steady him; they ascended above the bay waters leaning into the wind. Garren was nervous for if he shifted their balance unexpectedly, Traci could easily snap his ankles or wrench a knee. Showing off, Dana over clocked his gravity skates and skated rings around them waiting for them to reach the skater's elevation level, his tote-carry slung securely to his back.

Garren was having a hard time imagining how the Guards

up here could possibly patrol the city streets; you could barely see people like dots on the ground.

The sky cast a rosy glow on the city with dusk nearly complete, a crimson blend of brilliant color heralding the end of another day above Celesterra City. An elevation level below the skaters, fastrafts and private coaches sped their way within the city limits, bearing people home from their jobs and day time pursuits.

The fastrafts were physically incapable of defying speed limit laws, unless you knew override hacks, but private coaches were a different technology. Garren entertained himself by watching a pair of Guards flagging a private coach to a stop. The penalties for exceeding city speed limits started at piloting suspension and ultimately to a permanent grounding. A local hearing judge would decide their sentence.

Dana waved a hand at a not too distant pair of Guards patrolling together.

Most Guards covered their patrol areas in pairs, they g-skated randomly, interlinking in baffling skating patterns; giving Garren the impression a whole autonomous sub-culture existed up here in the skies above Celesterra City. A pair broke off from the pattern and zoomed an intercept course with his little travel group, Garren realized that since he was out of uniform, Traci and Dana could get Writ for flying a civilian in a non-emergency.

"UFB," one of the Human females cried, zooming so close Dana ducked out of her way. "Unidentified flying bodies! Halt or be charged for illegal evasion!" Her Human female skating partner crossed her path in a perpendicular zoom.

Dana and Traci halted, floating in as minimal drift as possible in the drafts. Garren felt a mild vertigo looking down at the building tops below. The hues of the sunset painted the city a beautiful landscape, Garren envied the gravity-skating Guards for being privy to this sight on their duty details.

The two uniformed women flew close, cloaks snapping

jauntily in the brisk drafts, both pretty with dark loosely braided hair disarrayed from the wind. They were wearing red lip colour and eye make-up, black eyeliner drew emphases to their mischievous expressions. They did not look like sisters, yet were so alike in attitude they could have been.

Wincing, Garren prepared for the dreaded wisecracks as the She-Commander smiled in such a way to let him know she recognized him from the rumours this morning. Instead of saying anything witty, she pirouetted on her skates and flew a ring around them. He followed Dana's lead as his friend kept his gaze on the one Guard still floating in front.

"Hi Terriane," Traci broke the tableau first. He added in a flirtatious tone. "What 's up .... besides us?"

Her body turning sidewise, she spoke over her shoulder in a sexy way. "Hello Traci," she drawled. She tilted her chin down, her irises half lidded under her lashes, looking coy and pretty. Garren wished the look would transfer to him. Lucky Traci! On his peripheral vision, he saw Dana marginally shaking his head, mouthing the words 'not worth the trouble'. Hmm? Garren's private thought in response was, 'maybe the trouble would be worth it.' Dana rolled his eyes in exasperation. 'Wait a mark, you are a telepath, aren't you?' Garren tried to project. There was no indicative symbol on Dana's epaulette pin to suggest telepath. He remembered something Keyth had said earlier, about Methusem liking to hide surprises. 'What damage could a secret telepath do to an enemy's plans?'

Dana assumed an overly nonchalant air, drawing the attention of the two ladies. He introduced them. "Garren, this is Guard Terriane, and this," he gestured to the hyperactive Commander, "is Commander Lisza. Newly commissioned Commander, I should add. And I'm sure her new authority has behooved her to behave in a much more decorous manner as befitting her rank." His tan brown eyes danced with quiet laughter; obviously he thought he was being facetious.

Commander Lisza did a pretty spin number on her skates

and posed in some semblance to a Guard on duty. "Why," she drawled in an accent similar to Terriane's, "are you carrying him," she threw a chin nod in Garren's direction, "when he's out of uniform?"

"You know, I was just talking to Methusem about that today ..." Dana began, the wind billowed his loose flowing long blonde hair in its playful whims.

Terriane gave a little chortle. "You and our Emperor were having a private chat?! Today was it?" In a graceful skating move, she dove under Traci's feet and came around again from above. Commander Lisza played the role of good Guard, while Terriane played naughty Guard.

"Terri, take notes for the scrapbook file, this excuse is bound to be too good to waste," Commander Lisza twitched her lips in a fetching smile. She seemed to know exactly how her smile affected the male of the Human species.

A voice bespoke in Garren's head, startling him, 'Don't let Lisza distract you. Keep your attention on Terriane.' Dana must have decided to acknowledge his telepathic ability. Another telepath! Garren felt surrounded by them today.

"Yes, and you were saying to Methusem today?" Commander Lisza knew Dana was savvy to her.

"I suggested to Him, the carrying of non-uniformed people could be left up to the discretion of the Guards," Dana mimed a pompous manner.

"This discretionary power hasn't been announced in our protocol statutes as of yet," Commander Lisza quirked her beautiful cosmetically shaped eyebrow.

"He seemed to go for the suggestion and agreed to subscribe to it as long as frantic chaos doesn't erupt over the skies of the City," Dana laughed, unable to keep up the pompous manner; a suspiciously surreptitious mimicry of Sovereign Minister Allons.

"Impressive Dana," Commander Lisza went around to Dana's back, he did not turn around to watch her. "Can you do an imitation of ole Nuben?"

Instead of a Nuben impersonation, Dana pirouetted on his skates and did an amazing imitation of Commander Lisza. The lights of his g-skates winked along the line of his boot soles as he did a tricky step movement, indicating his fancy foot work was requiring the skate's micro control crystal to over-clock.

The ladies both laughed at Dana's antics. "Aw, we'll let you off this time with a warning; don't pick up any more civilians. OK?"

"We just have one more person to pick up," Traci sounded very commanding.

"Wait a mille-mark!" Terriane exclaimed. "Do you see their epaulette pins?" She danced on her skates.

"Commander Dana," Lisza floated close to Dana to push her face to his neck. "Nice ring to it, eh?" She skated once more around the small travel group to brush up against Traci from behind. "And Commander Traci," she drawled.

Since he wasn't in uniform, Garren couldn't look forward to her checking out his epaulette pin, too. O, how he craved the attentions of a woman; to spend a whole night with her body pressed to his body, to feel the weight of her breast on his arm as she slept after satiating carnal passion.

'Don't fall for them mate,' Dana bespoke privately to Garren.

Lisza made an exaggerated groan, "we'll make sure we're on the other side of the city, when you pick up this one more civilian. Don't let us catch you."

'She seems nice enough,' Garren thought back, wondering if Dana would hear him. 'She's bending the rules for us.'

'One bend of the rules deserves another,' Dana responded telepathically.

Lisza skated away to give a little distance, then she performed a few aerial acrobatics to show off her moves. The moves were very sinuous and sexy; Garren forgot Dana's earlier warning to keep his attention on Terriane. He noticed Terriane flying downward and lost track of her as he watched Lisza.

All of a sudden, Traci surged upward in a gesture Garren

guessed was to protect him.

A pair of feminine hands sprang out of nowhere and pantsed him. His drawstring ship-pants were not up to the task of surviving the assault. There he was in the skies above Celesterra City with his pants down to his calves and no undies. He tried to grab his pants back up without upsetting Traci's hold on him, Garren didn't fancy free fall.

"Woo hoo," Terriane and Commander Lisza cried together. They both skated in close, circling for an up close look at Garren's bare bottom. "Woah, I don't see any of those famous five welts. There must be some Dragon healing here," Commander Lisza chuckled. "I guess this whole 'chat with our Emperor story' must be truth."

"Lisza," Dana was laughing so hard be was hardly coherent. "I thought you were going to give up this behaviour when you jumped rank."

"Nah, we vowed not to let a promotion change us," Commander Lisza cried, departing the scene with sparkles of humour flashing in her eyes. Terriane followed suit, and surprisingly Dana skated after them, leaving Traci to help Garren manage to redress himself.

Garren readjusted his initial impression of the ladies and gave into the joke with grace, laughing at his predicament, so much for a woman's attentions.

To offer solace, Traci said, "just be glad we aren't in the middle of a shopping galleria. You have been pantsed with the best of us mate. Women! You gotta luv 'em."

"It must be a private joke, I've never heard so much as a rumour," Garren shivered, it was too chilly up here to be exposed.

Dana caught up with the ladies without difficulty; he was one of the best g-skaters in the entire Guard and they all knew it.

"What's up Dana?" Commander Lisza winked shamelessly suggestive; she knew Dana to be too wise to ask her for a date. This must be kind of serious.

Dana didn't want to speak aloud, you never knew if the nanoscopic remotes were listening. He bespoke to both of them. They were not aware, until now, of his telepathic ability. 'Hullo, you gorgeous ladies!'

Terriane tchd, 'don't stop the flattery, keep it coming.' She hovered close to Commander Lisza, who threw an around her shoulder like she was a lamp post, standing as if they were standing on the street and not skating high up the skyline.

'Show offs!'

Personally, Terriane wouldn't mind sharing an evening with Dana between herself and her Commander. She made sure she thought that loudly. Dana knew better than to think he could handle both of them on his own.

The three Guards poised a moment in contemplation of their home city, a fount of fond tenderness filled their hearts with a moment of shared serenity.

Celesterra City was spectacular at night with light and colour. The downtown city buildings averaged 10 to 30 stories. The lively areas of the city at night, where dance clubs opened their doors of drink and music to adults, lit up sections of streets like mini-carnivals. Off the coastline of the northern peninsula side, the underwater restaurants glowed like under water ships, great spheres of light. The marine life was used to the spectacle and didn't bother to flee the artificial light. A pair of blue Dragons swam dreamily in the shallow depths, dividing the dining patrons into the too scared to eat their expensive meals group and the people who marveled at the Dragons' beauty.

Rivulets beginning high in the mountains lazily finished their journeys to the sea, passing first by the public parks. The parks where children played by day became the prerogative of lovers by night, the moonstone causeways with their arches transformed into perfect alcoves for couples to share interludes.

Feeling very sad to say it, Dana bespoke, 'listen ladies, Garren is being harassed by a nasty element in the ranks. I'd appreciate it as a favour if you could help me guard his back. Please keep it off the channels and pass the word only to those you absolutely trust.'

The ladies gawped; everyone in the Guard knew there was some corruption in the ranks, bespeaking telepathically to hide their conversation from their fellow Guards meant affaires were a lot worse then anyone suspected. The ugly specter of civil war reared its horrendous horns.

Dana remembered that the ladies training specialties lay in tracking airborne threats, making him think he should have a tracking specialist on his team. His team! The excitement of it distracted him from plots and intrigues.

"Sure we'll watch his back with pleasure," the ladies bore wicked identical grins, "and we'll watch other parts of him as well. Scrumptious bum he's got and scrumptious nethers, devastating combination with those storm gray eyes of his. How close you want us to watch him? Very close?" The ladies teased, but Dana knew they would heed his request. He saluted them before skating to rejoin Traci.

℘

Their rendezvous with Nerrys went without incident. Nerrys was waiting patiently at the construction mess; though Garren figured, to the experts, the mess of construction materials and framework were exactly in proper order.

Upon leaving the construction site, Traci decided to carry Nerrys, who was more an armful than Garren. Garren did not consider himself slighted in the height department; however, his companions seemed of a different race, Dana topped Garren by his jaw line and Traci and Nerrys by their collar bones.

They g-skated the night sky above their home City, Garren drank in the view. Dana wrapped both arms tightly holding Garren as their trajectory took a sloping descent. To save their friends from stomach dropping induced nausea, the gravity skating Commanders made their descent graduating, making a circuit of the Fountain Place Apartment Quadrangle.

Nerrys's family lived in Fountain Place, Delta 4, Apt 2901. Each of the four buildings was 30 stories in height, pentagon shaped with facades of smoke tinted transparent poly metal. The floors were divided into two and three bedroom family size apartments. Lovely fountains sang their soothing watery sounds to the building lobbies and an oversized fountain graced the courtyard geometry. Fountain Place was well known to Celesterra City as a residence for tele-kinetics; not exclusively so, for kinetic abilities didn't usually break latency in young children, not showing up until the teen years, plenty of time for parents to teach responsibility and courtesy etiquette towards sharing the city with non-kinetic neighbors.

Kinetic abilities were more prevalent in Humans and the Magical abilities usually prevalent in the Elf races, abilities did cross haphazardly to parents' consternation.

The soft kaleidoscope lamp light impressed Garren, attractively illuminating the courtyard's center fountain. The edges of the buildings were trimmed with understated glow lights; residents drew heavy draperies to keep their apartments private and to preserve night for sleeping.

Apartment balconies recessed into the buildings. G-skate certified Guards had special override codes to the balcony shields in their apartments, enabling them to fly directly to work. Visiting skaters may land on the roof and ride an inter-floor lift to their engagements. Violet vector lights flashed on the roofs as beacons for landing.

They skipped the rooftop landing and headed straight for Erin's balcony, conveniently situated one floor above Nerrys's family's apartment. Erin shared the apartment with his brother Samson, giving Garren a mild case of curiosity as to how the brothers had managed it for they did not qualify for a family size apartment. Traci and Dana started the final dive to the balcony. Garren shut his eyes against the sting of the wind and put all his trust into Dana's skating. If they were about to smack into the unyielding building surface, he didn't want to see it coming.

"Aahh!" Garren clutched his stomach. Telepaths! Dana went into a straight drop, Garren figured Dana overheard his thoughts and decided to make a joke. "Aah!" Their descent de-accelerated too quickly, Garren felt the pressure of gravity and hoped Dana wasn't about to lose his hold on him.

"See how lucky you are to be flying with me and not Dana," Traci teased Nerrys loud enough for Garren to overhear, making a great show of landing smoothly.

Lights winked on as they landed, the foursome invited themselves into Erin's welcoming apartment. Garren fought his trembling legs to hide his reaction to the plunge Dana had treated him to. There was no sign of Erin. No one was home. The apartment had all the messy glamour of a bachelor residence.

Traci made the introductions they'd skipped at the construction site. "Nerrys Nefeinn," Traci bowed from the waist to each in turn gesturing theatrically with one arm, "this is Garren Waysixth, Senior Fleet Commander of the Halçyon. Garren may I introduce Nerrys Nefeinn, tele-kinetic extraordinaire."

Garren looked up; he had to for Nerrys was of a height with Traci. His first impression was a vision of sternness and a low nonsense tolerance, a longer regard made Garren wonder. Nerrys appeared Human, had long white blonde hair parted off center with a barrette to hold a long lock pinned somewhere behind his ear; lots of wind whipped strands escaped the clasp. His brows were light brown, arched, and untouched by cosmetic shaping. Nerrys's eyes were a light amethyst, wide set, intelligent and penetrating. His cheekbones broad, complexion fair, and with lips that could make his face be sensuous or stern. Nerrys had the air of a man who brooked no nonsense, a mantle of authority you might find in a teacher or training

Commander, but a glitter in his eyes hinted at an intelligent sense of humour. Nerrys bowed politely, a languid movement, languid in a way that was subtly provocative. If you put Nerrys and Krizren in a room full of nubile females, their masculine sensuousness would start a swoon-fest.

A sigh came from Dana. Garren turned his face away, embarrassed to see the blatant invitation reaching out from Dana to Nerrys.

"Well Dana, I'm glad to see you remembered our existence," Nerrys said in his deep voice. "The kids can't wait to see you. And you Traci! Pleased to meet you Garren. I hear we're celebrating your promotion." He grinned to reveal white even teeth, erasing the impression of sternness.

"Not just mine," Garren pointed at Dana and Traci's epaulette pins.

Nerrys didn't gape, gasp, or fawn; he smiled wide with evident pleasure at his friends' good fortunes. "Congratulations!" He held out a hand to grasp wrists and he pulled each of them into a back slapping hug.

"Thanks," Dana's muffled voice spoke, managing to make his hug from Nerrys last longer than Traci's.

"It's still a shock," Traci added, smiling so hard, his lips barely moved as he spoke.

"Let's go downstairs, I have to get out of my work clothes and I desperately need a shower," Nerrys led the way to the hallway.

"Well, I didn't want to say anything as rude as suggesting a shower," Traci made a sniffing noise.

For no apparent reason, Traci tripped over a snag less carpet on clumsy feet. Nerrys stood ready to catch him. Traci laughed. Garren surmised there was a telekinetic prank involved.

They snubbed the inter-floor lift, using the shallow-stepped staircase instead. They climbed down one level, the stairwell walls prevented suicidal people from being tempted by the 30 or so floors separating them from street level.

Downstairs, Nerrys's apartment doors were invitingly wide open, a short foyer hall entrance blocked casual passer-bys from seeing inside, a guest's toilet closet faced the entrance.

The apartment's carpeting was a neutral brown and the walls were coloured neutral white. The first room they came to after turning right was a comfortably sized kitchen-living room combo. A counter divided the cooking area from the living room furniture area; a six-seater dining table took up a fourth of the space. A sectional sofa leaned against a wall, wrapped a corner, and came about to face itself. A smaller knee high table sat in the sofa area with children's games cluttering the surface. An expensive computer and entertainment center sat near the opposite wall. A hall branched off from the living room area, presumably leading to bedrooms and a hygiene room.

"We're home first," Nerrys swiveled his gaze to take in the mostly neat and clean room. "Want a tour?" He led them down the hall. Three bedrooms, one with a feminine décor, and one a young boy's room, opposite, Nerrys swept open a door curtain to reveal the shower bathing room. Three rows of three shower nozzles were set in a detached wall size partition at waist, chest, and overhead level; furry rug lined this one wall section useful for self back-scrubbing. Peering behind this center piece, a large oval pink bathtub faced a toilet closet.

Nerrys bent to pick up kid size clothes and tossed the items into a strewn pile in a corner of the room. The strewn pile neatened up with clothes fluffing by invisible hands, Nerrys's kinetic ability at work. "Ah, Jessie, I keep telling him the Guard won't accept slobs into their ranks." He shook his head, his eyes unfocused.

Traci made a noise in sympathy. "He's not interested in the construction trade?"

"Not since he was eight, I can't deny his decision hurt a bit."

"How old is he now?" Traci asked politely.

"He's twelve. He'll tell you 12 and a half," Nerrys smiled, love for his son making his expression very tender.

Garren felt a lump in his throat chakra. He turned away to admire a wall picture of a Mermaid combing her floating tresses with a shell comb, Merpages watching her with rapturous expressions. Dana stood peering over his shoulder to share the view of the wall picture. "Ah, Mermaids, what is it about them? Her long hair flowing in the water?" Dana sighed.

"Well, their tails certainly aren't convenient," Traci teased.

"Would you even recognize a Mermaid with her legs on?" Nerrys nudged Traci.

"Every girl he sees with long hair like that, he fantasizes is a Mermaid," Dana nudged Traci, too.

"I don't think I've ever met a Mermaid," Garren crossed his arms over his abs.

"Methusem is a Mer," Dana pointed out.

"Methusem is a Merpage," Traci nudged Dana with his elbow.

"Yeah, but Methusem is also a Were-Dragon, it's hard to distinguish his Mer traits from Dragon," Dana elbowed Traci's rib.

"Yeah, but Methusem's Mére is a Mermaid, Grand-Mére Dragoness is more remote by a generation," Traci elbowed Dana twice in a row.

"Mermaids are a breed of Demon, you know," Nerrys whispered.

"And natural adversaries of Dragons," Traci whispered, too.

"Not complete enemies, they came together; alas, Methusem is proof," Dana whispered.

"We never hear anything about the males that had to have come between Mére Mermaid and Grand-Mére Dragon," Garren spoke in his usual volume.

"I'm sure there is a good reason," Dana whispered. He shivered. "I don't know about you, but I'm scaring myself silly. If I start second guessing our Emperor's intentions, I'll lose my sanity."

They heard a female voice shouting, "ANYBODY HOME?"

To break the mood, Traci shook himself like a mammal shaking water off its pelt.

"YES SYRA!" Nerrys shouted.

"Syra is your daughter?" Traci asked politely.

Nerrys nodded. "Eligible daughter!" He behooved to mention.

"Has she shown interest in a profession?"

"My daughter takes life too seriously for such a momentous decision. The chopping of vegetables must be weighed and measured with due consideration," Nerrys smiled, his tender expression softening any hint of criticism.

"Attention to detail is a great skill," Traci said extra politely.

"Yes. Say that again while we wait for our dinner tonight," Nerrys led the way back to the living room. "I should help and win points with my wife. Jesse is still too young to trust with the kitchen appliances."

"DAD, DAD," a boy's piping voice and patter of feet accompanied Jesse's headlong rush into his Father's arms via throwing himself into the air.

Nerrys deftly caught up his squirming son, gave Jesse a hug and a kiss on the cheek.

"DANA!" Jesse shouted with joy.

Nerrys let the boy jump to the floor and Jesse threw a hug around Dana, pressing his cheek to Dana's stomach. "Dana I passed the math tests, I passed, I passed."

"Woah, fantastic Jesse," Dana congratulated.

Garren noticed a look of surprise on Nerrys. Had Jesse taken the Guard Entrance Exams without informing his father first?

Nerrys stopped in his tracks to study a spot on the wall, amethyst eyes a striking contrast to his tan face and blonde hair.

"Nerrys ... Honey," Nerrys's charming wife Nalira met them in the living room area. "Honey, are you OK?" She peered up into her husband's face, a soft expression of love on her face.

"Yeah, yeah," Nerrys snapped out of his fugue. "I just need a shower, ugh, can't stand myself."

"Honey you smell great," Nalira meant it, Nerrys smelt of the herbal water he'd doused in that morning. He usually took a shower coming home or going out. It was his way.

"Ah," he looked shy of a sudden in front of all these male visitors. His features took on a stern look, every bit the family man in charge of a house with two teenagers. The stern look softened as he gathered his wife into his arms for a fierce hug and welcome home kiss. He released her to head for the shower room. Nalira gave Nerrys a quick swat to his rear as he turned his back to her. Nerrys laughed, but that spank sound had quite a crack to it.

Dana sighed, he adored Nalira and loved her 'hello' hugs.

"Hi Dana, Traci," Nalira turned her cheery smile to the Guards. "This must be Garren?"

Garren held out both hands for a wrist to wrist greeting. Her grasp was very firm and warm. Garren swallowed a sudden lump in his throat; this family atmosphere was alien to him and he felt a little envy over it.

She turned to give hugs to Dana and Traci; again Dana managed a longer hug.

"Make yourselves at home; we be having some cooking to do! Hey Jesse, scamp, can you handle the vegetables?" She hugged her youngest child.

Jesse looked very, very pleased. The twelve year old must be craving some responsibility.

Garren remembered Methusem's words and wondered if Dana was really going to break the news to Nalira that she carried a child in her womb.

Traci gave profuse apologies, saying he had to go back to the Halçyon.

"Of course Traci, of course, don't be a stranger, eh?" Nalira gave him another hug, which meant she had to give Dana another hug. She giggled.

Syra giggled, too, watching from the kitchen area, she giggled around a stretchy taffy candy she held in her teeth.

"Don't forget to say good night to Nerrys!" Nalira called.

Traci looked back, "I think he's in the shower already."

"He won't mind," Nalira assured him.

&

Traci decided not to be conservative and accepted Nalira's words at value. He re-found the shower room and pushed open the privacy curtain. Nerrys was tapping water temperature settings in the shower pad. A confirm light lit bright yellow and the shower heads started a cascade of fresh mountain sourced water, heated to perfection, if Nerrys's long loud sigh of pleasure was any indication.

"Nerrys, I'm taking off," Traci waved.

Nerrys peeked out from behind his wet hair and gave Traci a loose wave and a smile.

Traci paused to give Dana and Garren each a hug, feeling awkward with Garren, then departed to return to Halçyon.

ᛯ

Garren felt acutely aware that he had put Traci off. He remained quiet and inattentive, sitting on the sectional sofa, while conversation around him buzzed. He startled when something bumped his knee. Garren looked up to meet the candid wide eyed gaze of the young boy Jesse. The boy's irises were a deep amethyst, his nose ended in a little slope. Jesse's brown hair had a life of its own, moving with every turn of his head.

"You're a FLEET Commander, Garren? Really?" Jesse's lips mouthed 'WOAH'.

"Garren is a SENIOR Fleet Commander," Dana laughingly corrected the boy. "And he is certified in the broadsword, which you would probably find interesting, you scamp."

Jesse jumped up and down. "Do you want to see my sword? Well, it isn't really a broadsword, but do you want to see it?"

Garren smiled, "you're certifying in the Archaic Weapons skills tract, too? Sure I'd like to see it." He did honestly want to see the sword.

"Don't take too long, dinner is almost ready," Nalira called, while Syra started mashing the mustard faster by raising the setting on the food processor.

Garren and Dana followed Jesse as he led them to his room. They passed the shower room, where Nerrys hadn't finished his shower, yet. The privacy curtain was still open from when Traci had pushed it open.

Jesse commented that his Dad's after work shower usually took a while, even for kinetics, construction work was very physical labour.

Nerrys bowed his head forward to let the shower spray sooth his nape; hands on the shower wall in a leaning pushup, shoulder blades pronounced and lower back arched, and with one knee bent against the opposite leg. Rotating his head under the shower spray, slowly throwing his head back, water smoothed his long blonde hair, - dirty blond and longer wet - , water cascading down his back and beading on his tanned skin. Nerrys's lips parted softly in absolute, but quiet, pleasure.

Dana said, "umm, he sure enjoys a shower." He noticed Jesse frozen and staring, as if Jesse had never seen his father before. The tall Guard gave Jesse a little nudge forward.

Jesse led the two Guards into his room, gradually regaining his normal exuberance; he dragged a long case from under his bed. The box looked shabby and the worse for wear. A brass toned metal plate decorated the cover, a signature etched in the corner.

Garren did a double take as he thought he read it correctly. His own excitement jumped into his throat and he swallowed reflexively. Roughly translated, it was inscribed with the Orb and Cross of Soling Vale. "Jesse," Garren mumbled under his breath.

Jesse looked up to see Garren's rapt expression; he smiled with pride as he opened the case. A strange sword of a strange alien craft lay without ceremony or dignity on a black cushion. It was a brassy colored looking metal, but definitely not brass.

One edge of the sword looked wicked sharp. Jesse lifted it up, his skinny upper arms bulged, showing how heavy the sword must be. He handed it without any reverence to Garren to try the heft of it.

Garren accepted it gingerly, wrapping his fingers around the hilt. The sword was indeed heavy, the metal of it beat up and scratched; it was not beautiful. The hilt was thick around for Garren's hand. The sword was meant for a taller/broader race of Human; Jesse would have to surpass his father in size to be able to wield the sword the way it was meant to be wielded. Garren guessed it might be a hunting sword. As he guessed this, a strange whisper sounded in his head, saying, 'couteau de chasse'. Garren quickly turned his head towards the whisper, but Dana was sitting on the bed and Jesse hadn't said it. All that was there was a plain oval mirror on the wall.

"This sword has been an heirloom in our family for forever," Jesse said with a child's grasp of time. "Its got Demon blood on it, or used to. Samson helped me scan it once, but we couldn't detect any blood. Dad won't let me leave the apartment with it." Jesse put a wealth of frustration in that last statement.

Dana clasped a friendly hand on the boy's shoulder, "your Dad surely just wants to make sure you have it to pass to your future children, Jesse."

"Yeah," Jesse ducked his head, and then wistfully regarded the sword in Garren's caressing hands. "Seems a shame though."

"Does that mean you're into the family glory thing?" Dana chided teasingly.

Jesse shrugged, blinking up at the tall blonde guard, for the first time comparing Dana's looks to his father's. He quickly hid his eyes from Dana without understanding why.

With a bow, Garren returned the sword to Jesse's hands, and then gave him the Guard's salute. He became inexplicably drawn to the mirror, feeling ridiculous, aware of Dana and Jesse observing his fascination.

"The mirror is an heirloom from my mother's side," Jesse

explained.

"Is it ... Magic?" Garren knew Magic came in strange guises.

"Actually, I dunno," Jesse's voice cracked on the 'dunno'. "I've never seen it do anything."

The disembodied voice whispered again to Garren's left ear, talking over Jesse's voice, saying, "you are ... fairest ... of all."

"Oh. Kay." Garren blinked and swallowed, wanting very desperately to leave the room. Was it safe for the child to be sleeping here with this thing?

Dana moved to peer directly into the mirror, nothing manifested. He gave it up and said to Garren, "it's been a rough day for you, mate, eh?"

A voice carried down the hall, "FOOD IS READY."

Jesse re-cased the weapon and put it away with the quickness of repetitive practice.

The trio returned together to the kitchen area. Food spread out on the table barely leaving room for the dinner plates and beverage mugs. To Garren's surprise Erin was seated at the table. Nalira sat at the end of the table. Nerrys sat at the opposite end, hair combed back wet from his long after-work shower and wearing a purple T shirt. An extra stool squeezed a plate space on the corner next to Nerrys, since there were seven of them. Dana hopped on to the stool, beating Jesse to it. Jesse tried to shove Dana off the stool, sending both of them into giggle hysterics. Syra sighed long suffering. A dinner napkin floated up and tossed itself over Jesse's face. Syra kinetically threw one of her kinetic's training balls at her brother.

Jesse clutched his chest crying, "she wounded my heart! Ahh!"

The boy's antics made Garren laugh. Nalira pointed Garren to the seat between herself and Syra to which Garren was perfectly amenable. Erin sat opposite him. Dana won the match for the corner; Jesse plopped down on the seat between Erin and Dana.

It was a cozy dinner setting; Garren enjoyed it immensely

and actually relaxed. Plates piled with steaming food floated slowly around the table, giving you a chance to spear what you wanted with a three pronged fork. Garren helped himself to some steaming cherry waffles, three helpings of peppered brioche, and a hungry man's dollop of mustard mash.

"How do you like the mustard mash?" Syra said as soon as Garren took a mouthful. She'd made it by herself this time.

Mumbling around the mouthful, Garren nodded his head and said how good it tasted. She smiled.

"Delicious Syra!" Nerrys claimed.

She basked in her father's praise.

Garren caught Dana's eyes and he projected the word 'What?' to the telepath.

Dana said directly to Garren's mind, 'I'm glad to see you happy. I don't know if you realize how infrequently you smile.'

Garren blushed, hoping his tan covered it.

Erin noticed Garren's strange reaction and misconstrued it. "Garren, I am so soo sorry about this morning," Erin's low sad voice carried a heavy apology. "I had no idea the Writ was illegal."

"I'm glad twas you," Garren said with all the sincerity he could muster. "Care gave you his highest recommendation."

"Oh?" Erin wiped his lips with a napkin. "I had the impression you weren't into that."

"No, I'm not into that, not the stuff Care is into," Garren was quick to say.

"What's this?" Nerrys spoke up.

"Umm, Garren was disciplined this morning," Dana answered the awkward pause.

"Disciplined?" Nerrys shared a look with Nalira. "Did you hear that Jesse? Discipline is part of life in the Guard."

"I'm not afraid of discipline," Jesse's young sincere voice made the statement sound wrong somehow.

"Jesse," Nerrys insisted on the point, "I've never hit you in your life. How could you possibly know?"

"DAD," Jesse's voice cracked. "I've passed all the entrance exams, all I need now is Samson to claim sponsorship of me and then I start the Guard school program."

"I just want you to understand what you're getting into," Nerrys wanted to protest that he wasn't trying to discourage his son, but realized that was exactly the point.

Dana received the distinct impression Jesse was keeping some secrets from his family. The boy's mind was shielded tight and Dana couldn't get a telepathic impression, the boy must be self-training to shield. 'Who was helping the kid train?'

"Samson is still out on his secret Rogue assignment," Erin put down his spoon and leaned back. "I would be honoured to sponsor you Jesse."

Jesse opened his mouth to say something, but nothing came out.

Erin smiled with understanding, "it's OK. I hero-worship Samson, too. My big brother sponsored me in the Guard."

"May I ask what Erin did to you?" Nalira said to Garren. "Unless, of course, it's inappropriate dinner conversation."

Garren made a motion with his wrist that could have meant anything.

Erin answered her, "single tail."

"Nalira was a Court Executor before we married, it is professional interest," Nerrys explained. He kinetically reached to dish another helping of cherry waffles.

Garren reached an arm over for more mustard mash, thinking life for kinetics was certainly convenient.

"Hey Erin?" Dana sat with straight posture on the stool, "you seem a little moody today, eh?"

"I guess I'm a little depressed," Erin admitted. "After this morning's fiasco, I skipped meeting with my Field Team. I hear my Commander is looking to trade me."

"What?" Dana echoed the shock Garren was feeling at the news.

"My stats have dropped too low, I might be better off

unassigned for awhile."

"No one is better off unassigned," said Dana, speaking from his new Commander position. "Hey -"

"Dana," Erin interrupted him, "if you were about to offer me a position on your team, I really appreciate it, but I just can't handle it for now."

"Oh, OK," Dana sounded disappointed.

"So, your brother is on a secret assignment?" Garren asked, genuinely curious.

"Yeah," Erin folded his arms, looking broody. His long brown hair was coming loose from its braid. "Samson is a Magic activator. It seemed an important qualification, but that's all I know about it." His attitude didn't leave much latitude for holding secrets from your brother, no matter how secret the assignment.

"Mom?" Jesse spoke for the first time in a mark. Atypically quiet, Jesse kept sneaking looks at his Father. "Is there Magic in your heirloom mirror? Garren seemed to think so."

The dinner party all gave Garren their attention.

Garren shrugged and started to disclaim the accusation.

"You saw it?" Nalira interrupted his disclaimer. She seemed amazed.

"What's this?" Nerrys verbally pounced.

"I didn't see anything … but I thought I heard …," Garren shrugged again. He really did not want to talk about this; kudos to Erin and Dana for being able to talk about their 'FEELINGS'.

"Did you hear weeping?" Nalira frowned.

"NALIRA!" Nerrys sounded angry.

Nerrys was alarming when he was angry. His amethyst eyes flashed and he frowned fiercely.

"It is nothing Nerrys," Nalira soothed. She wiped her hand on a napkin, then swept her short red hair back from her brow. "There is a presence in the mirror sometimes, a pair of red eyes that weep."

"A presence?" Nerrys slapped the table. A less trained

kinetic would be rattling the dishes by now, but Nerrys's self-control was absolute. "There is a possessed mirror in our son's room?"

"That presence has been in my family for generations beyond count," Nalira stood up and started to sound angry on her own behalf. "It's not just that mirror, it crosses into all the mirrors in the apartment. As far as it's concerned, this apartment is MY domain."

Nerrys's anger cooled in the face of his wife's anger. Garren suspected that as gentle as Nerrys seemed, he ruled his family with iron strictness.

When Nerrys didn't say anything further, Nalira sat down again and turned back to Garren.

"Did you see it weeping?" Nalira put a warm hand on Garren's forearm.

Garren knew her flashing temper was meant for her husband Nerrys, drowning into her brown eyes filled with temper was devastating to Garren; he loved her from that moment.

"Nalira," Nerrys warned gently. He knew exactly how it was to fall in love with Nalira.

"Um," Garren regained his self-possession, showing his quality as a Fleet Commander. "I didn't see anything. I ... heard a whisper." He shrugged again.

"It spoke to you?" Nalira's voice rose incredulously, both happy and sad for the mirror presence had never spoken to her or anyone in her family. "What did it say to you?"

Nerrys strode off, "that mirror can hang somewhere other than our children's rooms."

The rest of the dinner party waited raptly for Garren to answer.

"I thought I heard it say, "couteau de chasse"," leaving out the 'fairest' part, Garren's stomach rumbled loudly.

The females laughed in that knowing female way. "Ready for some desert Commander Garren?" Syra giggled. "Do you want mocha latte? A barista Witch lives two floors down, she usually does us the favour!"

"O, thanks Syra, but if you have chocolate, I'd be very satisfied with that."

She started clearing the table. Jesse jumped up to lend a hand.

"What were you doing when it spoke?" Nalira couldn't resist the mystery.

"I was admiring Jesse's sword and guessing at its type," Garren remembered, he had been thinking 'hunting-sword'.

Syra stopped mid-motion. "It recognized your sword Jesse!" The 16 year old girl's logic leaped.

"Yeah, but," Jesse didn't want to discourage his sister. "I've handled the sword plenty of times in front of the mirror." He didn't seem to mind having a haunted mirror in his room.

Nerrys came out with the mirror floating behind him.

"Ahh, life for kinetics," Garren joked with a little envy.

"I WANT DESERT!" Jesse yelled, making sure everyone heard.

Nalira dropped the mystery for another day. "Do you boys want to stay the night here?" She offered.

"You aren't afraid of this mirror, are you?" Nerrys said lightly, but with serious undertones.

"Of course not," Nalira protested. "Really Nerrys! I don't want our guests skating off, if we offer them liqueur with their desert. Plus, I would enjoy company."

"Well, I live upstairs Nalira," Erin begged off. "It is very kind of you to offer, I don't feel like I'm good company right now."

"Nonsense," she cried.

Dana said he'd like to stay over Erin's tonight. He gave the brunette Guard a big suggestive wink.

Garren understood that Dana wanted to cheer up his depressed friend and he did not want to crash with them while the 'cheering up' was going on. He also STRONGLY did not want to spend another night in the Junior Guard dormitory. He longed to spend the night aboard Halçyon, was she still berthed in the bay or was she floating in orbit by now?

"Oh, stay Commander Garren, please!" Jesse jumped up and down.

"I would be honoured," Garren accepted gladly and sat back down as Syra served up heaping plates of different flavored ice-cream and dishes of different toppings like crushed up chocolate cookies. Life didn't get much sweeter than this. He munched, while ardently hoping not to hear any more whispers from the haunted mirror.

XVI. TERRA-DATE 215.150 MORNING
:: Shopping mall. Garren ::

Garren lay in a contented quiet morning drowse, eyes open, and admiring a play of light from the window blinds. He lazed in the guest bed, sharing the bedroom with his hosts. The single size guest bed turned at a 90 degree angle from the double size bed where Nerrys and Nalira sounded deep asleep. The husband and wife slept quietly, barely a snore between them, Garren wondered if his own snoring had kept them awake half the night.

The kids were asleep in their own rooms. Jesse would have to learn to be an early riser, if he intended to go through with enlisting in the Royal Guard.

Garren wiggled his toes, watching them wiggle out from the bottom of the light weight sheet covering him from his pelvis down to his ankles. The bed linens followed a lavender and lilac theme. He guessed Nalira picked it to match her husband's eyes. He tucked his arm and elbow under the pillows, propping his head and shoulders higher, the linens were so soft, much nicer than the Junior Guard's dormitory. He shut his eyes tight, trying to imagine the domestic bliss of having a wife who chose bed linens to match his eyes.

He ran one hand down his contoured muscular torso, checking to make sure his abs weren't dissolving for he hadn't worked out since three days ago.

He mentally organized all the things he had to do today. He needed to go shopping for some pretty desperately needed clothes now that he had a commander's salary pay in his money account, at the moment he had on borrowed pajama shorts from Nerrys. The material was a mite thin for his comfort level, he felt his nethers were too free. Also, on the to-do list, he still had to transfer his meager belongings from the dormitory and send the stuff on to Halçyon. Keyth had taken charge of stocking Halçyon's supplies.

The Coronation Ball in Minister Ange's honor would be tonight and the Fleet's pre-launch party was set for tomorrow afternoon. By the Vale, he sorely wanted to get his Certification in Hand-to-Hand combat under his stats before launch. Nihera City would be packed with Guards making ready to go Deep Space, not to mention the Rocket Race fans already crowding the hotels. Would he find someone willing to help demonstrate his skills for the Exam and on a party day?

Garren reached out a foot to touch the sunlight, this simple pleasure would be unattainable in Deep Space. Deep Space in two days! Garren stretched all his limbs indolently, yawning deep and long.

Sounds of feet patter floated from outside the bedroom. The children be awake, he surmised. Garren rolled over the bed's edge and on to his feet, wrapping the sheet around his waist for his modesty's sake. But then again, Nerrys's 16 year old daughter Syra might be up. Not that he would try to seduce a 16 year old; it was just 2 short terra-years to 18. Would she remember him? Garren decided he could compromise his dignity in the hopes of a wife prospect. It took him two attempts to overcome come his modesty and leave the bedroom without the sheet.

Garren detoured to the toilet closet and after indulging his kidneys, turned and used the wash basin fountain to clean his teeth. Feeling freshened, he padded barefoot and braved the living room. Syra and the twelve year old Jesse were sitting at the counter, heads together and whispering. They startled when they saw Garren approach and suddenly stopped whispering.

"Goo-ood Morning," Jesse sang.

Syra studied Garren's face. In her opinion, Garren had the face of a heroic knight from a bardic ballad.

"Woah, Commander Garren," Jesse giggled, daring a glance at his sister. "Will I get a rippley tummy like yours if I keep training with my sword?"

Syra's gaze dropped to Garren's tummy, then lower. She covered her mouth in her palm.

Garren's bravado broke and he moved so the counter blocked the view. Jesse giggled, a deep belly laugh the way kids do, and Garren laughed, too, Jesse's laugh was contagious.

"Do you want to play a game?" Jesse begged. "We have 'Bop the Shell-Back'."

"Do you want to see me practice?" Syra focused on her kinetic's practice balls. She floated five of the balls and struggled with smaller ones.

Garren hadn't known that smaller objects required greater skill from the tele-kinetic.

"Has anyone offered to break your fast Garren?" Nalira said from behind him. He turned and admired her royal purple night gown, it made her mahogany hair look a deeper red.

"I was going to next, honest," Jesse jumped off the counter stool.

"Hey, morning folks," Dana strode in from the foyer, wearing a thigh length sleeveless tunic in a pale shade of grey, which flattered, amazingly, his white hair on white skin colouring. The tunic had fashionably cut holes on both sides revealing Dana's lower rib area to the top of his hip bone.

"Someone mentions food and here comes Dana," Nerrys joined them, totally nude and with his hair mussed.

Garren had to admit, if his inclination went that way, Nerrys's looks and aura would peak his interest. From the rapt expression on Dana's face, Dana had no reservations. This reminded Garren, no one had told Nalira the news Methusem had revealed yesterday. By Celesterran Society rules, it was a pregnant wife's prerogative to ask a friend to act as a sex surrogate partner for her husband; they almost always chose another man. Dana and Traci would probably be beside themselves with hope. There was also Guard Samson, if he returned from assignment.

"Food? Is that all you have to say after I bring you these tickets to the Coronation Ball?" Dana held up an engraved chip.

"Tickets for the Coronation Ball?!" Syra screeched. She jumped up and down and hugged Dana, dancing him around in a circle.

Dana laughed, letting her lead the little dance.

"Woah, Dana," Nalira broke into the dance to hug Dana. Dana milked the hug for as long as he could. "Thank you so much, but the Coronation Ball is tonight and it's half-way around the world?"

"Yes," Dana hugged the women to him and winked at Nerrys for his teasing presumption of the women. "Our friends aboard Halçyon," Dana winked at Garren, "promised to float us to the other side. So, we have to all be ready by Mark 15 this afternoon, on the roof, Traci will shuttle us over to the Fleet Bay."

"We're going on a Fleet SHIP?!!" Jesse screamed and danced with an 12 year-old's joy.

"Garren are you going to the Ball friend?" Dana asked. "We should find an outfit for you that will bring out the blue in your hair."

Garren laughed. "My clothes just have to be comfortable and functional."

"Yeah, I see that," Dana peered significantly at the pajama shorts, not really doing a job of shadowing Garren's significantly blessed nether package.

"Well, don't draw attention to it," Garren protested. Perhaps Nerrys had the right idea, by trotting it out in the open it lost its compelling mystery.

"O, Dad, can we go shopping? Please. Please. I got the

money Grandma sent, please?" Jesse pleaded.

"Well," Nerrys checked the time marker on the computer panel, "then we have to skip breakfast, time is moving ahead."

"Will you skip your morning shower?" Jesse teased his Dad.

&

The women decided they would rather spend their prep time at the spa being beautified by professionals; Nerrys, Dana, Garren, and Jesse headed for the Fountain Park Galleria; Dana tagged along solely to be Garren's fashion advisor.

Dana decided the promotion shock must have worn off Garren for the man was smiling frequently and broadly. He was so happy for his friend's happiness, Dana wanted to do something special to thank Methusem for being responsible for Garren's happiness; but what do you buy for the Emperor who has everything? Write a poem? Bake a cake? Methusem would be presiding at the Coronation Ball.

ɞ

"What?" Garren asked Dana for the third time. He was being treated to the regard usually reserved for Nerrys.

Garren was once again wearing the draw-string pants he'd confiscated from Halçyon's locker. He walked shirtless and wore his sandy-gray blue tinged hair back in a hair-tie Syra had lent him. She had offered to braid his hair for him and the idea of her hands playing in his hair had set his heart thumping, but Nerrys negated the offer, said they didn't have time. Garren thought his heart would go into shock at the missed opportunity.

As they walked to the Galleria 8 blocks away, Garren checked the streets for female prostitutes. He wanted a woman very keenly and he had just enough time this afternoon for a sure thing. He hadn't spotted a female yet, a male prostitute had whistled at him, to call the male prostitute 'not attractive' was a kind way of putting it.

Garren was not used to the attention his shirtless body was drawing from people on their casual business. A woman leaning over a second story balcony above Cardamom Rue Avenue definitely gave him an invitation to come up. The flattery to his male pride made him slowly smooth his hair back, his raised arm bulging cut muscle in a blatant gesture for attention.

In the lead, Dana stopped the whole party and waited for Garren to catch up. The bright sunlight beat down, all the contours to Garren's abs revealed in her bemused rays. Even the Goddesses be tempted, Dana romanticized.

Jesse stood with his hands on his hips, foot tapping, Goddess only knew what the 12 year old was thinking.

Nerrys treated Garren to an interested stare or two, to Garren's consternation.

♉

So, Dana thought, 'this is what it takes to get Nerrys's interest.' Dana was thin by genetic heritage; he would never be muscular in the warrior way. He didn't notice Nerrys by his side, until the man put an arm around Dana to pull him towards their destination and out of his distraction with Garren's physique.

♌

Nearly to the steps leading to the Galleria entrance, Jesse broke ahead in a run.

"Yayy!"

"Wait Jesse, where are you …," Nerrys stopped, Ruby's Toy Emporium was to the right and Jesse was running straight. "Jesse, the toy store is over here!"

"Da-add, I need clothes, not toys!" Jesse ran into the maw of the formidable Galleria Entrance.

Nerrys had stopped in his tracks. Garren turned to say something, but stopped when he saw Nerrys's expression. The man appeared to be choking back an attack of tears; his lower lip compressed a subtle tremor.

Dana put a comforting arm across Nerrys's back, hugging him. "This is the first time Jesse doesn't want toys?"

Nerrys took a deep shuddering breath.

Garren felt at a loss, not knowing how to give comfort, but wanting to.

"You know it's going to come, sooner or later," Nerrys smiled and looked blindly up at the brilliant blue sky. He was not accustomed to displaying his emotions so openly to anyone except his wife. "I'm going to get a cup of chocolate over there; I'll be right back, okay?" Nerrys's deep voice came out normal.

"Sure, Nerrys," Dana stepped back and gave the man some space.

Garren and Dana stood shoulder to shoulder watching Nerrys wait on line at a snack vendor.

Dana leaned close to Garren to speak quietly, "listen, Garren."

Garren peered into his friend's tan brown eyes.

"I was thinking, well, Lisza and Terriane will be at the Coronation Ball tonight," Dana said.

"Uh-oh, do I need to wear stronger pants?" Garren joked.

"Well, they seemed quite taken with your ... um ... embellishments," Dana suppressed a giggle.

Garren snorted.

"I was thinking we could hook up with them tonight, you know, invite them for a double date?" Dana leaned back to gauge Garren's reaction, his telepathic hearing didn't pick up anything. His common sense knew the idea was foolish, but he would risk it for Garren, sensing the man's intense need.

Garren became thoughtful, willing to swallow his pride to be with a woman.

"I have a friend with a water-craft out in Nihera Cove, we could skim the waves out there under the stars, drink a few drinks, make love to the girls; your last night planet-side and all," Dana smiled with a naughty gleam in his eyes, with Garren's help, he was sure the two of them could satisfy the girls.

Swallowing his astonishment, Garren said, "Dana, what a beautiful idea? Do you think they would really be into spending the whole night with us?" He felt overwhelmingly touched by his friend's thoughtfulness, "Dana, I don't know what to say!"

Dana drew out his PDA to send the invitation to the girls. He stepped to the side for some private conversation, the bustle of the Galleria crowd very light in the mid-morning was not intrusive. The crowd situation would alter drastically as time markers wore on; people all over the planet would be throwing parties in honour of the Coronation Ball. The Palace would be dishing out vegetarian feasts in the courtyards.

Nerrys rejoined them, two drinks in hand and one kinetically floating, he handed one to Garren and held Dana's, while the man was busy on the PDA. Jesse was nowhere in sight.

He seems recovered, Garren thought, thanking him for the chocolate drink. The drink was good, thought not as fantastic as Keyth's chocolate yesterday. Garren made a mental note to send a gift basket of chocolate to the 'would be' new parents. His face took on a smile, deciding if it was his place to break the news, it wasn't really, he just wanted to be the bearer of such wonderful news.

The sunlight glowed in Nerrys's amethyst irises, the fresh wind blew his hair about, and Garren bet Nerrys's hair never got to be so free on a normal day; for they had rushed this morning. The recent brush with tears made the tall man's lips softer and vulnerable looking. His eyes half lidded in the bright morning gave him a languid air, though, Garren knew for fact Nerrys had slept well last night and hadn't done any languid inducing activity. Garren felt uncharacteristically ... drawn, with a desire to kiss Nerrys full on the lips.

Garren shook himself briskly, sloshing some chocolate drink.

"Garren, I ...," Nerrys drew up to his full height and his expression turned very stern. Nerrys had a family history of being able to project sexual compulsion. It was damn illegal in these modern days. "Garren, I'm sorry."

"No, I'm sorry," Garren was totally confused. "I don't ..."

"By the Vale," Nerrys lowered his voice, "you are a gorgeous man." His only excuse for blurting such a thing was that his wife hadn't been in the mood for over 30 terra-days.

"Whah?"

"Um," Nerrys dumped the drinks he was holding into a nearby bin, deciding to bend to the whim, just this once. He put a palm to Garren's nape, under Garren's bound hair and moved his lips close. He brushed his lips to Garren's very sensuous lips, locking their mouths together.

Garren gasped into Nerrys's parted lips, taken literally by surprise; his intense need so overwhelmed him he began kissing back and lost his self-possession. He was kissing a 'married man' in a very public place. He almost pulled away, when Nerrys used his tongue to deepen the kiss, instead Garren locked his muscular arms around Nerrys and pulled their bodies together, moaning out of self-control.

"Nerrys?" Dana called, "umm, Garren? Umm, we have dates with Lisza and Terriane tonight."

"Mmm." Nerrys pulled apart slowly, touching his forehead to Garren's forehead before pulling away completely, caressing Garren's nape with his fingers. "Mmm, very nice," his eyes held a wealth of affection.

Garren swallowed, unable to marshal his thoughts into any coherency. His nipples were tightened, he sent up a prayer to the Goddess thankful for not letting his blood flood into his groin.

"Pretty hot friends," Dana remarked.

Garren blushed, his face hot with blood. With ill disguised relief, he motioned to the sight of Jesse returning with a strange companion.

Jesse walked, no, skipped, pulling his friend along. She was close to Jesse's height and perhaps his age, she moved ultra graceful and compact. She looked like a cross between a leonine Demon and an Elf, though, she wasn't a half Demon. She was of a race known as the Mynx, who lived mainly in the abandoned buildings of the old city. Her body fur was a light orange and her mane of hair a dark brown. She had a cute black button nose and whiskers on her elongated face.

The Mynx girl batted her sheathed clawed fingers at Jesse with playful familiarity.

&.

Dana had a private idea, now, of who was helping Jesse to train. The resources in the lawless Mynx population consumed not a little concern in Dana's mind. The Guards, nor almost the complete populace of Celesterra, did not venture into the labyrinth of abandoned buildings; if Jesse was going in there; GODDESS protect him!

℘

"Hey Dad," Jesse said, excitedly, "this is Miassa. She is my bestest friend."

"Your bestest friend!" Nerrys said in a voice reserved for talking to children, he offered her his wrist for a greeting.

She responded, very shy in front of the big Humans, and offered her wrist in return.

Garren thought she was adorable and he heartened at the obvious affection with which Jesse regarded her. Jesse spoke more, but his words were drowned out by a coach zooming in for a rooftop landing on the Galleria. The boy tried repeating himself, but three fastrafts and another coach vied for landing space, he shrugged and gave up.

Dana yelled, "the frenzy starts! They're insane, there 's going to be an accident if they don't take care."

The morning had worn on and Garren wondered if perhaps it was too late to do shopping.

"Come on," Nerrys grabbed the kids gently and hauled them back toward the Galleria. "Let's go inside and do what we came to do."

They tried a few different clothes stores catering to male styles. Garren remained passive, letting Dana hold up outfits against his body for whatever criteria Dana had in mind.

Garren only insisted he wanted pants.

Dana said, "why? You liked being pantsed by Terriane so much you want more?"

Garren conceded the point. The first thing he bought was a soft t-shirt, deciding to cover up his body for the day. It was still hard for him to imagine anyone getting excited over his half naked body. He never mentioned this to anyone from shame, but he was from a family of former Aristocrats. Among the society of his home planet, a combat hardened body was a sign of the lower classes. And since he'd started combat training at age 7, he'd endured plenty of ridicule. Actually, and Garren's face reflected these sad reminisces, the last two days were probably the longest span he could ever remember of being neither insulted nor ridiculed.

Dana observed Garren's mercurial change of mood with some alarm. He telepathically heard some of it. He shared a telepathic parley with a surprised Nerrys, Nerrys had not known of Dana's telepathic ability, but Nerrys had no guidance to offer.

"Listen Dana, do you want to meet up later?" Garren dragged his feet to a stop.

"No, let's stay together, eh?" Dana insisted.

"I'm feeling a little tired from all this trying on clothes," Garren insisted, just as stubbornly.

"We can nap at Nerrys's, right Nerrys?" Dana turned to their friend.

"Yes, absolutely!" Nerrys kinetically held up a bunch of clothes for Jesse, who couldn't make up his mind. Grandma's money gift only went so far.

Miassa was wearing a pretty brown jumper decorated with embroidered furry creatures, she seemed content with it, even though Jesse was insisting he buy her an outfit. Garren guessed she had little or no money.

Garren did not want to chance alienating his new found friends, but he was very ready for some alone time. He grit his teeth to endure the rest of their shopping trip.

The Fountain Park Galleria was an attractive shopping environment. The place was quickly filling with desperate shoppers. The black clad Guards in uniform were coming out in droves, too, along with some blues of the Juniors. He recognized several faces. The puckered face of one of Kraken's team peeked at him from behind a cologne display, and then moved on.

"I really have to sit down," Garren lost all heart in the shopping. "Can you just pick something for me? Charge it to my account."

"Hey Garren," Jesse's voice cracked. "There are some nice shady tables on the Plaza side, you want to go outside?" Jesse's air of concern so earnest, Garren's gloom broke a little.

"Aren't you still shopping?" Garren motioned to the floating clothes.

"We could use a break, too. We have time," Jesse shrugged up at his glaring Dad. "Miassa wants some ice slushee anyway."

"Cheery Cherry Cone," her strangely timbered voice added.

"Yum, cherry would hit the spot." Garren made sure Dana was okay with him going to sit down, while letting his friend do his shopping for him.

"Go ahead," Dana waved them away. He went into a huddle with Nerrys, discussing how to narrow down Jesse's selection to fit the budget.

Jesse held out his young hand to Garren, taking the Commander's hand, he led them out a side exit from the main Galleria lobby.

"Ahh," Garren sighed. It was much quieter outside and the tables arranged amid the terracotta plaza stones all had nice shady umbrellas against the sun's afternoon brightness. It was his first time in the area and he glanced around with mild curiosity. The far side of the Plaza had a few shrines set up for people to leave offerings. He found there was a shrine to Goddess Aphrodite and shrugging he decided he could use the feminine divine help.

"I'm going in there Jesse," Garren chin nodded.

"Okay," Jesse released his grip on Garren's hand. He had a knowing look in his eye that was out of place on a kid. "We're getting slushee ices, meet us right here at this table?"

Garren nodded and meandered off, thinking an ice might be better than going into some musty old shrine, but he was almost to the door. It was small as shrines went. A metal inlaid door stood ajar and he entered.

A faceless statue on the altar dominated the room, it had a suggestion of feminine curves. Dishes of incense burned dimly, the interior had no technological lighting and lit merely by candles and two flaming torches. Something in the naked flames touched a restlessness inside Garren. A small padded knee height bench waited invitingly for the prayerful.

He took up the invitation and knelt, he crossed his arms over his chest laying his palms open. He bowed his head forward and began beseeching the Goddess for some luck in his future. The incense smelled spicy and musky in a pleasant way. It was blessedly quiet and cool after the bright sunshine and loud crowd noises. He became comfortable enough that he didn't wish to move, yet eventually, move he must. He reached in a pocket for a few coins of the realm and dropped them in the offering dish.

The sound of the heavy door closing did not immediately quicken his danger sense. It should have.

XVII. Terra-Date 215.150 Morning
:: Flame and Claws. Garren ::

"Praying for a woman Command-DER Garren? Buying a woman, the only way you can get one?"

Ach no! Garren took his time to stand up and turn. Yep. It was Commander Kraken's team members blocking his exit. They were in uniform, which made them damn near invincible to Garren's hand-to-hand combat skills.

Did Cdr Kraken know what they were up to? Did they have their Commander's approval for their outrageous bullying? Was there something more sinister putting them up to harming him, someone from his home planet seeking to avenge an insult?

Garren measured his four opponents, if he could land a kick on their head, he'd have a chance. He wasn't good enough to get all four of them that way. Would they really try to hurt him?

"Waysixth, your surname has a familiar ring to it, don't it boys?" The Guard with a pinched face sneered.

Garren's heart fell, they knew of his Aristocratic background. He despised himself for it, how could he expect less from them?

"I don't have time for games today, lots to do," Garren paced the perimeter; the shrine was too crammed with five people.

"Oh, there is always time to play," another Guard cracked

his knuckles. He was nearest Garren.

Garren gave no indication of his intent, in the next breath he sprang into the air and landed a perfect roundhouse kick to the Guard's head. It was perfect aim and would have probably knocked the Human cold, but the uniform's helmet shield activated and Garren tumbled to regain his balance before they retaliated.

The Guards laughed, this was the kind of resistance playing they liked. They crowded Garren, pressing him into a corner behind the altar. Garren landed fist punches and kicks, but the uniforms absorbed all the blows.

"Are you winded yet? Need more practice?" Pursy sniggered.

"Practice, well, I do want to Certify later. Care to take the Exam with me?" Garren backed up as far as he could go in the small space. He had to trust that they weren't really planning on hurting him.

"Aww, is he trying to make friends with us? Aww," the biggest of the four Guards said this.

Garren winced and berated himself for letting his hurt show.

"Aww, we'll be friends with you Waysixth, did ya want us to spar with you?" He leaned too close for Garren's comfort zone.

"Ganging up on me when you're all in uniform is cowardly, don't you think?" Garren said quietly, intuitively he knew that if he tried acting out his Command rank, it would only incite them.

"Nah, let's keep our uniforms on, eh?" Pursy rummaged on the altar table.

There was some consolation to this; at least, Garren didn't have to fear rape from them.

"Well lookee here," Pursy held up a short knife, turning it to reflect the torch light.

"Put that down!" Garren ordered, "you don't know where it's been."

"We know where it's going to be," the big Guard sang. He

brought out a standard issue knife from under his uniform cloak.

"Two knives," Garren tried an arm twisting move on the big one. Again the uniform protected his target. There was no room to try a throwing move. Before he could contemplate any more plans, they were on him, grabbing his arms and legs, they dragged him through a hidden door behind the altar. They descended a sloping floor, going underneath the pleasant Galleria above. Garren struggled, throwing all his strength into it and began tiring. There were no torches down here and his night vision kicked in. He could see the smooth walls turn into rough rock. Oh no. He did not need anything reminding him of when he'd gotten lost in the Subterraneum.

Would Dana or Methusem have their telepathic ears open? Garren did his best to project a call for help. He tried a prayer to Aphrodite for good measure. He had more hope in Dana at the moment, had Dana heard?

Garren felt very vulnerable. He wore only a t-shirt and ship pants, the only weapon he had was perhaps the heel of his shoes. What were the knives for? Could he turn the knives on them?

They were coming to a turn in the pathway, at the end of this was a small room, it could be the basement of a house perhaps; they hadn't gone far at all.

"This is a nice place for some fun, ee heee," Pursy hoisted Garren up to reach his hands.

Garren re-energized his struggles as he saw the wrist cuffs. They managed to cuff his wrists together and his ankles, the length of chain between the ankle cuffs gave him enough line to spread his feet shoulder width apart; at that point, Garren would have liked his ankles chained as close together as physically possible. A hook was hanging in the center of the circular room from the underside of floorboards above. They draped the wrist cuff chain over the hook. Garren's heels didn't reach the floor, only his toes reached. His breath quickened. Where was help?

Should he mention that he could Writ them for this attack?

It could have the opposite effect of making them dump his body never to be found. Yet, he still believed they wouldn't seriously hurt him, there was a certain degree of bravado games among the Guard, had it ever gone too far? He didn't know.

The biggest Guard with the standard knife made to start cutting Garren's shirt.

"Hey, this shirt is brand new!"

The protest did no good, they looked at him with a look that made the belief they wouldn't hurt him evaporate in musty air. They sliced off his shirt, they cut off his pants, and then they sliced off his shoes. He yelled at them, for they made shallow cuts on his feet and shins with the removal of his shoes.

All the playful taunts weren't playful anymore.

"Don't move my little aristocrat," the big one said. "Don't want to get cut now."

Garren's fury made him kick, it only made them laugh and it made Garren more furious.

Pursy and the big Guard both used their knives to trace random lines up and down the length of his body. Garren felt small trickles of blood tickle his skin as some of the knife play cut him. All the cuts were shallow and were more irritating than painful. It felt like lines of ice trailing over his body, highly sensitizing his skin as the lines came close to areas like his armpit and knee back.

The third Guard who hadn't said anything yet, put his lips to a bleeding cut, licking the blood from Garren's skin.

"STOP!" Garren did not like it one bit. He started shaking with unspent fury, unable to land a kick or punch or even bite.

The last of the Guards raked his nails down Garren's skin, he knelt behind Garren and took some ass cheek into his mouth and bit down, leaving teeth marks.

Garren yelled at them to stop. "COWARDS!" He was now bitten, cut, and scratched, and he became afraid they could rape him with a knife handle.

The knife cuts were bleeding from everywhere now;

stomach, chest, his arms, legs, and back. The big Guard chuckled low as he started moving the knife into Garren's pelvic region and into the patch of hair near his groin. Garren kicked again, not caring if he got cut because of it.

The Guard behind him knelt again and took one of Garren's testicles into his mouth, bearing slowly down with his teeth.

Garren yelled at the top of his lungs in fury and humiliation. The teeth pulled painfully, but didn't bear enough to cause actual damage.

Was this after all, just a game? Garren's eyes burned crying without tears, not caring at this point, he just wanted them to stop touching him, wanted it to stop very badly.

"Before we leave you here," Pursy began; he slammed the knife into a wooden beam, until it stuck there.

"No," Garren panted in a tone of dread, "don't leave me here."

Guard number 3 pulled something black from under his cloak.

"Have you tried the new tawse yet?"

Despite all the bleeding cuts, Garren blanched anew. "You mean the new tawse that can drive a Human insane from pain," Garren whispered. He searched for a place in his mind to hide, a place not attached to his body.

"It's just a rumour, no one's proved it, YET." Pursy unrolled a limp piece of black rubbery substance. There were strange ridges chiseled in the implement. He paced around Garren's body, on the third loop he stopped behind Garren. Garren tried to turn and face him. The big Guard put his two meaty hands on Garren's thighs and held him still, his face too close to Garren's groin.

"You better not sit there, eh. He'll probably piss once he gets this on his Aristocratic arse."

Garren screamed in rage, shutting his eyes tight. 'They won't really do it, not really.' He cursed as he heard the whistle of the tawse on the air, just before the most incredible burning pain laid across his ass cheeks. Fire!

"The full pain doesn't blossom right away, it should hit one … two … now."

"Aaaa," Garren screamed and contorted his body as the searing pain filled all his awareness.

"Well, that's one, ready for the next fourteen?" The big Guard put his big hands on Garren's neck, holding his face still for his study.

"Here comes two," Pursy struck the next agony on Garren's ass with a laugh of pure glee.

Garren became consumed with hatred for these Guards as the pain drove any last ray of hope from his heart. O, it burned, it burned. It felt like his skin was trying to crawl off his body. Tears and sweat poured off his agonized body, the salt in his sweat stung in the shallow cuts from the knife, inconsequential compared to the fiery pain dealt from the tawse.

Guard number three warned of a light down the underground path.

"Do you think we should leave now?" The big Guard reluctantly released his hold on Garren.

"Mmm, our job here is done," Pursy made a show of leaving the tawse on the ground. "Let's leave our buddy here as an offering to whatever comes. Maybe you'll be lucky and get some sex play."

Garren didn't react.

"We'll leave this tawse here for who comes your way, eh? Tis a shame though, if we leave it we won't have it to use on your little friend Care."

Garren roused from his agony at those words. "You leave Care out of this. You'll get no mercy!"

"YOUR friends," Pursy drawled, "should choose their friends more wisely."

"NOO, COWARDS!" Garren yelled as they left him there naked, helpless, and bleeding; with only the approaching light for company.

He did his best to ignore the pain, after all they'd done to him, they really hadn't injured him. The blood loss from the shallow cuts was the worst of the physical damage and it was minimal. He remembered Keyth saying that the pain from the tawse was excessive, but caused minimal physical damage. Abandoning him there, for whatever came, was the worst crime they'd committed against him.

The light approached, ever brighter, Garren didn't trust it to be rescuers. He managed to hop on his toes, a few trial hops got him high enough to grab the hook with one hand, he swung there and managed to get the cuffs chain over the hook and he dropped to the floor, falling prone, because he was shaking so violently.

An unreasoning dread grew in his mind, he scrambled on his elbows and keeping his ass off the ground, backing up as the light arrived. He drew breath to scream, but there were no screams left in him to scream. The light came from two flaming eyes, the eyes belonged to a creature of silver fur and big shaggy head. It was naked and a horrible oversized penis lifted ready for a helpless victim.

Garren didn't have to be a scientist to recognize that this was the Demon Methusem had described yesterday. They knew it was roaming the subterranean passages. Why not show up here somewhere under the Shrine of Aphrodite?

Somewhere, Garren rediscovered his courage and he closed off the silent screams.

The Greater Demon Ariel bowed at the waist to put its face closer to Garren's, sniffing. "I thought I smelled Dragon. You smell of Dragon Magic, of Dragon King," its painfully low voice rumbled. "It pervades these passages. It drew Me here." It reared back, flames licked around its body, barely missing torching Garren.

IT laughed and Garren's courage faltered for an instant.

IT stood there considering its thoughts for a short while. It reached out a huge clawed hand to grab Garren's ankle and it lifted him and dangled him, examining him. To examine Garren more closely, IT used its power to undo the cuffs on Garren's wrists and ankles, before dropping Garren back to the ground.

Garren gasped, breathy with barely contained panic. He crawled on his belly and elbows to get away from the Greater Demon. He should be thinking of ways to destroy this Thing, no ideas came to mind. The thing laughed again and Garren trembled so violently he couldn't crawl anymore.

"You ... you wear your fealty like a stink, fealty to your Dragon Master. How loyal is your fealty?" Ariel spoke in a deep voice that made Garren's ears ring. "Would you take this flesh?" Ariel held his own penis in its clawed hand. "Would you take this glorious ravishment upon your body to spare your Master?"

Terrified beyond remembering any of this, Garren passed out cold. He lay naked and bleeding, and limp as a doll. So limp and unmoving, that when his unlikely rescuer showed up, Jesse thought Garren was dead. The young boy screamed in rage. He carried a torch from the shrine, Miassa stayed back in the tunnel, too afraid to come forward.

Jesse waved the torch threateningly at the Greater Demon, not recognizing IT for what IT was, not recognizing ITS power of fire element.

Ariel regarded the Human whelp and its fire dance. There was something familiar about this whelp, not a Dragon smell, something else, it would take some pondering to recall.

"What did you do to my friend?" Jesse cried, standing over Garren's body, waving the torch.

"I did none of this to your ... friend," Ariel deigned to answer. "Your own Human kind did this to him. Fear not little one, for your friend doth lives fleetingly."

The scent of the Dragon King on the prone Human was too irresistible to Ariel and its penis swelled to its full ponderous desire. Ariel approached Garren where the Human laid waiting,

Garren's unprotected ass inviting ravishment, raising claws to strike the boy away like an insect.

Miassa jumped like a spring, attacking the raised claw. Ariel flicked his claw and she was thrown, she landed harmlessly on her feet. Ariel lashed out with tongues of flame, she was too quick and escaped into the pathway and cart wheeled around a corner.

Throughout this attack, Jesse screamed his hatred at the Demon. Jesse swore vengeance at it.

Ariel raised a flaming hand to smite the young Human.

Jesse was the son of two powerful tele-kinetics, generations of tele-kinetics from both sides of his family tree. Kinetic powers didn't break latency in children, not until after puberty. It was an inkling of the man Jesse would grow up to become, that in his most desperate need to save Garren, he dragged the power within himself from dormancy. He was able to call forth his power and swiped a blow of pure energy against the Greater Demon Ariel. Jesse beat the kinetic force against Ariel, deflecting the fire attack and pressed the Demon backward.

Ariel got a whiff of something most unexpected, unexpected and exciting, and it decided on the role of patience. It decided to save its consummation of lust on the Dragon tainted Human for another time. It sped away from Jesse like a flame on a wind.

Miassa rushed forward, "Jesse, Jesse." She ran to him.

Forcing his kinetic power early came with a price, blood dripped from Jesse's nose. He dabbed at the blood with his sleeve. A small trickle of blood dribbled from his ears and another small trickle from his eye, he pressed his other sleeve to it and it staunched the blood.

Miassa purred encouragement at Jesse. He smiled at her purr, it was one of his favorite sounds.

A line of blood dripped down Jesse's leg, small internal hemorrhage leaked from his bowels and urinary tract. The bleeding was brief enough that they did their best to hide it, not even sure why he should, but Jesse had grown use to hiding his doings from everyone and it was habit.

"Garren," Jesse fell to his knees, remembering and railing at himself for tending to himself first. "Garren, Garren, Commander Garren." Jesse and Miassa stared dismayed at the lines of cut skin all over Garren's body. Garren's rear cheeks were a mess of broken capillaries and blotched bruising.

Garren stirred, very intense pain shocked him fully awake and he cried out.

"Garren," Jesse cried. "O, I'm so glad you're awake. Come on, we have to get you outside and get a healer."

"What? No, I don't need a Healer," Garren didn't remember anything after the initial strike of the tawse.

"Garren, it's okay. Let's get out of here first," Jesse tugged on Garren to get him up.

Garren gasped, when he tried to sit up. He looked down at himself, the light from the torches to Garren's night vision as clear as the full light of day. He had to acknowledge he understood Jesse's insistence for a Healer. But the Launch on Halçyon to Deep Space was only two days away. Any action on his part requiring testimony would make him miss the launch. He did not want revenge on Kraken's Team badly enough to miss it.

"Listen Jesse, please," Garren kneeled. "I can't go to a Healer, I can't report this, not right away. I launch in two days. I can't miss it, I could be left here terra-years waiting for the next Deep Space assignment."

"Garren, but, the Emperor has to know this," Jesse was only 12 and a half years old, yet, he could understand Garren was talking crazy.

"Please Jesse, No, I'll miss the launch," Garren repeated. "They'll make me stay for hearing testimony. Have you ever wanted something so bad that pain won't stop you?" He prayed Jesse would agree. "I'll report everything from space. Only two more days! Please?"

Miassa spoke up, she did not understand Garren's plea, but she understood his desire was stronger than his suffering. "There is a Mage Healer in Nihera City. One who will heal your hurts as if it never been. But she must be kept secret, you must not reveal her to anyone. And you must bring a tithe gift." Miassa cocked her head in a cute gesture. "She likes the pretty jewelry, bring to her and she will Heal."

Garren tried to re-think the whole situation. Was he insane? Here he was begging children to hide misconduct in the Guard. A Mage Healer sounded great right now. The agony on his ass was driving him to stupid decisions, he couldn't concentrate on any sane rationalization.

"Miassa," Jesse wrapped his mind around the details of the plot, dabbing occasionally at his nose during the conversation. "How are we going to get him there? If he takes a ship, they'll see him and know! And the Ball"

"O," Garren swallowed down an urge to weep, he was so very tired. "I really don't care about making the Ball."

"We have a Crystal-Magic Port-Way to the far side," she said with pride. "You cross the threshold and you are in Nihera City." Before leaving the area, she swept up the abandoned tawse and rolled it up to fit in her jumper pouch.

Though Jesse's common sense knew this scheme was irresponsible, they helped Garren to the Crystal-Magic Port-Way; it wasn't far from the shrine. Miassa explained that the shrines nearby the galleria, concentrated the Magic in this area. Her Magic knowledge was impressive for a young girl.

Their path took them through a basement storeroom and they snatched up a discarded table cloth they found for Garren to use as a wrap for his nudeness.

At the port way, a very thin light band drew a man sized oval on a rock face. Miassa gave Garren directions to the Mage Healer. Jesse promised Garren he would tell Dana he'd gone ahead to Nihera City, but not how exactly.

The children were half-way back to the Galleria, when a

radiant smile pasted on Jesse's face. His kinetic powers were finally his, he could sense it, touch and feel things with it. He felt fantastic, and no false sense of pride, it was real.

And as far as Jesse thought, he'd beaten down a powerful Demon. He would take down that sucker, just wait.

Care Ethaynen

Born Terra-Year:: 193

Race:: Human / Unidentified Non-Human

Special Abilities:: Classified Latent Unknown

Mission Specialties:: Gravity Skates
Independent Operative

Home Residence   Planet Celesterra

Oᴨ ᴛO ᴛHE FAR SiDE OF OVR PLaᴨEᴛ

XVIII. TERRA-DatE 215::149
Daylight on the Planet's farside
:: Nihera City, Care's impressionable first impression ::

True to Traci's word, Krizren had floated Halçyon to orbit, then to Nihera City. Going along for the ride were Care, Rhiannon, Minister Ange, Vylara, Emperor Methusem, and Starra. Vylara and Care both suffered a mild case of stomach ache from demolishing too many snack chips.

Care and Rhiannon had disembarked from Halçyon and were now strolling along the heart of Nihera City, enjoying a pleasant late afternoon bask under the summery sunshiny sky. They had gained extra sunlight time by landing on the far side of the planet. Care heartened at the gorgeous blue skies and wispy white clouds. Buoys marking the race route perched glittering in the sky going up and out over the Meridian Sea as far as the Human or Elf eye could see. Care jostled elbows in the crowd gathered here for the Rocket Races. Rhi had quietly cast some buffer Spell on his person and was not being jostled.

There were laws against Magic use in public thoroughfares. Rhi flouted these laws. Care couldn't decide if it bothered or pleased him, and not doing anything about it as a Guard made him criminal too. Oh well.

The gathered throng of people dressed in colors to reflect their favorite Rocket pilots. Children sat atop adult shoulders, waving pennants or holding on for dear life. The flavorful ice treats being slurped by many within his periphery had Care's mouth watering for one.

Huh?

Rhi was looking up and not at the Race Lane. The sea birds, too small and impuissant to be threatening wheeled in the sky, crying their melancholy caws. Two dark shadows passed over the crowd, shadows shaping a monstrous wingspan. Adults gasped and children cried out in pleasure. Care joined the gaspers as a pair of Dragons soared above, heading northward. Before Care could make out details of color and wing iridescence, the pair were already too distant. Woah! The Dragons only bespoke with Emperor Methusem, anyone else was potential appetizer. It was whispered that in the time of the conquest, Methusem had fed slavers to the Dragons, but no written history text confirmed it.

"Do you think Methusem's temper reaches here, even?" Rhiannon wondered.

A Human male next to them replied, "o it twas dismal weather here yesterday. The Palace hasn't offered any explanations and the Guards aren't answering any questions t'on it."

Speculation and rumour were spreading rampant amidst the city, nay, prolly the whole planet. Care shrugged. Now that you mention it, the crowd's general mood seemed a bit jittery, the adults anyway.

Suddenly, a clear voice nearby rang out, "hide the aphrodisiacs," and sniggered.

Care turned, almost recognizing the speaker, seeing a Commander he couldn't quite remember. Physically, the Human male had no distinctive qualities. The statement was clearly meant for Rhiannon's pointy ears. Rhi was either completely indifferent to the snide bait, or hiding any ill feelings well. Ungh, the name was on the tip of his brain.

The movement of a black uniform in the crowd drew his attention. Another Commander? Care quickly surmised that Commander Kerlin wasn't the only Commander at the Rocket

Races courting interviews.

How Care wished he was savvy enough to hack the Commander's Registry. He wished. He wished. Hmm. Could a law flouting, cool-headed Mage-Elf, hack the most highly encrypted database in the Realm?

Rhi quirked a quizzical eyebrow at Care's sudden unblinking stare. "I'm not telepathic Care."

"O yah, um," Care smiled beguilingly. "Are you savvy with computers?"

"No!" The most annoying Commander spoke up again. "He's savvy on computers, I mean lying on top of computers on his belly. It's what this Elf likes."

Care frowned. How did obnoxious idiots like this get to be Commander? Well, at least Minister Ange made a start yesterday. If it weren't for Rhi's buffer Spell, he'd plant a big wet sloppy kiss on the Elf. Answering this creep's snide bait would only make it worse, but Care was never one to be passive.

The Commander was studying Rhi, who was still ignoring him. 'Uh-oh'. If he detected Rhi using Magic, they'd be in big trouble. O no!

"What's this? Is this Magic I perceive?"

Rhi stoically ignored him.

"Answer for yourself," he scowled seeing Rhi's new epaulette pin. Apparently, Rhi's promotion had gone unnoticed by the registry monitors. "Well, Senior Guard?"

Rhi looked the Commander straight in the eye. "Yes!"

This Commander almost failed to hide his grin of satisfaction. "Do you know what the Discipline Writ is for casting Magic in a public thoroughfare?" He hovered so close to Rhi he was breathing on the buffer Spell.

Care was just about to step in between them when Rhi answered. "Why would it be relevant? It isn't as if I was casting Magic in public. Why would I care what the punishment is?"

"There is a Spell on you!!" The Commander practically shouted in an attempt to exert authority.

"Which I cast early this morning aboard ship in orbit, aboard the Halçyon in fact, far away from the public," Rhi retorted.

Care knew this to be an absolute completely totally blatant lie. His admiration for his Elf friend leapt to a new emotional apex. Rhi lied perfectly, which was kind of weird, since the Organization of Elf Affaires publicist extolled their virtues by claiming Elves never lied.

Fortunately, the Commander decided not to call out a truth testing telepath.

"And how long do you plan on wearing this Spell?" The Commander backed down.

"Well, obviously I can't dispell it here. I'll have to wear it awhile yet." Rhi shrugged with an air of perfect unconcern.

Care studied the Commander, who was still staring at Rhi as if he could stare down the Elf. Everyone on the planet knew you couldn't out stare an Elf. Care felt glad for the buffer Spell. There was a look in the Human's eyes as he stared, not blinking. A raw look of need, not exactly lust. It was time to whisk Rhi away.

"We got things to do Rhi," Care led Rhi away, pleased to find Rhi would let him lead them. The Commander didn't pursue them, the raw look in his eyes now veiled with something else. Did the guy take any responsibility for his obnoxious behavior?

Care felt his morale slip, two assholes in as many days. He cheered up when he remembered the fate of yesterday's asshole. His ass fired! Hah!

O! Care saw Rhi slump his shoulders. An emotion of supreme sadness seeming to weigh him down, only for a moment, then it was shrugged away to hide. Then and there Care decided, if Commander Kerlin declined Rhi's application, well, officially Care's docket still assigned him Rogue Fielder; he would use his freedom to bodyguard Rhi, until this mess within the Guard was fixed. Now he understood how Garren must have felt yesterday. 'Am I in luv with this Elf? Woah!'

All thoughts of love scattered as the first rocket moved into position for the race. It smoothly hovered in to take its position at the first lane pylon. What a beauty! The rocket had a snub nose, red and silver markings detailed a sleek body and fins. Care had no concept of what the spiraling fins did for a rocket; he hadn't done well in aerodynamics theory.

The whole antigravity science wasn't as sexy as combat classes. Care's technical major made him an expert in weapons engineering. His zippy little hand cannon was his proto-type. Officially, he was supposed to hand it in to the weapons lockup between assignments. He couldn't bear to part with it, so far, no one twigged he'd kept it and kept it secret. Did he actually trust Rhi enough to reveal it to him? 'Yeah? Woah!'

Many of the spectators in the crowd had their ear speakers and PDAs out; some wore the glazed air of the telepaths. Care did not care enough about the race to join them. He liked the rockets though. It was unnerving to watch the crowd 'ooo' or 'ahh' and seemed to sway in response concertedly to something invisible, though, of course, Care knew they were responding to the excitement of the rocket race.

"I can't tune in the soundtrack," a female voice nearby was saying. Her companion mumbled something.

Care wore a slightly bemused expression. A Human nearby noticed Care's expression and explained, "they race to a sound dub customized to match the racecourse; the pilots know when to bank and adjust acceleration by the beat of the music. It's more exact then relying on sight. Crescendos and all help."

"Ah, Ok. Thanks." Care smiled at her.

His interest shifted to a female standing by this helpful person's shoulder, feeling her interest in return, his body reacted in a positive way. Rhi took an interest, too. Not being in uniform made them off duty and raised possibilities. Or would she be too interested in the race? Had the pesky Commander gone far away?

She smiled winningly at Care and managed to include Rhi in the smile. Her blue lips, blue eyes and dark blue hair left her white-ish with blue undertones skin very pearly looking. She was slender with fulsome breasts and questionably Human. Care peered more closely at her hair, he couldn't tell if feathers were decorating her hair or if the downy feathers were part of her hair; silver rings tangled in the long strands, catching light from the noonday sun. Silver earrings dangled from her ear lobes, strands of silver decorated her neckline and wrists, each finger adorned with a silver ring with stones in topaz, amethyst, and citrine. The jewelry ensemble was very eye catching and pretty. A see through light pink smock dress gradually became more opaque and shadowy the further down it went; her feet were bare on the shiny stonework of the plaza ground. A nearby public fountain randomly sprayed a refreshing mist on them as they stood near it.

Her come-on was fast, even too fast for Care's experience, but she wasn't wearing the gear of a pro. Mebbe she was a prostitute taking the day off for the races?

"Um, who is the smile for sweetie?" Care winked.

She giggled. "Bozh you boys. I like zhe two boys at zhe same time."

Care almost jumped at this statement, spoken with no trace of shyness. Rhi giggled beside him. His Elfin giggle had a sweet sound to it.

"H'm? What do you think Rhi?" Care pushed his glossy locks behind his ears.

"Nah!"

"Huh?"

"There he is, over there," Rhi pointed to someone on an elevated platform, one of the pay per view vantage points for the races.

"You mean Commander Kerlin?" Care cried, voice cracking in excitement. "Are you sure?" This person was facing away from them.

"Yes. His hair, it's a unique shade of orangey-red," Rhi pushed his way through the crowded plaza, threading a straight line towards this orangey-reddish haired Human.

Care offered rueful apologies to the pleasant Blue Lady and followed his friend's lead, heart hammering, to Commander Kerlin. The next chapters of his life would be determined on the whim of this stranger.

The duo came only so close to the stairs leading to the platform before the crowd throttled their progress. Even the buffer Spell didn't help at this point.

"Ach, Care are you wearing your gravity skates?"

"Yeah, but we can't use them we're out of uniform..." Care trailed off. Rhi's expression said, 'don't be ridiculous'. "Well, alright, if you're ready to risk 75 whaps from a stiff paddle, I will too."

"Did you say 75??" Rhi drooped his posture in consternation. "I forgot the penalty was this severe on Celesterra."

Surprised, Care politely hid his reaction. He personally did not consider 75 whaps severe. Rhi's whole body language yearned up to the platform.

"I'll carry you," Care offered.

Rhi blinked at Care. "A very generous offer Care, but I'd have to cast a dispell, which isn't worth a serious flogging over." Rhi tapped his narrower than Human foot. "Ach, rotate it." Before Care could cry "NO", Rhi had already used his Magic.

Quicker than Rhi, Care activated his g-skates with a deft stepping motion, wrapping his arms around Rhi's slender waist, carried him aloft.

Rhi protested briefly, then yielding with grace he automatically rested his feet on the tops of Care's feet, taking the strain of all his weight off Care's arms.

They reached Kerlin very quickly. Their situation was compounded with Care realizing there wasn't actually room on the pay per view platform for 2 more bodies. He deposited Rhi and stayed on his skates, literally waiting for the local Guards on duty to come arrest him. Moments went by, yet no Guards showed up, this could mean none of the local guards were Certified for g-skates. And Kerlin, so intent on the race, hadn't turned or noticed them yet.

Taking his time, Care studied this Kerlin. Orangey-reddish hair? Personally, Care considered the shade more a ruby, especially; in this bright sunlight. Kerlin's hair was cut straight across the straightest of lines, the length reaching at where his under arms started and from what he could tell from this angle, straight cut bangs above his arched eyebrows. His hair was sleek and flowed wonderfully vital in the breezes. He wore a billed cap with the logo and colors of his obviously favorite racing pilot. On this warm sunny drenched day, his jacket had long sleeves with more racing colors; black, yellow, and white and black checkers. The pants were also in racing motifs. A belt encircled his waist; again yellow and black. Kerlin's head and hands were raised, binocs held steady and at length to his eyes. Care could see charm bracelets on both Kerlin's wrists; the charms were a collection of various racing emblems.

Care grinned; he enjoyed watching people who could totally immerse into their hobbies.

At this point in time, either a rocket had reached its finish line somewhere beyond orbit, or Kerlin decided to notice them.

Care felt a moment of panic, unreasoning dread, based on recent experiences.

Commander Kerlin checked out Rhi first. Who wouldn't? It gave Care another moment to study Kerlin more. Racing emblems decorated the front of Kerlin's jacket, racing emblem pins tacked the jacket collar. Care looked down and found the unmistakable blinking of g-skate lights on Kerlin's boots. Care's hopes soared up to the racetrack markers.

Reluctantly and with pounding heart, Care started the journey to meet Kerlin face to face, as his gaze reached Kerlin's belt buckle, shaped like a rocket racer, Care's hands went clammy and his breathing became shallow. Pins and needles sensations made him shiver. He reached Kerlin's face, meeting light brown eyes, two wells of intelligence and something else. What was it? Kindness? Care found Kerlin watching him with a warm welcoming smile softening Kerlin's lips.

Forcing his breath out, in, out; Care did something silly you never should do on g-skates. He fainted. The last thing he remembered was falling face first. And thinking: 'This isn't -'

♌
♏

Aloud, he mumbled, "- My best first impression."

"It surely was the most impressionable first impression," the unfamiliar voice had a teasing tone to it.

Care turned his head towards the voice by his shoulder, peeking under his eyelashes. Huh? *Groan*. The voice belonged to Commander Kerlin, seated on a stool beside whatever furniture Care was lying on. He weakly raised a hand to his forehead and discovered a damp cloth across his brow.

Kerlin lifted the cloth and replaced it with a cool damp one.

Where was the med-tech? Being med-maided like this by his maybe new Commander was major-ly embarrassing, nay, sort of fun. Care's sense of the ridiculous asserted itself. The cool damp cloth, "hmm, that feels nice ... um, can we rewind, reset this day and start over?"

"What? No." Kerlin's medium low voice held a note of laughter matching Care's. "Then the outcome of the race might change."

Care smiled cautiously, thinking; 'so far, this is the best Commander ever, I wonder what he's like in combat', as Kerlin leaned over Care to check a bio-monitor on the opposite side of the pallet.

Kerlin was dressed in a no-sleeve shirt of a wafer thin material, suitable for the warm weather outside, a deep royal purple, well; the new royal colour was actually blue. Kerlin's perfectly even trimmed hair flowed gracefully. The movement of Kerlin's reddish hair made for a fascinating study. His face shone smooth with the clear skinned pale complexion of a redhead, high cheekbones, eyes perfectly set in a heart shaped face, a narrow nose with a slight upturn, and eyebrows with a barest suggestion of an arch. Those brown eyes transferred their regard from the monitor to Care's face, holding alertness, kindness, and dancing merriment in them.

Somewhere in this sublimely rapturous study, Care came to realize he was falling in ultimate love with Commander Kerlin. But instead of thundering heart and sweaty palms, Care's heart beat with an increasingly steadfast strength, his nerves resolute with mind clear and ready for anything. Oh, and passion, it was there, the kind that burned self-perpetually and wouldn't make a nuisance of itself. Care never knew passion could have a life of its own detached from physical need.

Kerlin sat up from the stool, his movements precise and controlled, like an acrobat, the muscles forming shape under his skin, understated and solid, the motion of Kerlin getting up a gliding motion, an impression of flight about to happen.

A med-tech finally came in through a pair of whooshing doors, taking Kerlin's place, waving a scanner a finger's breath over Care's skin. "When was the last time you ate a meal?"

"Ate?" Care repeated absently.

"Yeah, as in food? The fuel that keeps us complex multi-celled organisms from dying," the med-tech spoke with a hint of sarcasm

"He ate some chips yesterday afternoon, at the least," Rhi said from somewhere.

Care craned his neck to find Rhi seated on a stool by the wall, a great wide window behind him, tinted against the sun's heat. "Ach." For the first time he noticed Minister Ange was with them. They weren't in a true med office. This must be a private lounge for the paying racing crowd. A chuckle came from Minister Ange; he was staring at the ceiling, lost in some private scheming.

Rhi left the room, the whooshing door stayed open. A buzz of voices came from the hallway, a dulcet female voice saying, "this is why females make better technicians." A male voice replied with high humour, "really, why is dat?"

"Cuz-cuz, we have more patience. If you'd read the instructions..." the pair faded away.

A loft covered half the room with a poled railing along the balcony edge and stairway. Kerlin went towards the railing, instead of using the stairs, he jumped to grasp the balcony's middle rail and swung his legs twice for momentum, then in an impressive display of gymnastics swung himself legs first up and over the upper railing to the upper level.

Propped up on an elbow, Care let his admiration show. The whole maneuver had been a song in motion, exquisite and graceful.

Minister Ange chuckled again. "You mean you have not read Kerlin's profile?"

Care shrugged to acknowledge he hadn't.

"Yet, you applied to his Field Team?" Minister Ange's piercing regard was very disconcerting.

"When I read the posting, it just felt like the right thing to do," Care shrugged again, meeting gaze for gaze without blinking, - like an Elf.

"Are you a Fore-Gleamer young Care?"

"I'm a dormant latent unknown," Care flopped on his back, pulling the thin coverlet to his chin, then added lamely, "I am not young, I'm 22."

The med-tech snorted. "Well, any rate, I can't let you up, until you eat something nutritious, unless you want an injection."

On the last, Kerlin came sedately down the stairs laden with a snack tray. He handed Care a mug of steaming liquid.

Care took the proffered drink. He really didn't want a hot drink, but accepted it with a polite "thank you", being waited on felt weird.

Rhi returned to the room, his pale skin looking even paler than normal; accompanied by Minister Ange's most able assistant. Care for the first time noticed the assistant was now wearing the emblem of a Jr Minister. She had to be the youngest ever.

Her demeanor was natural, so Care deduced the reason for Rhi's distress was personal and not a threat relative to life on their planet. 'I don't think Rhi's worried about my health to this degree'. Had Kerlin declined Rhi's application to the Field Team? What a quandary!

Vylara looked to Minister Ange, who smiled gently at her and nodded with a huge grin on his elderly face. The young female Elf's somber face hinted at a shadow of a responding smile, she touched a tentative finger to her Jr Minister emblem seeming to gain personal empowerment from the feel of her Authority.

Her dark hair was now gathered tight into a topknot with bangs stopping atop her eyebrows; the last time Care had seen her, her hair had flowed freely. Earrings with tanzanite stones were modest and tasteful weights on her ear lobes. Her petiteness gave her Elfin features a pixyish look, very cute. She reached into her mustard colored robe and pulled out a small titanium box. It was one of those boxes that were locked from the inside, an item popular with dexterous kinetics or dexterous Magic-users. The lid was engraved with the Royal Crest of Celesterra.

Kerlin made a small sigh, avidly watching her hands. "I haven't had the pleasure Milady Minister."

"Vylara," she blushed at handsome Kerlin. "My name is Vylara." Not taking her eyes from Kerlin's face, -a cute and sexy look, Care thought. - she tilted her face to the box and gently breathed on it in a low huff. They heard the inside latch click.

Woah! Care had heard of Breath Magic, but had never seen it in action. Interesting party trick! What could she do to his insides with her breath?

Vylara flipped open the lid and held it up to face Kerlin.

Care sat up to see what was inside. The inside was lined

with a twilight dark sleek material; five mini-pennants laid out in a perfect row, a matching row above these were 5 pewter metal epaulette pin settings. Four of the pennants signified Guard rank, the fifth signified Command-Second. In a ritual dating back to the beginning of Emperor Methusem's dynasty, Commander Kerlin would give these pennants to the applicants he chose for his team. The Guard would keep the pennant when accepting the assignment, or would return the pennant if declining. A Guard may not answer for a requisite two days, giving both sides of the party time to think their decisions through.

It would be Commander Kerlin's prerogative to appoint his Command-Second. Oooo, the epaulette pin setting for Command-Second was certainly beauteous. Care would like to pin that to his collar. His current epaulette pin would fit into the setting, his half indicating rank and special ability if any, the setting that would be the bottom half was engraved with Kerlin's Field Team initials. The Command-Second pin had a layer for the extra engraving. Very spiffy!

Kerlin touched a fingertip to the engraving, much the same way Vylara had touched her Ministry emblem. He was clearly having a moment, his expression rapt in quiet joy. "Awesome," Kerlin breathed.

Care bit back a startled exclamation. That breathed "awesome" told Care a few things about his maybe new Commander. He'd been raised in Celesterra City and was close to Care's own age group, perhaps ten terra-years between them.

A quiet chuckle of glee came from Minister Ange. "Well now," the Sov. Minister brought forth a similar box, but bigger, from his own vanilla coloured robe pocket. "Of course, your promotion is official." The Minister fell into his officious sounding voice, "I dare say, you will be requiring this for your uniform." He opened his box close to his chest, no one could see into it. He kinetically lifted out an epaulette pin before closing his box and returning it to his pocket. When Kerlin didn't approach him, he added, "Commander Kerlin, are you declining your promotion?"

With an alacrity that made them all laugh, Kerlin stepped forward, then shyly held his palm open to receive his brand shiny new Field Team Commander's epaulette pin.

"We'll dispense with the whole ceremony since you are not in uniform," Minister Ange's eyes twinkled. "I commend you with all the very best wishes of our Emperor, young Commander."

Commander Kerlin didn't protest being called young. "I..." Commander Kerlin bowed low and with arcane ceremony to the Minister. Jr Minister Vylara handed Kerlin's epaulette pin box to him again, because he'd forgotten to take it from her earlier. Kerlin repeated the arcane bow, this time to the Jr Minister. She giggled. The giggle turned the high-powered moment into a peaceful moment of pleasant camaraderie.

"Well," Minister Ange said with great regret. "We must return to Celesterra City to attend ministerial matters. The Commanders of The Halçyon are graciously ferrying us to and fro. We shall rejoin you on the morrow."

"For your Coronation Ball and ceremony," Vylara reminded.

"Ah yes, I dare say, hum, hem," Minister Ange's pale cheeks took on a blushing coloration.

XIX. :: Night in Mihera City.
Viglia
:: Care takes half the blame ::

"Have you appointed yourself Night Watcher or are you just practicing your Magic?" Care joined Rhiannon on the hotel's rooftop. Care's teeth gleamed in the moonlight, there was enough light that he could see the Mage Elf was still upset about something. He was confident he could coax his friend out of it.

Rhiannon looked at his toes.

'Silly', thought Care. Across the way was much more fascinating. A jetty on the coastline, very close to the hotel, shone bathed in light from the barely waned moon and the lights from the nearby Park. A pair of Dragons, at least thrice the mass of a Human or Elf, was sitting with their double wings folded peacefully betwixt their shoulders. The Dragons appeared to be deep in a speechless conversation, the occasional grunt or huff punctuating whatever point they were trying to make. A few Human sized figures stood pretty close. Too close! "Who is that down there?" Care asked his companion.

"Our Emperor conferencing with the Dragons," Rhi scuffed the ground with his boot, the lights from his g-skates twinkling happily in contrast to the Elf's mood.

"I can't imagine what a Dragon would want to conference about." Care chuckled. "I hope they aren't complaining about their diet."

Rhi managed to giggle, trying to imagine the Dragons at a table with bibs around their great necks waiting for a tavern wench to plop dinner plates on their table.

"Well?" Care moved close to see Rhi's eyes, the Elf's eyes glowed in the dark, Rhi had the loveliest aqua-green eyes.

"What?" Rhi stepped back, not yet used to Care's extroverted way.

Care moved again to reestablish the close eye contact.

"Are you going to tell me what is bothering you?"

"No," Rhi ducked away and pouted. "Not if I can help it anyway." He had a feeling Care would trick it out of him.

"Are you upset with me for fainting? You don't want to be on a Field Team assignment with me?" Care teased, or hoped he was teasing.

"Of course I'm not upset."

"Well, that is a relief," Care made an exaggerated show of mopping his brow. "Do you need sex?"

"No!" Rhi cried with some exasperation. "Not now, anyway."

Care whipped out his PDA from a hip pocket, the little screen winked in the dark of Nihera City. "If only I could hack the Commander's Registry."

"What? Why?" Rhiannon said.

Care hummed.

What a treat that would be! He settled for the Guards' General Registry, using the couple of hack codes he'd broken to access the Court Executor data. Click-click clack tippy tap. Uh oh. "Wait a tinker's dam, this isn't right. You didn't ride your g-skates out of a uniform, I did!" There was a Writ in the Registry for Rhi, a chastisement of 75 with a stiff paddle. It was a negligible Writ, but Care guessed Rhi's tolerance would be low.

"So, you were going to take a punishment that should have been meant for me and not say a word?" Care sounded teasing, hiding the seriousness of his question.

"Yes..." Rhi started to say – Care interrupted with a "tchd". Rhi continued, "anyway, I'm guilty of using Magic in a public thoroughfare, so I consider this getting off light." Rhi folded his arms on the roof-side's protective rail and buried his face.

"Aw Rhi," Care put an arm around Rhiannon's narrow shoulders and gave a reassuring hug. He clicked one handed into the PDA. "There, I petitioned to take half the Writ myself, I'd take more, but they only allow you to take half."

"Or thirds," Commander Kerlin stepped off the hotel inter-floor lift and joined them at the rail, squeezing between the two Guards. His gaze was drawn irresistibly to the Dragons. "Twenty-five each."

"Huh?" Care and Rhiannon said in unison. "But you're a Commander, you can't do that," Care continued. "It's too undignified."

"Is it?" Kerlin's question held a lot of humor. "Tonight is the end of my second day as a Commander." He mused. "Besides, it's been a long time since my last chastisement, it'll be a reminder for me."

Rhiannon stared out at the Dragons. Personally, he thought spanking and paddling were ridiculous ways to treat the Realm's Guardians.

"How did your interviews with the other potentials go?" Care tried to sound nonchalant, but failed.

"No body impressed me," Commander Kerlin sighed, then he winked. "No one fainted, it was quite dull."

"Aww," it was Care's turn to scuff his boot on the ground.

"Actually, the first time I saw Rhiannon here, he had collapsed, very bravely done. Hmm? What did I hear you say about hacking the Commander's Registry?"

It took a moment for Care to recompose himself. "Umm."
"Mm?"

This awkward pause reminded Care of why he was giving up the Rogue Fielder life. He was supposed to be quick thinking, in a Field situation his cover would have been blown for not having a ready answer.

"Umm."

"Take your time," Kerlin mimicked Rhi and let his chin rest

on his forearm.

"Well, I just thought that if I had access to the Commander's Registry, I could see which Disciplinarian they are going to dispatch, professional interest and all. You know I'm Certified, too."

"Yes, I read that in your profile ... in the Commander's Registry," Kerlin smiled towards the Dragons. "But being Certified yourself, don't you already have access to that info?"

"Ah."

"You're cute when you're caught out," Rhi giggled.

Care chuckled.

"Here, lemme see that," Kerlin held out his hand for Care's PDA.

Wondering if he had just destroyed his career, Care handed the little instrument over.

Commander Kerlin tippytapped at it and then handed it back.

With some trepidation, Care looked at the screen. "Woah!" A cursor block blinked, the prompt for the Commander's Registry log on said 'successful'. Oh Joy! He became so intent on scrolling the data, he didn't notice the Dragons taking off or the whoosh of their great iridescent wings.

"What do these little numbers mean?" Care bumped shoulders with Commander Kerlin to show him which numbers he meant.

"Those are your stats. They're supposed to help us Commanders put together a well meshed Team, though personality conflicts are inevitable."

"Oh," Care felt dismay. According to his 'stats', he was an undisciplined wretch.

"Don't worry, these stats were updated yester-terra-day. It looks like your involvement at Garren's hearing made you unpopular with some officials."

Rhiannon looked at Care, he hadn't heard about the hearing yet.

"Tch falaetin officials," Care almost let his ire divert him from the joy of reading the Commander's Registry. "I wish our Emperor would do something about them."

⅋

For a little while it was just the sound of their breathing, the ocean breakers, and Care's tapping in the night. The night time temperature felt very mild for an ocean side location. Rhi looked up waiting for Orbital Station Alpha Lunam to make its last pass for the night. He peeked sidelong glances at Kerlin. 'Would this Human allow a Mage Elf of his condition on a Field Team?'

β

"Woo hoo, Erin Tomick is on his way to do the honours!" Care announced happily.

"You know this person?" Kerlin stood up straight. "Let me see what the Registry says about him." To his credit, Kerlin admitted, Care handed the PDA over with little reluctance. "You can browse it again later."

Care looked for the Dragons. "They left?"

"Hmm," Kerlin said, deep into studying his PDA. "The Field Team Manual highly discourages having two Discipline Certified Guards on one Team. Erin is a minor telepath, minor kinetic, ah; and Certified for g-skates too."

"Care and I are both Certified for g-skates," Rhi said excitedly.

"Yes, I can see that, very auspicious," Kerlin winked, the wink went unnoticed in the dark. "Well, I'm not a sadist, lemme end your suspense." And he reached into his hip pocket and held forth two miniature pennants.

"Woah," Care and Rhi exclaimed for joy. They took a pennant each. The pennant symbolized a formal Offer of Assignment to Kerlin's Field Team. After the requisite two days, they would keep the pennants to Accept, or return them to Decline.

"So we're sorted then. Would you both accept an invitation

to have supper and drinks in my suite?"

And two very happy Guards followed their Commander to the Hotel's descending lift, wincing as their pupils constricted to the sudden light.

Methusem had just returned home to His Seaside Palace from his conference with the Dragons. Day was breaking and he disdained sleep for the day.

"Her Ladyship, Ysette of Galatea is here to see you," Princess Dawn announced, barging into Methusem's personal Royal chambers.

"An Ambassadress?" Methusem turned from his contemplation of holographic stellar maps. "I am not expecting a delegation from the Galatea quadrant. It is chaos around here without Minister Angélus managing my appointments."

His daughter, the Princess Dawn, peeked curiously at the stellar maps. Methusem waved a hand and the maps dissolved. "She is here as an applicant," Princess Dawn pretended disdained interest in Methusem's maps. "To petition for a position as your wardrobe Minister."

"Quoi? I need a new Minister of Royal Appointments, not a Minister of the Royal Wardrobe. Let Nuben assume the tasks." Methusem sank gracefully into a cushioned chair.

"Ole Nuben?! He can't even dress himself," Princess Dawn came close to pouting. She rolled her eyes and sighed loudly for emphasis.

Princess Dawn was an extremely pretty girl of 16 terra years. Her long sleek hair, gleaming with natural highlights was bound neatly atop her head into a fountain like spray of brunette, revealing her semi-pointed ears. Her blue eyes were keenly alert and full of curiosity. She was dressed in a white long sleeved top of silk and lace, white short shorts, white sheer leggings, and against her parent's wishes; wearing a pair of custom made gravity skates.

His daughter, Methusem did not have it in either of his hearts to scold her. He gazed upon her with great affection, Dawn and her twin's mere birth were a miracle of nature; descended from a Mer / Dragon on Methusem's behalf and an Elf / Human from her other parent.

"Should you not clear it with me first, before you create a Minister position and advertise?" Methusem mildly scolded her. "You think I need a wardrobe assistant?" He added with some doubt.

"Methusem!" All his children call him by name. "That plain tunic you're wearing fits about as well as a spud sack from the hydroponic farms." Princess Dawn sounded like any other teenager in Human history embarrassed by her parent.

"Fine," the Emperor caved to daughter pressure, just like any Dad in Human history. His soft voice lilted in his exotic accent, "you interview her and you attend to all the details."

"Fine, I've already met her. She is great for the job."

"Fine, then the two of you can put your designer senses together and buy me something to wear for Ange's coronation ceremony."

"Methusem! I love you," she sounded a mite wistful.

"I love you too Princess," he rose from his satiny cushioned chair to kiss her forehead and with great tenderness he brushed her fringe of wispy bangs to press his chin to her cheek; memories of her baby smells now supplanted by her expensive perfume.

"Methusem? Do you think I will ever have Dragon wings like you?"

He briefly listened for the Great Knowing, it remained silent on the subject. "I do not know, luv." Methusem moved to his writing desk and sat gracefully on a stiff backed seat. "I have to tell you, unsheathing wings is extremely painful, I dare to hope you will be spared. Are you not happy on your g-skates?"

"Well yes. But! Your wings are so pretty; prettier than the Grand Dame Brynnhilde." Her smile was teasing. She was not too naïve to be aware of the effect the Grand Dame had on males, even on the cute Guards. She sat, fidgeting restlessly, waiting for Methusem's full attention.

"What is it, my daughter?" Methusem waved a computer quill.

"Those were maps of Tarraconensis just now."

"Maybe twas, maybe twasn't."

"Are we going to conquer Tarraconensis, next?"

"Mm," Methusem made a noncommittal noise.

"Planet Tarraconensis is in the middle of the Outlaw's Badlands," Dawn said, overeager to prove to Methusem she was no slouch. "If we conquer the planet," she sprang to her feet to pace the room like a campaign veteran, "we would be dividing their territory in half. On the other hand, we will be vulnerable from both sides; it will be difficult to protect our borders. Do we have the reserves?" She pounced eagerly on Methusem, leaning over his desk where he was scribbling onto a computer screen.

Methusem quirked a smile, trying very hard to resist her wiles, she was like an ancient feles sitting on the book you were trying to read.

"Are you auditioning for a Fleet posting?" Methusem used the fluffy end of his computer quill to tickle Dawn's nose. She crinkled her nose. "Now there is a thought. I do need to create a rank higher than Fleet Commander, someone for them to be answerable to. And I have just the Human in mind … when he comes back from his Rogue Field assignment." He shooed at his daughter to get her off the desk.

"Methusem? Do you want me to join the Guard, so I can help?"

"My daughter, your offer is most generous. Actually, I was rather hoping you would consider a governorship over one of our planets. I trust you to look after the best interests of our civilians."

She smiled, overjoyed at the praise, and then she realized what it entailed. "But that means I would be living on another planet, away from you!" She moved close to tears, the mercurial moods of a 16 year old.

"By then, you will be old enough to travel the corridors. You would be only footsteps away."

"Woah, really? ... I could open a portway with crystal Magic." Princess Dawn clasped a palm around her dainty crystal pendant.

"Dawn," Methusem admonished, "you should trust your own Magic. Not the crystals."

"Yes Methusem," she said, not at all sounding heedful.

Methusem sighed and watched her pace around his chamber.

His chamber was full of antiques, situated on the top floor of the Seaside Palace. Down the hall was the Eternity Chamber, a circular room where he could randomly view his Realm on real honest glass. Directly across the Hall two guest rooms sat empty, also very old fashioned. Methusem made a mental note to ask Minister Hannah to update his private decor to reflect the modern day.

"Methusem, I want to use my power for the good of our Realm," Princess Dawn stood at attention, clasping her hands behind her back.

"Which power?" He got up and took a seat in front of the fireplace.

"I'm a catalyst. I can activate latent powers in the Guards." She said, even though Methusem was well aware of what a catalyst does.

"Sweetheart," he put an around her shoulders and drew her close as she sat beside him. He cast a quick little fireball spell to start a cheerful blaze in the fireplace hearth, dispelling the morning chill. "We are not so pressed to force latents into their powers. People will embrace their abilities at the time they are ready, and sometimes," he gave her an extra squeeze, "especially in the case of Humans and Elves, the time never comes."

"You always are so very wise Methusem," she kissed him on the lips, resting in his arms, the most comforting and protective place in the meta-verse. "I guess I would get angry if someone forced me into abilities I wasn't ready for." A voice of the Great Knowing touched her, she startled for it was a family gift that rarely touched her. "That is what the Empresses of Catharra did to you, wasn't it? They forced you into your power." She hid her face in the crook of Methusem's neck, horror struck, grasping him tightly; despite her education and maturity, she was still only 16.

Methusem felt quite abashed, he would never have revealed this to her. "Yes, they came and took me from my birth planet and dropped me on Ancestral Earth. Into circumstances so brutal, I came into my power very young." He hugged his distraught daughter. "Shh. Tis a great consolation for their plans have failed."

"What plan?" Dawn whispered.

"Once I claimed the Throne of Prophecy and ruled Celesterra, they came seeking marriage; believing they would take control of our Realm. As you can see, it did not and will not, ever happen. Hush and do not dwell on history, twas two centuries ago."

There came a small commotion outside his chamber, the new door Guards announced Minister Angélus and the privacy curtain fluttered aside to admit the Minister and his Assistant Junior Minister.

"You are returned early from Nihera City? Did you lose your money on the Rocket Races?" Methusem smiled warmly.

"Indubitably, indeed," Minister Ange bowed from the waist to his Emperor and Princess. He was holding a computer tablet under one arm and Vylara was holding a bundle of velum and folders in her arms.

"Oh, the hotels, you know, at Nihera City are quite booked, you know, what with the Rocket Races and all, so, I took the liberty of engaging the Royal Suite for our new Field Team Commander, Commander Kerlin," Minister Ange's clear blue eyes took on a sparkle. "And I took the liberty of securing a chamber with Palace funds for one of our Field Trainers, Guard Donné. He's worked quite tirelessly and is deserving of some quality leisure time. I hope you don't mind my presumptuousness in these matters?"

"Not at all," Methusem grinned. "It is not like you are practically throwing Donné into Commander Kerlin's path."

"A-hem," Minister Ange readjusted the computer tablet he carried. "It's quite handy to travel with Halçyon able to flit to orbit and to the farside in no time. We came back to attend a few matters and then we shall be returning to Nihera City for the party."

Vylara shyly smiled behind him, obviously, happy to be going to the Coronation Ball.

"And where are you taking your office?" Methusem nodded at the bundles of paperwork.

"Well, you know, I am most honored by my recent appointment, tis wonderful and enjoyable. However; in order to really concentrate on matters at hand and to settle such matters in a timely manner," Minister Ange paused to take a deep breath.

Methusem took the opportunity to interject, "petitioners are driving you out of the Palace?" It wasn't hard to surmise this, yet, the Emperor hesitated to discourage petitioners. You never know when something brilliant would present itself. Methusem did not have the born imagination of Humans and Elves and he required their initiative for the growth of Pan-Jupiter.

"Ah yes, quite right," Ange bowed again.

"Do you want me to carry that for you Minister?" Vylara gestured to relieve him of the computer tablet.

"O, Vylara, very gracious, we can both see you have quite an armful already, I can handle carrying this, in fact; I'm sure I could take some of those folders from you." He reached to kinetically take some of her burden, but she tightly held to the files.

"No, I have it under control." Vylara protested.

"Ahem, well," Minister coughed politely. "Well, well, we stopped here to inform you there is a Rogue Fielder returned from extra-stellar tour, he is quite anxious to interview with you. I came here myself, otherwise; he would have to wait on protocol delays."

"Samson is back?" Methusem leaned forward. He kinetically doused the fireplace fire for the risen sun was quickly warming up the day.

"Not Samson," Minister Ange apologized. "It's Guard Tamkin; he was traveling undercover in the Merchant Navy."

"I shall interview him today." Methusem laid a hand on Dawn's knee, "and what are your plans today Daughter?"

"I'm going on a study tour of Goddess churches today," she shrugged, knowing it sounded silly for a moderner to be into such things.

"And where are you taking your office today?" Methusem said to Minister Ange.

"We're going to the park, not very imaginative surely, we just need a few marks peace to get this lot sorted," Ange shrugged. Vylara looked pleased to be included in the 'we'. A pompous Minister like Minister Allons was always 'I' this and 'I' that.

The Minister and his Assistant bowed again before taking their leave.

Princess Dawn giggled and leaned close to Methusem's ear. "Do you think he has any idea how Vylara feels about him? Her love is so sweet."

"Our dear Minister ...," Methusem left the sentence unfinished.

ॐ

"Illustrious Highness!" Her Royal Highness Princess Luna hurried into her parent's private suite, carrying a toddler held snugly in her arms.

Princess Luna was the identical twin sister of Princess Dawn. Physically, they resemble each other to the point no one could tell them apart; however; their demeanor made them individually unique, Luna was the more serious and quieter of the two.

Today Luna was dressed as befits a Princess, her ivory gossamer lace gown swept to her feet hiding her slippers and a dainty understated tiara neatly graced her long black hair.

Methusem gave his daughter his immediate and full attention, his children usually addressed him by name; for her to call him by title meant she must be very upset. He did not recognize the Elf child Luna held, the utterly terrified little girl circled Luna's neck with her arms. Meth recognized the child as an Aramys Elf, a race of Elf native to the Empire of Catharra. Methusem was evolved enough not to transfer his bitter hatred of the Catharran Empresses to the child.

It was times like these Methusem regretted some of his youthful decisions. He had worked too long at suppressing his gleaming powers that it did not come readily to him now.

Princess Dawn went to stand near her sister.

Emperor and Princesses, all three being powerful telepaths, dispensed with audible speech and switched their conversation to telepathic subspeach.

"How did this Elf child come to be here, Luna?" Methusem besaid.

"I granted their ship permission to berth in the bay," Luna projected this with apology. "They came in with your Rogue Fielder," she quickly added before her parent could scold.

"Minister Ange mentioned an anxious Rogue Fielder had come in," Methusem made sure only his clear and calm thoughts telepathed across.

"There are more children, fifty-four in all. They desperately need asylum," Luna bespoke, fighting back tears. She took a deep steadying breath.

The little girl tucked her head under Princess Luna's chin, but kept her gaze on Methusem. Many children shared a strange fascination for him as if an innate instinct in children sensed his Dragon King Magic.

Dawn put her arms protectively around her sister and the child.

"Methusem," Princess Luna besaid, a wash of emotion telecrossing this plea, "I pray you will grant me means to start an orphanage for these children; at least, until you can act on their behalf."

Methusem was not exactly sure where this was leading, but he could not deny his daughter. "Granted ... and I appoint you Minister of all Celesterra orphanages. Hire whomever you need." He kissed her face, brushing away her tears. The little Elf girl put her pudgy little hand out to touch Methusem's cheek, staring at him with a single-mindedness that might have unnerved a Human.

"What of this ship's pilots? Can they explain their need for asylum?"

Princess Luna closed her eyes, making Methusem and Dawn feel heartsick even before she bespoke. "There was one pilot, she died; our medics didn't get to her in time."

"Died? ... Died?! ... Someone died?" Methusem said this aloud.

"She made the final sacrifice to bring these children here."

Methusem brushed his fingers over his eyelids and sent a telepathic call to his Rogue Fielder, finding him eating in the buffet hall, bidding him to come and report. Aloud he said to his daughters, "please, do what needs to be done to care for these children." The twins and the Elf child departed silently.

The Emperor of Celesterra clenched his fists in a Human like gesture. He did not have the Fleet resources to fight a war; not with the turmoil in the Guard, morale at an all time low, and a brand new untried Minister of the Royal Fleet in charge of manning his newest and brightest Ships of the Line. And the new hospital ships still in drydock and unequipped.

But, whatever was chasing children into the night of a foreign Empire to seek asylum; well, he would have to manage a way to wage this fight. Somehow.

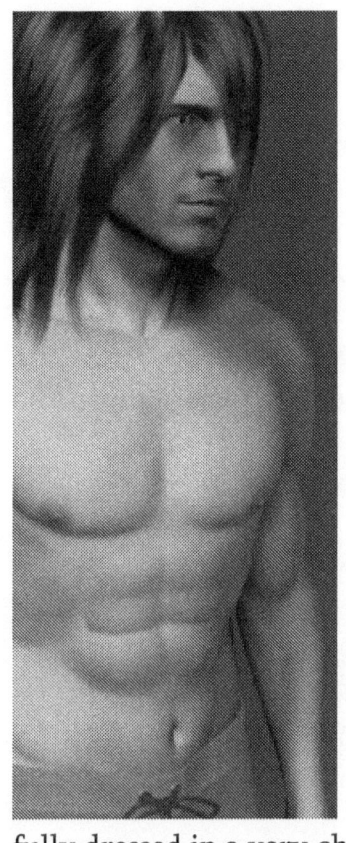

XXI. TERRA-DATE 215::150
Dawn
:: Nihera City, Care ::

"Wake up Rhi, let's go check out the sights," Care gave Rhi a shake.

"Go AWAY!" Rhi turned over.

"Are you going to just stay here and brood all day?"

"I need extra rest after I cast spells," Rhi mumbled and drifted back to sleep.

"Oh," Care said lamely.

A curtain whooshed aside and Kerlin came out of the bathing room fully dressed in a very chic racing motif.

"Nice suite you have here, I can't remember if I mentioned it last night" Care remarked.

The hotel suite had a balcony overlooking a park. Full length windows slid open to the balcony.

The bedroom had two big square beds with room enough for four people a piece; the beds were undressed in blue and white satiny linens and rumpled from being slept upon.

There was a lot of blue in Nihera City, probably in honour of the colour of Emperor Methusem's Aura Spectrum. It could have been worse; history texts say purple used to be the Royal colour.

A computer screen took up most of one wall, the better to watch the races with; if you did not want to go outside, in truth;

from outside you only saw the start of the race. The rockets aimed straight for orbit navigated strategically placed obstacle pylons guiding the way. The racecourse ended somewhere near the Emerata Vale.

Kerlin went to Care where he sat on the bed, fidgeting with a bracelet. "Care could you help me with this?" As Care cheerfully fastened the clasp on the racing motif charm bracelet, Kerlin added, "gotta envy the kinetics, bet they don't have trouble with jewelry clasps."

"Actually, it takes a very skilled kinetic to handle something this fine," Care finished the job and let his fingers brush the little charms of different rocket models.

"You're pretty savvy Care," Kerlin complimented. "You are an excellent choice for a Field Team."

Care ducked his head, "aww." He waved jauntily as Kerlin started to leave the room, so jaunty Kerlin paused to ask, "Whah?"

"I am really looking forward to today," Care jumped to the bed Rhiannon wasn't sleeping on and started giving the mattress motion stabilizers a workout, jumping high enough to touch the ceiling.

"Today? The Coronation Ball?" Kerlin guessed.

Care shook his head, negatory.

"Um," Kerlin cocked his head in a cute gesture, and then chuckled. "You mean the visit from the Disciplinarian?"

Care grinned. He was fond of Erin and if Kerlin offered a team position to Erin? Woah, awesome!

"Well," Kerlin's brown eyes danced in merriment, "he's coming HERE to administer the Writ, so let's all be here by Mark 13. I have time to catch a few races. Cya later!"

Yeah, it sort of sucked that his third of the Writ only called for 25. 'Would Erin bend the rules and dish me all of Rhi's 25?' Guessing the Elf had a low threshold tolerance, though he didn't think Rhiannon would go for it, Care could already tell the Elf was pretty stubborn.

Mark 13, hmm, it was only 5. What to do with himself? A fresh pay deposit waited in his money account, some souvenir shopping could be worthwhile. Money unspent was money wasted. Nothing like junk! And he hadn't found an apartment to keep his junk. Before his Rogue Assignment he'd roomed with Guard Jace, Jace was sharing with Jenny now and he doubted Jace would want male competition living with them. Care had heard gossip that Emperor Methusem had pardoned them for being in the station lounge when the Planetary Alarms went off.

Care jogged to his own hotel room for a change of clothes. He thought about giving up his room, since the hotels must be booked, he decided to hold the lease in case a friend needed it. He dressed in pale brown shorts and sleeveless top, wishing he had something in racing chic. Oh well. He checked himself in a mirror. Sunlight bathed the room and emphasized his yellow irises, it was Care's eyes that betrayed the fact he wasn't entirely Human. He had never met his parents, had no idea who his family might be, genetic tests were inconclusive. Care never worried about it. The Guard was all the family he would ever need. His friend Krizren had once tried to after-gleam his past for him, it didn't help; for it showed only his parentless childhood. Krizren's gleaming limit reached to twenty terra-years.

Ahh, mysteries, Care smiled to the mirror. If he had a chance, he'd like to delve into Garren's mystery. There had to be more motive behind the hostility directed at Garren than Garren's semi-charming personality, he liked Garren, even if Garren was a TRIFLE off-putting. Care snorted. It would make Garren a great Fleet Commander.

He heard kids screaming from outside. He opened the balcony door and leaned over the railing. The swimming pools were all on this side of the building, occupied to the max by playing tourists. From this view, he could see the jetty where the Dragons had been conferring last night. He'd never met a live full blooded Dragon. Would they be walking around the souvenir shops buying souvenirs? A chill of excitement thrilled him.

Not wanting to waste another mille-mark, he activated his g-skates and glided over the railing and down to the stone paved pool level. Knowing Erin was in town to dish discipline gave Care an incentive to invite trouble, especially, with a fantastic Commander like Kerlin, Care was pretty confidant Kerlin wouldn't care how much trouble he got up to as long as it was harmless.

Some of the children witnessing his skating waved enthusiastically, screaming their encouragement. Parents smiled, too. It was hard not to show off, though he was no way near as fancy a skater as Dana. Hmm, could he coax Dana to the city early? Dana surely wouldn't miss the Coronation Ball.

'Woah, is that ...?' Care did a double take as he recognized one of the swimmers. It was Starra climbing from the nearest pool; a fair Elf female, she was barely age forty, pretty, blonde, and very pert breasted. Her bathing bottoms were a collection of pink strings, very fetching on her. Last he'd heard, she was assigned to the Astrogation Console serving under Commander Bel. She'd been along for the ride on Halçyon yesterday, she'd ended up spending all her time with Emperor Methusem and Care hadn't had opportunity to chat with her. Did she have an Empress fantasy?

"STARRA, STARRA," Care shouted. He skated up to her, braking with his fanciest move.

As she recognized him, her face lit up with pleasure. "CARE! Oh, it's soo good to see you." Her arms wrapped around Care for a tight hug.

Care felt the strength in her arms, you couldn't tell it

without experiencing it. She pulled back a little to plant a flurry of kisses on Care's face. She was a very affectionate girl. Care couldn't stop hugging her, o, he was crazy about her. He only stopped, when the kids started pointing at them, teasing and singing, "kiss the girl!"

"So," her high voice took on a teasing tone, Care was Starra's favorite Human to tease. "That was you skating, out of uniform! Are you inviting it again?" Starra knew exactly what Care was into, sharing some of it.

He laughed in answer, he knew she knew.

"Are you staying at this Hotel?" Care asked with high hopes.

"No, but close by. I'm here for the pool," she shrugged one shoulder. Her hair was drying quickly in the bright summery morning, her ringlets were appearing. Her neck looked really too slender to hold up all those tresses.

Care curled a strand of it around his fingers, peering into her upturned blue eyes. She coyly bit her lower lip and blinked her eyelashes at him. She spoke softly, "I have a lovely new very stiff hairbrush."

Care let out a long sigh that made her giggle in delight. When Starra talked about hairbrushes, she didn't mean she wanted her hair brushed.

She playfully pulled on the waist band of Care's shorts, tucking her fingers in against his mocha brown skin, smiling unabashed. She had a small space in between her front teeth, which in Care's opinion gave her smile a planet's worth of character. Her pointed ears were a midge longer than average and her hair curtained apart by her ears. She usually wore her hair gathered into a topknot, all her glorious ringlets cloaking around her, it was a treat to see her hair down. Ooo, he wanted to kiss her ears.

"Anyhoo," Starra winked an invitation. "I'm staying at a charming tavern inn called the Rusty Wheel. It's very historical."

"Wheel? You mean those round things?" Care knew

perfectly well what a wheel was, he just wanted to see Starra roll her eyes at him and he wasn't disappointed. He laughed with high spirits.

"Want to meet me for breakfast? My treat? Say in three marks?" She gave a fresh tug on his waistband.

"What time is it?" Care deliberately delayed an answer.

She knew Care was going to say yes. "It's mark 5.30."

"Mm," Care stared up at the blue sky as if thinking about it. Was she falling for it? "Is there a hairbrush in the offer?"

"There is always a hairbrush," Starra giggled. "For you!" She dropped her voice to a husky timber and rose on tiptoe to peer very close into his gaze as she said, "oh, yes, a very stiff brush!"

"Okay," Care laughed, as if he hadn't been holding out on her. "The Rusty Wheel? Charming."

"It IS," Starra slapped a backhand on his stomach. She moved away without so much as a cya later.

What a gorgeous day!

People were really enjoying the summer morning. It was early for most non-morning people, but just about everyone had some plan to celebrate the Coronation Ball in the evening. The anxiety Care had sensed yesterday seemed to have evaporated. Everyone knew Emperor Methusem would be arriving in the city soon today; the Emperor's presence bestowed a sense of safety and security to many.

Care strolled in the general direction of the Merchant's Quarter, the oldest and most historical section of Nihera City; he learned this from reading a mounted street plack. The city had originally been founded by a species now extinct for hundreds of terra-centuries. Their descendents survived to the present day in Hybrid-Humans, people like Dana, or perhaps in Care's own genetics. Genetic testers were baffled by Care's genetics; his ancestor was something obscurer than Dana's; yet, they didn't classify Care as a Hybrid like they did to Dana. Hybrid usually meant sterile. As far as Care knew, his own workings were fertile.

There was only pedestrian traffic on the streets of the Merchant's Quarter. A very limited fastraft circuit was the only means of transportation and it was designed discretely to minimize distraction from the historic ambiance. The streets were rather tight and the shops narrow and standing shoulder to shoulder. Care enjoyed it immensely. A sense of excitement pervaded his morning, owing to the promises of Starra. In his moment of personal sublime rapture, a danger sense prickled his nape hairs. Huh??

He became instantly alert, but did not see anything disturbing.

A very short Medusan child ran up to him, pushing a token at him. "Token for the Goddess Aphrodite, Sir. Free prayers, Sir." Little snakelets lay content around the child's head, a few yawning in adorable affectation, not a hiss on his head.

Care pushed the token back at the kid. "No thanks. I prefer my life WITHOUT divine intervention."

"Sir, Sir, Tis the Goddess of Luv!"

"I don't need it, go run along and bother some other gullible tourist," Care became mildly annoyed.

"Free Sir, Free prayers!"

Care moved on, rude, yes, sometimes you have to be with the pushy types. He took notice of uniformed Guards gathered under the awning of a pastry shop, he decided to go chat them up.

The Nihera assigned Guards were friendly enough, smiling and recommending Peppered Brioche to be followed by soothing Berry Swirls. "Mmm," Care beamed. The Berry Swirls were warm from the oven, bringing out the tartness of the berries. A witch brewed Mocha Latte layered his palette over the sweetness of the pastries. He peered at the signage. The little pastry vendor called itself the 'Luv N Ov N', a painted picture of steaming brioche loaf underscored the lettering.

It was a pleasant conversation with the Nihera Guards. They talked about the races, women, the new tawse, and

Dragons. Sometime in the conversation, Care noticed the nasty Field Commander from yesterday in the street talking to the Medusan kid. Care casually asked one of his companions if he recognized the Commander.

"That's Barett," the Guard said with derision.

"Barett," Care repeated. Now he remembered, Barett was originally from Quinterra, the same planet Garren hailed from. Was he accepting Aphrodite's Prayer Token? Should he follow the Commander? What could he possibly learn? "Hmm."

"Hmm, what?" Care's breakfast companion asked, biting down on his fourth Berry Swirl.

"I wonder what he's up to? I don't trust him," Care admitted, perhaps not wise to say out loud, curious to know what the local Guards thought about the obnoxious Commander. He gulped down the rest of his mocha latte and prepared to leave the shade of the pastry shop awning.

"His team is pretty awful," the local Guards were in concerted agreement on this.

"Just don't use your g-skates, out of uniform, eh?" One of the Guards mumbled around a hot bread roll.

Care grinned wickedly; he twitched his feet and glided up, hugging the building wall.

One of the watching Nihera Guards slapped himself in the forehead, he pulled out his PDA, and started a Writ.

"Yes," Care congratulated himself. There weren't any shadows to hide in up here for tailing Commander Barett. He would be better off on the ground hiding amid the crowd.

The trail led to the local Shrine of Aphrodite, it was located in an out of the way courtyard off Delaine Rue. A quaint public water fountain took up the center, tourists dipped their hands in to pat down their faces with the fresh cool water. The summer sun heated up the morning.

Care contemplated going inside the Shrine or waiting outside. He was out of uniform, then again, his clothes made him out to be on a casual stroll. He decided to go in, he cautiously stepped through the arch of the Shrine's entrance. Huh? The small room was empty. Where had the Commander gone?

Hanging fabrics decorated the walls, brushing them aside one by one, he found a hidden door. He hesitated again. On a Rogue Field assignment, he would have went straight through, today he was on vacation, darn it! This wasn't an alien planet, he was on home soil. Care pulled out his PDA. He tapped in a text message to Commander Kerlin, as casually as he could mention it, he messaged that if he wasn't at the Rusty Wheel by Mark 9.30, then he would be officially missing in action. The message was suspiciously cryptic, no help for it.

Feeling reassured, Care pushed the hidden door, it swung forward and he stepped through it. A stairway led down. There was another door opposite, Care decided to try it before going down in the dark.

He listened first and upon not hearing any voices, he advanced deeper into the Shrine of Aphrodite. Actually, it didn't feel like the Shrine anymore, this must be a connected building. There were no windows in here. There was a vent for air; a chalice of incense burned on the floor, the smoke had to go somewhere. Care found it odd, there was no idol to represent the Goddess, just some plant matter on a table, about twenty lit candles lit the enclosed space from shelves affixed to the walls.

"This is a surprise," a voice from behind him made Care whirl.

"Where did you come from?" Care shrugged his shoulder to relax the sudden tension.

"I was downstairs," none other than Commander Barett paced the small space, studying Care. "I thought you didn't need divine intervention."

'Now, why would Barett know of my words to the Medusan?' As soon as the thought began, Care dove for the exit. A body stood in the doorway, blocking him. Cursing himself for falling for such a stupid trap, Care jabbed an elbow at the Human Guard in the doorway. The Guard blocked Care's move readily enough. Three more male Humans squeezed into the room. Care had a craving for fresh air. "Step aside and let me pass," Care's normally playful tone came out very steely.

"Oh come now," Commander Barett spoke. "We just want to give you some of what you like."

Care stared at the Human. He acknowledged that Guards played pranks on each other, to find a Commander involved; it was outrageous. Care considered going for his weapon, he had it hidden in his boot. The fit was snug enough that he needed a distraction to pull the weapon free and aim it.

"Come on," Commander Barett cajoled. "Lower your shorts a little and bend over the table."

"Absolutely not!" Care folded his arms. "Do you have the time?" Was it Mark 9 yet?

One of Barett's Team snorted a laugh.

Commander Barett grabbed for a rod that had been hidden in a dark corner of the room.

Care backed a step, it was not a standard Disciplinarian issue implement, he'd never seen a rod like it before.

"It's only resin, hardly a torture instrument," Commander Barett was talking in mild conversational tones.

"You tried to set me up, using the Medusan to lure me here!"

"Yes, but it didn't work, remember? Or did you come here to follow me?" The Commander seemed to find this very interesting.

"Why me?" Care stayed on the offensive side of the questions.

"You need to choose your friends more wisely."

"Who?" Care said, obtusely by the expression on the Commander's face.

"Your new buddy Garren Waysixth"

"Garren?" Care was astonished. "Aren't you from the same planet? Shouldn't you be allies or something?"

Commander Barett didn't answer this. "Lean over the table, come on."

"Absolutely NO WAY!"

"You like this. We promise to do a good job."

"I don't like YOU and I'm not into rods."

"Come on, what, you want hand spanking? A little lame, eh?" The Commander paced a perimeter, his Guard Team standing in a semicircle herded Care toward the table.

"Lower your shorts, trot out your little package for us!" A couple of the Guards started breathing hard. They were becoming anticipatory.

"I am not trotting anything out," Care's patience for the patter was nearing nil. Something moved and he startled. Was that plant moving? In distaste, he dodged away from the table, reaching for his boot. He'd almost got the hand-cannon out, when vines closed around his wrists and ankles, dragging him gracelessly over the table on to his stomach.

"You're a Mage?" Care said, though he hadn't heard any Mage tongue.

"No," the Commander explained. "I'm a Cleric."

Care struggled against the vegetation. This sucks. He was flat out on top of the altar table, his wrists and ankles stretched to the 4 corners.

Commander Barett did the honours himself. He pushed Care's shirt up to his shoulders and tugged down Care's shorts to his knees.

"You're going to lose your Commission for this," Care spat at them. They laughed, then paused to admire the sights.

The candle light glowed off Care's medium brown skin and gleamed in his glossy brown hair. Locks of Care's hair covered his face, his yellow irises peeked out, looking very animalistic in the flame light. It was carnal and exciting to the Quinterran born Guards.

Care was not excited at all.

"Here, we don't want your face to get dusty," one of the

Guards slid a clean scrap of cloth under where Care's face was raised.

The resin rod was sliding along the skin of his back. Care's breath caught, "I DEMAND you RELEASE me."

"And we can't see your package; you should be comfortable with that?" The Commander leaned his face close to Care. He pulled his face away before Care could finish gathering spit.

A rough hand moved on the back of his thigh, petting up and down, getting higher up his body with each pet. Care kicked, the vine didn't give him enough slack to raise his booted feet.

"What kind of Cleric are you? Whom do you serve? Where's your loyalty to Emperor Methusem?"

"I honour my loyalty to Emperor Methusem. Please don't mistake this harmless fun to mean otherwise. My power comes from the Goddess Astra." Commander Barett rubbed both hands down the skin of Care's back in a soothing rhythm like a spa masseuse. Care was not relaxing.

"Astra of the Astra Vale?" Care said, curious despite his anger. The Commander's hands felt very large. "We're in a Shrine of Aphrodite."

"The Divine Goddess Aphrodite doesn't seem to mind, SHE has never manifested." Commander Barett moved his hands to Care's ass cheeks. "I must complement your skin care regime, you are as fine and smooth as a girl."

Care stayed absolutely still, assuming the psychology that if he didn't react, they would get bored.

"I was offered a very attractive bribe to do serious damage to your person," the Commander said with some reluctance. "It isn't in my nature to do such a thing; in fact, I'll probably be made to suffer consequences for not delivering. I'm telling you this to warn you."

"I don't care how much you warn me, you're still going to lose your commission for this," Care's voice rose in anger.

"You know what ...," Barett bent to lay soft kisses on Care's skin.

"Ew, yuck, stop kissing me, ugh, disgusting," Care squirmed.

The whole Guard team now had their hands on Care.

Commander Barett continued to speak as he put his hands between Care's thighs to cup his balls, he squeezed Care's tender instrument together to the point of extreme discomfort. "I don't really mind losing my commission. Guard service is pretty boring, except for times like these."

"Please let me up," Care's whisper became pleading. This was awful. Someone else was licking his skin, he twisted around as far as he could go to shake him off. "Aphrodite help me." Where was divine intervention, when you needed it? This mess was going to put him off the mood to meet Starra later.

Fingers tickled the backs of his knees. Care did not laugh. "STOP IT!"

"I think our friend is ready for the rod!"

The hands and kisses and licks stopped touching him, for which Care was grateful. "I don't want the rod!"

"We tried to obtain the new tawse for you, alas, it's too tough to acquire, none of that sensual feast for you today." Commander Barett sighed as if sorely disappointed.

Care sent a prayer of thanks for the small miracle. No matter how hard he pulled, he could not pull free. He started bracing himself for the resin rod. He lay his cheek down on the cloth scrap, groaning his anger and misery.

"There we are, you embrace it," Commander Barett said with so much satisfaction that Care swore he was going to punch the guy's lights out.

"No, you can crack my spine or chip my bones with that thing!" Care panted with the beginnings of panic.

"Relax, I said I don't intend to damage you, I meant it," Commander Barett rested the rod across Care's ass cheeks, ready for the first blow.

"No, you'll chip my tale bone," Care freaked.

"I know how to use this," and he struck the first blow.

Smack!

Care jumped like a spring board. "Yikes! Please use something safer, please."

One of the Guard team members spoke up, "maybe he's right? I'd be more comfortable with something standard issue."

Care cringed, tightened his hands into fists and shut his eyes tight enough to see lights.

A small argument ensued among his captors, until Commander Barett capitulated. One of the Guards brought out something; he held it for Care to inspect. It was a heavy three fingered tawse. It was an implement much heavier than he would normally play with and he hated it. But he wouldn't fear for his bones from it.

Care turned his face away from it, choking on his own saliva. He nearly hyperventilated when he felt it brush against his ass on top of the welt from the rod. It brushed him softly three times, then came whipping down on him. "Yoww!" Laying flat meant his skin over his ass was loose, increasing the stinging sensation, if he'd been bent over, his skin would have been tighter and not as hurtful. Again the tawse struck. Oww, it stung. The impact hit the meat of his buttocks. Thud.

Three! Four! Five! On exactly the same spot on his right cheek. He screamed in outrage at the tenth strike on the same spot. The fingers of the tawse moved to his left cheek, repeating the 3 soft ones, then came whipping down. Care arched his back trying to line up a different stop for the next blow, but Barett had perfect aim. The tawse moved up his ass a little, careful to not hit his tale bone and Care forced himself to relax. He was going to have to surrender to the tawse or it would overwhelm him. SMACK, ten times on each ass cheek. The sting was immense.

The tawse moved down to exactly the area where he would sit, and whipped down on his sit spot for ten more. Moving upward again, Commander Barett skipped over Care's kidney area and went for the meat of his back under his shoulder.

Care lost track of the beating. Hot silent tears he couldn't hold back poured down his face. He thought he would pass out soon.

Barett seemed to sense this for he finally put the tawse down. "Wasn't that great?" He was very breathy with excitement. He started to kindle a lust for Care. "Have you ever had it so wonderful? We can do that any time you want."

Care shuddered. The guy was insane. Care tugged his hands, but the vines still held him tight. "Can you let me go, now?" Care managed to speak between gasping breaths. His back and ass felt like one big raw bruise, it hurt terribly. He'd never taken such a thrashing. Playing at spanking wasn't like this.

"Do you want that hand spanking now?" A Guard said. They crowded around and started smacking his ass, legs, and back randomly.

Care tried hard not to, but he started wailing his anger and pain.

A noise as of several people climbing steps reached their ears. Had someone heard his yelling? Why hadn't he yelled sooner?

Through the haze descending on his mind, he became aware of singing, a chorus of feminine vocals. They were very soothing, not soothing enough to make him forget the bruising on his skin. At any other time, the singers would have thrilled Care's curiosity.

The beating had stopped. Care twisted around and saw the soon-to-be-ex-Guards standing in trance, as if under a telepath's compulsion. It would be so much better if they would take their hands off him.

What's this?

The vines were loosening their grip. The singing must be calming the vines, too. He pulled and jerked to hasten the process. He crawled forward, off the table, and swung to his feet.

Spitting angry, Care felt it would serve the Guards right if he used his hand cannon on them. He wondered why he wasn't being susceptible to the singing as the others. He rearranged his clothes, wincing as his shorts touched his skin, refreshing his urge to fire his weapon at his tormentors.

The tempo and timber of the singing changed, the Guards had enough presence of mind to say "Pardon" as they brushed passed Care in their haste to obey the call of the Sirens.

Care dearly wanted to see the legendary Mermaids, but wisdom overcame the desire. He decided to wait; perhaps it was moot for something approached the doorway. Care backed against a wall, tempted to draw his weapon, yet, not wanting to elevate the violence level unduly. To his surprise it wasn't a Mer, something with wings crowded the room. Care relaxed, exhaling a huge breath of relief. He recognized her from the news broadband. It was none other than the Grand Dragon Dame Brynnhilde. It was hard to take in her full beauty in the dim room. The dim candle light added to her supernatural looks, a soft shine emanated from her. She wore diamond jewelry and a diadem, otherwise her statuesque figure stood proudly nude.

"You are Care?" Her voice was a throaty contralto and quite fascinating.

"Yes," Care shook himself. "You know me? I mean, you were looking for me?" He was astounded such a magnificent person would be here for him. Had she brought the Mers to rescue him?

"I am in this vicinity to conference with the Water Demons. A Medusan child came to me and told me a strange tale."

"A little kid sent YOU to rescue me?" Unaccountably in his own mind, Care felt re-threatened by tears. He dabbed at his eyes quickly, sniffling. To his surprise, she embraced him close and to his impression very maternally. He resisted the urge to cry. It was quite nice to be held like this by a sympathetic person, one who could kick serious 'bad guy' butt if need be.

His nose reached the hollow between her breasts. He felt disrespectful pressing his face there, but there was no neutral territory he could reach.

The singing outside had lowered to a low hum, voices humming in perfect harmony in mixed octaves.

Brynnhilde petted his hair, avoiding the skin of his back, Care's shoulder length hair refused to cooperate and didn't stay petted behind his ears. He thought he felt a kiss on the top of his head. His face screwed up and this time he did cry a little. After a moment of lovely comfort, he reluctantly pulled away. Surely a Dragon Ambassadress had better things to do than nursemaid a crybaby.

"Tis pleasing your genetic heritage grants you immunity to the Siren's song. Never forget they are Demons, to remember will bide you well," her head nodded slightly as she spoke, her ankle length cascading tresses moved as if stirred by a breeze.

"Really?" Care smiled, his personality started to recover from the mind burden the assault left on him.

"Come," she beckoned, "I will lead you to a Mage-Healer in this city. She will bestow her Healing gifts upon you. Only you must avow to never reveal her and you must offer her tithe to her liking." Dame Brynnhilde winked. "She is quite fond of jewelry."

They exited the room and came to the room with the stairs leading down. Care was gathered to Brynnhilde's side by her wing snuggling protectively around his body.

Care did his best not to stare, but then decided they were worth staring at. Women of an otherworldly nature were mingling with his tormenters, six of them. They all had very long tresses to their knees. Three of them were narrow of waist with high breasts and long legs. Three of the women were more rounded in the waist, their breasts and thighs fuller. They were all completely nude, except for necklaces of a pink stone. These were Mermaids with legs. He knew from his schooling that they could shape change at will between a dolphin like tail and

Human legs.

They had sang the Guards out of their uniforms. It greatly appeared an interspecies orgy was about to take place.

Care crossed his arms and his face went glum. After what these bad Guards did to him, they were about to have this heavenly reward. Brynnhilde's wing tightened around him like a reassuring hug.

The Siren song stopped. They each bowed respectfully to Grand Dame Brynnhilde and the bows were returned. Care bowed beside her, best way to treat a lady you just met.

"Greetings, Water Demons," Brynnhilde swept her tresses behind her shoulders. Care couldn't see her expression.

"Greetings Great Dragon Mistress," three of the Mermaids spoke in perfect unison.

"On behalf of the Dragon King who rules here, may I know why the Water Demons are roaming these dry lands?" Brynnhilde tilted her head in a questioning pose.

"It is said, an ancient and most powerful Elemental Fire Demon has come to torment the land of the Demon Lord, we seek to find if the rumours be true," the other three Mermaids spoke this time, also in unison. "We smelt the wet tears of this young one with the smell of Fealty on him, as token gift to the Demon Lord we came to see what we may do to serve."

"Ah," Brynnhilde said. "If this Fire Demon is ancient and powerful as you say? Is it prudent for your coven to seek confrontation with such a fiend on dry land?"

During this, Commander Barett started, looking at his surrounding in some alarm. The Mermaid nearest him started humming and he relaxed into patience again.

"We do not know if IT has immunity to our song," three Mermaids raised their arms high and sang a sweet pure note in perfect harmony.

The singing sounded sensational to Care, it did not move him the way it moved Barett and his team. Care wasn't aware that his yellow eyes began to shine, making him look supernatural as well. Two of the Mermaids bowed to Care, who became perplexed at the treatment.

"As tithe, we bring this small offering for your Lord, please bring these to Emperor Methusem with our greetings," a Mermaid moved forward with a small chalice and offered it to Care.

'What? Were they calling Emperor Methusem a Demon Lord?' Care accepted the chalice, a little put out that he was going to have to carry this thing around all day.

"Ah, pearls!" Dame Brynnhilde offered to convey the chalice of pearls to Emperor Methusem. "This will please him greatly." The Great Dragon Dame bowed again. The Mermaids returned the bow.

"May we ask," three of the Mermaids spoke, "why the Great Dragons are wandering the underground? It is legends persevering all the Ages, Dragons rule Skies and Merfolk rule the Waters."

"I did come to confer with you, the Water Demons; I think now I may have been hasty in my reasoning," Brynnhilde said this with an air of confession. She continued, "the mischievous ways of the Merfolk are also legendary."

At this, the Mermaids stood to close ranks, shoulder to shoulder. Care tensed, but did not interfere with the Ambassador babble; negotiations and treaties were beyond the scope of his training. He would only make it worse. Could Brynnhilde handle six Water Demons? Care was losing his romanticized notion of Mermaids. Yet, they had come to rescue him, he sniffed at himself. They had smelled his scent and came all this way? Too bad for his ass they hadn't made it sooner.

A small chuckle came from Brynnhilde and she looked sidelong at Care.

Care's sense of the ridiculous came to the fore. He groaned, greatly exaggerating it.

As one, the Mermaids seemed to stand down; five of them gave their attentions to Barett's Field Team, the sixth gave a mysterious smile to Dame Brynnhilde.

"Truce," the Mermaid said, tossing her lovely green hair, drawing Care's attention to her locks. She had no whites to her eyes; they were a solid shade of glittering green.

"Truce," Dame Brynnhilde echoed.

"In honour of our Truce," the Mermaid spread her hands in a theatrical gesture, "perhaps, we may assist the Great Dragons to respond to this mischievous harm done upon them?"

Dame Brynnhilde grasped her hand, for the first time giving a hint of internal anxiety. "Dragon Kin would be honoured to accept the gracious assistance of the Water Demons. A harm HAS been done upon us." Dragon Lady and Mermaid held each other's wrists. "A young one, one of our cubs has gone missing. Originally," Brynnhilde shrugged an apology under the weight of her tresses, "we assumed a Mer had lured the cub away for one of their … jokes." At this Brynnhilde darted a telling glance at Barett and team, it was difficult for Care to hide his reaction to this. A joke, eh? He began feeling better about Barett's pending orgy with the ladies.

"A lone young Dragon cub?" The Mermaid showed some emotion at this. Children were very precious to Demons, since they did not breed often. "I vow, on behalf of my sisters and I, we will seek for your cub as we prowl for the Demon. We will safely return any cub we discover."

Dame Brynnhilde nodded, clutching the chalice of pearls in her one hand between her breasts. She seemed overcome for an instant. She bowed and smiled.

"Come young one, it is time we see to your Healing," Brynnhilde bowed again and offered a brush of lips to the Mermaid's cheek. The Mermaid bowed low, sweeping her shining locks to the floor.

"I'm 22 you know," Care heard two of the Guard Team giggling like virgins as Brynnhilde guided him down the stairs. He wanted to go up, not down, he trusted her though, trusted her implicitly. The underground passage was intermittent with glow moss, making Care assume the people living in Nihera City must use the passages for shortcuts or something.

They walked maybe 50 steps, when Care blurted his thoughts. "They aren't REALLY about to have a good time, are they?"

Brynnhilde turned her head towards him for a moment of study, then she smiled, "depends on their preferences."

"What do you mean?" Care felt like taking his shorts off, his shorts hurt, rubbing his skin as they walked.

"All right, I will tell you this tale, but you must promise to keep it close. It might amuse you to know this and distract you from your discomfort."

'Discomfort? It hurts like crazy.'

"I offer you apology for not healing you myself. Dragons heal each other as foreplay to mating, I do not intend insult, but I will not mate with another species."

"Please, no insult taken, I understand," Care said in all seriousness. He did not expect the Grand Dragon Dame to sully her hands on him.

She gazed at Care with a meaningful side glance.

Care smiled, was he being teased by a Dragon?

"You are quite sweet for a Human type," Brynnhilde may, or may not be, teasing as she said, "tender and tasty little morsel."

Care cleared his throat, "umm, something about a Mermaid joke?"

"Yes," she fell into a bardic cadence. "You may recall the Legends. Mermaids, since ancient times by mortal reckoning, use their Siren song to lure Humans to them."

"Not ... not to their deaths surely," Care didn't think so, but could use a lil confirmation.

"No, they find their new joke more entertaining, even the young Dragon Kin fall for them," Brynnhilde sighed heavily. "You were witness to the power their song has over your Kin."

"Well," Care needed to qualify this, "technically they aren't my kin."

She hugged him to her with a wing, making him laugh in happy surprise. Care thought she was fantastic.

"They devote festivals to their entertainments and contests to award the Mermaid who lures the most males."

"But, what do they do with them? It looked like orgy time back there," Care was torn, he didn't want Barett's Team hurt, yet, he wanted them punished. "So, they lure them with a Siren song and then give them an orgy?"

"They lure the men with their Venus legs, yes," Brynnhilde's smile turned sly.

Apparently she was amused by the joke, too. It must be a female thing, Care was thinking. Venus legs?

"Do you mean they have other kinds of legs?" Care couldn't imagine.

"They lure the men into their embrace with their Venus legs, then after they get comfortable, the Mermaids shape change to their Adoni legs."

Care wasn't comprehending.

"To enhance their joke, they over-endow their Adoni legs and they take advantage of their captive."

Care initial reaction was to laugh uproariously, but as he thought about it, he stopped abruptly; feeling wrong about laughing, rape was no laughing matter.

"Is it rape if they lie down willingly?" Brynnhilde answered his unspoken thoughts.

"In this case, I would have to call it rape. Tis not much different from a woman luring you home with sweet promises, only to find her husband home and waiting for his desert. We have an obscure little law, says iffn you perform sexually with a married person, you have to provide like service to all the spouses."

"Does this happen among your Women Kin for festivals?" She asked politely.

"If they do have festivals, I haven't received an invitation," Care cringed at the idea.

He considered carefully what he should do, he honestly felt he should report the Guards in trouble, but … Guard uniforms weren't proof against the Siren song, Care would be sending his fellow Guards into danger. The best suited to rescue them was himself, if he was truly immune to the Siren song. Hmph! They would have to sit tight, until after his Mage Healer visit. Barett will have to reap the consequences of his plot. Care felt cruel, yet, he could live with it in this case.

Dame Brynnhilde stopped walking and sniffed the air.

Care raised an arm to test whiff his arm pit, nothing unduly obnoxious, he did note it was time for some depilatory maintenance.

"Another of your Kin! Blood wounded," she said. She back tracked a passage and to Care's total surprise they met Garren.

"Heya Garren," Care called.

Garren whirled and gave Care such a look of palpable relief, it was strange.

"Care … Care," Garren gasped, his voice hoarse. "Are you okay? I should have warned you, they are attacking my friends. My friends … have you seen Dana? Can you contact him?"

"Woah, shoo," Care was relieved to find he still had his PDA in his pocket. "Relax Garren, Dana is a lot smarter than both of us." He grinned.

"I wouldn't blame you, if," Garren whispered, "it would be safer for you, if …"

"Garren!" Care couldn't believe his ears. "I am not about to blame you for what Barett did to me. Are YOU okay? Did they damage you? Are you bleeding? Is that a curtain you're wearing?"

"Tablecloth," Garren made light of it.

Good, if Garren can kid around, he can't be too hurt. Care checked the time first, still a mark and a half to Starra. Was he still in the mood? YEAH!

Brynnhilde beckoned and the two friends followed, Care trying to admire her wings and read his PDA and walk at the same time. They came to a stairway leading up.

"You're Kin here knows the way to her sanctum. It is right above. Don't forget to bring a tithe. And if perchance you learn her name, do not speak it, utter it, or breathe it." The Grand Dragon Dame Brynnhilde said the last in a tone loaded with warning.

It gave Care ghost-bumps.

XXII. T<small>ERRA</small>-D<small>ATE</small> 215::150
Late Morning
:: Care and Garren at the Mage Healer ::

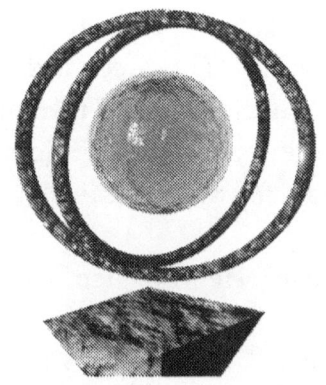

They climbed the winding stairway up to street level and pushed through a hanging curtain to find themselves in a tiny cul-de-sac. Care thought there must be lots of these nook and crannies around the historical city. Garren swayed on his feet and Care caught him.

"Garren, speak to me," Care held Garren from collapsing to the dirt ground. "Which is the way to the Healer?"

The mumble reply sounded like, "blue."

Care made a quick visual scan of their surroundings. A high surrounding wall embraced the cul-de-sac, an archway in one wall led to a main street. There were various shops, each with an arched entrance and a shingle to proclaim its subject wares. One did not have a shingle next to it, the opening covered by a blue portière. "Blue!" Care hoisted Garren gently (bending from the knees) over his shoulder and headed for the blue archway.

Inside the foyer of the place, the floor was stone tiled and covered with a center area rug, the rug was blue ovals radiating concentrically with scraggly fringe on the edges. Shelves and eclectic dressers were strewn with a riot of clutter; lots of crockery, clay baked knick knacks, candle sconces, bead necklaces, pretty seashells, 3 tea sets in different motifs, and more stuff. Three overstuffed cushiony arm chairs were positioned randomly in the room, facing in odd directions. Lanterns filled with glow moss hung from the walls, shedding a comfortable level of illumination in the room. Musty smells from dried herbs engendered a desire to sneeze in Care's nostrils. Care decided he wanted his next apartment to be just like this room! The clutter made him feel cozy. He especially liked the pell-mell seating arrangements.

Care very gently lowered Garren to the rug. The tablecloth un-tucked from Garren's limp body and Care saw all the shallow knife cuts marking his friend's skin. "Those cowards!" Care shouted furiously. "Those stupid –" It did no good to rant and rave. "Garren, I'm going to call emergency medical services, I don't think you're in a condition to wait for a mythical Mage Healer."

"No," Garren said, his voice very hoarse. He struggled to sit upright.

"Wait, okay, we'll try the Healer, relax," Care put an arm around Garren's back to help, alarmed at seeing Garren thrashing his limbs helplessly.

"Is there any water?" Garren croaked.

"Water?" He gently helped Garren lay on the rug, then searched the room for a water source. Care found a tap extended from the wall. It was a very plain tap, purely functional with no décor value. He rummaged a crockery piece from a shelf, filled it with water, and carried it to Garren. "Here Garren," Care said gently.

Garren rolled on his side and propped on an elbow, eagerly took the water vessel and drank deeply, not coming up for air as he gulped the water down greedily. He gasped. "Thanks Care."

"Garren I have to get our tithes for the Healer. I don't want to just leave you here."

"I want to come, give me a moment, please," Garren closed his eyes and let his head loll back. "One moment, okay?"

Care sat next to Garren on the floor and watched him anxiously. A quarter mark of time slid by, then Garren moved true to his word.

"Okay," Garren smiled weakly, climbing to his feet with all the effort of climbing a hill. He rewrapped the tablecloth around his body under the armpits and tucked in the ends; if you didn't look too closely it could resemble a sarong.

Care gave Garren a doubtful look. "We'd better limit our search to the shops in this cul-de-sac."

"What is a cul-de-sac?" Garren joked.

At least, Care thought Garren was joking. "Where are your boots?

Garren groaned in irritation. "My PDA is lost." He would be docked for a replacement, then he remembered he was drawing a Senior Fleet Commander's salary grade, he cheered up.

The two men exited the strange room, Garren walking gingerly. Care offered Garren an arm to lean on, and it seemed to Care with great emotional pain that Garren accepted the offer.

The late morning sun was very bright. This little out of the way area was virtually empty of tourists.

"Why don't you wait here Garren? I'll go check right over in the souvenir shop." Very glad he was not as broke as usual, Care hurried into the shop across the unpaved way. He hurried as best he could; the knowledge of Garren waiting outside behooved him not to haggle with the merchant.

The store had knick knacks and assorted stationary and souvenirs of Nihera City and the Rocket Races. First thing Care grabbed was a pair of shorts about Garren's size, all the clothing options were in racing motif, and a pair of all purpose beach shoe flats. He bought two of the most expensive necklaces in the shop, which took care of his money account. As a side tithe, he had just enough illumes left over for a pretty yet rather plain jewelry box. The Mage Healer would surely like this for her tithes.

He returned to Garren and they went into the blue lair and waited for the Mage Healer.

To his utter surprise, the Mage Healer was none other than the Blue Lady he'd met in the racing crowd yesterday, the Lady who said she liked two men at the same time. 'Trust me to remember a detail so vividly.'

Garren let Care do all the talking.

Care presented their tithes, the two necklaces. "Oh, I hope you don't have those already, perhaps it hadn't been best to buy jewelry right next door to where you live." In high hopes he followed the tithes with his other token gift to the Mage Healer; a pretty jewelry box, basically a plain box with a mirror under the lid and a pretty cameo adorning the lid. Instead of the pleased response he was expecting, 'uh oh', Care thought, - the healer just stared at the box.

"BOX?!" She closed her eyes and turned away, then spun back to face Care, her long blue hair swinging like a whip with the little silver rings tied to her hair ends adding weight. "Just for zhe record, ZHEY pinned me wizh zhat bad rap. I never opened zhe BOX!"

"Huh?" Care smiled his special smile, which usually scored for him with the ladies. The Healer was not impressed. She was muttering under her breath, saying confusing things, like, "not my fault damning no world."

After these comments, she had Care and Garren strip totally nude and she paced around them with a view for their wounds. She shook her head at Care's back and ass. "Zhis mess was not consensual?" She spoke with a very peculiar impossible to place accent, her 'r's rolled and her 'a's sounded like 'ah'.

"No." Care choked on saying anything more.

The Lovely Blue Lady gave her attention to Garren, circling him several times, lightly touching fingertips to a few of the knife made cuts.

These cuts horrified Care. He would make Garren's

tormentors suffer.

The Mage Healer sniffed at Garren, vaguely at first, but then sniffed and snuffled. Her eyes widened and she clucked her tongue with a shipload of sympathies. "You poor boy!"

"MiLady, what is it? What did you smell?" Care sniffed at Garren, he only smelled dried blood.

"You may call me Aneena."

"I can speak it?" Care asked overly politely.

"Yes," she winked. "You boys, come hizher wizh your smells of Demons and Dragons upon you. It be interesting tale for tea time."

"You smell Demons on Garren?" Had Garren encountered Mermaids, too?

"Come, I have busy day. Let me attend you boys quickly."

She twirled the tithe necklaces around her finger like a propeller and led the way to a room with a bed in it. The bed had metal slats on the head-board and foot-board. The room was empty of anything else save two long curtains adorning a high-set window.

"You boys, lay zhere!"

She raised her arms and closed her eyes, preparing to call her Magic, Care guessed, either that or she needed a good stretch and a yawn.

The two naked Guards climbed on to the bed. Care sighed at the soft cushiony quality of the bed covers.

"Your healing needs are on your back, eh?" The Blue Lady "tsked".

"Um, good point." Care turned over to his stomach. Garren mimicked him, giving Care the impression his mind was not really paying attention to their surroundings.

She walked around to the head of the bed carrying two sets of chain and bracelet bondage restraints. She wrapped the chain around the top slat in the headboard and asked for Care's wrists. He complied with a shiver of dread. "Um, tis this truly necessary?" He made a fist, but she waited until he relaxed his hands before the bracelets clicked and locked. She was no slouch to the tricks.

"Young one, you never Mage Healed before? Hmm, virgin? prrr," Aneena grinned wicked amusement. But the expression in her blue-on-blue eyes were kind and Care blew out a deep relaxing breath. "Zhis is for your safety and mine, alas."

She snapped the same bracelet arrangement on Garren, then moved to the foot of the bed to attend ankle bracelets avec chains.

Care craned his neck to watch as she let her filmy dress drop soundlessly to her ankles. She raised her arms and stretched. Care smiled. He lost his fear at that point.

Aneena climbed on the bed, one knee between Care's legs and wedged her other knee between Garren's thighs. She threw herself forward and she landed with her body partially atop Care and Garren. She pushed Care's hair aside and kissed his nape, then she bit him there. Care clenched his teeth to keep from crying out. He hoped the Healing would erase her teeth marks, he projected this thought very loudly in case she was telepathic in any sense. She licked at one of Garren's dried blood wounds.

She sighed and a forceful wind whipped the window curtains and filled the little room. Care buried his face in the bed covers. It felt like the winds high above the city. The wind became cold, wind from the mountains perhaps? This new wind was laden with cool mist.

His back, ass, arms, legs, and feet felt cold, except for where her body touched him. Her body felt very warm and the contrast made him dizzy. A quite wonderful feeling started in his skin. A sublimely rapturous feeling, Care classified this feeling up there with sex and spanking. He heard a deep throaty moan come from Garren. Garren yanked his wrists and ankles, bucking against Aneena on his back.

She laughed joyously and purred. She was enjoying this a lot, Care didn't need her to say it to know it.

The wind grew heavier bearing cool moisture. Then something gritty slapped at Care's skin. Sprinkles of it hit the bed covers by his face. Was it ... dirt? Common variety dirt, like from the road outside in the cul-de-sac. Wind, Water, Earth, and Care squeezed his eyes shut, was fire coming next?

A feeling so rapturous made Care buck against her, he raised his hips then slammed his pelvis down on the bed. "Oh, gracious Lady, Oh OH!" Care tried not to move, but the next wave of wonder crashed over him again. Barely coherent, "this is a little Mage Healing?" This was an elemental Sorceress mighty with power. What was her secret and why was she tucked away in this tiny out-of-the-way cul-de-sac?

CARE AND STARRA PLAY

XXIII. TERRA-DATE 215::150
Early afternoon
:: Nihera City, Rusty Wheel Inn ::

At the beginning of a hard spanking, Care's thoughts always run to, 'Goddess, why am I doing this? This is the last time. Would it be rude to ask her to stop now?'

"Ow oww, oh! Oooo!"

"Ow is not a safe word," Starra paused, laying the hairbrush on his ass cheek, it vanished to Care's perception and she rubbed the flat of her palm over Care's smarting skin in soothing circular patterns. Care mentally leaned into the sensation, when her fingers brushed into his dividing cleft, he sighed. All too soon the flat of the hairbrush returned, then resumed its rain of smacks. Starra alternated left, right, left, right, and then middle. The middle one jarred the meat of his backside and he felt a deep tremor in his flesh. Starra kept it moving, never hitting the same spot twice in a row.

Care tucked his head down near the floor, closing his eyes. Starra was sitting on the foot of the bed and Care was turned over her to lay cross her knees. She didn't say anything, leaving him undisturbed to concentrate on the smack of the hairbrush.

She sped up the pace and after several fast smacks Care clenched his ass cheeks together by using obscure muscles. As soon as Care did that, Starra stopped to rub his smarting ass cheeks again, then resumed the spanking slower this time.

Care began whimpering with every landed blow. She

alternated with soothing his bottom more frequently, sensing he was near his limit. He was more aware of the sound of his ass being smacked now, more than the feeling of it.

Starra made a pleased sighing noise and put the brush down next to her on the bed. She gave a little bounce of her knees, giving Care a ride. He was flying too high to laugh or talk. She used both her petite hands to rub Care's lower back and thighs.

Care lay limp and unmoving, breathing as if deep asleep.

"Mm," Starra murmured, tremendously pleased with herself, quite confidant she had Care completely dominated. She ran her fingers, thumb and middle finger spread into one line and caressed into Care's cleft. She teased the fine little hairs around his ass opening. He moaned.

She reached under him, between his legs to gently cup his balls. There were no teasing touches now, her hands were firm and knowledgeable, her strokes sure and insistent.

Sounds came from Care's throat that were beyond describing in words. Starra put her arm under Care's chest and pulled him to a sitting position. Care sat on his heels, groaning cuz it hurt, beside her legs and resting his face against her arm. He was shuddering in reaction. She pushed her lips against his face, planting kisses and licked playfully at him. Two of her fingers caressed one of his nipples and then pinched his nipple until it was an acute point of concentration. He gasped and Starra then kissed the new soreness she'd created.

Care's erection strained for release, hard, hot, and standing straight up by itself. He felt too blissful to even touch himself.

Starra smiled at Care's cock with tender emotion. She loved every bit of Care's body, the skin of Care's cock was a lighter shade of brown than the rest of him and the skin couching his balls a darker shade. He depilated most of his body hair and it was a great pleasure to her; every bit of him kissable, lick-able, and caress-able.

Starra put her two hands under his armpits and gently lifted him over the bed up to his hips, his legs bent at the knees over the edge. She pushed Care's thighs apart to kneel there. She moistened her lips with her tongue then lowered her lips to wrap around the head of his cock.

Care arched his back, quite un-expecting this. It was not something he experienced often. She licked a line up and down over the big vein on the underside of Care's cock. His carnal cries were a mixture of moans and sobs. Tears leaked from his eyes as Starra took him into her hot sweet mouth again and again.

Starra put one hand under Care's ass cheek marveling at the heat. The spanking brought blood to the area. He would be bruised.

Care was close to coming. Starra gazed down at Care's near to release cock, Humans were thicker in the shaft then Elves, Elves have the benefit of length in compensation.

Paying attention to her own body, Starra realized her body was quite agreeable to having Care's cock inside her, her pussy already wet with invitation.

She dragged more of Care on to the bed, throwing him down, almost rough, a display of her dominance. She threw a leg over his groin to straddle him. Getting to her feet, she squatted over Care's cock. She took the head of his cock in between her legs first, then bearing slowly down, until her own moisture made Care's whole length a comfortable fit.

"Ooh," Starra groaned as she sat with the full power of Care's maleness inside her. "Ah ... ah." Did all Humans feel this good? This could be addicting.

Care cried out, he was fighting not to come and give Starra a chance to catch up. It was a loosing battle. He had no leverage to thrust his hips up to meet her. She was in complete control, and she was quick moving, and coming down hard on him, her bones hitting him as she completed their connection.

Care opened his eyes to witness the exquisite beauty of her. Her eyes were closed and her mouth opened in a silent 'O', her cheeks flushed. Her wild blonde ringlets danced around both their bodies and her pert pink breasts bounced.

She screamed and her pussy squeezed down on his cock and that was all Care needed to explode. "AHHH!"

Care cried anew as the release came and struggled to relearn how to breathe. He'd never had sex with Starra before, it was mind consuming that spanking him had moved her so. She opened her eyes and Care drowned into their blue depths.

"Woah," Starra breathed.

"Woah," Care echoed. He gasped, feeling a throb from his bruised ass. He might need another healing before his Discipline Writ later.

"Do you want some A.P.?" Starra leaned down to whisper in Care's ear, pressing her cute breasts to his chest. "Huh, sweetie?"

Care thought about a.p. – artificial penis. He really wasn't into it, but the way she looked at him, her pupils dilated and the soft pleading in her tone made Care realize this was something she wanted. He nodded and then closed his eyes. He would do anything to please her, but he wasn't looking forward to this.

He kept his eyes closed as her heavenly body weight left him. He heard a dresser drawer open, it beeped as it opened and closed. A moment of waiting, he imagined she must be putting the holster belt on.

"Are you sure you want this Care?" Starra asked him sweetly. "I won't think less of you for not wanting to take it."

Care opened his eyes. She stood at the foot of the bed in a panty harness, a very realistic penis hung where it normally would on a Human or Elf.

"Yes!" He lied.

She smiled a beaming smile at him. "Okay." She giggled.

Her pleasure made Care glad he'd lied.

"Turn over then."

He groaned and obeyed. He crawled completely on the bed and tucked his arms under a pillow.

"Oh, no," she giggled again. "Hands behind your back."

He obeyed the order, burying his face in the soft bed pillow. He sincerely hoped this wasn't going to hurt.

Starra nudged Care's thighs open with her knees. "Bend." She made Care bend his forearm across the arch of his back, did the same to his other arm. With one hand she managed to get her Elf fingers to hold both Care's arms together by his forearms

Care tested her strength and found her physical strength to be superior to his. He was prisoner; he could not break free if he wanted to. 'Did I really consent to this?' He struggled and she giggled at him. It was a game to Starra and Care wondered if he had a right to panic. He felt the a.p. lying on his ass cheek. It was hard and pretty warm. "Ah," he whispered, for once at a loss for words.

"Is it too hot?" Starra asked. "I'll lower the temperature setting." She slapped the thing against him a few times, a strange sensation.

Care felt something warm and wet, Starra was smearing lubricant on him down there. Breathe, breathe, Care exhaled. She was moving into position. She was panting with excitement. He was panicking and he moved.

"Care," Starra scolded. "You have to keep your back straight, keep your colon straight."

"Uh," Care was beyond speech and not even capable of making a joke. He was totally pinned now, with her hand holding his arms immobile and the a.p. starting its penetration. It slid in pretty easily and Care was a little upset about that, feeling it should be more difficult to be used like this.

"Ok, I'm turning the vibration feature on."

Care cried out. "Oooo."

She thrust into him very gently in half thrusts. She penetrated Care completely with the a.p. and only pulled out half way.

Care heard her moan, the vibration action must be doing something for her. "Mmm."

Care relaxed into the pressure moving in his ass opening, giving over complete trust, wondering how long he had to endure it.

"Mmm," Starra lengthened her strokes.

Care bit his lip not to whimper.

"It has a nub for your prostate, try not to move. I'm turning it on."

Care screamed in reaction. He cried out with every thrust and muffled his cries by pressing his mouth against the pillow, way passed whimpering.

She finished quick.

Care sobbed into the pillow. Starra released his arms and turned him over. She took off the a.p. and tossed it to the dresser. She lay with her length pressed to Care, arms around him, nestling as much as she could of him.

They lay on their sides; Care's reviving erection between them. Starra wrapped her hands around his cock, even while kissing Care. He panted into her mouth. She stroked him, until he came again.

"Do you want me to ...?" Care offered, whispering.

She kissed him tenderly on his lips. "Hearing you make those noises makes me come," she said shyly, a strange moment to become shy all of a sudden.

A short while later, Starra sat up to look at the time-marker, then lay back down, snuggling Care in her arms.

Care mumbled, "you have stuff to do?"

"No. Your after-care is more important."

He smiled, Care did love Starra's after-care. "Aww, I'll be okay. I've got to get up pretty soon anyway."

"I'm not hurrying off," she stated. "Mmm, you are fantastic you know."

"Aw," Care bashed. "You devastate me. Say, the hairbrush is safely stored away, right?"

"No, it is still on the bed with us, actually," Starra said sweetly. "Incorrigible, trying to tempt me. We did too much!

You may hate me tomorrow."

"No, no," Care argued. "It was perfect." And he sighed and curled his toes.

Starra giggled and played footsy with him. She combed fingers through his hair. "You feel so good. All over every bit of you! Are you sure you aren't part Brown Elf? And you are so KISSABLE." Upon these words, she captured Care's mouth with her own for lots of kisses.

XXIV. TERRA-DATE 215.150 LATE MORNING
:: The Rusty Wheel Inn, Kerlin ::

Kerlin whiled away the morning by catching races from his pay-per-view vantage, he could become spoiled pretty easily, enjoying this lifestyle. The morning sun was heating up the day. The sunshine made him feel overheated in his souvenir jacket and he decided it was a good time to sit for a leisurely breakfast at a shaded eatery.

The table he sat at was a modest bistro affair with two chairs in wrought iron motif. The Nihera City eateries were packed to the brim with people enjoying their vacations. The crowds were mostly Human, intermingled with Elf, and Kerlin even saw a few Medusans.

Kerlin overheard snatches of conversation. The hot buzz topic was the pending Coronation Ball. People were hopeful of catching a glimpse of Emperor Methusem. Kerlin was looking forward to seeing the Emperor, too. He'd had opportune conversations with Emperor Methusem on occasion, not often enough to feel he had the privilege to drop by the Palace without an express invitation.

Eating his last bite of breakfast, Kerlin sat back in the café chair and took an appreciative sip from a fresh Witch brewed coffee, extra light. Kerlin wondered what their Ancestral Earth forebears had been thinking to go out into space and leave coffee behind, not that he wasn't grateful they'd remembered the chocolate. Fortunately, the Barista Witches preserved the coffee drink Spells. Yet, how did the Barista Witches know what true coffee really tasted like?

Brightly coloured aviary life fluttered around the oversized flower urns propping up the café's awning pillars. Puffy ferns and flower petals attracted the creatures, not at all shy of the people crowds. Kerlin enjoyed watching them go about their business.

Someone behind Kerlin called, "there you are!"

Kerlin looked up to see two Humans in guard uniform, a male and a female. The male had dark hair pulled back in a hair scrunchee. The female wore her thin blonde hair in a single braid wrapped around her head, not a strand out of place.

"Congratulations on your promotion Commander," the male held his hand out for a wrist to wrist greet. "I'm Jace. This is my partner Jenny."

"Hi. Thank you," Kerlin offered his wrist in return.

He recognized their names. These were the two who had failed to raise the Planetary Shield Vale during the planetary alarm. He looked at their uniforms' epaulette pins, the insignia engraving indicated they were assigned to inner city security. Apparently, the fiasco hadn't ended their careers.

"Sorry to interrupt your breakfast," Jace pulled a carry-all from his shoulder and rummaged in it. "We have here," Jace pulled something out, "your new command issue PDA." Jace tapped on it a few times. "This one is now activated and your old is decommissioned. Do you have it on you?"

Kerlin pulled his PDA from a hip pocket and traded for the one Jace held, feeling sentimental at letting it go.

"Good luck recruiting for your Field Team," Jenny said. The two moved away before Kerlin opened his mouth to invite them to join him for coffee.

The new PDA had the same functionality as his old one, the display screen had a higher resolution and bigger display area. The first thing Kerlin did was log in to the Commander's Registry for a little research. A friend of Care's had come up in last night's conversation, a guard by the name of Erin Tomick.

Erin Tomick's profile listed him as a low-level telekinetic and low-level telepath. Low-level telepath usually meant the telepath communicated mainly in pictures.

The clincher that made Erin interesting was his certification in gravity skates. Skating was a necessity to Kerlin's vision for his Field Team. From reading the registry, he discovered Erin was on shaky terms with his current team. A prime opportunity to lure Erin over.

The Guards' private broadband hosted a bulletin board for available missions commanders could request for assignment, eligibility was based on a Team's certifications and special abilities. Some missions were more exciting and rewarding, some not so much.

Erin's special abilities would help qualify Kerlin's Team for a wider range of mission requests.

If he could manage to have his Team assigned to a mission Erin would find interesting, would it entice him to join? The Commander's Registry didn't list much information for Erin's likes and dislikes. The guard was a certified disciplinarian, a common certification for guards trying to qualify for Rogue Field assignments.

A Rogue Fielder, in addition to being dispatched on sensitive missions for the Emperor, were out and about in the galaxy to be called upon by Fleet Commanders and Field Commanders in need of reinforcements. One of a Rogue Fielder's duties was to satisfy Writs. A guard couldn't escape a whipping by being urgently transferred to a border lying space station.

All Kerlin could find concerning Erin were a few posts raising concerns over the absence of communication from his brother Samson. Samson was a Rogue Fielder on secret assignment out in deep space. Samson Tomick could be anywhere in their galaxy's yonders. It couldn't hurt to investigate Samson's status.

Kerlin made a bold move and sent an email to Minister Angélus, suggesting a little investigative mission to ascertain if

Samson was indeed, in need of some assistance. All he could do after tapping the send key was wait for an answer.

Browsing his new PDA's menus, he found new email in his folder, including a new one from Care Ethaynen.

Kerlin sat up and focused his attention, shifting out of vacation mode. The message said, if Care wasn't at the 'The Rusty Wheel Inn' by mark 9:30, then Care should be classified missing in action. Kerlin couldn't come up with one reason why Nihera City would prove that hostile an environment. What was Care up to? He checked the time marker. It was near 10:. A flag next to Care's profile showed Care had incurred a new Writ. Kerlin tapped in his Commander's override code to un-redact the charges to be able to read it; 'skating out of uniform'.

Kerlin reviewed over the messages Care had sent yester-terra-day. He became suspicious of the message asking Kerlin to okay an assignment for Care's friend Garren Waysixth to a Field exercise in archaic arms. This lead Kerlin to look up Garren in the Commander's Registry. Yesterday's Jr guard was now ranked with the Senior Fleet Commanders. Kerlin rubbed his smooth chin, running his thumb up the side of his heart shaped face, pondering the significance.

A promotion leap like this one could only come directly from the Emperor. It could be to show the Realm Garren had the Emperor's favour, or it could be another move to counter corruption in the ranks? Perhaps, a combination of the two reasons.

What could be the bigger picture here?

Kerlin asked a waiter for directions to the Rusty Wheel Inn. It was close, he decided to jog. He would have preferred gravity skating, but he was out of uniform. Skating out of uniform would break a protocol statute, leading to a Writ of corporal punishment. The thought reminded him of the 1/3 Writ he had volunteered to spare from Rhiannon. Kerlin had only been paddled once in his life. He needed time to mentally prepare for it. No time, now.

Arriving at The Rusty Wheel Inn only a little out of breath, he found it had a historic charm, what it lacked in amenities it made up for in character. The inn didn't have a pool. The lobby's sitting area was generously furnished with over-plush seating sectionals.

A Human male was sitting alone on one of the sofas, eating from a snack tray. Kerlin recognized Garren Waysixth, looking a lot larger than life than his thumbnail led one to believe. Garren had a highly defined muscular physique with broad shoulders and rippley abs, though in no way was he top heavy. He moved his eating utensils around his snack plate with a grace you saw in hand to hand combat specialists. Those archaic arms exercises were rigorous and physically demanding. Kerlin could see all this, because Garren was wearing only shorts and beach flats footwear. Garren was watching the broadband news as he ate. The monitor's antique frame made the monitor seem not too incongruous to the historical décor.

Kerlin heard the high pitch of female Elf giggles. He followed the sound to the inn's souvenir shop. Standing on the doorway frame, he recognized Starra from Commander Bel's crew. Starra and a female friend were sifting objects among a stuffed toy animal display. The two Elf maids were average height, topless, and wearing short pink skirts. Starra's long blonde ringlets were a wild armful, draping down her arms and shoulders to cloak her upper body.

Kerlin didn't recognize her friend, she had the correct posture of a Guard.

The friend was saying, "Starra, did you leave Care in your room by himself?"

"Oh yes, our boy is sleeping peacefully," Starra giggled, the giggle had a double entendre ring to it.

"Did Care let you use your ...," the friend leaned close to Starra's hair to whisper.

Kerlin couldn't hear the whisper, but it was relief to hear

Care was out of harm's way.

A breeze teased the air, drifting in from the wide open shutters of the shop's window and wafting a scent from the Elf maids' expensive perfume. Kerlin left them to their gossip.

Returning to the lobby sitting room, he considered interrupting Garren's meal to introduce himself. The hotel lobby was bright and sunny. The shutters were open to welcome the day. Ceiling fans stirred a breeze. It was a tempting idea to sit for a snooze.

"Hello. Garren Waysixth? Pardon me for intruding on your meal."

Garren looked up, mouth full and chewing, he waved a welcoming hand gesture.

"I'm Commander Kerlin, pleased to meet you. Do you mind if I sit with you?"

Garren swallowed before answering. "Please, sit. Are you hungry?" Garren turned a little in his seat as Kerlin sat in the corner chair.

Kerlin sat back and relaxed, sinking into the plush cushions. "Thank you, but no, I just ate a huge breakfast."

Garren was busy chewing and didn't try to talk with his mouth full. His gaze was very direct and Kerlin could see Garren's eye color was the storm gray of a sky heavy with thunder clouds, very striking on his suntanned face, he had sandy dark-blonde hair with blue tinged streaks working as highlights.

Kerlin didn't form the impression Garren was the type of man who would tint his hair, the blue must be natural. According to the Commander's Registry recent database update, Garren's profile listed his special ability for night vision. What must it be like to never know darkness?

"What?!" Garren muttered through a mouthful of food.

Kerlin didn't detect any defensiveness in the question. "I was just wondering what it must be like to have night vision, never knowing darkness."

"You read up on me?" Garren gulped at a mug of chocolate zabamilk. He wiped the resulting milk mustache off on a napkin.

Kerlin nodded. Garren sounded more curious than bothered by Kerlin's presumption. He took a liking to Garren. There were some hyper sensitive people you had to watch your words around, Garren wasn't one of these.

"I can't see in a complete absence of light, but in dim light I see quite clearly," Garren explained.

"It's an impressive ability, it must come in handy on night missions," Kerlin said.

"I inherited night vision from my grandfather," Garren added, and then looked embarrassed. "Please, don't let me ramble on about my family."

A hotel staff person intervened during their strangely awkward pause, coming up to them to ask them if they wanted anything to eat or drink. "We have a Barista Witch brewing up fresh. Her specialty Spell is mocha java."

Kerlin caved to the temptation. "I've never tried mocha java. Sure, I'll buy one."

"Me, too," Garren added to the order before the waiter walked away. He told Kerlin, "I'm going to eat my whole pay raise if I don't start moderating."

"I know what you mean. I haven't gotten used to my new pay raise, either," Kerlin confessed. "The trick is to not change your lifestyle too much."

"Your rank is new?" Garren asked.

Kerlin counted the days on his fingers, "yep, confirmed three days ago.

"Ah," Garren made an appreciative noise as the mocha javas arrived.

The waiter placed two steaming mugs on the snack tray, frothy peaks made for a swirled topping on the coffee drinks. Unless he used a spoon, Kerlin couldn't figure a way to sip the drink without getting froth on his upper lip.

"Ooo by Astra, those drinks look yummy-lici-ous," Starras joined Kerlin and Garren, giggling with her friend as the two Commanders turned their smiles and frothy mustaches at her.

"Hello Starra," Kerlin greeted. "It's lovely to see you." He used the little drinks napkin to wipe away the froth mustache.

The Elf maids controlled their giggles with obvious effort. "Congratulations Commander(!) Kerlin."

"Thank you. Are you on the launch schedule for deep space?" Kerlin asked, making polite small talk.

"Yes. Our Commander Bel accepted a commission for one of the brand new ships of the line. We're soo happy, but it's a huge amount of work to move all our gear."

"You're launching The Equinox?" Garren spoke up. "Isn't that right?"

"Yes, we are," Starra turned to Garren. "Are you friends with Care Ethaynen? Fleet Commander Garren," Starra said, becoming a little shy.

"I'd like to think I am. Please, call me Garren," Garren's voice dropped into more serious tones in front of the ladies.

Starra's friend asked, "is it true Garren, you're launching The Halcyon?"

"Can you believe they assigned me to her? My first commission. She's been docked over fifty terra-years. I'm looking forward to deep space exploration."

"Don't you mean deep space adventure?" Starra teased. "I've seen you practicing your sword skills in the training yards."

Kerlin surmised, beneath the giggles, Starra was an astute girl. She must have special qualities, something Care Ethaynen felt drawn by. "Is our friend Care still sleeping upstairs, Starra?"

"Yes," she bashed her eyelashes. She made it pretty obvious by her reactions, she and Care had shared an interlude together.

"Are you waiting for Care?" Starra asked.

"I just wanted to make sure he's okay. He sends some cryptic emails, a habit with room for improvement."

"He seemed okay to me," Starra hugged her bag from the

souvenir shop.

The Elf maids shared a glance, it looked like a telepathic conversation.

"Commanders, you're both welcome to relax upstairs. Our rooms share a lovely balcony, nice shady lounge chairs with a lovely view," Starra offered.

"See you later," Starra's friend said. "Room 201." The ladies waved as they took their leave.

"Should we accept their offer?" Kerlin asked Garren.

"Are you sure it's okay to be up in their room?" Garren hesitated on getting off the sofa.

"It'll be fine."

Both Commanders picked up their mocha java mugs, way too tasty to leave behind.

&

Upstairs at the inn, Kerlin took off his racing souvenir hat. He shook his ruby red hair, trying to alleviate a severe case of hat hair.

"I'm going to freshen up in the shower," Garren called out.

"Is it real water?" Kerlin asked.

"It has a choice of water or sonics," Garren answered from inside the shower room.

By the sound of it, Garren chose water.

Kerlin stepped out on to the balcony. He peeked in the balcony door to Starra's room.

Care was laying still, bed linens twisted around his legs. Starra was leaning over the bed, but she left without waking Care.

Kerlin returned to Starra's friend's room. The room was cooler than the balcony. The sun was at its midday zenith. He turned on the room's broadband monitor to watch a few races.

Garren came out of the shower, dressed the same as he was before, going out to the balcony for a nap on the lounge chairs.

A few marks later, Kerlin threw a pillow at the monitor. The odds off pilots were winning the day's races. Kerlin refused to concede the tiniest of doubts the races might be pre-determined, somehow. It was illegal for Gleamers to use their pre-cog talents to predict races. Plausible deniability? Kerlin didn't bet on the races, to-terra-day, he was doubly glad he didn't suffer that imperative urge to bet.

Kerlin stared at the time marker, considering if he had the commander's prerogative to wake up a team member. Would Care be awake by now?

:: Care Ethaynen ::

Care woke, the light had shifted in the room. Uh-oh, he wasn't sure what, but sure he was late for something. Starra had left. What's this? Something fuzzy rested in his hand.

"Tch," Care clicked his tongue and smiled. It was a child's toy, a fuzzy dragon toy with a mane and a brush for the toy's hair. Sniff. There was a spicy scent on it, one of the pricier perfumes. He held the fuzzy thing close to his nose. He hugged it.

Shadows moved on the room's balcony and he heard voices, definitely Garren's voice and perhaps Kerlin's as well.

Care turned over on to his back, clutching the toy. His ass throbbed and the skin there felt tight. Starra's spankings were incredible and he savoured it. She'd said it had been too much this time. 'For her to say to 'me' it's too much, it must be pretty bad.'

Not for the first time, Care asked his subconscious why he had this need to be punished all the time. Some people used spanking to enhance their sexual play. Care didn't give himself that excuse. It was punishment, plain and simple.

He turned on his stomach and quietly cried on the fuzzy dragon, feeling bad, because he'd fallen asleep on Starra's after-care and because he didn't understand. He had better stop this crying, Care scolded himself, before Commander Kerlin came in, the extremely last thing he wanted was to be sent to a

psyche-tech. 'Ooops, too late,' he thought, as Kerlin exclaimed
–

"CARE ETHAYNEN," Kerlin said, totally exasperated. "What in Goddess's name happened to your ASS?!"

Care's weeping turned into a chuckle. He laughed into the toy. It was extremely funny to hear his Commander yell "ASS!"

"Care?" Kerlin sat on the side of the bed. "Did you forget you volunteered for a third of Rhiannon's sentence Writ? Not to mention the extra 75 you incurred this morning. I feel like smacking your ass myself."

Care lowered the toy to his nose, chuckling and admiring the graceful way Kerlin moved.

"Are you laughing at me?" Kerlin slapped a hand on the bed.

Kerlin was smiling kindly through the scolding, which Care appreciated. The last thing he needed was one of those judgmental sneers.

"I can take it. Rhi will be okay."

"You can't 'take it' in this condition!"

"I'll be fine, honest," Care smiled winsomely.

Kerlin put a hand to Care's face, moving the toy and gave Care a penetrating study. He used his thumb to brush tears from Care's lashes.

Care's face crumpled, turning back to the toy.

"Is this her price for having sex with her? Your Elf friend?" Kerlin asked gently.

"NO. Absolutely NOT," Care was horrified to think Starra might get blamed. "She just understands me. Prolly better than anybody ever!"

"Care, Care, Care!" Kerlin paced. He paused at the balcony door. "Well, Erin is a professional, we'll let him decide if it's best to postpone your Writ."

Commander Kerlin whipped out his PDA for some light reading; Care figured this out when their conversational pause stretched.

Care turned on his side and tucked the toy under his face.

The fuzzy dragon would need a name.

Commander Kerlin put his PDA down on a side table; he took off his racing motif jacket and removed his racing motif pants. He had on a light silk tank top and silk shorts. Kerlin stretched out on the bed next to Care, on his side with his head propped in his palm. His brilliant red hair fanned around his arm and shoulder.

Care watched all this with some curiosity, he didn't worry for Kerlin's warm brown eyes danced with that combination of merriment and kindness Care had grown to love in the one day he'd known his Commander. A fierce conviction blazed in Care's heart, knowing he would sacrifice his very life to protect that look in Kerlin's eyes. It was unusual to swear fealty to a mortal Human, but Care silently swore it.

A sudden wind gust invaded their room from the balcony door, riffling the linens and their hair.

Kerlin's eyes widened. Was it a trick of the wind or light? He thought he'd seen something move in Care's strangely alien, yet beautiful, yellow eyes. He knew from Care's stats in the Commander's Registry that Care was a latent unknown. What power could it be? Would Care's latent abilities ever catalyze?

"All right, I'm dizzy with curiosity," Care mumbled behind the toy. "Why did you undress down to your underwear?"

"Oh yeah," Kerlin pulled his mind away from his contemplations. "Did you and Starra do the after-care thing?"

Care caught his breath. He hesitated to answer, but Kerlin waited patiently. "I fell asleep," he finally dragged out the confession. "She left me this toy!" Care said in wheedling tones.

"It's certainly cute and very fuzzy," Kerlin reached to pet the toy. "Are you going to take it Deep Space?"

"We're going Deep Space?" Care couldn't believe it.

"My very first mission request and it's already been approved." Kerlin smiled happily.

"Can you tell me?" Care held his breath as Kerlin's hand left petting the toy and reached unhesitant to pet Care's glossy brown hair. Care bet Commander Kerlin did everything he did without hesitation, absolutely fearlessly.

"We've been approved by the Emperor to track Guard Samson. He was last seen on a commercial cruise line. I'm booking us passage to connect with the cruise yacht's next boarding stop. Technically, it's not an assignment, though," Kerlin was a little disappointed over it, "we're officially on pre-assignment leave. But, Minister Ange has arranged for the Palace to pay our fares."

"You mean Erin's older brother Samson? Is that how you plan on enticing Erin to join our team?" Care's eyelids drooped. Kerlin was petting his hair, then his nape, traced his ear, strong strokes down Care's arm and side. His touch completely devoid of any sexual suggestion, it was extremely comforting.

"I had an exciting day, you know," Care smidged over, almost embracing Kerlin's total body.

Kerlin smidged over to close the slight gap, he enfolded Care to his body and tucked Care's head under his chin. "Hm? It's up to you if you want to talk about it. This after-care is verry nice, by the way."

Care started speaking, timidly at first, then sped up as he got into the rhythm of the telling. He told Commander Kerlin everything. And at the end he cried more tears.

XXV. TERRA-DATE 215.150 LATE AFTERNOON
:: The Rusty Wheel Inn, Kerlin ::

Care Ethaynen had fallen asleep. Kerlin un-wrapped his entwined arms from Care as gently as he could manage. The 22 year old Guard did not waken.

Commander Kerlin Lantanthen sighed and strolled to the balcony. The outdoor breeze played with Kerlin's chest length ruby red hair and the sunlight constricted the pupils in his brown eyes to pinprick sized dots.

Kerlin heard a snore, following the sound, he found Garren Waysixth a snooze on a lounge chair

The little awning attached to the chair back was pulled up to shade Garren's face from the bright sunlight, and he was dressed in a pair of racing motif souvenir shorts in the colours of the last in place pilot.

Kerlin gave Garren a close inspection. There were no marks on the new Fleet Commander, except for a couple of dark freckles near his ribs. By Care's account, Garren had a good excuse for a midday snooze. The Mage-Healer must be mighty powerful for Garren's skin looked flawless.

Garren opened his eyes and merely blinked upon finding Kerlin's face close to his skin. It didn't take a scientist for Garren to figure out Care must have confided in his Commander. "Do you think I'm an idiot for not reporting it?" Garren grimaced.

Kerlin studied Garren a bit longer before answering. "To be honest, well, I wouldn't say id-ee-ut." Kerlin parked his butt on the balcony railing with an acrobat's confidence in heights.

"You plan to report the attack after the Launch?"

Garren shrugged. "They didn't damage me. Honestly, I don't remember what happened after the first tawse strike." Garren huddled and laughed to pretend he was exaggerating.

Kerlin wasn't fooled and made sure Garren knew it. "You think they didn't damage you, because you were out of it before the Mage healing. How did you get to this side of the planet? Did you meet Fly13?"

"Huh? Remind me later to send a Gift Basket to Jesse's family?" Garren stood up and paced. He stopped close to Kerlin. "Please, I meant to say. Maybe I should get into this spanking thing too, teach me some social graces."

Kerlin chided, "you aren't socially unfit Garren."

"Thanks," Garren said with a load of doubt. Garren leaned over the balcony to hide his face.

"No. You are suffering culture shock. I hear Quinterra Planet has a broody, strictly conservative society." Kerlin leaned back, his legs tucked in the railing securing him to his seat, trying to see Garren's expression. He saw Garren swallow what was surely a stubborn rebuttal.

"It never occurred to me, perhaps you're right," the man said softly.

"How did you get to the Healer this morning?" Kerlin asked one last time, if Garren wasn't ready to talk, he wasn't about to force it out. If Garren's mind was hiding things, it was best left to a Senior Psyche-Tech to sort it.

"Jesse Nefeinn, of all people," Garren explained when Kerlin shrugged. "Nerrys's 12 year old son and his Mynx friend led me to a Crystal-Magic Port-Way, a portal."

"Awesome," Kerlin was impressed. "Does the portal work in reverse?"

"I dunno."

The bustle on the street below the balcony of the two Commanders started to calm as people began patronizing the restaurants for supper. The little kids were going indoors and the vacationing grown-ups were taking over the streets.

Kerlin fetched his PDA from inside. He took up a lounge, folding his legs on the leg rest, while he worked. Pleasantly surprised, he found a message from Fly13 inquiring after the racing excitement.

Garren sat back down again on a lounge with no urge to do anything.

"Heya Garren, do your skills include Stats Meshing?"

"I've studied it," Garren admitted.

Kerlin shoved his lounge chair next to Garren's and resettled on it, they shared the view of the PDA screen. Kerlin tapped at it, scrolling data.

"You have half your team together." Garren commented. "This is Rhiannon? We met aboard Halçyon yesterday."

Kerlin nodded.

"According to these stats, he has difficulty obeying authority. I know, since my stats look like this," Garren joked.

"Well, Rhi is an Elf Princeling," Kerlin found it curious when Garren didn't react in the slightest. "Rhi is still adjusting."

"A very kind way of terming it," Garren smiled. He appreciated Kerlin's world view. "It says here Rhi is an erotamanic? I didn't know there was such a thing."

"Another coin of what Care enjoys."

$\wp$

Garren sat up in his lounge when they scrolled Care's stats. Since the Hearing – was it yesterday? - Care's stats had tumbled; Garren knew it was his fault. "Care's discipline record is worse than mine, these stats are my fault. ... Care is an unclaimed orphan?"

$\wp$

"Yeah," Kerlin said sadly. "He has unidentified non-Human genetic ancestry. I guess fear of the unknown could put off adoption seeking parents." He held his PDA up higher. "And this is Erin. The registry says his Commander is looking to trade him. My problem is, I have no trade options."

"I met Erin yesterday, too; he's decent people."

"I don't understand his stats," Kerlin admitted. "Do you have any idea why these are so low?" Kerlin hoped Garren wouldn't hold back on confiding.

It was Garren's turn to study Kerlin. Finally he said, "well, yesterday he seemed depressed to me. But Dana spent the night cheering him up."

"Ah," Kerlin nodded. "He isn't conservative, then?"

"I didn't form that impression," Garren confirmed.

"Good to know! I can't afford to have a sexual conservative with Rhiannon and Care on my team, t'would be an ill fated combination." Kerlin smiled, peering deeply into Garren's storm gray eyes, and asked, "what do you recommend for my overall Team Mesh Stats?"

"You need someone with a very level head. Beyond your gravity skates requirement, I wouldn't try to assign Special Abilities, Magic-Users, or latents. You need a stabilizer. Erin has a very high ego stat and Rhi is up there, too. But Erin's high ego may drive Rhi's down if he can assert the proper dominant attitude."

"Thank you Garren, I'm so glad I asked you." Kerlin put his PDA back inside the Inn room. He came out with two ice cold waters.

"Thank you," Garren drank the whole mug in record time.

"You need more?" Kerlin laughed, without waiting for an answer, he hopped right up to fetch a whole pitcher of ice cold water.

Garren was impressed; no matter how many times Kerlin sat down and got up, his energy level never varied.

"What about you Garren? Are you going to assign any Guards to your ship?" Kerlin held up a finger to stall Garren's reply. He fetched out two pillows for their lounge chairs. "You were saying?" Kerlin prompted, hoping Garren didn't mind conversation for conversation's sake.

"I don't believe it's Halçyon's destiny; four Fleet

Commanders on one ship, hard to figure out what it means."

"Well," Kerlin folded his arms and put a hand to his smooth chin.

Garren leaned back, fixing the pillow under his back, enjoying watching his new friend think.

"I read something in the Fleet Dispatch, a columnists rumour only. Emperor Methusem is creating a higher level rank above Senior Fleet Commander. A Sovereign Commander, title will come with a crownlet, just like a Sovereign Minister."

Garren swallowed the news.

Kerlin clucked his tongue on the roof of his mouth and smiled.

"You figured something out?" Garren sat up. The pillow fell lower.

Kerlin shook his head, indeed, but it wasn't his place, besides, he could be wrong.

Both Commanders leaned back in their lounges, eyes closed, relaxing in the late afternoon's summer warmth.

Garren rekindled the conversation. "You will have two Discipline Guards on your team; Erin and Care are both certified."

"Yes, and you won't have any on Halçyon."

"True, I can live with the situation." Garren smiled in Kerlin's direction.

Kerlin thought Garren's face breathtaking, his whole face transformed by the smile.

"I'm assuming Erin can keep Care disciplined into behaving. He gets flippant with our protocol statutes," Kerlin laughed, "even the ones that count."

"Yes, only the convenient statutes count."

The Commanders shared a long laugh.

"Alright, you have an opinion to share regarding Erin and Care?" Kerlin said on the tale end of the laughing bout.

"Well, they know each other, know each other's likes," Garren grinned as he spoke.

Kerlin finished, "in other words, I won't have effective discipline, they'll be pleasuring each other."

"Weird, eh?"

Kerlin folded his legs, hugging his knees, grabbed his ankles and rocked as he gave thought to the problem. He stretched out again and went limp. "I have to Certify in Discipline, in something that will frighten both of them. It has to be so simple I can learn it in a day."

Kerlin saw Garren blanch. Discipline Exams meant volunteers.

"Hmm, I bet Starra would be a good person to ask." Kerlin paged her on his PDA.

"Hullo Commander Kerlin!" Starra's happy sweet voice rang clear as a bell. "How is our friend Care?"

"Our boy is sleeping peacefully, cuddling with a fuzzy dragon."

"Aww, Care is soo a cutie," Starra giggled.

"Starra, I have a sort of serious question for you, I need advice," Kerlin said.

"Yes, of course, Commander," Starra tamed her giggle a bit.

"The hairbrush thing you were using today, is it a standard issue implement for Disciplinarians?"

"There is something similar still listed in the Exam Catalog. It's the same size and weight, it doesn't have a bristle side to brush your hair," Starra went into new peels of Elfin giggles.

Kerlin couldn't help adding a giggle of his own, her giggle was infectious.

"Does it take much practice to learn?" Kerlin asked.

"Not at all, there is an anatomy chart to study; it diagrams safe body areas to punish. The chart is nearly identical for Humans and Elves. No one certifies for it anymore. Tis considered ridiculous," Starra became coy. "Commander," she said breathlessly. "Are you going to certify for it? You'll collect quite a groupie following."

Kerlin laughed, "maybe." He winked at Garren, who turned

nervously. "What is the highest limit certification?"

"The highest?" Starra squeaked. "300 hundred smacks. I don't know if you could find a volunteer for that Commander."

"Would 300 influence Care's behaviour, do you think?"

"Well, with me, we've never gone over maybe 180 at the most. Yes, I would say you might slow Care a bit with a threat of 300." She went into new giggles. "Oh, our poor boy!"

"Starra, would you have time to give me a quick lesson?" Kerlin asked politely, with all due seriousness.

"Sure, it won't take more than a 5th mark. Um, the Exam Halls are booking fast, you should schedule your Exam right away, if you want to do it today. I'm sorry I can't recommend a volunteer to help with the Exam."

"Thanks Starra. I'm still in your hotel room."

"It is a nice place, isn't it? Everyone is making fun of me, because of its name. I'll be there p.d.s." (pretty damn soon)

Garren artfully kept his face turned away from Kerlin.

"Garren?" Kerlin tried to get his friend's attention. "Have you considered certifying in some Discipline before going Deep Space? You'll never know when it will come in handy."

Garren sighed deeply and turned his face to connect line of sight with Kerlin. "Actually, I want very much to certify in Hand-to-Hand Combat before Launch. It's all I have time for, if I can find a partner." Garren shrugged a shallow apology. He'd posted on the Exam roster bulletin board for a partner, so far, no one had messaged him.

"I am certified in Hand-to-Hand Garren. I would be more than happy to be your partner. And tisn't necessary to volunteer to be my Exam partner, ok. It's too harsh to ask that of someone." Kerlin sighed. He added with mild sarcasm, "I can't imagine why no one certifies in this hairbrush thing." Kerlin laughed. "What certification grade are you looking to reach in Hand-to-Hand? I am Certified Master. I'm very limber, it helped loads." Garren did not answer right away, Kerlin kept talking into the pause. "So, is this your second day as a Commander? This is my third; Minister Ange gave me my pin yesterday. Have you met Junior Minister Vylara? She is very nice."

"Commander Kerlin," Garren whispered, Kerlin had to lean his ear closer to hear him. "Do you really want to partner me on the Combat Exam?" He sounded very serious.

"Of course, Garren," Kerlin put hand out to give Garren's shoulder a reassuring squeeze. "It's a fun Exam!"

"You must know by your conversation with Care that some nasty sorts are attacking my friends. It's not very wise to associate with me, because ..."

"Garren, don't be daft," Kerlin smiled kindly, giving him another reassuring pat.

Garren breathed deep and said, "I would be honoured to volunteer for your Discipline Exam."

"Thanks for the offer, but I realize now it's much too harsh to ask of anybody," Kerlin shrugged.

"But, Starra is on her way to demo for you."

"No matter, she's a sweet girl, she won't be angry."

"Kerlin," Garren argued, "you need this certification to keep discipline on your Team. Like you said, you never know when you'll need it. Besides," Garren spoke over Kerlin's protests, "I've already experienced the new tawse, just one of those has to equal 300 smacks with that little hairbrush thing. Trust me."

"Garren ..."

"Please Commander Kerlin, I'll be upset with you if you don't accept," Garren closed his eyes and leaned back, pretending to nap.

:: Care Ethaynen ::

It was nearing the end of a sunny day in Nihera City. Care quietly dressed in the Inn room.

Upon hearing the murmur of voices from the room's outside

balcony, he decided he seriously wanted to avoid his Commander for the time being.

He headed down one flight of stairs to a discrete side exit of the Inn. He carried in his hand the little plush dragon toy Starra had slipped under his fingers earlier, while he'd been napping. The toy smelled of her expensive Elf-Maid perfume.

He paused on the stair landing, a mirror hung on the wall where the staircase u-turned, to check on his outward appearance before stepping out to the street. Tan brown silky shorts hung half way to his knees and a sleeveless brown tunic reached to his hips.

He 'tchd'.

There were a few blood stains on his tunic, most likely from when he'd carried Garren over his shoulder earlier in the day. Care's outfit finished with his guard-issue gravity-skate boots. He wasn't fashion savvy enough to tell if the clothes did anything for his mocha brown complexion. His glossy dark locks reached to his shoulder blades. He descended the last steps two at a time and reached the outdoor sunshine.

Walking made his shorts chafe his ass cheeks. He was sore and bruised from Starra's spectacular hair brush spanking on his ass. Care grimaced as he tenderly rubbed the seat of his shorts, yet, also relished the feeling.

Care looked around for any friend in sight from whom he could possibly borrow money, another visit to the Mage Healer was a tempting idea. He didn't want to appear too obviously physically inconvenienced in front of their Realm's Royalty.

Tonight's plans included a party for Minister Angélus's Coronation Ceremony. The Emperor had promoted Minister Angélus to Sovereign Minister of the Royal Fleet, the sovereign title came with an honorary crownlet.

The promotion was a terrific leap from Minister of Royal Appointments. Care was very fond of the kindly busybody, but still, a twig of doubt concerning qualifications crossed his mind. The Fleet embodied the Realm's accumulation of inter-galactic space technology.

Care appreciated the challenge it was for the Emperor to maintain discipline without thinning personnel in the ranks. Managing seven planets must be a tough job.

He grinned.

He recognized a wild mop of long blonde ringlets. Starra was heading towards him, turning the corner of Rue De Zure. His grin widened as she came closer. She was wearing her bathing outfit, which was a collection of pink strings obscuring her bottom nethers. A towel draped around her neck, the ends laying over her pert breasts.

Starra's almond shaped eyes were a candid blue. She was returning Care's grin, the smile Care imagined she saved just for him.

He knew, she knew, he was waiting for her. The noise of her beach flip-flops made a fancy rhythm on the cobble stoned rue. She ran the last few steps into his arms and covered his face with a flurry of affectionate kisses.

Care was moved more than usual and held tightly to her. Had they had fantastic sex only a few marks ago? Care realized he was feeling extra feelings for Starra t0-terra-day. Did she reciprocate at all?

But, she was assigned to a Fleet ship, Astrogation-Tech for 'The Equinox' under the command of Commander Bel. And his own Field Team would be going deep space in a few terra-days.

Starra was an astute girl, she must have read something in his eyes, or in his quiet. "Care?" She began. She rose up on her tip toes.

Care expected another flurry of kisses, instead she pressed her lips to his for a more intimate and meaningful kiss than they'd ever shared before. After a moment of bliss, she drew apart from him, reluctant to do so.

Starra reached around him to put a hand on Care's butt cheek. He groaned in pain, greatly exaggerating it to tease her.

"Still good?" Starra smiled sweetly.

A little gap in her front teeth gave her smile all the character in the world, Care loved her smile.

"Oh," Starra became serious. "I received a hush word concerning Garren Waysixth."

"Hush word?" Care knew what the 'hush word' meant, but had never heard one before. It was news passed from Guard to Guard within their network of friends, news you didn't want carried on the communications broadband. There was some corruption within the ranks and it seemed to be taking the Emperor forever to sort it out.

"The word is to watch Garren's back," Starra whispered close to Care's ear, making sure she tickled with her breath. "Garren is your new friend, eh? What's going on with him?"

"I don't know the whole story," Care leaned close to her pointy Elf ear, making sure to tickle her, too. "Kraken's team members attacked him this morning. They used the new tawse on him."

Starra inhaled sharply. "Poor man. I dearly hope I never have to experience that monstrous new implement, unless I'm wielding it. Well, I'll keep alert for him."

"Thanks Starra," Care gave her another hug, 'ooo', he was crazy about her.

She became shy of a sudden, bashing her blond eyelashes at him. "Care ... would you? Would you ... want to trade bracelets? Before we go off on our assignments." She became too shy to meet his eyes.

"Yes," Care answered without any hesitation. "Charm bracelets with little hairbrush charms?" His words set her off on peels of Elfin giggles.

"Cya later at the Coronation Ball, Care," Starra dashed off to her hotel room. She turned back to flash him a smile, looking like she had a secret. She disappeared into the Rusty Wheel Inn with fresh giggles.

What a glorious day!

Care's own smile turned rueful. Now, he really needed

money, first for a tithe for the Mage Healer and then for a girlfriend bracelet.

XXVI. Terra-Date 215.150 Late Afternoon
:: Exam Hall, Kerlin ::

Garren Waysixth passed his Hand-to-Hand Combat Exam with the highest marks in Guard history for a Human mortal. For the first part of the Exam, Garren had to win in 24 moves. The second part allowed him 12 moves to win. The third part was a question and answer session, mostly scenario questions about the best way to handle different types of confrontational situations; including, when physical force was uncalled for. For the fourth and last part of the exam, he had to win the upper hand offensive in 4 moves, which he did.

He was a much more skilled fighter than Commander Kerlin, even at Kerlin's Master level. Kerlin did not take it personal and Garren admitted he'd been training vigorously and religiously since age seven. Garren started out in a very good mood for Kerlin's exam.

The Discipline implement for Kerlin's exam was an oval object with a handle. It was little bigger than Kerlin's palm and fingers combined, made of a wood material, polished smooth, and as thick as Kerlin's forefinger. After letting Garren examine it and giving him plenty of excuses to change his mind, Kerlin accepted the thing back and they made their way to the appropriate Exam room.

There was quite a buzz in the Exam Halls among the Guards for Emperor Methusem had been the volunteer for the new tawse exams. Both Commander Kraken and Senior Guard Erin had passed the exam. According to buzz, Emperor Methusem had burst into screams on both exams after the 11th and 12th strike of it. The Emperor had healed himself straightaway. In a quite unexpected surprise, Emperor Methusem had requested the assistance of the Dragons to donate Healings. Prince Wenrik, brother to the Dragon Ambassadress 'Grand Dame Brynnhilde', was waiting patiently in an antechamber of Exam room #107 to heal the volunteers. Even with the incentive of experiencing the Healing powers of the handsome Dragon Prince, no one else was certifying for the new tawse.

Commander Kerlin made a point to introduce Garren and the Prince before going in for his exam, to reassure all individuals involved that the Prince would be waiting close by to heal Garren straightaway afterwards.

Prince Wenrik was in Were-Dragon form, his wing membranes were the colors of a sunset, the whirling glyph patterns tinting more to gold than silver, colors very well suited with his bright gold short length hair and green-blue eyes with pupils of molten silver. He was dressed in a tan soft fibered loincloth and tan sandals. His physique resembled a dancer's muscular definition. His apparent age mimicked a Human of perhaps 30 terra-years, but it was misleading. He came across as too haughty for casual conversation and his actual age remained a subject of casual speculation among the Guards present.

Kerlin's name was called for his exam and he led the way into the chamber, Garren following and muttering something like, "third time in two terra-days for this nonsense." There was a block near the judge's tables to position Garren upon, complete with restraints. Having read up on Garren's infamous Hearing, Kerlin did not want to subject Garren to the block, since there were no written exam guidelines to the contrary, Kerlin pulled up a chair from a side table and set it in front of the judges. The only rule Kerlin knew was strictly adhered to was 'no hand touching' of the Discipline-e beyond restraining him or her.

Garren didn't comment on Kerlin's non-standard arrangement, he gracefully bent into position across Kerlin's lap without evincing any outward indication of discomfort for the situation. Garren was wearing a standard court smock, Kerlin made quick work of unfastening the back clasp of it and waited for the judges to make the 'begin' announcement.

The first fifty paddle strokes across Garren's bare bottom, Garren didn't move. The second fifty he squirmed a bit and Kerlin put hand on Garren's side to hold him steady. By count one hundred Garren started gasping and his hands balled into fists. By one fifty he started whimpering.

Kerlin paused, ready to stop; Garren whispered to Kerlin to go on with the exam.

Feeling pretty awful about the whole thing, Kerlin continued. He would have to do something very, very nice for Garren to make up for this. It seemed the exam was going to finish smoothly, by stroke number 200 Garren was crying out in pain. At the 220th stroke Garren screamed, "NOOO, I REMEMBER, PLEASE." He sobbed a heartbreaking sound and Kerlin stopped.

An elderly Human woman on the panel of judges nodded. "Exam satisfied. Congratulations Commander Kerlin, you are now certified to Discipline 300 by Ashwood Paddle."

Kerlin was surprised. "The whole 300, Lady?"

"Yes Commander," she nodded to her fellow panel judges. "A great part of the responsibility of a Disciplinarian is to recognize when the subject is close to breaking. We want to Discipline our Guards into obeying the statutes, not destroy their constitutions.

I'm reading here in the Registry you've invited Care Ethaynen to join your Field Team. I speak for all of us here in congratulating you on your choice of Exams. A standard issue Disciplinarian kit will be forwarded to you. Pleasant Evening Commanders."

Garren awkwardly lurched to his feet and tried to stand on shaking legs. Kerlin detached his uniform cloak and wrapped it around Garren's body, lifting Garren up to cradle him in his arms, he quickly made his way to the Prince. Kerlin became alarmed for Garren wasn't protesting being handled, Garren had a great deal of pride and Kerlin feared Garren might be damaged by the events of the last few days.

Without any ado, Kerlin settled Garren on a padded table in the antechamber. Prince Wenrik was already glowing with Dragon Healing Power and to Kerlin's eyes the Prince looked quite spectacular with the glow on. The Prince touched his hands directly to Garren's backside. Garren writhed from the Healing power's touch, but he didn't vocalize any response.

Had Garren said he 'remembered'? "Garren," Kerlin hugged the man's shoulders. "Did you remember something from your attack? The part you said you forgot?"

Garren writhed, but Kerlin held him with all his strength.

"I remembered the eyes, eyes and red flames," Garren whispered, quite unlike his usual self.

"Red flames?" The Dragon Prince spoke in a flat voice. "You encountered the Fire Demon? Where did this take place?"

Garren had trouble focusing his own eyes on the Prince. He whispered, "under the Shrine of Aphrodite, Celesterra City."

The Prince took on the dazed look of an actively communicating telepath. "My Dragon Kin will search there for the Fire Demon. And my sister tells this news to the Water Demons. We shall defeat this ancient evil."

"Oh, I should have thought of this before," Kerlin brought out his PDA. "Fly13, please answer this message. We're searching for a lost Dragon Cub. I'd consider it a great favour if you would sensor scan anything regarding our search in your travels." A blerpy sound came in response.

"Let's get you back to the hotel Garren, my friend. I don't know about you, but I really don't feel like going to the Coronation Ball."

Garren smiled tremulously. "Me neither, go figure, eh? Would you mind if we ..."

"Yes. What? Anything Garren, anything!"

"Would you mind if we stopped at a pastry shop?"

"Absolutely positively on our to-do list!"

He gave Garren an affectionate brotherly hug.

A court clerk found them as they were dressing Garren in street clothes and handed them two engraved placks. Garren's plack was engraved with his new Hand-to-Hand Certification listed under all of Garren's other Archaic Arms achievements. Kerlin's plack started a list for his brand new Disciplinarian Skill Tract. In addition, Kerlin was given a polished ashwood paddle.

Kerlin chuckled, "when Care sees this baby, I don't believe discipline will be a problem on my team!"

Outside the Exam Halls, Kerlin and Garren stood on the steps. Kerlin was about to flag a fastraft, when his PDA Blerpied the Blerpie that meant a Guard issue was being broadcasted. To his pleasant surprise a notice of statute had been re-issued. The matter of Guards on gravity skates being allowed to carry civilians or fellow Guards out of uniform in a non-emergency, was now up to the discretion of the Guard.

Great news! Commander Kerlin smiled at Commander Garren, Garren had the advantage of size over him, but Kerlin felt confidant he could carry Garren without dropping him.

Garren felt confidant in Kerlin's strength, his only trepidation was that he didn't want his enemies to see him being that friendly with Kerlin; for Kerlin's safety's sake.

They walked. Stopping at three different pastry shops on the way, Kerlin insisting Garren put his illumes away and Kerlin paid for all the treats. Laden with parcels of Peppered Brioche, Berry Swirls, Sugar Bombs, Whimmy Chips for the crunch, and Jillysnap Sours; Garren confessed to missing his workout for the fourth day in a row. Kerlin pointed out that the Hand-To-Hand Combat Exam proved Garren wasn't losing his edge.

"So, where are you staying?" Garren licked granules from

the Sugar Bombs off his lips, his tongue darting out artlessly.

Kerlin couldn't help wondering if Garren had been sweets deprived as a child. "Courtesy of Sov Minister Angélus, I'm enjoying the hospitality of the Royal Suite at the Hotel New Ranger."

"The Royal Suite?" Garren feigned being star struck. He smiled wide.

That beautiful smile, Kerlin thought. Garren must have swept aside his plaguing worries.

They arrived at the hotel, Kerlin looked straight up, it was a straight elevation line to the Suite, but they were carrying packages and their placks and one ashwood paddle. Matters of discretion aside, they rode the hotel's inter-floor lifts to the Suite.

"Sweet," Garren complimented.

They skipped the bedroom and settled in the courtesy living room area. There were two sofas, two cushy recliners and a desk table with a swivel-ly chair. The fabrics, walls, and carpets were in an indigo and vanilla motif, very restful to the eyes. One wall was entirely of window, the kind that doesn't open, with a long stretch of window blinds. Kerlin asked the room service computer to close the blinds. Night outside had descended and he hoped the closed blinds would guarantee some privacy.

With a great sigh, Garren dropped like a sack, - a graceful sack -, into a recliner, he extended the leg rest with a button. He held the sweets parcel open in his lap, eyes closed, digging blindly for a sweet. His hand was still in the parcel, when he drifted off into dreamland.

Kerlin smiled with great affection for his new friend. He gently moved the parcels to a table. Garren didn't even twitch. Checking the room's closets, Kerlin found a fluffy knee blanket and tucked it around Garren's body.

The sound of splashing came from a connected room. A dual door archway stood open to an area with a modest sized pool. The walls were black marble, the floor tiled with thumb sized mosaic beads of mixed purples. A line of waist high cabinetry stood against the back wall of the room stocked with pool toys and bathing luxuries. Rhiannon the Elf was sitting on a cabinet, fully dressed in long sleeves and pants, kicking his legs to some inner tempo. Three sets of balcony doors were open to the well lit night, boisterous voices floated from the park outside, everyone celebrating the coronation in one way or another. Kerlin felt a little bad about missing Minister Ange's ceremony, he was quite fond of the old busybody.

Kerlin smiled at Care, who was doing the backstroke in the pool. Only about four body lengths long, Care flipped on to his tummy to do a breaststroke on the return lap. Kerlin wasn't sure, but it looked to him like Care's severely bruised ass cheeks were back to normal. Had Care visited his Mage Healer again? By Care's own admission, he'd spent all his money on the first tithe for the Healer. Had Care found more tithe money and from where?

Which reminded Kerlin, hard pressed to hide a grin, he retrieved his new certifications plack and ashwood paddle from the living room area of the suite. This was going to be a treat. He returned to the indoor pool area, gently tapping the paddle on the plack, making little clacking noises.

Care completed two more laps, before he registered what Kerlin was holding. He completely froze and sank under the water. He came up sputtering, standing, the pool was only hip high on him. A few soapy suds slid down Care's arms and chest.

Rhiannon watched this quietly from where he sat. He hid any reaction remarkably well.

XXVII. Terra-Date 215.150 Early Evening
:: Nihera City, Hotel New Ranger. Care ::

Chest tight and knees weak, Care Ethaynen hopped out of the pool to examine his Commander's plack. The plack listed one entry for Kerlin's new skills tract.

"THREE HUNDRED," Care cried. "What idiot volunteered for that Exam?" He resisted believing, denial can be bliss.

"Our friend Garren," Kerlin said quietly. He felt pretty awful, but also feeling relieved he had this certification; Care's reaction boded well for his team's discipline.

"Garren?! No WAY!" Care was practically sputtering. He stared at Kerlin, trying to gauge his Commander's intent. Then he broke into a broad smile. Did he dare court a 300 smack Writ? What could he do to justify it?

"And I don't mean to use this lightly," Kerlin put as much seriousness as he could muster into the threat.

"Um," Care gulped. "O, Hi Erin!"

A uniformed figure skated in from the balcony, skimming over the railing. It was Erin Tomick, the disciplinarian on duty scheduled to perform the Writ of Sentence.

※

"Heya Care," Erin Tomick was tall, Human, wearing his brunette hair in a braid reaching to his waist. He smiled his pleasure at seeing his friend again and telepathically sensing Care's anxiety, looked for the source of it. He became sidetracked by Kerlin's ashwood paddle. Ahzo! "Nice, I haven't seen one of those in the field." His voice was mild and semi-deep and sounded like he found most of life amusing. "May I?"

He held up a hand.

Commander Kerlin offered the paddle up by the handle, smiling at the newcomer. He took a quick look at Erin's epaulette pin and smiled wider when he saw the team setting missing. Erin was officially unassigned.

"Nice polished finish," Erin handed it back, jauntily waving it to watch Care's eyes follow its trajectory in the air.

"Well, who is first to satisfy their third of the Writ?" Senior Guard Erin said as he set down his backpack. He drew out a stiff leather-like paddle, he flicked it swiftly on the air with an air of lots of practice and it didn't flex at all.

"I am," Rhi's voice sounded dry.

"You are?" Erin smiled at the fair Elf. "Those cabinets will do nicely, don't move." His long legs carried him swiftly to the end of the room.

β

Care was sure Erin's professional judgment didn't miss the disguised fear in the Elf's body language.

Kerlin winced and Care was sure his Commander was wracking his brain to figure a way to spare Rhiannon.

Suddenly, a PDA blerpied! It was coming from Erin's and Kerlin's PDAs in unison. Erin whipped his out first. He clucked his tongue. "All Writs are here-by cancelled in honour of the Coronation Ball. Can you believe that? I missed the crowning to take care of this and spare you guys the angst of waiting." He shrugged, his shoulders shook.

Care curled his body into a ball, leaping into the pool. When he came up he saw that he'd accurately doused the laughing Disciplinarian Guard. Not that the uniform let water drip down the collar.

"Erin, may I have a private word with you?" Kerlin called out, he'd put his trophies on the floor.

Erin gave Commander Kerlin a curious, yet, knowing look. He winked at Care as he followed Kerlin into another room.

An incredibly happy Elf stripped and jumped into the pool,

swimming circles around Care and splashing as much as possible. Care made great sweeping splashes with his arms. The teammates to all intents, were trying to drown each other.

The pool's monitor activated its water jets, replacing the lost water. Care and Rhiannon stopped to catch their breath, laughing like two truant teenagers.

"Do you want ta see my handstand?" Rhiannon took a deep breath and dove under, his legs came straight up out of the water, but he couldn't hold the pose and he fell over. He came up with a hand pressed over his nose for his laughing accidentally made him snort water up his nose.

"Um, I wouldn't perform for the judges just yet," Care laughed.

Erin came in just as Rhiannon jumped on Care to dunk him, Care wondered why Erin looked teary. Was he touched by Commander Kerlin's offer to track Samson?

Care wrestled with Rhiannon under the water, when they came up Care had an arm around Rhi's neck in a playful head lock.

"Do you mind if I swim with you?" Erin asked.

"Yayy, Erin, hop in! Are you giving up on the Coronation Ball?" Care lost his hold on Rhi as the Elf twisted and Care went under for another dunking.

"Wait, I have to breathe," Care called time out. He backstroked and Rhi did the same.

They watched Erin as he stripped, unbraided his hair, and stepped naked into the pool. Kerlin came into the room naked and carrying a computer tablet.

Care watched Kerlin move, there were muscles moving in places on Kerlin's body that Care never knew Humans could have in those places.

Erin held a deep breathe and went under, he came up smoothing his waist length hair back on his head. Without his hair by his face, his brown eyes looked huge and thoughtful. And he looked ten terra-years younger. He swam to hug the pool rim next to Care and Rhi, all three exercising by kicking their legs, very respectfully NOT splashing Commander Kerlin.

Kerlin pulled a pool side tray open and settled the computer tablet on it. He lifted the screen up and started his project, whatever it was?

Care gave Erin a happy grin. He mouthed, "did he give you the pennant?"

Erin mouthed, "Yes."

"And?" Care whispered in excitement.

Erin nodded vigorously.

"Yes!" Care took a breath and went under, testing his lungs to find out how long he could stay under. He must have made Erin nervous for the tall guard put a hand to Care's armpit and pulled him up. Care bulged his cheeks, refusing to breathe. Erin put his hands to Care's cheeks and squeezed, making Care do a spitting sound as he laughed out the breath he was holding.

Care swam a couple of laps, his curiosity growing as he watched the intensity with which Kerlin was working on the computer. He swam up behind Kerlin, "may I watch?"

Kerlin glanced quickly at him, smiling, "sure! You haven't lost your enthusiasm for the Commander's Registry?" He teased.

Moving closer, Care watched Kerlin scroll through layers of stats. A laughing shriek from Rhiannon grabbed his attention a moment. Erin was grabbing Rhi by a foot and they both went under water, the water churned like rapids water, then they came up embracing tightly and kissing like lust crazed teenagers. Their scene was pretty hot, but the Commander's Registry lure pulled Care's attention back to it. The Commander's Registry was awesome and Care was awestruck that Kerlin would let him read it.

Commander Kerlin was editing Erin's profile, he adjusted the stat numbers, mostly going up and one down. Care was too unfamiliar with it to recognize what each stat symbol stood for. It came turn for Care's own record, Kerlin bumped most of them up, close to or higher than they had been before Garren's hearing. A few stats went down.

"Is going down good for those stats?" Care asked, wild with curiosity.

Kerlin looked sidelong at Care with a cryptic smile. "You came under discussion at the Exam Halls, while I was waiting. I'm anticipating your stats changes."

Care gulped. "Lil ole me?"

Kerlin's brown eyes sparkled with affectionate humour. "Lil ole you! Her advice to me was, 'a lil preventive medicine'."

Care's breath caught. "Preventive? Whah? I don't think that is legal, Commander!"

"So," Kerlin continued as if Care hadn't spoken. "We will start with every fourteen terra-days for your dose of 'preventive maintenance'. That is in addition to any Writs you invite and in addition to your play with your friends, be it known playing with Erin is NOT an exception to this rule. Be prepared for tomorrow morning and your introductory dose by ashwood paddle. I believe you will be behaved at the Fleet Launch Party tomorrow."

A wicked grin flashed on Care's young face.

"You'd better save that grin for a different occasion Guard Care!" Kerlin tried hard to not let a smile ruin his stern impression. Unfortunately, Kerlin groaned, Care was too intuitive to be fooled. "May I ask you something personal Care?"

Care nodded, he had an idea what Kerlin was about to say.

"I am more than thrilled to have someone with a Rogue Fielder's experience on my team, but there is nothing in your records to give a clue as to why you gave it up. You worked so hard to make all the qualifications for it. Would you be willing to talk about it?"

"Um," Care became serious. "I don't think I'm ready yet, to talk about it, I mean. Basically, though, even though it was fun, I got tired of being alone." He sighed and sank down to his chin in the water.

"Okay." Kerlin gave Care a reassuring hug.

Care was aware of a sudden that they were both naked in warm sudsy water, but Kerlin seemed completely oblivious.

"Okay, let's see how these stats Mesh," Kerlin told Care with some excitement. He clicked a key and the stats scrolled in a flash. A percentage bar began filling itself out from left to right. It stopped in the 80 percent quartile. "Oh," Kerlin blew out a deep breath. He sank under the water for the first time and stayed under a bit. He came up lost in thought.

Care tried to think of something helpful to say. He heard a voice shouting outside, drifting from the balcony, it sounded very irate and exacerbated, quite a different timber from all the other merrymakers.

Someone shouted, "hey, how were your Juniors? Did everybody pass?"

The irate voice shouted back, "I never want to see another Junior again, keep them away from me, so help me! They all failed, every single last one of 'em!"

Care chuckled. "It sounds like Donné complaining! Actually, I was surprised he accepted that training class."

Kerlin startled, "do you mean Field Trainer Donné? The one from the archaic arms exercise?" Kerlin pounced upon the computer keyboard, pulling up Donné's stats and added them to his Mesh.

Hitting the key again, the percentage bar recalculated. It ended its bar in the 95 percent quartile.

Kerlin hopped out of the pool in a flipping hand spring from the pool edge, almost faster than the Human eye could track. And almost as quick, he dashed into the bedroom and came hopping out, hopping into his g-skate boots, hopping towards the balcony.

"Writs! Commander! Writs! Skating out of uniform!" Care shouted. "By the Vale, you're a fine one to lecture me in preventive medicine!" Kerlin flashed an apologetic smile at Care before skating naked and wet with suds over the balcony railing and out of sight.

Erin spoke, "is he always this tempestuous?"

Care whirled, he'd completely forgotten his teammates who were both floating with very relaxed smiles on their faces. Care grinned. Going Deep Space with this Team was going to be FUN!

There was shouting and smatterings of applause from outside as Kerlin returned from his leap.

"How'd it go?" Care asked, though Kerlin had returned way too soon for it to be encouraging tidings.

"He closed his balcony doors in my face," Kerlin flashed a grin, not at all discouraged. "I know which room he's in, anyone want to come?" He dove quickly for a cabinet and grabbed a hotel provided bath towel. Kerlin wound the towel around his sprightly body.

Holding back a laugh, Care followed suit, feeling the challenge. Kerlin was now wind dried, but the three Guards were dripping suds as they crowded, towel clad, into the inter-floor lift. They didn't excite any comments as they trekked the halls.

"This is it!" Kerlin rubbed his palms. He knocked on the door. They waited. They waited some more. Kerlin pounded on the door.

"Go AWAY!" A voice shouted.

"Cranky little thing, isn't he?" Erin said wryly.

"We have to get in there and talk to him," Kerlin glared at the door's security keypad.

"Hm," Care's 'hm' drew Kerlin's attention. "Do we use kinetics or Magic to break and enter this room?"

Kerlin put a hand on the door latch. "Hm. No, I can't ask you to do that, technically, the requisite two-terra days aren't over. The responsibility wouldn't fall to me."

"Actually, I think the two day wait requisite is just a suggestion and not really a rule!" Care said, and Rhi nodded an agreement.

Kerlin shook his head, then he pulled Care and Rhiannon to his body for a fierce hug. "You are fantastic!" Erin held back, but Kerlin extended an arm to bring Erin into the group hug. Kerlin had just let go of their hug, when the door behind him opened.

The four new teammates and the Human in the door regarded each other.

"Go AWAY! This is not a subtle hint."

Care waved, he'd met Donné a few times before this, but never to stop and chat. The person in the door had the colouring of a Human native to Strata-Terra. Snow blonde hair, alabaster complexion, gold eyes, and a slim figure. This Strata-Terra born may have been near mid-twenties in age. He was of a height with Commander Kerlin. Donné stood looking a bit ragged and worn, hot and dusty, and in sore need of some stress reducing non-activity.

"Those Juniors can be a handful, eh?"

Donné 'tchd' and huffed. He made to close the door, but Kerlin got his boot in.

"Donné, let me introduce us, I'm Commander Kerlin," Kerlin began.

"STOP! I am not in the market for a Field Team, please, leave me at peace," Donné made to slam the door, but Kerlin's boot didn't move. The exhausted Field Trainer took another survey of the towel clad foursome and seemed to relent a little. "You could have put some clothes on, before barging down here, where you aren't wanted!" He turned around to go back to his room and Kerlin took the opportunity to barge the rest of the way in to the room.

Care tried hard not to laugh, but a snort came out.

Kerlin made a tour of the tiny hotel room and Care followed with his eyes. The room was definitely low budget economy, completely opposite of the opulent luxury of the Royal Suite to which they themselves were privy.

"Are you done now? Are you leaving?" Donné was all but

stamping his feet.

"This room doesn't even have a bathtub." Care chided, as if it was Donné's fault.

"It has a sonic shower."

Care clucked his tongue. "Ugh, no water?"

"Hey, I'm lucky to have this room. You do realize that every planet side Fleet Guard is in this city right now?" Donné started tugging off his boots as he said this, the unmistakable lights of gravity skates twinkling from his boot sole lining.

"We're staying in the Royal Suite upstairs, lovely indoor pool, sudsy," Erin nodded and smiled as he said this, as earnest as a souvenir salesperson.

"The Royal Suite?" Donné didn't seem to believe him.

"Yes, we were enjoying it ourselves, when the unmistakable voice of a fellow Guard in need of a little down time made us realize we were being selfish. Come on up and cool down, eh?" Care said this very nonchalantly, shrugging a shoulder.

"Please, you don't need to thank us," Kerlin grabbed the gear backpack Donné had thrown to the floor and hadn't had time to unpack yet. He hoisted it to his shoulder and led the way.

"Wait! Bring my stuff back here," Donné tramped after Commander Kerlin, nagging all the way to the lift.

Care and Rhiannon shared a glance and laughed. Donné was certainly lively, even when fit to drop with exhaustion. Erin came up behind Care and Rhi, like a rear guard. Care glanced at Erin behind them and felt wonderful; feeling like someone had his back, then thinking he should establish his place now. He waved Erin to go ahead of him and Care took up the rear guard position. Erin caught on pretty quick and tried to wave Care ahead. They were still ushering each other as they gained the inter-floor lift, it slowed down their progress. Kerlin had Donné's backpack over his shoulder, Donné leaned against the lift wall pouting, and Rhiannon took a place at Kerlin's side. Rhiannon was giving Erin smoldering looks, perhaps, thinking back to their recent play in the pool. Care couldn't stop smiling.

He didn't think he could be any happier.

Care paid attention to Donné's expression, he wanted to see it when they opened the door to the Royal Suite, but Donné was too tired to react.

Kerlin dropped the backpack in a closet and closed the door and locked it with keypad code.

"Keeping my stuff hostage is not going to work!" Donné's temper was working up to spitting mad. He stomped into the living area and stopped when he saw Garren sleeping in the recliner.

He did look really cute, Care thought, and vulnerable. He'd turned on his side with the blanket doing half a job, candy and pastry wrappers littered the table next to him and on the floor.

Kerlin set a fresh pitcher of ice cold water on the table side and he re-tucked the blanket around Garren's chest, hips, and knees.

"Isn't that the Junior you tried to assign to my Field Exercise the other day?" Donné said quietly.

Care wondered if Donné was as moved by Kerlin's caring gestures as he himself was.

"He's a Fleet Commander now," Kerlin answered just as quietly.

"FLEET Commander?!" Donné seemed out of touch with current events.

A multi-terra-day Field Exercise can do that to ya! Care moved on to the pool. He whipped off the towel and jumped right in. "Aahh!" The water was still fantastic.

Donné folded his arms, "big tub, eh?" He was either too tired to keep up the temper, or he was starting to be impressed. He looked so tired and it looked like a chore as he started undressing. Donné jumped into the water and let out a long sigh.

Kerlin jumped in next.

"Is there a chair in here?" Donné closed his eyes, letting this pushy Commander push him around.

Rhiannon sank into the pool, peeking at Erin from under his blond eyelashes, his almond shaped aqua-green Elf eyes pools of need. Erin was fully able to empathically read those emotions and he seemed perfectly willing. Care smiled at the noises coming from Rhi, even Donné cracked open a tired eyelid to peer at the noisemaker.

Donné became self-conscious that Commander Kerlin was acting like a chair, just so he could relax. He pushed away and swam a few laps, sinking under to wet his hair. "Mm," Donné broke the surface and whistled with pleasure.

Care shared the sentiment. The water was warm and embracing as a womb. The mildly perfumed soapy mixture made his skin feel soft and slick. He ran his hands all over his body. He got out of the pool for a scrubber cloth and quickly hopped back into the water, careful now not to splash. Even though Rhi's thrashing about made the water a trifle turbulent.

Commander Kerlin was holding his last team pennant. "Here Donné, why don't you just hold on to it for a couple of days? You never know how you'll feel about it by then."

"Yeah, yeah," Donné stuck the pennant behind his ear, his long snow blonde hair helping it to stay. He sank and Kerlin grabbed him.

Kerlin backed up to lean on the side of the pool and wrapped his arms around Donné, just holding him.

Care moseyed up to his Commander; the room lighting made Kerlin's skin moonlight pale and his red hair looked very dark from the weight of the H2O molecules.

Kerlin greeted him with a warm smile.

"Commander?" Care began, artfully not quite meeting Kerlin's eyes. "You were only teasing before, about the preventive medicine thing, right?"

"Oh no, I was completely for real!"

"But, you wouldn't even consider going the three hundred?" Care found it hard to believe Garren had made it that far in the exam.

"It's a possibility," Kerlin said softly. "What are you thinking about right now?"

"Um, I'm thinking about the sudsy pool water."

"You aren't thinking about 'inviting it'," Kerlin used the lingo. "Not like you did this morning when you skated out of uniform for absolutely no qualifying reason?"

"I did have reason," Care protested, politely not reminding Kerlin about the earlier skinny dip over the balcony. "I was tailing Barett for Garren's sake." He said in complete honesty. Gasp! "Barett's team and the Mermaids!" Care scrambled for a PDA. He paged Barett. "Barett! Barett! Acknowledge! Do you require assistance?! Barett!"

♋

Kerlin's heart hammered as he listened to Care's conversation. The consequences for Care did not bear contemplating, if irreparable harm had been done to Barett's Field Team.

♋

"Barett!"

At last a tired sneering voice answered. "Care! Are you ready for more?"

"How did your dates with the Mermaids go? Did you get along okay?"

"They let us go after they finished with us. Do you know what the penalty is for abandoning a civilian to the mercy of an enemy of the Realm?"

Kerlin closed his eyes in horror.

"Like your buddies, Kraken's team did to Garren?" Care said harshly.

Kerlin opened his eyes, listening with great admiration to Care's quick thinking.

Care continued, "and they weren't enemies, they are loyal to Our Emperor." Care left off the Demon Lord bit. "And you were in uniform."

"They sang us out of our uniforms," Barett's voice took on

volume. "We were civilians when you left us!"

Care was thinking fast. "You looked like you were headed toward a consensual orgy! And after what you did to me, it rankled pretty harshly to my mind."

"Why hasn't Kraken's Team been arrested?" Barett asked as if it was of no consequence.

"Garren thinks it was a harmless prank."

"It wasn't. I told you about the bribe I was offered to harm you."

"Who offered the bribe?" Care asked with hope Barett would spill it.

"I don't know."

Care was crushed.

"He was a Cleric, and not a Cleric of Astra." Barett's voice changed to a pleasant coaxing. "Come trot your shorts for me again, play, and I won't report the abandonment."

Care went cold. "You better watch your mouth Barett!"

"You'd better watch your ASS, Senior Guard."

At this, Kerlin grabbed the PDA from Care. "Barett, this is Commander Kerlin. I am watching Care's ass now, you watch yourself or you'll be staring down a one way trip to Dragon gullet!"

A pause.

"Commander Kerlin, enjoying your two days as a new Commander?"

"Three days. I'm nominating you for a demotion."

"Be ever careful in the dark luscious Kerlin. O, yes. I can offer you this warning, seeing as how friendly I am with your teammate Care. Rumours are a Mermaid was asking about you, she asked of you by name. From what I overheard, she was close enough to smell your blood and lust for it."

The PDA link cut.

Care's chill went down to his bones, the warm pool water didn't help dispel it.

"Interesting Team, eh?" Erin said. He, Rhi, and Donné were

wide eyed at the exchange they'd just witnessed.

"DON'T BACK OUT!" Care cried, hiding the fact that his heart was shattering into pieces. "I will."

"Whah?" Erin exclaimed in all seriousness, despite his bantering tone. "I wouldn't miss this for the Realm!"

Rhi nodded.

Donné added, "I want to be where I'm needed, if you feel my presence on the Team will help, count me in."

Kerlin put an arm around Care, hugging him against his side. "We can handle Barett!"

A Blerpie broke the shared silence. Kerlin moved, "that's mine. I should change my Blerpie tone to something original."

"I'll fetch it Commander," Erin offered. He kinetically lifted the PDA from where it had been left on the tiled floor, floating it to Kerlin's open palm.

"Awesome," Kerlin smiled in wonder. His lips opened on a silent 'O'. "It's Fly13." He said to Care, "it thinks it may know where the Dragon Cub is!"

"A mission Commander?" Care said, all excited.

"Well," Kerlin read the desire in Care's eyes, sharing it. His four team picks were watching his face trenchantly. "I don't know if I want to make a wrong start with my first team. I only gave Erin and Donné pennants a mark ago. And Donné is exhausted."

"Ach!" Care splashed.

"We'll inform our Emperor, he'll send someone to Fly13, in fact; he'll probably go himself."

"What is the Writ standard for jumping the requisite?" Donné looked at Erin, one of the Disciplinarian experts.

"It has never happened," Erin bit his lower lip. "An untried statute is usually judged by the Emperor in person."

Kerlin dispatched a high priority emergency message to Emperor Methusem, he sent it with the planetary emergency code, he was sure Methusem wouldn't mind his presumption. "There." He faced a very sourpussed and disappointed Care.

"Officially, Care, you are still a Rogue Fielder, so you can go. And I'm a Commander, there is nothing to stop me from going either."

Suddenly!

All the PDAs blerpied. "What is this? Planetary alert?" Kerlin mumbled. Nothing so drastic. Every Guard going Deep Space were to turn in their uniform for an upgrade. All uniforms were being spelled with counter-kinetic jinxes. Rogue Fielder Tamkin had reported in with a warning stating that pirates currently at large were some of them endowed with powerful kinetic abilities. The uniforms needed the extra protection.

"I'm not going outside without my uniform," Rhiannon said adamantly.

"It wasn't a request Elf," Erin said with a tone of authority.

"I don't care Human."

"Rhiannon," Kerlin chided. "You can't walk around in uniform all the time."

Rhi sank in the water up to his lower lip.

"Let's do turn our uniforms in, we'll go together," Kerlin moved to climb out of the pool.

Erin mumbled to Care, "he's definitely not a procrastinator, is he, eh?"

"Nope, makes a decision, then wham," Care mimed a racing rocket speeding off the start marker.

"O by the way Care, that message you left me this morning was too cryptic, more details next time," Kerlin slapped his hand into his palm for emphasis.

They walked through the living room area, Garren stirred despite their efforts to be quiet.

"Hi, did I miss anything?" Garren's voice sounded very vulnerable. "Are you going out?"

"Hey Garren," Kerlin stood by Garren's chair to rub Garren's shoulder. "We're being ordered to turn our uniforms in for some jinxing."

"Oh," Garren smiled wanly, lifting his head up and feeling around to orient himself, looking groggy. "They haven't issued me a uniform yet."

"Commander," Care said in a normal voice. "I'm going to hang with Garren, I'll do the uniform thing tomorrow." He plopped down naked in the recliner opposite Garren, pushing the button to raise the leg rest. "Are those candies Jillysnaps Garren?"

Garren grinned and reached to hand the bag of Jillysnaps over.

"Thanks!" Care grabbed at least four Jillysnaps in a single dip into the bag.

"We'll turn in your uniform for you, Care. Garren, I hope you can keep Care behaved while we're out. And remember what's waiting for you tomorrow, Care." Kerlin slapped a hand on his hip to demonstrate a hint of the matter waiting for tomorrow.

"O yeah, Garren, I must sincerely thank you for volunteering for my Commander's Discipline Exam. To take three hundred, you have my eternal respect for that."

Garren winced. "Have you met Prince Wenrik?"

:: Care and Garren in the Royal Suite ::

Garren Waysixth and Care Ethaynen chatted quietly, hanging out in the Royal Suite, eating from the bags of candy and sharing some memories of Guard Training. They ordered room service twice, torn between chocolate and alcohol, they finally discovered a drink that combined both. They ordered up a whole pitcher of Mudtini.

"O, I owe you money for the tithe," Garren remembered. "May I borrow your PDA?"

"Ach, it's nothing Garren."

After passing a mark or two of talking, snacking, and

drinking, their mutual friend Dana Atuin came swooping in from the balcony of the pool room. Dana joined them in the living room of the suite, a step of his feet deactivated his gravity skates.

Dana stood a full head taller than Care or Garren, he was classified as a Hybrid-Human. His alien genetics derived from a people long extinct. He was slim, leggy, with long blonde hair reaching to his hips, his eyes were a tan brown.

"Garren!" Dana exclaimed.

"Hi Dana," Garren smiled, genuinely glad to see his friend.

"Hi Dana," Care said, giggling, sipping from his third, no fourth mug of Mudtini.

Dana dropped a fair sized parcel on a sofa as he said this, "I hope you like the clothes I picked out for you." He added wistfully, "Garren, I can't handle Lisza and Terriane by myself."

"O, by the Vale Dana, I am so sorry, I can't believe I forgot such a thing," Garren looked genuinely contrite. He apologized profusely.

"What's this?" Care asked.

"Yester-terra-day, Dana arranged us for a double date with Terriane and Lisza," Garren explained.

Care poured out an extra Mudtini for Dana. "I know them both. They pantsed me once in the Mall. Invite them here Dana, by all means. If I'm an extra body, I can trot down to my own hotel room here."

"Of course you aren't an extra body," Dana sipped at the drink. "Mm mmm."

"Dana," Care said with a mischievous twinkle in his yellow eyes, buzzed from the alcohol and sugar rush. "You better take off your uniform if you be intending to drink, or you'll get Writ."

"Do you feel up to it Garren?" Dana noticed that Garren was not his usual self. "I'm sure they won't be upset if we beg off."

"No, please, do you think they would want to come up here?" Garren wiped a chocolate mustache off his lip with the back of his hand.

"Don't forget to tell them about the fantastic private pool!" Care said with sincerity. Woah, it was fun to get drunk once in a while.

Dana smiled at Care and finally noticed he was naked. "Hey, we should all be naked for when the girls get here, won't they be surprised. Ooops, I better page them or it's moot."

The ladies were agreeable to the suggestion and arrived fairly quickly. The women were both pretty brunettes, red lip color and eyeliner drew your attention to their mischievous expressions. They were surprised to find their fellow Guards naked and pitcher deep into their Mudtinis.

Garren paged room service for two more pitchers, ordered some appetizers and a pot of witch brewed mocha latte, and very pleased to find Mustard Mash on the menu.

"Isn't mash usually a side dish?" Terriane padded barefoot behind him. Garren turned to her and found her naked. He stood stunned, his storm-gray eyes gathered a look of hunger. The look thrilled Terriane to her toes. Goddess, he was scrumptious, the hunger in his gorgeous eyes made to stir a little fear, but in an exciting way. She raised her fingers to Garren's male breast, spreading her fingers, his strong chest was more than she could cover with one hand. Her open lips dove straight for his nipple.

Garren gasped and staggered, breathing labored. He put a muscular arm around her petite body, crushing her against him, the feel of her soft body against his excruciatingly sensitizing. She raised her face for his kiss and they fell on to a sofa together with Garren on top. Completely oblivious when room service arrived, Care got up to get the door as he told Garren not to bother getting up.

Care poured himself a fresh mug and dollop-ed out a helping of Mustard Mash. Dana was busy with Lisza and Care felt a little odd man out.

Dana raised his head and telepathically sent Care an

invitation to join them. "Huh? You're a telepath?" Lisza raised her head to look at Care with a steamy invitation in her eyes. Her legs were entwined around Dana's waist, but she held a hand out to Care.

Care and Dana took turns making love to her, riding her to orgasm after orgasm.

Garren gave all his efforts to Terriane. After his first orgasm, his second erection lasted a long time. His fingers danced over her clitoris as his cock thrust into her pussy, coaxing the high pitched moans and wails he so loved from a woman.

Dana brought out his favorite lubricant and massage oil. The five of them poured handfuls from the bottle.

After Garren used some of the massage oil on his cock, he found he could manage to slip that extra bit into Terriane's pussy he'd held back for fear of hurting her. She threw back her head and cried out a carnal cry that almost made Garren come immediately, but he managed to keep it going vigorously a little while longer.

Eventually, the five of them lay panting and spent, shoulder to shoulder, moaning and in some cases crying from the intensity of it, and after a bit of that, they sat up to eat the now cold appetizers and to refresh a buzz-on from the drinks. Care ordered a fresh batch of warm munchies. The night was half over and Care felt sad, but then brightened after realizing they still had half a night to go.

"Hey, you wanna dip in the pool?" Care suggested.

"Hey, yeah," Lisza's drawl was heavy with afterglow.

Laughing, they carried the food into the pool room.

Dana stopped drinking, if they were going to swim drunk, someone had to play lifeguard, just in case. The warm water felt soo good.

Garren's cock was ready again. Lisza tapped Terriane on the shoulder. "Mind if I cut in for this one?" Commander Lisza asked her best friend politely.

Terriane sighed and reluctantly let Garren loose. Garren

captured Lisza's mouth with his lips, tasting her, and wrapping his muscular arms around her yielding body. Dana grabbed Terriane's hand and let his brown eyes fill with invitation.

Terriane had always been very attracted to Dana and she hopped, throwing her legs around his waist, the hair around his balls was the silkiest thing she'd ever touched. Dana carried her to the edge of the pool, where she laid back submissively and gave over control to Dana.

Care helpfully handed the bottle of lubricant to Dana. Dana politely thanked him and instead of rubbing it on himself, he spread Terriane's pussy lips for it and dribbled it on her, smoothing the stuff in and on her nooks and crannies. She was very languid from the sex with Garren, and she let her limbs go limp, riding the sensations; she got a great deal of satisfaction just by the fact it was Dana touching her so intimately. He cautiously, yet expertly, slipped his cock inside her, milking the sensations for every drop. She screamed loudly in ecstasy. After Dana came, he let some of his weight rest on her body where she laid, her legs dangled in the water.

The people in the park outside their pool room balcony were still partying. There was some enthusiastic applause in response to her screaming. Terriane smiled and laughed. She crawled on to all fours and got up. "I'm gonna go take a nap," she whispered, flying on wings of satisfaction.

Dana whispered to Care, his eyes cast down, "Care would you ...?"

"Of course Dana," Care stood behind Dana in the pool. Dana handed him the bottle of lubricant and then bent over the edge of the pool, he dropped his face on to his folded forearms. Dana cried out when Care initiated his move, moaning and making soft sobbing noises intense with sensation.

Lisza turned her face towards Dana and Care to watch them. Her cries rose in pitch, holding on to Garren as he fucked her into another screaming orgasm as Dana's noises moved her. She'd known Dana since early training and she'd always desired him.

Garren's lips were seeking hers and she surrendered to this scrumptious man. She sighed deeply, completely sated. Garren buried his face in her breasts, kissing her there tenderly, rolling her nipples gently in his teeth, flicking the points with his tongue. "O Garren," Lisza sobbed. "You're taking me up to where the Goddess sings." And she screamed as his fingers found her clitoris and rubbed her in circles, while he worked suckling at her breasts.

More applause sounded from under the balcony.

"Woah, there be some serious rocking in the Royal Suite," someone shouted. "Hey come out and take a bow," someone else shouted.

Garren whispered to Lisza, panting softly in her ear, his hot breath drove her wild, even in her sexual exhaustion. "Will you sleep the rest of the night with me?"

She brushed her splayed fingers in his gorgeous full bodied hair. "You dear man, yes!" She wrapped her arms around his neck. He rose from the pool, carrying her in his arms, dripping pool water as he did so.

Dana and Care were resting on the pool's edge.

"Wait," Dana called gently. He picked up a clean fresh towel and patted Garren and Lisza dry, so they wouldn't drench the bed linens and be uncomfortable.

"Thanks Dana," Garren said with much emotion. "Thank you." He offered his lips to Dana for a friendship kiss, they kissed over Lisza cradled in Garren's strong arms. She giggled, a very spent sounding giggle. They went to bed.

Care and Dana stayed up a while longer, finishing the pitcher of Mudtini, it was much too delicious to resist. Then they went to bed, too, flopping down to sandwich Terriane between them.

The good natured rumours of the party in the Royal Suite that night, spread through the Guard like a computer virus, by morning, every Guard on the planet had heard about it.✍

Dragons Cubs and Virgin Blood

XXVIII. Terra-Date 215.151 Early Morning
:: Hotel New Ranger. Kerlin ::

Kerlin's Team, upon returning to the Royal Suite and finding the beds taken, empty pitchers of chocolate smelling alcohol, empty snack trays, and empty bags of sweets; were vocally miffed at missing the party.

Erin, Donné, and Rhiannon crashed on the sofa and recliners in the living room area.

Kerlin braved the bedroom, hoping not to find any more after-party debris.

Two women he recognized by reputation were leaving Care, Garren, and Dana sound asleep in the beds.

"Poor exhausted boys," Terriane teased Kerlin with a wink as he watched the ladies skate off into the early dawn, departing via the balcony.

The morning summer sun had noticeably cooled since the previous day. A brisk breeze from the open balcony doors tangled in Kerlin's tousled hair, feeling caressing and comforting.

Kerlin took his time in the toilet room, splashing soap-wash on his face and cleaning his teeth with oral hygiene rinse. He changed into fresh shorts and crawled into the huge bed where Garren slept like an innocent cub. Before drifting off into slumber to sleep the day away, Kerlin read through the morning's announcements on the Guard's circuit broadbands.

The Royal Space Fleet's pre-launch party was scheduled for the afternoon, but the Launch Event itself was delayed, due mainly to the fact it would take approximately three days to Spell all the uniforms for protection against kinetic pirates.

Guards certified for gravity skates were all upset for they had to turn in their boots. The Spell casters pointed out to the Guards complaining on the message boards, how much more unhappier they'd be kinetically dangled by their boots. Kerlin felt like he'd left a best friend behind, when he'd left his skating boots at the Spell labs.

A public announcement was issued for kinetic volunteers to help test the uniforms' effectiveness against kinetics powers.

Kerlin heard a rustle in the next bed.

Dana Atuin was getting up and dressing, shifting his own PDA from hand to hand as he pulled up his sleeves. Dana said he regretted having to run out. After last night's Coronation Ball, Nerrys Nefeinn had stayed in Nihera City with his family. Nerrys, his wife Nalira, and his daughter Syra were all volunteers to help with the counter kinetic jinx testing. Dana's mail held a message from Nerrys, asking Dana to keep Jesse company and a Nihera City sightseeing tour seemed a worthwhile idea.

"Oh yes," Kerlin remembered Garren mentioning Jesse only the day before.

Kerlin's PDA blerpied with a text message from Emperor Methusem.

The missing Dragon cub, a five year old named Freegelda had been rescued yester night. She was unharmed.

A Demon Summoner known as Kanuenos had trapped her under a Deja Spell deep in the Subterraneum underground. The

Spell worked by returning her again and again to her starting point, it was a Spell adapted to prevent escape into the crossroad corridors. In fact, Freegelda was now grounded by her big sister Brynnhilde for wandering off in the first place.

The Summoner was officially on the 'most wanted' list; though he hadn't been seen nor heard from at all. Methusem's private speculation to Commander Kerlin was that Kanuenos may have gone down a Dragon gullet. The Dragons, however; weren't fessing.

Methusem included a private request to Kerlin to please, keep in touch with the lonely Fly13. A message once in a while would cheer the shuttle. Kerlin smiled at that, he didn't mind a bit for Fly13 was a convivial personality.

Methusem signed off the message by wishing Kerlin's Team well being and wrote he looked forward to seeing them at the Pre-Launch party.

Kerlin had a feeling his Team would be sleeping through the party, he hoped the Emperor wouldn't be upset with him for missing two parties in a row. He returned a text message to mention Garren was staying with them in the Royal Suite.

The last thing Kerlin was thinking as he drifted off to sleep, he wondered if it would be safe to introduce himself to the Lady Mage-Healer for he very much would like to make her acquaintance.

☞

Kerlin woke a few marks later; the blinds were drawn and he wasn't able see if it was still daylight. He didn't want to open the blinds and risk waking Garren. He got up to go into the living room and was satisfied to see the sun still up and well arced in its zenith. He found Care was awake and doing callisthenic exercises.

Care gave his Commander the famous grin.

"O, don't think for an instance I forgot about your preventive medicine. Did you?" Kerlin fetched up the ashwood discipline paddle.

"Commander," Care whispered with a wide eyed look of innocence. "The noise will wake our teammates." He gestured to the Guards sleeping on the sofas.

"Haven't you a room registered in this hotel?" Kerlin raised one eyebrow.

Care's breath caught. He was stuck for it. He groaned.

"Lead the way," Kerlin beckoned, crooking one finger.

With trembling legs, Care led the way.

Once in Care's economy sized hotel room, Care went to bend over the side of the bed.

Kerlin put a stop to that, "we're not here for you to get comfortable."

Care rolled his eyes. "This is where Erin would tell me to grab my ankles."

"Well, let's do it then," Kerlin held the paddle and stood next to Care.

Care stayed standing and bent over, his hands on his knees.

At first, Kerlin paddled Care over his shorts, using the same stroke intensity he'd used during the exam. He couldn't tell if Care was reddening and Kerlin found it necessary to tug down Care's pajama shorts. He resumed the paddling.

Care started a quiet whimper. "You give excellent discipline," Care's voice wound very tight. He was careful not to say anything teasing or sarcastic, afraid it would make Kerlin stop.

"I hope this works, Care. This preventive medicine is your reward for *not* breaking our protocol statutes." Kerlin stopped with Care's ass cheeks in the red zone, not wanting to cause bruising. He sat down on the bed and took a deep breath to steady his nerves.

Care pulled up his shorts and stood with his arms crossed. "I understand."

"The thing I don't understand is," Kerlin chose his next words, "you have friends to do this for you. Why do you still need to invite discipline?"

Care took a deep breath. "It's different. Playing has safe words to make it stop. Official discipline, there is no stopping. You have to take it, no matter how much you want it to stop."

Kerlin tried to absorb the concept.

"Is this why you're giving up your Rogue Fielder assignment?"

"NO!" Care turned away from Kerlin. "You can take back your team pennant, you know."

"Care. I *do* want you on my Team. Did I make you angry with me?"

"You're implying that my personal issues would interfere in my duty to our Emperor."

"I know your loyalties are above reproach." Kerlin brushed back his hair. "I've only been a Commander for a few days. I don't have the experience I need to properly understand some of our Team's personal issues."

"Let's go back to the suite, eh," Care said.

♋

After this dose of firm 'preventive medicine', they returned to the Royal Suite. Care flopped face down on a sofa and gingerly rubbed his ass cheeks. For a new disciplinarian, Commander Kerlin had done a thorough job.

Erin, Donné, and Rhiannon were awake and dressed in lazy day casual chic. Erin and Rhi were in a heated argument over which entertainment band to watch on the jumbo sized computer screen. Kerlin interrupted this argument by asking who had started it. Erin and Rhi stood silent. Kerlin turned his question to Donné and without any apology Donné pointed straight at Erin.

Kerlin tapped the ashwood paddle on his palm and bade Erin to follow him. Biting his lower lip in consternation, Erin followed, albeit slowly. When they returned, Erin sat very stiffly on a recliner chair. The computer screen was off.

Feeling very lazy, they all resumed their afternoon napping.

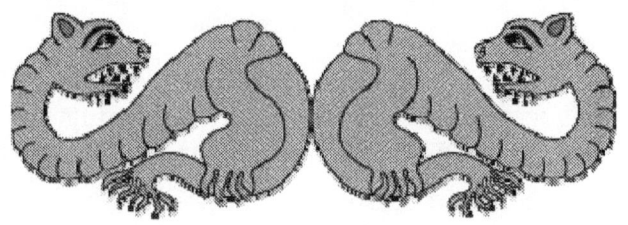

They were still napping when their unexpected visitors arrived.

Commander Kerlin and Care jumped up into a fighting stance, instantly alert. Kerlin stood down first.

Care grimaced a little, sitting down was not his first choice, he removed himself from present company to get dressed.

Kerlin waved a cheery 'Hello' to their Emperor, followed by Sov Minister Ange and his assistant Junior Minister Vylara. Traci and Dana followed next and to Kerlin's surprise, Sov Minister Allons also joined the entourage. A Guard wearing the deep burgundy coloured version of their Guard uniform walked in, almost mechanical in his movements. He had full bodied long dark hair and expression on his face was hard to detect. The burgundy uniforms were worn by the immortals serving in the Guard. And lastly, to Kerlin's vast dismay, Commander Kraken and Commander Barett were joining them.

The presence of the last two made Commander Kerlin feel extremely put out at their Emperor, even though this was the Royal Suite and their Emperor could be expected to hold meetings here.

Kerlin quietly followed Care into the suite's bedroom, needing to calm his mixed emotions before confronting Kraken and Barett. Erin, Rhiannon, and Donné filed behind him.

Kerlin paced the bedroom, making an incomplete circuit around the two beds.

Care and Erin sat gingerly on a settee by the huge window, comparing notes on Kerlin's discipline techniques. Rhi and Donné listened to Care and Erin with a morbid fascination for the subject.

Garren woke and pulled a pale blue sheet over his body and thought vaguely about getting up, entertaining an idea to not move, until the last mark to launch. He'd become emotionally attached to Care and Kerlin and almost wished he could join their team and give up a career assignment on Halçyon.

Kerlin snapped shut the privacy curtain to the bedroom, greatly wishing the curtain would turn into a solid door to physically bar the two rooms apart, - did Rhiannon know such a Spell?

The curtain rustled and Dana entered, he gave Kerlin a mixed smile of happy and sad. "They brought the meeting to you, since you weren't at the Pre-Launch Party," Dana stood awkwardly. "Are you angry?"

"Honestly, I'm put out that Methusem brought THEM here," Kerlin paced anew. "Barett and Kraken."

"You haven't filed a Writ request against them?" Dana said. He wasn't aware of the details of the attacks on Garren and Care. Some people are born naturally proof against telepaths, Kerlin was one of these as Dana discovered.

"I'm filing nominations for their demotions."

"They aren't Field Team Commanders any longer. Methusem has assigned them a commission to ready the Hospital Ships. In reality, desk jobs."

Kerlin was about to ask, readying for what? The door curtain again fluttered. He braced himself to be professional for handling the unpleasantness. His heart rate sped up.

Prince Wenrik appeared first, poking his head first through the curtain, then followed by the rest of his body. His wings were completely sheathed; he might pass for an Elf if you weren't expecting anything extra. The Dragon Prince wore the same loincloth and beach sandals as yester-terra-day.

Following him, the cutest little Were-Dragon fluttered her wings. She appeared equivalent to a five year old Human with a mop of short riotous blonde curls shrouding her face. She had one set of wings, the membranes bore a resemblance to what Kerlin remembered of Prince Wenrik's wings. She wore a cute little jumper dress reaching to her knees. She zoomed around the room flying near to the ceiling. She sniffed, her cute little nose rather pointed in the center of her face. She sniffed and snuffled and fluttered by Kerlin's elbow.

Kerlin extended his forearm for her to perch upon.

She settled, blinking lazy eyelids. She hummed under her breath, like some children do when they were wrapped in their own universe.

During his preoccupation with the cub, Dame Brynnhilde had joined them. Kerlin recognized her from the news broadbands. The computer images didn't do her beauty justice. Kerlin decided she was quite spectacular in person. She wore breast plate armor like a halter, chain mail draped from the bottom of her breast cups to her upper thighs.

"Yayy," Care spoke first, a wide happy grin flashed ear to ear.

The Grand Dame opened her arms to Care like you would to a child.

Care grinned and ran to her with no trace of embarrassment, surrendering his body to her embrace. Under her wings and ankle length tresses, Care became practically hidden from view.

Prince Wenrik spoke. "You are the Human Kerlin, friend to the entity Fly13?"

Kerlin inclined his head, he would have bowed but for the little girl on his forearm. "I am so honoured." Kerlin had taken only one protocol class in Training and he felt highly unqualified for this meeting. Well, he wasn't one to stand on ceremony.

"On behalf of Castle Utfordring and reigning Dragon King of our Lands, Lord Fafner, we offer our gratitude and our Dragon Family Kinship to you and yours." Wenrik gestured to include everyone in the room.

Dragon Family Kin-ship? Kerlin knew how rare this honour

was bestowed. He was so touched, he didn't know what to say.

"This is Freegelda," Brynnhilde's husky voice introduced, her pronunciation heavy on her consonants. "The young one your wisdom helped us to rescue from the Demon Firedrakes enthralled to the Summoner."

Kerlin petted the girl's hair and his wrist came close to her nose. She sniffed and seemed to swoon.

"Please, we offer apologies on behalf of our sister Freegelda. The scent of virgin blood is highly intoxicating to us and she is young and inexperienced."

Every Guard in the room swung their staring amazement at Commander Kerlin.

Kerlin shrugged.

"Come Freegelda, we must tell the Human's Dragon King of the roving Firedrakes." Brynnhilde beckoned to the child and the child sweetly obeyed.

Prince Wenrik stayed with the Guards, standing polite and reserved. Care started a chat with him.

Dana mentioned aloud that Nerrys and Jesse were planning on visiting today, adding, Jesse was excited to hang out with Fleet Commander Garren. Dana winked at Garren.

Garren smiled in do part to the familiarity, he would never forget Dana's thoughtfulness and friendship.

"Dana," Kerlin's mood was much better than a moment ago. "What were you saying about readying Hospital Ships?"

"Tch, Commander if you would deign to attend the meeting you could catch up on events," Dana teased.

Well, Kerlin thought, if he's teasing it can't be too serious. "Could you please just tell me?"

Care snorted. He called out in a laughing voice, "be happy you aren't wheedling information out of Traci!"

Dana agreed loudly.

"Well?" Kerlin drawled.

"Sixty terra-days hence, some of us are invading a bio-lab in the home space of the Empire of Catharra."

"Whah?" Kerlin said.

"And what do you mean, some of us?" Care latched on to that bit.

"Well, your team isn't going," Dana shrugged an apology. "Traci and I don't have teams yet, so we're going as Rogues. The immortals will be our back ups, they are supposed to assist us as we need them, but not engage directly in the battle. The 'Scooter Brigade' are being called into action."

Rhi chimed in, "what horrific thing is happening at this bio-lab?" He asked, but he cringed waiting for an answer.

Dana only said, "there are children involved. We're delaying for the Hospital Ships and there is heavy argument over the decision."

"Did they want me in their meeting? Seems odd if we're not invited to the battle," Kerlin said in a rebuking tone.

"Kerlin, you are respected as a strategist. I think Methusem wanted your input in the planning," Dana lost his usual smile.

"O," Kerlin kicked the floor. "Heya Erin, want to give me some return discipline with that ashwood thing?"

Erin rolled his eyes thinking Kerlin was joking, he'd missed the conversation. He and Donné were deep in a private chat about Field Training.

"It is not too late," Dana slapped Kerlin's arm good naturedly.

Kerlin, about to heed Dana's encouragement, stopped to stare at something strange out the window. He asked the room service computer to open the blinds and the window blinds completely opened.

Wenrik shouted in a most earnest voice, "DROP TO THE FLOOR!" He grabbed those nearest him, Care and Rhiannon, and pulled them to the floor. Garren rolled off the bed and hit the floor. The rest of the Guards reacted just in time as the windows and sliding doors shattered into glittering shards of transparent poly-metal.

Kerlin clapped hands over his ears, the swift shift in

barometric pressure weighing on his ear drums. He squinted his eyes open, desperate to witness the sky. The sky had turned a strange shade of purple, a storm of incredible power. Just as Kerlin thought his ears drums would burst, the weight lifted and the purple lightened to a normal shade of gray gathering storm.

Methusem ripped through the bedroom's privacy curtain, his Dragon wings unsheathed and poised to spread, his aura spectrum glowed blue, the Emperor's power upon him and becoming greater by the instant. Methusem leaped from the balcony, rising rapidly in the sky, he became shrouded in a blazingly hot blue lit mist and from this mist a magnificent Dragon emerged.

In Dragon form, Methusem was a dreamy cobalt blue with a sky blue underbelly, a hue hard to detect with naked eyes on a neutral weather day. His mane of hair, reminiscent of an equine, was the bleach white of stratus clouds.

Dame Brynnhilde came running behind the Emperor; she too leaped from the balcony and morphed into her full Dragon form, her aura spectrum a pale green. Her Dragon form matched her aura in colour and her mane matched the halo gold of her Were-Human form hair.

Prince Wenrik unsheathed wings of light from his back, the light coalescing into two sets of wings, panting from the pain of the energy searing his skin. He remained in the room with the Guards, taking deep breaths to recompose his manner.

Kerlin arched his back and performed a back handspring to gain his feet and looked out the window. Strange bodies of flame were zipping high in the sky. "Our Ministers," Kerlin shouted above the roar of thunder. Though, he didn't believe Emperor Methusem would have left them dying on the floor.

Kerlin ran into the living room area, the windows in here were also shattered. Minister Ange and Vylara were bravely sitting on a sofa together. The Were-Dragon girl huddled under the desk and looked very rebellious about it. Cdr Kraken and Barett stood protectively by Minister Ange and Vylara. The immortal Guard was nowhere to be seen, nor was Minister Allons.

Kerlin spotted Traci skating not far from the window. Dana zoomed passed Kerlin on hobby skates and joined Traci in the air. The two of them skated off in a pair, both Guards were weaponless.

Cursing, Kerlin fumed, missing his own gravity skates. He put on a smile for Minister Ange's and Vylara's benefit, then, he heard wild shouting from the bedroom and he turned toward the sound. He saw Ange stand up and aim his hand like a weapon.

Something slammed into Kerlin's back, knocking him to the floor, he cushioned his head with his arm, and narrowly avoided cracking his skull open on the floor. He rolled automatically to his feet. He had a chance to admire the Minister use his powerful telekinetic ability on something long, limber, and licking with flames.

Unfortunately, a second such creature invaded the room, it wrapped a tail around Kerlin's waist, despite Kerlin's best dodging efforts. Kerlin's waist suffered an awful painful squeeze. The creature whipped Kerlin behind it as it spit itself back out the window. A flame touched his leg and Kerlin decided not to hold back the scream building in his lungs.

Searching the sky for a hopeful sight of a Dragon to rescue him, his gaze was drawn to the sight of a larger than Human sized creature, perhaps a Leonine Demon, high in the sky, Emperor Methusem in Dragon form chasing at its heels. The thing Methusem was chasing held someone limp under its arm.

A black Dragon Kerlin didn't recognize was heading to join them, but was too far away yet to help. The green Dragon wasn't in view.

Kerlin gasped as the Firedrake holding him whipped its tail around. Kerlin put his hands to his neck to prevent his neck from being injured by the velocity of the whip like momentum. Kerlin kicked and writhed to no avail, he couldn't loosen the

Firedrake's hold.

Someone was aiming right at Kerlin and the creature carrying him, someone very blonde. It was Donné veering in close, wearing hobbyist's gravity skates, not at all up to par with Guard issue skates, and wielding a penta-shield and a training sword. Donné's efforts were only irritating the creature.

From below, Prince Wenrik swooped into the fray, still in Were-Dragon form, a ball of energy coalescing over his fist. "Firedrake Demon, I challenge you!" The Dragon Prince shouted!

Another nearby Drake winged in close and flew at Wenrik. Donné rose up on his skates and closing in on the Drake's flank, jabbed his sword at it. The thing rolled in the air, incredibly agile, and opened its toothy maw. Expecting a fire attack, Donné raised his shield, but a wide jet of water attacked him instead. The shield didn't look to be helping against this attack and Kerlin thought in horror that Donné was drowning.

Prince Wenrik threw his energy ball at the creature attacking Donné and followed through by physically slamming his body against the Waterdrake, driving the Waterdrake off without successfully doing much damage to it. The collision broke the Prince's wing and he tumbled from the sky.

Donné was desperately wiping his eyes and didn't see the Prince falling.

"Donné," Kerlin screamed. The creature holding Kerlin swung him in its tail and Kerlin fought an urge to throw up. He screamed for help for the Prince.

Below them on the ground, Kerlin saw a kid with brown hair look upwards. The kid raised his arms and during this gesture the Prince's freefall slowed to a harmless velocity. The Prince landed safely on the ground with one wing bent at an excruciating angle. The kid dropped to the ground in a faint. A blonde man came screaming from a building and ran to the kid.

The Dragon that was Methusem broke off his attack on the Leonine Demon and sped towards the unconscious kid.

Methusem flashed his aura, touching both the boy and the Prince with his dragon healing magic. The boy moved and the crying man hugged him close. He lifted the boy in his arms and ran towards the building. The kid struggled, he looked raring to continue the fight.

The Prince fluttered his wings, having some trouble righting himself, while lying on his back.

Kerlin watched Rhiannon run to the Prince and help him stand.

On a powerful down beat of his wings, Prince Wenrik launched into the air, when he gained sufficient altitude, he shape changed into his full Dragon host. As a Dragon, Prince Wenrik's hide was a tan brown with a lighter tan underbelly and straw colored mane.

Meanwhile, Methusem scanned the sky, the Leonine Demon had disappeared from sight. Methusem spotted Kerlin in the clenches of the Firedrake and charged at them. Kerlin waved as cheerfully as he could at his Emperor to show he wasn't hurt.

The Firedrake apparently decided that to engage a charging Dragon King not to be wise, it threw Kerlin. Kerlin first went upwards, riding the initial momentum and then started the downward arc. Methusem flew directly under Kerlin.

Kerlin rotated his body in a half twist and hit the back of Methusem's neck. Scrambling for a hold to stop his slide into freefall; Kerlin tangled his hands in Methusem's soft stringy mane and held on. He got a leg over and sat up, feeling disrespectful about riding his Emperor this way.

His Emperor's Dragon hide was soft to the touch, but a sparser furred area felt pinch-y; like Human hair bristles growing back after a recent shave.

Donné gave a salute with his Training sword.

Methusem bore Kerlin down to the ground by the hotel's park and took off after Kerlin safely stood on his own legs. Kerlin resisted an urge to rub his inner thighs where Dragon fur had prickled. He gazed up to watch the action in the sky.

The branch of Guards affectionately referred to as the 'Scooter Brigade' arrived and jumped into the battle. Their transportation resembled an antique chariot without the wheels nor burden animals to draw them. These Guard issue fighting vehicles moved incredibly fast and were more secure than g-skates, if you listened to the Scooter Brigade boast.

Shuttles designed for battle began arriving, these shuttles were designed to carry six Guards a piece.

The Firedrakes and Waterdrakes proved incredibly agile, however; and it was the g-skaters who scored the best against these airborne threats.

A shuttle touched down near Kerlin's Team and a voice bellowed, "raring to join the battle? Hop aboard."

Kerlin hesitated. Where was Care? He noted the rest of his Team were hesitant to enter this shuttle, alas, something felt wrong about it. A woman's scream came from the inside of the shuttle and Kerlin had to decide then and there to chance it. They were out of uniform and unarmed. The scream came again. Donné skated to Commander Kerlin, knees bent and crouched for speed. He looked to Kerlin for instruction. "One of us has to do it!" Donné had only a training sword to work with.

Kerlin's heart hammering, he made his first life and death Command decision for his team. He acknowledged a 'go ahead' to Donné. Kerlin gave him a brief head start then headed after him. He motioned the rest of his team to wait outside, of course, they didn't obey. Would he ever have iron hand discipline? Most likely not.

Inside the shuttle, Kerlin saw Donné attacking a Guard in uniform, whom Kerlin recognized as one of Kraken's disbanded team. Donné's flurry of sword blows had the traitor pressed into a corner. It was a losing battle for Donné, the one in uniform only had to wait for Donné to exhaust himself. There was time enough to get a hostage out.

A figure wearing a green cloak huddled near the flying

controls manned by two more of the disbanded team. A fourth man in Guard uniform, Kerlin recognized as Pursy, stood in the doorway of the toilet closet.

The shuttle took off for the sky with Kerlin's Team aboard. Care leaped aboard just in time, Kerlin had no knowledge of how much Care was missing his negatron hand weapon prototype.

The cloaked figure dropped its cloak, a woman of supernatural appearance stood naked, a necklace of pink stones draped between her breasts and around her throat, yellow hair draped to her ankles. This had to be one of the Mermaids. Weren't they supposed to be loyal to their Emperor?

"There he is!" One of Kraken's team pointed at Kerlin. "A virgin, just like I promised you!"

The Mermaid sniffed, she shuddered with desire. "Yes, yes!" She took two steps forward and stopped. She closed her eyes and bowed her head, then took back the two steps. "He is Mortal and Human, yet he wears Fealty."

"So," the ex-Guard exclaimed. "Does that make him less delectable?"

A shout came from Donné, Kerlin whirled. His newest team member lay unmoving upon the floor. Care was landing hand to hand blows to no avail on one of their kidnappers. Erin telekinetically hoisted Pursy to the ceiling with a gesture of his hand, then the kidnapper went flying out the shuttle. Erin had tossed him to his probable death. There was a chance the uniform would save the one from a freefall death landing. If the Guard had turned in his uniform for the counter-kinetic jinxing as he was supposed to do, well, the point was moot, now.

Rhiannon took Erin's tactic as a hint and tried to get his target moving towards the exit for a nice one way trip into freefall. Before he could complete this goal, the Mermaid started to sing.

Everyone except for Care stopped to listen to the siren song. Care used the distraction to kneel by the fallen Donné. When everyone stood becalmed, she stopped singing. Kerlin used the moment of distraction to plan a counter attack.

"What are you waiting for? We brought you this offering of alliance, eat him!" Kraken's team member cried at her with impatience.

The Mermaid shifted her gaze to Kerlin, her eyes were the colour of seaweed with no white. "What manner of Lord are you that you command Fealty?"

Kerlin ignored her and knelt at Donné's side, feeling for his neck pulse. His next intent was blocked from her sight by Care, Kerlin grabbed for Donné's sword. He aimed its point at the Mermaid and ran it at her. Kerlin ran the sword through her torso.

She screamed and staggered a few steps, but did not fall for she was immortal. It would take more than a single blow of the sword to finish her. She started singing again, but her singing had pain in it and lost its power.

Care ran at her and threw all his weight at her to push her towards the open exit. He caught a glancing blow, he was body checked by an attack from one of the uniformed corrupt Guards. Care's head slammed against the wall of the shuttle, he went down.

They were now flying over the Meridian Sea, the city lost to view. The Mermaid didn't wait for the next push, she leapt for the exit, her legs shimmered and a marine mammal's tail appeared in the shimmering mist. She vanished over the edge of the shuttle hatchway.

The kidnappers attacked in concert, whatever the plot they had hatched with the Mermaid was now undone. They should have just surrendered, but they didn't.

Denied the time to cast a Battle Spell, Rhiannon went down next under the assault.

Kerlin refused to let anger cloud his combat reflexes. A blow landed on the back of his skull and he screamed inside his mind, then, knew nothing.

♌

Erin alone had managed to keep on his feet. His kinetic mind pulses were near exhaustion and he despaired of saving his teammates.

But, as Kerlin went down; their attackers started grabbing at their temples and twisting their bodies. They hit the floor of the shuttle and were laying in contorted positions.

Erin had never seen such a spectacle. His teammates lay unmoving on the floor. His mind threatened to go numb, but he remained purposeful. He sat at the piloting controls and brought the shuttle about to head back to Nihera City. He sat in the pilot seat and kept his hands on the steering controls, gripping it tight, his knuckles white.

Kraken's ex-Team started making strange sounds, drooling, and mumbling nonsense.

♌

Emperor Methusem flew with his mighty Dragon wings fully extended, gliding the air currents. He reached the shuttle, while it was still hovering the sea. He leveled directly above the shuttle and stretched his healing aura to encompass it.

He'd witnessed the falling bodies. His dread was that he had lost a loyal Guard. He shape changed into his Were-Dragon form and then sheathed his wings, his feet planted firmly on the roof steadfast against the wind. Grabbing the edge of the shuttle roof, he swung himself inside the hatchway.

The first face Methusem gazed upon was Erin's. Erin's handsome face started to regain signs of life when his teammates began stirring. Methusem felt for Kerlin's team with his telepathic senses and put his hands over his hearts. They would be fine.

Kraken's ex-team members, however; were in a state of mindlessness; physically, his Dragon Magic had healed their brains, but the filling was gone. Methusem could not feel any sense of their personalities or even speech recognition. He recognized the damage from a Telepathic Mind Rip. Methusem knew Erin was a minor telepath, yet, the Human did not have the power to do this damage. One of the others had done this thing. Methusem's powers could not reveal who exactly, not without violating his vows. He knew it had to be either Care or Kerlin.

Kerlin, Rhiannon, Donné, and Care were starting to revive.

Methusem hastily passed judgment upon his treasonous Guards. Carrying out the sentence immediately. Methusem dredged forth the power for a high level Spell Casting.

PERFIDIA SOLVENOUS.

The Transformation Spell took hold. The mind ripped ex-Guards' flesh turned to mist and from the mists came insect sized creatures. An ancient Earth historian would have recognized a swallow tailed butterfly. The wind from the open exits on the shuttle dragged the delicate winged creatures into the Nihera City dusk.

Erin watched silently.

Methusem stood framed in the shuttle exit, standing with his toes over the edge and one hand leaned on the aperture frame on his right. The lights from the city and a passing luna station glittered a reflection in the Meridian Sea as they approached the Nihera City Cove. His knee length midnight hair whipped around his nude body by a strong wind into a hopeless tangle. Lights reflected off some of the strands, glints of white light. His peridot eyes wide with unshed tears shone like jewels in the dusk.

♌

Methusem's flawless copper colored skin was very warm and comforting to the touch, Erin found as he put an arm around his Emperor to steady himself, stepping upon the edge, implicit and utter trust in Methusem's mighty strength to keep him safe. Erin leaned closer to Methusem's body, drawing in the warmth. The layer of Erin's borrowed tunic whipped in the wind brushing between them.

"How is Garren? The Leonine Demon took him ..." Erin's

anxiety faded.

"Garren is well, Dana and Traci took his care upon themselves. And I battled the Felled Angel Ariel. I banished the whence 'Angel of Punishment' to a Sub-Realm, where His immortality will drain away. He may or may not ever reappear." Methusem's eyes flickered and he gazed up at his handsome Guard, indulging a breathless moment to caress the life-spark in Erin's mortal body, bathing Erin in the essence of his Aura. A mortal body, but a life-spark as ancient as time itself. "The Immortal Felled are not our greatest, nor worst, enemy."

Erin closed his fingers tightly on long strands of his Emperor's wondrous hair. "I know, I've heard this one. Our greatest foe is the Enemy Within."

"Yes. Enemies within our own Guard. I will do all in my power to ensure civil war does not come to pass," Emperor Methusem closed his eyes against the buffeting winds caressing his body as he leaned upon the brink of the sheer drop from the shuttle.

XXIX. TERRA-DATE 215.152 EARLY AFTERNOON
:: Mermaid in the fountain. Kerlin ::

Kerlin learned a new appreciation for telekinetic construction workers. The kinetics mentally lifted the transparent poly metal into the empty frame. Kerlin and Care fixed the window sheet in place with sealant gump.

They were twenty stories up from street level, hovering on their gravity skates.

Actually, the window situation wasn't as bad as at first estimated. The higher story windows needed replacing. The terrible barometric storm front had been localized.

The specific cause of the atmospheric abnormality wasn't yet a matter of public record. Kerlin was suffering an intense curiosity, he conceded he may never be qualified among the need to know ranks. Trying not to think about it, Kerlin found himself enjoying the physical labor of repairing windows. He'd had an awful headache since the shuttle fight, the fresh air was helping him to feel better.

Glancing down the building, Kerlin saw a figure dressed in the burgundy colored version of their guard uniform floating up to their elevation. Kerlin and Care shared raised eyebrow expressions. The burgundy indicated the guard was an immortal. The figure appeared to be Human male with long wavy brunette hair. They didn't see the light of gravity skates and the figure didn't have wings. Exactly how the dude was flying, baffled them both. The figure met them at eyelevel and just hovered there a moment.

Kerlin knew the immortal's name only as Four. If there was

a Three or a Five immortal, Kerlin had no idea.

The immortal's face wore the expression of an actively communicating telepath, but Kerlin didn't hear anything in his mind.

Four seemed to be struggling with spoken words. He merely said, "you are wanted."

"That's nice," Care shifted on his skates, hovering protectively near Commander Kerlin. "It's nice to be wanted."

Kerlin nudged at Care to move, "you don't need to shield me." He didn't want to nudge Care too hard, if Care lost balance on his skates he could sprain an ankle or wrench a knee.

Having declared his mini announcement, Four fell from the sky, faster than natural free fall, he slowed close to the ground and made a smooth transition into walking away.

Kerlin quickly finished applying the window gump, then started to skate off in Four's direction.

"Wait!" Care cried. "Where are you going?"

"Care, you're being a bit over protective, eh? Four is a Royal Guard, I'll be fine," Kerlin saw Care was genuinely upset.

"Kraken's Team were guards, too!"

Kerlin wasn't exactly sure how to calm Care's fears. "It might be our Emperor who wants me. I wouldn't want to keep him waiting."

"Methusem would talk directly to your mind, if he wanted you to report. And I know, I was a rogue fielder, remember?"

Kerlin believed it. He said the only thing he could think of to reassure Care's worries. "I'm in uniform. Freshly counter jinxed"

Care had to agree Kerlin was safe as can be. He nodded once and skated off, going up.

Kerlin skated to follow Four. The immortal was nowhere in view. He landed on street level and pulled out his PDA. There were no messages waiting. Someone wanted him who didn't have access to the broadbands?

A sense of something brushed his mind, a sensation hard to

explain.

"You are unharmed!" The words came to his mind without a voice. Telepathy.

"Who is this?" Kerlin said aloud.

"Oh, I am hurt. You don't remember me?" The voiceless words floated in his mind. It felt like words on the tip of his tongue.

An image of a mythril bangle bracelet showed in his mind's eye. "Caithlin?"

Kerlin felt her delight transmitted over the telepathic link. Talking with telepathy added depth to a conversation. 'Where are you?'

He felt a tug, an urge to follow something pretty, an intangible dangling in front of his nose. The urge he followed was a straight line, there were plenty of obstacles in the way; buildings, statues, and what-have-you's. As a test, Kerlin resisted the urge. After figuring out he had a choice, he chose to continue following the urge.

He heard a fountain before he saw it. An archway led off the main rue and into a private courtyard. No stores, the courtyard led to private residences. There was only the blue canopy of open sky above.

The fountain was a grand one with spouts of architectural artistry, the water sprays were all toward the center, the brief arc of the water fell with soothing sound effects. Kerlin was able to stand at the edge of the fountain without getting wet. He estimated the fountain could comfortably fit ten or fifteen Mermaids.

A Mermaid was in the fountain, in full Mermaid form, her tail glistened in the sun touched water.

"You remember me, do you?" Kerlin smiled at her.

Caithlin was completely submerged in the fountain water, her ankle length tresses floated to the surface. At first Kerlin thought maybe she couldn't breath air in full Mermaid form, but then remembered Caithlin and her pregnant friend had been breathing air in the cave last terra-week.

"It's a delicate partial transformation', the explanation came directly to his mind. 'And." Her face rose from the water, she leaned her folded arms on the fountain edge, splashing Kerlin a bit. "Tis rather a rare ability to partially transform our upper body." She said this last aloud.

The technical details were fascinating. "Can you only change when you're exhaling? What happens when you're lungs are full of water the moment you shift to air breathing?"

Caithlin laughed with her eyes. "We manage it," was all she said on the matter.

Kerlin clicked his teeth to stem the tide of questions wanting to run off his tongue. Somehow, gazing into her Mermaid green eyes, Kerlin discovered he had made a friend.

"Remember," Caithlin turned coy. "Remember, you did not accept my bracelet for a gift?"

Kerlin pretended not to remember.

"You can not fool me this way,' she spoke into his mind again.

"How and when did I become telepathically bonded to a Mermaid?" Kerlin bespoke.

"By your lucky fortune," Caithlin listened to hear if Kerlin was angry.

He shook his head, errant fountain mist darkened his ruby red hair. He scooped a handful of the clear fountain water and splashed, using the water to brush back his hair bangs.

A voice rang out, "ACH NO!"

Kerlin turned to find Care Ethaynen skating toward them. "Care," Kerlin said sternly. "Did you follow me?"

Care didn't take his eyes off the Mermaid. The yellow color of his eyes shifted with vague shadows.

A curious whistle came from Caithlin, looking genuinely surprised, and she seemed fascinated by Care.

Intervention time? "Care! Care!" Kerlin shouted twice.

Care finally flicked his glance at Kerlin and nodded. He

jabbed a pointing finger at Caithlin. "If you ... DARE ... try ... your Mermaid joke on my Commander, or anything even remotely a joke. ... I WILL come after you. You are warned!"

Kerlin was taken aback by the outburst. Caithlin seemed to understand. At that moment, Kerlin believed Care would murder the Mermaid, if it came to it. He had no idea what Mermaid joke could make Care turn into this deadly serious threat. He decided the wisest course of action in the situation was to heed Care's experience in the matter.

Care gave Kerlin a concerned look. He retreated without another word.

It took a few quiet moments for Caithlin to recover her talkative mood. "A Nymph?" She rose up out of the water to her waist line, her open scarf dress dragging in the water, leaning her wrist on the fountain's edge. "It was believed they were all lost at the crossroads."

"Nymph? Are you saying Care's unidentified non-Human genetics is Nymph?" Kerlin didn't want to frighten her away by pouncing on her with too many questions.

"Yes. It is well he protects you. I was worried for you."

"You were worried for me? Why, though? You haven't known me long," Kerlin shook his head. "Wait, forget about me. Do you know more about Care?"

She nodded. "The Nymphs were descendents from Ancestral Earth," Caithlin put a hand on Kerlin's arm to calm him down. She could sense the waves of intense curiosity thrumming with energy in his body.

Kerlin was entirely enraptured by their conversation. "The crossroads? Do you mean the crossroad corridors? The ones the immortals use to step between worlds?"

"Yes. Know, not all immortals can step. It takes a certain flavor of power and a fearlessness about becoming lost."

"And the Nymphs became lost?"

"The mystery has not been delved to conclusion. When the Mers and Dragons forsook ancient Earth, it was thought the

Nymphs were crossing, too. But, it is written in Lore, the Nymphs did not step behind nor beside us."

"Someone made it through, if Care truly is part Nymph," Kerlin was finding Caithlin an easy person to talk to.

"And therein it lies," Caithlin said, sounding mysterious.

"Therein lies what?" Kerlin leaned closer to her, resting against the fountain's edge.

"To you, I am a person, Nymphs are a someone. There are many among Humans and Dragons, who would not note the distinction."

"Oh," Kerlin moved his leg, it was starting to cramp. "I think I understand."

Kerlin was leaning close enough to Caithlin to kiss her, if the thought came to cross his mind.

Caithlin was a Mermaid, yet, also a woman. She sensed his lack of interest in her charms. "This close to a Mermaid, and you haven't once thought of sex at all, have you?"

"Sex?" Kerlin laughed. "Our conversation is too interesting to think about other things."

She rolled her eyes in a gesture she must have picked up by living among Humans. Still, Kerlin's attitude was refreshing.

"What forms has your Nymph chosen?" Caithlin asked.

"Forms?" Kerlin raised an eyebrow. Did she mean ...?

"Shape changing!" She shape changed to demonstrate her meaning. Her tail shimmered with a green halo of light, legs took the place of her dolphin like tail. She perched her backside on the edge of the fountain. Her wet scarf dress clung to her body like a second skin. It created a striking enhancement to her ethereal looks, but, what would it take to make this Human Kerlin notice her figure?

♋

"Care's power is latent. He doesn't shape change," Kerlin felt elated. Shape changing would be an awesome stat for his Field Team.

Caithlin looked sad. "How old is he?"

"22. Why?"

"Oh," Caithlin's sad expression turned nonplussed. "Perhaps, I have misunderstood my Lore studies."

"What does Care's age mean in terms of shape changing?"

"A Nymph must choose their forms, two forms, and change by their twenty first solar solstice."

"What happens when they don't?" Kerlin guessed, "will he lose his shape changing ability?"

"He will sicken," Caithlin grew sad, again. "And die."

Kerlin's pulse sped up. Caithlin inhaled deeply, practically tasting Kerlin's pulse on her tongue.

"Care is twenty two," Kerlin grabbed her hand and held it. "His Human genetics must be saving him. He's too incorrigible, he likes to be an exception to the rules."

"Perhaps." Caithlin agreed. "Or Celesterra's solar sun does not hold sway over Nymph biology."

Kerlin exaggerated a sigh of relief. He sat next to her on the fountain edge, touching shoulder to shoulder. "It is odd, eh?" He mused aloud. "Emperor Methusem didn't recognize Nymph in Care."

"I do not have the rank to be allowed to read the Tome of Lore on Methusem. But, I did hear a story from the Mer Bards. Methusem declined, many times, invitations to the Court of Nymph. Therefore, may be, he has never met a Nymph in person. According to the legend, hmm, how to translate this? The refusals truly pissed off the Queen of Nymph."

Kerlin laughed. They shared a telepathic mental image.

He was still holding on to her hand, his thumb absently rubbed her knuckles in a caressing motion. "There is a Tome of Lore on Emperor Methusem?"

"Yes. But. It was stolen."

"Stolen! By whom?"

"I'm not in the need to know."

"Oh. I know how THAT feels," Kerlin sighed. "You study

Lore for a hobby?"

"Yes. Much of Lore reads like bedtime stories. Too enjoyable to miss when opportunity presents."

"I would love to talk all night and listen to your stories?" Kerlin tried to think of a way to coax her into hanging out all night.

"I can't," she said.

"Oh? Why?" Kerlin felt keenly disappointed.

"For your safety, alas. All I smell is your blood, all I hear is the flow of blood in your body, I can see the blue of your veins under your fair skin," Caithlin fought an internal battle to keep her eyeteeth at un-aggressive proportions.

Kerlin sat quiet a moment to decide how much he really wanted to hear her Lore stories. "How much blood are we talking about? Sips? Swallows?"

"NOOO! YOU CAN'T!" A little girl's voice yelled. Wings stirred the air and swooped close.

Kerlin recognized Freegelda, the Dragon cub in were-dragon form.

"Another person in your fan club?" Caithlin laughed so hard she had to hold her sides.

"He is my honoured Dragon family, his virgin blood is for me," Freegelda continued freaking out.

"You can not feed on him," Caithlin barely caught her breath back. "You are young and inexperienced, you do not know when to stop taking."

"I CAN, TOO. I CAN TELL," Freegelda's wild riot of short blonde curls fell all in her face as she beat her wings.

Kerlin interrupted their argument, "you can stop taking blood before you hurt me? We need to be absolutely sure on this."

Caithlin froze and Freegelda landed on the courtyard cobblestones with her wings half extended.

Caithlin froze, because she saw Kerlin was totally serious about inviting her to drink of his blood. Freegelda quieted, because she was swooning at the scent of Kerlin's virgin blood.

"You would trade blood to hear Lore?" Caithlin questioned.

"Depends on how much blood we mean."

Caithlin almost swooned, right next to the five year old Dragon cub. "A trickle, a long, slow, salty, trickle. You wouldn't even feel lightheaded."

Kerlin considered the proposition. He liked Caithlin. And he liked the little Dragon cub, who was technically honorary family. It was difficult for him to fathom why a trickle sized taste of his blood could excite them this much, and that it was connected to the fact he'd never had sex in his life. For him, it hadn't been a lifestyle decision, there was always something to do, more interesting things.

♋

Caithlin perceived this was going to be a package deal and decided she'd rather share Kerlin's virgin blood, than have none at all. "I could monitor her, make sure she stops before taking too much."

To give Kerlin a chance moment to think on it, Caithlin started pulling her hair from the fountain water, hand over hand.

"Do you need help?" Kerlin offered. What a novelty this was!

"If you want to help me wring the water out, twist my hair gently in sections," Caithlin demonstrated.

Kerlin followed her instructions. "This is heavy, your head can really hold this up?"

Freegelda started to help, too, starting at the ends.

"This is a historical first, a Dragon helping a Mermaid with her hair," Caithlin wondered if it was possible to be friends with a Dragon. "Well, we can not stay in this courtyard all night."

"No. I want to change into regular clothes." Kerlin grabbed another section of Mermaid hair. It was thick as a rope. The strands caught the light, reflecting shades of green, jewel colors, rather than a solid indistinguishable mass of solid green.

"Oh. Change into night clothes? Is this what Humans call a pajam-my party?" Caithlin exclaimed.

"Are you saying you want to have a Human style pajama party?" Kerlin couldn't resist the sense of fun in the Mermaid's voice. "What about Freegelda?"

"I HAVE PAJAMAS," Freegelda said with patience.

"Won't your parents miss you if you aren't home tonight?" Kerlin was careful to talk to her as an equal.

It didn't help. She still looked at him like he was a dim witted idiot.

"You were kidnapped all that time," Kerlin explained his reasoning. "They may be missing your company."

"Kerlin, you do not understand family life for telepaths," it was Caithlin's turn to explain. "Her parents will know where she is and can talk to her mind anytime," Caithlin added, teasing, "as long as evil Summoners aren't blocking."

Freegelda stuck her tongue out, but then she laughed. "I am grounded, but I am allowed to be near to our Dragon family." She gave Kerlin an almost shy look.

It was a relief to find the girl had a sense of humor, Kerlin had begun to doubt. "Jammy party it is," Kerlin realized he had to buy pajamas. All his sleeping clothes were back in the Guard dormitory in Celesterra City. Much had happened during the last terra-week.

♋

Kerlin skated to the Hotel New Ranger to change into street clothes, shorts and a tunic. The Dragon cub and the Mermaid waited for him by the fountain, or rather, were supposed to wait. Freegelda followed his every move.

Dusk fell on Nihera City. The street lights switched on their glows and were outdone by the shops' lighted windows. The racing season was over, as well as the Palace sponsored Balls and parties. The shop doors were wide open like overly enthusiastic prostitutes, optimistic the vacationers still had money to spend.

Kerlin stopped at a kiosk to check his account balance. He

negatively effected his balance by withdrawing illumes. The kiosk converted his money and dispensed coins of the Realm.

For three people intent on a pajama party, actual pajamas were the missing element. Kerlin hoped the handful of coins would be enough for three sets of pee-jays. Even the most basic necessities were outrageously overpriced in the historical part of the tourist town.

Before leaving the kiosk, Kerlin checked hotel room availability. His doubts were allayed, there were plenty of rooms with the racing fans leaving the city. The Rusty Wheel Inn was more expensive, but closer than the Hotel Looloo. He decided to splurge on the Rusty Wheel.

Kerlin strolled with his two female companions, browsing for shops selling pee-jays. Freegelda retracted her wings, she resembled a Human child, wearing a brown jumper dress, backless to her waist. Caithlin modestly draped her scarf dress, covering up her breasts, not to give Elf women an inferiority complex in their under abundant breast measurements. Kerlin and Freegelda both helped to keep a watch on Caithlin's ankle length hair, it had a tendency to catch on things.

Hearing Kerlin's unspoken thoughts, Caithlin explained, "having my hair cut doesn't help for as soon as I change my legs to my Mer tail, my hair will automatically grow back. It is the same for Merpages. Does this not happen to Emperor Methusem when he shape changes?"

"I've never witnessed Emperor Methusem change into a Merpage." It was a fascinating detail to learn, listening to her Lore stories would be worth a little blood trading.

Turning the corner by Rue La Mour, they strolled by a line of shops standing shoulder to shoulder on the narrow stone lined street. Kerlin was disappointed to see a few franchise stores in the historical section of the city; a Goo store, a Sockatorium, and a toy store called 'More Toys'. The back of the toy store sold pajamas. A clearance rack was selling one-size-fits-most-Humans night shirts. The material was summer light, soft, and comfy. Kerlin read aloud the slogans printed on the shirts. Caithlin chose the shirt with 'Mermaids Gone Mana' and she cajoled Kerlin into buying the shirt with a cartoonish Dragon head quoting, "Tasty Morsel".

Freegelda was fighting with another young female customer over the last pink flowered child sized pee-jays. Kerlin couldn't see Freegelda's face, she was facing away from him, but the little girl let out a shriek and ran outta the store. Freegelda turned, holding the pink pee-jays, a mere hint of fang showing. Caithlin winked at Freegelda in approval, careful not let Kerlin see the wink.

Kerlin ended up carrying the shopping bag. They walked by an ice scream stand, Kerlin offered to buy. The ladies weren't interested. He bought one caramarshocream pop for himself.

Watching Kerlin lick and slurp at the pop, made all sorts of fanciful notions cross Caithlin's mind. A casual humming song came from Freegelda.

Kerlin licked the last bit of his ice treat. They stopped in front of a store window. Caithlin was staring at a seashell converted into a decorative hair comb. Kerlin considered buying it for her, until he saw the price listing. "Ouch."

"But, here is an idea," Caithlin proved she understood the value of Realm coin. "At the Inn, Freegelda can fly up to the balcony, this way the Inn will only charge for two of us. It will save money."

"You mean, the money we save from the Inn, I could spend on this hair comb. How does Freegelda feel about this plan?" He glanced down at the Dragon cub.

She was ogling a stuffed toy dragon. It was a hot toy this season, it came with a tiny toy brush to groom the toy's fur.

Kerlin felt helpless to say, 'no'.

The time it took for Freegelda to make up her mind which color dragon toy she wanted, Kerlin could've eaten two more caramarshocream pops. Caithlin fussed with her new hair comb in front of a full length mirror.

The Elf male working at the shop tried to interest Kerlin in a new charm for his racing emblem charm bracelet. "Maybe next year," Kerlin said. He'd bought enough souvenirs.

Kerlin stood at the shop doorway to usher the ladies out first.

"Thank you Kerlin," Freegelda said very sweetly. She put the Dragon toy in a pocket of her jumper dress.

Returning to the rue, Kerlin visually scanned the upper story levels, wondering if Care might be trailing him from up there.

Caithlin said in amusement, "more of your fan club?"

Seeing Kerlin staring right at him, Rhiannon skated down.

Embarrassed at being spotted, Rhiannon said, "I'm not as good at this as Care. I should have hid under a Spell."

"I appreciate my Team looking out for my welfare," Kerlin sounded indignant.

"Commander, you're not even in uniform," Rhiannon stood stiffly.

"Is this your alluring Elf mage?" Caithlin put her hand possessively on Kerlin's elbow, leaning close.

Rhiannon eyed her suspiciously, a light blush crept into his fair complexion.

"Your commander is protected by a Dragon and a Mermaid. He is safe in our care," Caithlin said, she didn't need telepathy to sense the Elf was not reassured.

"Care has already threatened her," Kerlin said quietly.

Kerlin was one of those people, the quieter he became, the angrier he was in contrast. Rhiannon knew this, yet, angry was better than harmed.

"If anyone of my Team intrudes on my privacy again tonight, I'm disbanding my whole Team. Understood?" Kerlin meant every word and conveyed it to Rhiannon.

The Elf blinked, didn't say anything in response, he skated up, up, and away.

"Chantal is away from this city. Your Team may rest their fears tonight," Caithlin petted Kerlin's arm.

"They wouldn't like you feeding us blood," Freegelda unsheathed her wings in two soft bursts of light. "I will follow and watch from the sky."

"It's not necessary," Kerlin called to the flying Dragon cub. Freegelda either hadn't heard him, or, she was ignoring him. "Now, a five year old child is protecting me. The other commanders will make fun of me," he tried to make light of it.

"Freegelda is five, but she will be a fully grown adult Dragon before she is ten. They grow so very quickly," Caithlin sighed.

"She's almost an adult?" It was hard to believe. Kerlin wondered if it would be considered rude to ask her Prince Wenrik's age.

"His birth announcement issued forth thirteen terra-years ago, alas, I wasn't invited to the hatching. He would be about twelve terra-years of age," Caithlin answered his unspoken question.

"Prince Wenrik is twelve? He looks almost thirty," Kerlin wondered if the Mermaid could be teasing him.

"He will remain the same for 500 terra-years. Longer, if he inherited his father's immortality."

"How do they know if he's immortal?"

"When he is killed, or, if after 500 terra-years he does not age."

Simple answer.

"He hatched?"

"Yes."

"Hatched ... from an egg?"

"Yes. You did not know this of Dragons?"

Kerlin admitted he did not. "Are Mermaids ..."

"Yes, we are born from eggs. We are water demons, alas."

"But, you were raised by your Mother, right?"

"Of course," she didn't take offense at the question. "We are close to the Inn, I see the big wheel up on the roof sign." Caithlin tugged on his arm.

While they strolled the last few blocks, Caithlin told Kerlin a story about a Mermaid falling in love with a land Prince. By the time they reached the Rusty Wheel lobby, Kerlin's mood rebounded.

Kerlin figured out the story was meant to manage his mood. He was frustrated with his Team's overbearing protectiveness, but, wouldn't it be ironic if something happened to him after all the protesting.

They approached the reservation desk, a Human female desk clerk greeted them on behalf of the inn. The desk clerk gave them a bright smile, all ready having love on her mind, to her mind Kerlin and Caithlin were like, totally, romantic together.

"A room for the two of you," the desk clerk winked. "I have just the room, we call it the candle light room. Please, wait in the lobby, we'll call you as soon as the room is ready."

There were a few people seated on the plush furniture, eating from snack trays, and watching broadband news.

They'd just finished arranging Caithlin's hair, so she wasn't sitting on it, when a staff person came to lead them to their room. He led them up three flights of stairs.

There were only four doors on the third floor. The staff person threw open the door and stood back to let Kerlin and Caithlin enter.

Kerlin stopped short on the threshold, the room was worth a moment of appreciation.

Candlesticks were lit, rows of them, on dressers and the bedside tables.

One corner of the room had a bathtub shaped to fit the corner. The Inn staff had taken the liberty of filling the tub. Suds frothed the top, reminding Kerlin of a mocha java. Lit candlesticks and a small bowl of individual soap balls sat in the inner corner recess. A single candle floated on the bath water.

The bed silks were turned down in an invitation to lay down and get cozy.

An archway to the balcony was open. A bistro table was set with a bucket of ice chips and a wine bottle. A whoosh of wings and Freegelda was standing on the balcony table. She scooped a handful of ice chips and started eating them.

Caithlin stood near the dresser top, waving a hand to test the heat of the candles. "Humans are fond of these tiny open flames?"

"I believe," Kerlin was feeling a mite overwhelmed. He cleared his throat, "the inn is trying to make our stay romantic for us."

Freegelda retracted her wings, the brief breeze made all the burning candle flames flutter. "PAJAMAS!" Freegelda grabbed the shop bag holding their new pee-jays. She made very quick work of changing into the pink flowered night shirt. She climbed on the bed and settled between pillows, resting against the headboard. She looked dwarfed by the big bed. She smiled fang at Kerlin.

The fangs didn't make Kerlin too nervous, he did wonder if he had the prerogative to change his mind about letting a Dragon and a Mermaid feed on blood directly from his veins.

Caithlin dropped her scarf dress, she peeled it from her body in slow movements, despite her efforts, she sensed more curiosity than anticipation in Kerlin's mind.

Kerlin watched her, he sensed her slow motion striptease was deliberate. The candle light reflected in her mermaid green eyes, cast warm tones on her fair skin, her hair. Her ankle length tresses were the only hair on her body, she was completely smooth, even the area between her ... Kerlin coughed.

"Do you want help changing clothes?" Caithlin took tiny steps toward Kerlin.

She grabbed the hem of his tunic and pulled it up and over his head. She playfully left his face tangled in the cloth for a moment and pressed her soft breasts against Kerlin's muscle toned chest. Kerlin had ripples and definition in his torso, arms, and shoulders.

Laughing, Kerlin pulled the tunic off his head.

Caithlin tucked her fingers in the waistband of Kerlin's shorts, paused in the act of undressing him. But, there was no catch of his breath, no sense of yearning for her to lower her touch. She could've been a mother undressing her child for all his reaction to her.

She gave Kerlin's shorts a tug down and it fell to his feet. Caithlin made a show of admiring his cock, not too small, not too big. She felt desire for him, alas, his cock did not lift for her, not a twitch.

They stood nude, facing each other. Then, Kerlin picked up the night shirt with 'tasty morsel' printed on it. Caithlin grabbed the night shirt away from him.

"Did you want to sit in the bath?" Kerlin suggested.

"It's not worth wetting my hair," Caithlin searched the night shirt for the head opening. She pulled it over Kerlin's head.

Kerlin stood submissively while she worked to guide his arms into the short sleeves. The one-size-fits-most-Humans night shirt hem hit him below his knees. The wide open neckline slipped off one shoulder. He wondered if it made the blood vessels in his neck more inviting.

"Is it my blood alone drawing your interest to me?" Kerlin asked.

Caithlin pulled the 'Mermaid Gone Mana' night shirt on. It took the two of them to pull her hair out to drape over the outside of the shirt. "I should have dressed feet first, it would have been easier."

Kerlin gazed into her eyes, wishing he understood how to make the telepathy operate.

"Tis not your blood alone. Kerlin. I like you."

"What, then? Why?" The were close to the same height. He leaned close to her face, searching her expression for answers.

"It started in the Subterraneum."

Kerlin thought back to the cave and the Siren Song. "You said my resistance to your Siren Song was a challenge. Is that it?

I'm a challenge?"

"Tibetha said you were a challenge," Caithlin reminded him. "My feeling for you started, when you gave me your name after your friend Amé warned you of the danger. You were either incredibly foolish, very naïve, or, you were putting your trust in me."

"I trust you," Kerlin said softly.

"I know," Caithlin leaned the extra smidge to kiss Kerlin full on the lips. She kept her lips pressed to his, until she realized he was letting her kiss him, rather than kissing her back. She pulled away and sighed.

Kerlin cupped her butt with his hands and lifted, carrying her to the bed. He tried to crawl on the bed, carrying her, but the night shirt caught under his knees. He fell on her, laughing playfully.

The Mermaid laughed, too, freed her knees from the material to climb far enough to reach the pillows. She grabbed Kerlin by his armpits and dragged him to the pillow.

Freegelda pounced on them, she grabbed Kerlin's wrist. She curled up against Kerlin's hip and holding his wrist to her face, she started licking the skin over his pulse.

"It tickles," Kerlin twitched his hand, but didn't pull away. Her grip was very strong, it hadn't occurred to him she could physically overpower him with her Dragon strength.

Caithlin leaned the length of her body against Kerlin's opposite side. She pressed her hand up the inside of his night shirt, rubbing his belly and cupping caresses on his inner thighs. It was soothing. She sensed he was finding comfort in her touch without any hint of sensuality. She refrained from letting her hands roam close enough to his groin to molest him and let her hand rest on his hip, her thumb made caressing circles. She dropped her chin to rest on his shoulder.

"Do you want a once-upon-a-time story?"

"Once upon a time?" Kerlin's voice turned breathy.

"Yes. There are many stories starting with those words,"

Caithlin spoke softly. Was a sensual sensation starting to stir within Kerlin?

Caithlin moved to let her breath touch the skin of Kerlin's throat, under his ear.

A reflexive reaction made him pull back. He didn't move far.

Caithlin moved her mouth to his other ear, her faced pressed the left side of Kerlin's head against the pillow, trapping him.

"Are you okay?" Caithlin asked.

"Ah huh," Kerlin licked his lips, his face was being buried under her hair. "Are you going to bite me soon?"

Caithlin reached her telesense to touch the Dragon cub. No stranger to telepathy, Freegelda sweetly accepted the touch.

Freegelda sank deeply into blood swoon. Very gently, Freegelda pricked her eyeteeth into the soft hot flesh of Kerlin's wrist. Hot blood splashed into her mouth, the unbridled goodness of virgin blood with all its untapped energy. The energy points in Kerlin's body flowed pure, free, and untainted by the touch of another.

Kerlin felt like a livewire had plugged into his wrist. A current flowed up his arm. It stopped at his heart as if it didn't know which way to go from there. The touch of two sharp objects were at his throat. Caithlin's eyeteeth. It felt like the stinging hot needles of a too hot shower.

"Oww," his cry choked off. The current of energy poured to all his limbs. His groin became the focal point, drawing heat away from his throat and wrist.

Blood pumped to his groin and he felt an erection starting, trapped under the weight of Caithlin's body, the smallest movement rubbed his cock between them. He became so hard he ached.

It was Freegelda who pulled her teeth away first, being careful not to damage or traumatize Kerlin's flesh. It was Freegelda who used the telepathic link to the Mermaid to remind Caithlin to snap out of the rapture and stop drinking blood.

Caithlin cautiously retracted her teeth from Kerlin's neck vein, she held her tongue over the teeth puncture wounds, waiting for Kerlin's blood to start clotting in the wound. Caithlin then felt the heat of Kerlin's erection. At last. She yanked their night shirts up between them, his naked cock rubbed against the smooth skin of her pubic bone. Sensing how near to orgasm he was, she gyrated her hips in small movements and was rewarded by his half stifled cry. Warm fluid started trickling over her pubic skin.

Kerlin put an arm over Caithlin's back, hugging tight. His breathing was shaky. "So, I'm not a virgin anymore."

Caithlin bit back a laugh. "You're still a virgin dear."

"No, oh, what a mess I made."

"Trust me, you're still a virgin."

"By what criteria?" Kerlin breathed.

"You didn't penetrate my aura, and we haven't penetrated yours. You remain pure, untainted."

Freegelda curled up in a pile of pillows near the bed's headboard. "Thank you Kerlin," she said in the same tone she'd used to thank him earlier for the toy.

"Do you want a story now?" Caithlin resettled their night shirts and cuddled Kerlin close.

"Yes, please."

"Once upon a time," Caithlin began.

Weakened by blood loss and an intense orgasm, Kerlin fell asleep somewhen between once and time.

♋

"This Elf with the alluring features," Caithlin handed Kerlin's shirt to him.

"Alluring?" Kerlin accepted the shirt and pulled it over his head. "Doesn't every Elf have alluring features?"

"No, they do not," Caithlin glanced at the Dragon cub sound asleep on the bed. She mentally kicked herself for feeling an oogle of maternal instinct.

Kerlin leaned to give Freegelda a little kiss on her head, careful not to wake her. Her pointy eyeteeth were showing, her bottom lip curled under her upper eye teeth.

He stood up to finish dressing. Caithlin watched him, a happy half smile tugged her mouth at the corners.

"When next we meet, after your journey to the stars, you will be virgin no longer," she said.

"I won't? I mean, I will?" Kerlin stood submissively still to allow Caithlin to arrange his clothes, fluffing his shirt hem neatly over his shorts.

"Your alluring Elf mage will see to it."

"Does this mean you won't want my blood?" Kerlin put a hand to his neck. Were tooth marks showing? He turned his wrist, there was faint redness and swelling. People might not notice it.

"Freegelda is young, she does not have her full healing powers. And yes, I will always swoon for your blood. The three of us are bonded now. A strange bonding. Her Dragon King, the Black Dragon, may object, but there is nothing the Dragons can do. The only way to break the bond is to kill you." Caithlin laughed pleasantly.

Caithlin threw her arms around Kerlin for a hug, wishing she could keep him for a pet.

Kerlin hugged her back. He would miss her. Miss them both.

Caithlin wanted to hug him harder, but was very conscious of his fragile bones. She felt his kiss on her head, much like the kiss he'd given the five year old.

"Will you be gone long?" Caithlin asked.

"No. I'll be back in a terra-month or so. You will find me, right? With your telepathy, like you found me yesterday."

"Yes."

They released their hold on each other and Kerlin walked away. He turned to wave once, a warm affectionate smile on his lips. Then, he was on his way to the stars.✍

Garren Waysixth stood alone and despondent, leaning his elbows on a bar height table in the Luv N Ov N pastry shop, propping his head on his palms over a mug of witch brewed mocha latte and inhaling the aroma for comfort. He was wearing regular street clothes, a soft t-shirt and sturdy canvas pants. An awning in front of the shop shaded the outdoor tables.

He took a bite of berry swirl and chewed. He was feeling sorry for himself. He'd been unable to fight in the Drake battle and even worse, he'd needed rescuing. One more ridicule he'd have to endure.

He'd said his 'goodbyes' to Kerlin that very morning. They'd made promises to keep in close touch and Kerlin gave Garren a permanent invitation to adjunct with his Team at any time he felt like it. It had been an interesting conversation. Kerlin had asked who had sworn Fealty to him for that had saved his life. Care shyly admitted to it and Kerlin had looked choked up with emotion.

Garren looked up at the sky; wondering if his friends were shuttling their way to an orbital station by now. His own ship Launch was scheduled for tomorrow and he hadn't been issued his new uniform as of yet. Sigh.

He'd given his farewells to Dana and Traci. They'd left for Celesterra City last night, escorting the Sovereign Ministers home and accompanied by an immortal Guard known only as 'Four'. They were participating in the planning of an invasionary force scheduled hence to destroy a Bio-Lab in their unfriendly neighbor's home space, Empire of Catharra.

The Bio-Lab was reportedly using Elves for biological experiments. A ship full of Elf children asylum seekers were living in an orphanage, founded by Her Royal Highness Princess Luna, in the heart of Celesterra City. Within the shadow of the Seaside Palace, there was probably no safer place for the children. Our Emperor's ethereal, yet, mighty Dragon wings embraced the capital city.

Amid all these farewells, Garren had spent a few marks times with Jesse and his Dad Nerrys. Jesse's tele-kinetic talent roused from latency, Garren had barely lifted a finger yesterday, not with Jesse levitating everything in sight. Garren worried unnecessarily for awhile, but Nerrys did not try for any tongue kissing, again. They'd said their affectionate goodbyes and the Nefeinn family were on their way back to Celesterra City.

Garren took another bite of Berry Swirl and washed it down with a large gulp of lukewarm mocha latte, the while mentally kicking himself for being an idiot. Junior Minister Vylara had stopped by last night to ask after his health and she had brought him a single blooming long stemmed Red Delilah. At first Garren had felt very happy at the prospect of making love to the pretty (and eligible) Elf maid, but a conversation beforehand had revealed her feelings for Minister Ange and Garren realized she was only looking for a casual relationship. His mercurial mood swing swept him into a sulk and Garren had begged off by saying he was still tired from being dragged off in the clenches of Ariel. He'd slept alone last night. Sigh.

Locally assigned Nihera City Guards were stopping by the pastry shop intermittently, it was a hot spot apparently, his mood must be putting them off for they didn't stop to chat. Methusem had promised a visit before the Launch, Garren did not believe the Emperor would have time to sit down for a chat for he was busy using his powers to help rebuild a lot of broken windows.

He wondered if Prince Wenrik would be amenable to a visit. Garren closed his eyes and tried to rebuild his personality into the semblance of a Senior Fleet Commander. He had to be tough; a Commander shouldn't be lamenting his lack of social options.

Unaccountably, Garren felt something invisible brush his back, something barely tangible. Was it a ghost? Was someone hiding under a Glamour Spell? The strange touch didn't repeat and Garren let gloom overcome him once again.

He gave his full attention to finishing off the mocha latte, deciding he'd go wallow in self-pity at the beach cove.

"There you are!" A vaguely familiar voice shouted from the pedestrian crowd.

To Garren's amazement, it was Keyth shouting and he was accompanied by Krizren and someone who at first glance Garren thought was Donné, but this StrataTerra person looked younger and less finished in his figure and slender enough to swap clothes with Methusem.

"Do you have any concept of how hard you are to track? We hacked into your PDA and trailed it, you wouldn't believe where we found it. Is there a story there Commander Garren?" Keyth hammered Garren with this flurry of questions.

Krizren held out his wrist and Garren held out his own and they clasped grips on each other's wrists in greeting, Garren was sure Krizren could feel his pulse hammering.

"This is Amé. We boldly go where no StrataTerran has gone before," Krizren introduced their latest shipmate with a nod of his head and an ephemeral smile. He sounded insincere, but humour lit his candid ocean blue eyes.

Keyth kept up a monologue, "Garren, did you actually feel my astral presence? You reacted. Do you know how rare that is?"

"You used your astral-kinetic power just to find me?" Garren rudely interrupted.

Keyth nodded, standing shoulder to shoulder with Krizren

and they folded their arms in similar poses. Amé grabbed a Berry Swirl off Garren's plate without so much as a 'by your leave'.

"Why? What's happened?" Garren gathered his self-possession. Was another attack imminent?

"Nothing." Keyth lifted his face to a breeze, all breezes to be duly appreciated on this bright sunny morning.

"Why did you need me then?" Garren asked, genuinely puzzled.

"Do we need a reason? You are our shipmate, aren't ya?" Keyth and Krizren shared the same smile in Garren's direction.

Garren swallowed.

Krizren linked his arm to Garren's elbow, Keyth crooked Garren's opposite elbow. Amé picked up what was left of Garren's pastries.

"Come on," Keyth chatted on as they pulled Garren along with them. "The benefit concert is starting soon. Have you ever watched the Brook Dancers? They are amazing to watch, they stand in a line and do lots of fancy foot dancing in unison and they tap and it makes for a great rhythm."

Stuck between two of his shipmates by the elbows gave Garren little choice in the matter of where he was going to spend his planet-side afternoon. Halfway down the block, Garren's gloom broke and he smiled the smile that transformed his face from mere male beauty to a legendary knight of ballads.

Several marks later into the night, Krizren and Keyth stopped walking in their tracks and took on the glazed look of actively communicating telepaths. They gazed at each other, then slowly turned to Garren with regretful expressions.

"Sorry to relay this to you Garren," Keyth began.

"WHAT?!" Garren almost dropped the bag of jillysnap candies he was holding.

"Halçyon's launch is being delayed."

Garren closed his eyes in quiet personal horror and couldn't' quite hide his sudden misery.

XXXI. TERRA-DATE 215.154 LATE AFTERNOON
:: Celesterra City, Collier Building, Care ::

"I demand an explanation for your Team," Care Ethaynen stood in the interim office assigned to Commander Kraken.

"Ex team," Cdr Kraken spoke from his chair, not bothering to look up from his computer. Papers and folders were strewn about the desk.

Care lurched forward and with a broad sweep of his arm, he swept the papers off the desk. Grabbing handfuls of folders, he tossed it all into the air.

Cdr Kraken stood up, his face mottled with rage, "I'll have you Writ beyond your wildest nightmares for that."

"Go ahead, I dare you. Our officials may not hold you accountable, but I DO!"

"You are declaring TREASON!" Cdr Kraken reached for Care in a hand-to-hand combat attack move.

Care spun beyond reach, then initiated an offensive stance of his own, preparing to move in retaliation. His beautiful, yet alien yellow eyes held a strange shadow in them.

Before Care could attack Cdr Kraken, Commander Barett's silhouette filled the doorway. Assessing the situation quickly, Barett wound his arms around Care and called upon his Clerical powers for the strength to contain Care's anger. "Stand down."

"No," Care struggled. He dropped to his heels to slip under Barett's hold. The move didn't work.

Cdr Kraken shouted, "I want him arrested and sent to the stasis cells."

"You tried to kill my Commander, I don't believe you didn't

know your team was up to murder," Care struggled with all his might against Barett to no avail.

Cdr Kraken moved to a recessed wall kiosk to call for Guards to arrest Care.

Before he reached it, Barett said, "no Kraken. I'll deal with him."

"Not good enough, Barett."

"I say it is," Barett's voice was mild, light, and pleasant as always.

Cdr Kraken stepped back to the office window, as far as he could get away from Barett and Care and be in the same room.

Care's anger became superseded by curiosity, he twisted in Barett's hold to look at the man's face. He stopped struggling, "your eyes?!"

"You should talk," Barett pulled the suddenly pliant Care out into the corridor.

"Wait. I demand explanations," Care insisted. He yanked away from Barett and hurt his shoulder in the process.

"My eyes bleed to blue, when my Goddess is upon me," Barett smiled, very eerie considering his bled blue eyes had no pupils showing in them.

"You look blind," Care remarked, working on a calm distraction as he planned for a second chance to attack Kraken. "Why didn't your Goddess help you fight off the Mermaids the other terra-day?"

"I was within the influence of Aphrodite's Shrine," Barett admitted this weakness to cleric powers.

"Oh." Care took a step toward Kraken's office, but Barett was paying attention and blocked him.

"Let us go quickly to the Palace, I believe Kraken will indeed enter a Writ for your arrest," Barett grabbed a hold of Care's elbow and nudged him to mirror his pace.

"What good will going to the Palace do?" Care was practically spitting angry.

"Our Emperor will countermand the Writ in time to do you

some good." Barett dodged into an empty office, pulling Care along, and swooshed closed the office privacy curtain.

They heard running boot treads.

"Those will be the Guards Kraken summoned to arrest you. The fool," Barett's voice was heavy with derision. "By the way, aren't you supposed to be in orbit right now, waiting for your transport to deep space?"

"There is time. I told my Commander I had to fetch something," Care rubbed his sore shoulder, talking to Barett like he wasn't sure quite how to react to the 'Goddess upon him' thing.

Barett laughed quietly. "Your Commander Kerlin swallowed your excuse? He must be more complacent than most of our Field Commanders."

"What's going on here Barett?" Care sounded young and vulnerable as he said it.

"Palace politics. There is nothing to fear, our Emperor can handle Kraken."

"Handle what? Kraken's Team tried to blood sacrifice my Commander to a Mermaid. They attacked Garren and left him at the mercy of Ariel," Care swallowed like he tasted a bitter pill. "You attacked me."

"I sincerely thought I was doing what you liked," Barett offered half a shrug for an apology. "I haven't discovered Kerlin's significance in the petty schemes," Barett continued. "As for Garren, they are content to merely make him suffer; for now."

"Why? Who? Why make Garren suffer?" Care's voice rose at the unfairness of it.

"Shh," Barett hushed him. "To understand, you'd have to understand Quinterra Planet's culture."

They heard running bootsteps again.

"Our Guards are not stealthy," Barett mocked.

"We can't stay here," Care said.

"True."

Care braced for the unpleasantness and moved towards the curtain.

"Not that way," Barett said with great patience, he body checked Care before the younger man went any further.

"What way then? Out the window? It's too small to fit through."

Barett sighed deeply and seemed to dangle his arms out. "It's a relaxation technique," Barett was moved to explain by Care's expression. He found it hard not to laugh at the earnest twenty-two year old Guard.

Care couldn't tear his gaze away for fascination. Was he about to see Cleric powers? He hoped it was more spectacular than controlling weeds, like those vines in the shrine.

Another noise came from Barett, he tilted his head to the side, his brunette waves at almost shoulder length were floating in the air. The noise coming from his lips sounded on the edge of an acute orgasm of the female kind. Care surmised using Cleric powers must feel good.

Something was happening to the wall beside the window. The stone work started to spit gravel. The mortar crumbled to dust and the larger building stones crumbled into pebbles.

"Awesome," Care whispered. "I meant it as a compliment."

A Human sized hole gaped in the wall, sunlight streamed from the outside. The two men stepped over the dust and rubble.

A non descript shuttle came hovering towards them, its side door slid open. By the plates, Care could tell it was a private coach. "How did this show up so conveniently?"

"With my Goddess upon me, I can speak mind to mind."

Care stood with his boot on the edge of the shuttle, hesitating as he saw the occupants. Barett's former Field Team were all accounted for, though, this time they weren't in uniform. Care vividly recalled the last time he'd been with these five Humans from Quinterra Planet.

"Relax," one of them called. "We don't hold a grudge, I for

one, had a great time with the Mermaids."

Barett stood close enough behind Care to breathe on his neck.

Rounding the corner of the building they were escaping, a group of Guards came running. Care decided he'd rather take his chances with them.

It was Commander Lisza and her Command-Second Terriane leading the hunt.

Holding her PDA high, Terriane cried, "told you we'd track him down." She gave Care a big suggestive wink. "Hi Care, throwing any royal suite parties lately?"

Care's anger slipped away and his sense of the ridiculous returned. "I'm in uniform, you can't perform your infamous 'pants me' move!" He teased.

Cdr Lisza 'tchd', "we've already seen what you're packing, remember?"

Barett snorted.

The ladies managed not to stare unduly, when they noticed Barett's strange bled blue eyes for the first time.

Cdr Lisza shrugged and shook her long dark hair. "Care, you should go straight away to the Palace. I mean it."

"Whah? Aren't you going to arrest me?" Care didn't understand.

"Nah," she 'pshhd'. "No one around here is going to listen to Kraken's orders. Seriously."

"He is certified in the new tawse, y'know."

Someone came pushing through the crowd. "Let him put his authority to the test."

"Garren!" Care twitched a grin and looking bashful he said, "are you, umm, still mad at me?"

Garren shook his head. "No," he said simply. He checked out Barett a moment. "Is it Barett I'm talking to, or his Goddess?"

"We are both here," Barett said after a moment of looking condescending.

"Ri-ight," Care felt ghost-bumps.

Two more figures came pushing amidst the group. A male and a female voice shouting. "Pardon." "Coming through."

"Jace and Jenny," Care greeted them with undisguised pleasure.

"Hey Care," Jace clasped wrists with Care. His brunette hair was tied into a hair scrunchee high on the back of his head, his short hair bobbed with his head movement. "Are you headed to the Palace?"

"Could you float us along?" Jenny nudged in front of Jace. Her blond hair bound neatly into a sleek braid.

Jace added, "she has a theory on why the shield generator failed the other day."

"Sure, squeeze in," Care changed his mind about boarding the shuttle, feeling okay about it with his best friends along.

The overcrowded shuttle lifted off, heading towards the Palace and flying on auto-pilot.

Jenny sat on Jace's knees. They were talking engineering tech stuff; transmitters and reflective energy frying oscillation crystals and the like.

Care and Garren sat on a sideways bench, sandwiched between Cdr Barett and one of his ex-team members.

Barett spoke into the conversational void, "Care, if you do have ass sex with Garren, he'll like it best on his back."

Care froze in disbelief. Garren didn't react. Care couldn't decide between following Garren's example, or punching Barett, Goddess or no Goddess.

Jenny made the nasal noise uniquely Human female, "I've never heard anything more obnoxious in my life."

Care smiled at Jenny, admiring her personality.

Barett seemed very content with himself.

Care put an arm around Garren's back for moral support.

Barett spoke again, "life in Celesterra City won't settle down to her normal simple routine, until you leave the planet." He paused and added, "son of the manor."

To Care's surprise, Garren responded to Barett, "then the next terra-days life will be complicated."

Jace and Jenny were still fuming on Garren's behalf. "Where did that statement even come from?" Jace accused Barett. "Garren isn't even into sex with males."

At this Garren shifted in his seat, he looked very depressed to everyone looking at him.

"I ...," Garren said in a raspy voice, speaking too low to be heard and some words were lost. He quickly brushed his thumbs over his pinched closed eyelids.

Care regarded him with a worried frown. "Garren, are you okay?"

Garren nodded.

"Garren," Barett said fiercely. "Did someone hurt you?" His reaction caught Care by surprise, considering the extremely rude things he'd been saying.

Garren insisted he was 'okay'.

Neither, Barett, nor Care were convinced.

CONTINUED IN REALMS AND GALAXIES #11 HELLFIRE

Publisher's Note:

PLEASE CHECK OUR WEB PAGE FOR PUBLICATION DATES.
http://groups.yahoo.com/group/BonCoeurPublishing

Author's Note:

MISTY LARA PRENOVILLE

BORN: 1964   Resides in Long Island, NY

Ms Lara reads her messages on the Yahoo Group:

ScreamsBeneathePandora
Please join at url: (Membership is Free.)
http://groups.yahoo.com/group/screamsbeneathepandora

www.ingramcontent.com/pod-product-compliance
Lightning Source LLC
Chambersburg PA
CBHW020932020726
47495CB00002B/458